Dancer

Something warm and wet dripped onto the center of Fiona's lower back. "What—"

Wolf Shadow's deep laughter rumbled close to her ear. He seized her and rolled her over in the soft grass.

"What are you doing?"

"I promised you honey," he said.

He parted her vest, and she giggled as she felt the warm drops on her bare breasts.

"You're dripping honey on me," she squealed.

"You must shut your eyes. This is an important part of the bee tree ceremony. You must obey my instructions without question."

His hands were everywhere on her body . . . moving over her . . . touching . . . caressing . . . teasing.

"The most important part of the ceremony," he managed between long, hot, deep kisses, "is that every drop of honey must be licked off."

"No matter where it is?" she asked.

"No matter where."

Moon Dancer

Judith E. French

AVON BOOKS 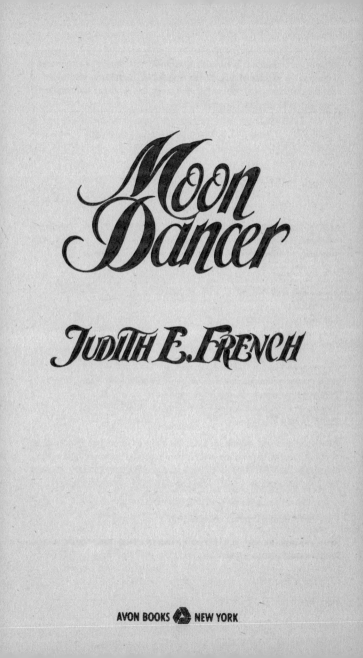 NEW YORK

MOON DANCER is an original publication of Avon Books. This work has never before appeared in book form. This work is a novel. Any similarity to actual persons or events is purely coincidental.

AVON BOOKS
A division of
The Hearst Corporation
1350 Avenue of the Americas
New York, New York 10019

Copyright © 1992 by Judith E. French
Inside cover author photograph by Theis Photography, Ltd.
Published by arrangement with the author
Library of Congress Catalog Card Number: 91-93015
ISBN: 0-380-76105-X

First Avon Books Printing: March 1992

AVON TRADEMARK REG. U.S. PAT. OFF. AND IN OTHER COUNTRIES, MARCA REGISTRADA, HECHO EN U.S.A.

Printed in the U.S.A.

RA 10 9 8 7 6 5 4 3 2 1

For my grandfather, William H. Faulkner,
the greatest storyteller of all

There was never any yet that wholly could escape love, and never shall there be any, never so long as beauty shall be, never so long as eyes can see.

LONGUS

Moon Dancer

Chapter 1

Maryland Colony
February 1730

Red-haired Fiona O'Neal held her breath against the stench of the unwashed fur-clad trappers as she pushed aside the ragged deerskin curtain between the store and the public room of Jacob Clough's Indian trading post. Fear curled in the pit of her stomach and stretched cold fingers up her spine, but she pulled her homespun shawl up over her hair and entered the low-ceilinged room with a face as expressionless as that of the drunken Huron brave slumped against the fireplace wall.

Jacob Clough banged his battered tin cup against the sagging trencher table. "Damn you, Fiona!" he roared. "What took you so long? My customers are thirsty." On the far side of the table two filthy, bearded white men leered at her and held out their mugs as she poured the rotgut whiskey with unwavering hands.

You'd be proud of me, Grandsire, she thought. She could almost hear his gravelly voice in her mind. *Steady. Steady hands,* he'd growled at her a thousand times. *A woman with trembling hands is as useless as a horse with three legs.*

The nearest man, his scarred features almost hidden by yellow, tobacco-stained whiskers, caught hold of Fiona's arm below the elbow. "Pretty little thing, ain't ye, girlie?" He laughed, exposing broken, green-scummed teeth.

She twisted, trying to free her arm from his iron grip, but his long, dirty fingernails dug into her flesh with the tenacity of a bulldog. His companion snickered.

"Feisty, too, ain't she?" Fiona's captor gloated. He yanked her closer, bringing his bearded face so near that she gagged at the smell of his foul breath.

Fiona slammed the jug of whiskey down on his other hand, smashing his fingers against the oak table. Yellow Beard yelped with pain and let go of her arm. In a heartbeat, she was halfway across the room.

"What the hell—" Jacob shouted.

"I'll not be handled by filth such as that!" she shot back. She was trembling now—not with fear but with anger—and her green eyes were as hard as Sligo flint. "Bondwoman I may be," she spat in fiery English, heavily accented with the lilting pipes of Ireland. "I'll cook, and scrub, and tote your stinking slop buckets, but I'll whore for no man."

A movement by the blazing hearth caught Fiona's attention, and her head snapped around. The Indian brave's sloe eyes were open wide, and for an instant their gazes met, and the green of the Irish sea washed against gleaming obsidian. In the savage blackness of dark eyes that were more like a wolf's than a human's, she read compassion. The shock was so great that it rocked her back a step, but when she looked again, the painted Huron's eyes were expressionless, and his face showed the slacken waste of a drunkard.

"What did I tell you, Karl?" Jacob demanded of the blond trapper. "She's cherry. There's none so pure as an Irish virgin. Papist, she is, and certain she'll burn in hell does she lift her skirts for an honest romp.''

Fiona felt the heat rise in her cheeks. Damn Jacob Clough to the deepest pit in hell! Who was he to shame her before these animals just because he'd bought her indenture in Philadelphia? This was supposed to be a land of opportunity! What kind of government would permit such injustice? Even in Ireland, she'd been treated with more respect by the occupying British troops. ''You'll not do this to me, Jacob,'' she swore. ''Not if I have to cut your black heart out to stop it.''

''We'll take 'er,'' Karl said.

His partner, a hulking bear of a man with a patch over one eye, leaped to his feet and drove a hunting knife into the table between Jacob's thumb and index finger. ''Not so fast. He said the one he sold us two years ago was cherry too, but she was worn as an old shoe—red-haired slut. Jacob's partial to redheaded women. Ain't no chance of nothin' old enough to breed being virgin.''

Jacob drew back his hand and blinked. His face had taken on a pasty shade of white. ''No need to carry grudges agin' old friends, Nigel,'' he sputtered. ''This one's different. I got me a squaw to look to m' needs. She cooks what I tell her to, and she spreads her legs when I say so—without givin' me any backtalk. I got no need of such fine-bone spirit as Fiona's. 'Course . . .'' He grinned. ''I ain't spendin' the winter in the mountains with only Karl to keep my backside warm.''

''How much?'' Nigel demanded.

Jacob stepped away from the table. ''Dear. Fiona'll come dear. I gave you a bargain on Gerty 'cause you promised to sell her back to me come spring. Who cheated who on that deal?''

''Wolves et her,'' Karl said.

"Not what I heard." Jacob shook his head. "Word was that Frenchman Roquette bought a scalp off you, Nigel—a white woman's scalp with hair like a blazin' sunset."

"Karl tole ye wolves et her. Didn't say they et her hair." Nigel grinned. "No sense wasting a good scalp, was there? Not with Roquette paying hard silver for hair."

"Gerty sure didn't need it no more," Karl added.

A wave of back terror washed over Fiona, squeezing her chest so tight that she could hardly breathe. Abequa, Jacob's plump Ojibwa wife, had warned her that he had sold another bond girl to these two fur trappers. Abequa had advised her to be nice to Jacob, to let him feel her breasts and buttocks—even to bed him if he wanted her.

She'd refused. The last time Jacob had tried to touch her, she'd spilled hot bacon grease on him. Nothing would make her submit to being mauled by a man. She might be a bond servant now, but she didn't intend to remain one. And being a servant didn't make her a trollop.

Unconsciously, Fiona's hand went to the amulet at her throat. It was her last tie with home . . . her only friend. Her necklace had been a source of strength when her grandfather had died in Dublin, leaving her destitute. And the familiar charm had helped when Jason Bryant, the kindly Philadelphia apothecary she'd been apprenticed to, had succumbed to typhoid and her indenture had been auctioned off along with the contents of the shop. Now the amulet offered nothing. It hung around her neck like a lump of coal.

"You can't do this," she protested desperately. "I'm no whore! I'm a trained apothecary. I'm a healer. If you have no need of me, then sell my indenture to someone who does—not to such men as these be."

"Fifty pounds," Jacob said.

"You're mad as Roquette's horse," Nigel said.

"Look at her." Jacob's voice became as silky as oil running over a cast-iron skillet. "Look at those hips. Turn around, Fiona, so the gentlemen can see your hips."

"Twenty," Nigel offered.

"Show us her tits," Karl said. "I like a woman with big tits."

Fiona's knees went weak. She tasted the metallic dryness of fear on her tongue. *He's going to do it— the bastard's going to sell me. He'll make the devil's profit,* she thought with black Irish humor. *Jacob paid twelve pounds for my indenture, and he's asking fifty.*

"She'll fight you like a cornered badger," Jacob said, "and when you get in the saddle, she'll be as tight as wadding down a musket barrel."

Tears gathered in the corners of Fiona's eyes. Every instinct bade her to run—but where could she go? The trading post stood alone in hundreds of miles of trackless wilderness. There wasn't a road or a white settlement for days.

Beg Jacob to keep you, a voice in Fiona's head cried. *He's a coarse pig, but he's better than these two. If you go with them, you'll die. Tell Jacob you'll do anything he wants.*

Another mocking voice chimed in. *What did you expect? Are you any better than your mother? You can make a purse from a sow's ear easier than you can make a lady of a whore's bastard.*

Jacob lifted the hem of Fiona's skirt, exposing her black-wool stockinged legs to the knee. "Look at these legs," he coaxed. "A lonely man would kill his own grandmother for legs like these to wrap around him on a snowy night."

Karl's hot eyes and whispered oath of admiration yanked Fiona from her trance. She spun away from

Jacob, leaping not for the doorway as he expected, but instead running to the fireplace and seizing a flaming brand.

"By Mary's robe," she swore, "you'll not sell me for a bawd and live to tell of it!" She whirled the flaming log around her head and bashed him across the shoulders with it. He screamed and fell back against the doorway, beating at a spark clinging to his shirtfront.

Karl howled with glee and plowed over the bench to grab her, but Fiona saw him coming out of the corner of her eye. She twisted around and struck him across the side of the face. His laughter turned to cries of pain. With his beard on fire in two places, Karl plunged through the outside door to bury his head in the knee-deep snow.

Panting for breath, Fiona backed against the far wall, nearly tripping over the drunken Indian. Jacob barred the way to the store and living quarters; Nigel stood between her and the door through which Karl had escaped. "Don't come near me," she warned Nigel. "I'll kill you if you come near me!" She was too frightened to realize that she'd lapsed into Gaelic, or that she was standing inches from a wild savage.

"Put it down, woman," Nigel said, taking a step toward her. "Put it down, unless ye want to feel the weight of my fist."

Sweat ran down Fiona's face and dripped into her eyes. She wiped her forehead with the back of her hand. Her skirts were very close to the flames; she could feel the intense heat through her stout leather shoes. "I mean it," she said. "I'll kill you."

Karl appeared in the doorway. "You bitch," he said. "You bloody bitch. I get her first, Nigel. She's mine."

Nigel lunged at her, and she flung the brand with all her might. The log hit his chin and right shoulder, but he kept coming. Fiona feinted left, then ducked right under his arm and ran toward Jacob. He staggered up and spread his arms to catch her, and Fiona balled her fist and punched him square in the nose. Blood flowed.

When Jacob grabbed his nose, Fiona turned sideways and tried to squeeze through the opening, which led to the storeroom. She knew Jacob kept a loaded musket under the counter. I may not get them all, she thought, but I'll shoot the first one.

She was three-quarters of the way past when Nigel grabbed her thick braid and yanked her head back. She screamed and struggled to get free. Her teeth closed around his hand, and she bit down hard. With a cry of rage, Nigel drew his fist and slammed it into her jaw. She went down in a crumpled heap.

Jacob sniffed loudly and wiped his nose. "Thirty pounds," he offered. "I told you she was a wild one."

Nigel didn't answer. He stepped over Fiona's still form and went into the store, returning with an Indian trade blanket of red wool. He spread it on the floor, picked up Fiona and laid her on it, then rolled the blanket around her. From a bag at his waist, he drew four silver crowns. "Twenty," he said. "Take it or leave it." He slung Fiona over one shoulder and glanced at Jacob.

"Twenty-five," Jacob bargained. "When will the likes of you find a woman like her?"

Nigel started for the door.

"Done," Jacob cried. "Wait, I'll fetch her papers for you."

Nigel tossed the coins to the floor. "Don't need no damned papers where I'm takin' her," he said. He glared at Karl. "Bring them mules around and fetch me some rope."

Jacob followed Nigel out into the snowy twilight.

"No need to leave tonight," he said. "Sleep here until morning. Me and my woman won't be no bother to you."

The Indian opened his eyes partway and watched through the open door as Nigel tied the unconscious woman across a dun-colored mule. The trappers mounted their animals and rode off into the forest, leading another mule. Wolf Shadow remained motionless as Jacob Clough came back inside and stomped the snow off his boots.

"Ungrateful bitch," Jacob muttered. "Serves her right." He scowled and looked around the room. "Abequa! Abequa!" Jacob's voice rose to a shout as he called to his Indian wife. There was no answer. "Now, where in hell's that lazy squaw?" Jacob glanced at Wolf Shadow, then pushed aside the deerskin and stalked into the next room.

Wolf Shadow opened his eyes again and stared at the outside door. The red-haired woman had the heart of *meshepeshe*, the panther. She had put up a brave fight—she deserved better treatment than she would receive from the two white men who had carried her off.

He took a deep breath and flexed his cramped muscles. White women were none of his concern. He'd come here to Jacob Clough's trading post for a much more important reason than interfering in the sale of a woman. He should be thinking about Jacob and the two white men who worked for him—the bondman Harrison and the squint-eyed one called Zeke. Wolf Shadow hadn't seen Zeke for several hours. Zeke carried a knife, and he threw it with the skill of an Iroquois. Wolf Shadow knew that if he wasn't cautious, he could pay for his recklessness with his life.

Nevertheless, the woman's pale freckled face with its green cat eyes haunted him. Troubled, Wolf

Shadow leaned back against the logs and went over the scene again in his mind's eye.

He remembered with shame that once—for a flash of time—he had looked into the white woman's eyes, and she had looked into his. She had gazed at him in a way that made him wonder if she knew he was not a Huron as he pretended to be. As if she knew that he had not drunk the firewater, but only poured it over himself and pretended to be imprisoned by the liquor's evil spell. But if she had read the truth in his eyes, she would have exposed him as an impostor . . . wouldn't she?

The green-eyed woman was a great puzzle to him, and it was just as well that she was gone from this place, he decided. Still, the scent of her seemed to linger in the air, and he could not help but wonder what her thick red-gold hair would feel like sliding over his fingertips.

An hour later Harrison, the bond servant, entered the public room. The fire had burned to a single glowing log, giving little light. Wolf Shadow didn't need much light. Harrison didn't notice him until he clamped an arm around his neck and pressed the point of his steel knife against the bondman's spine. "Make noise—you die quick," Wolf Shadow threatened, deliberately using broken English.

Harrison gasped with fear, but he made no outcry. In seconds Wolf Shadow had the white man facedown on the uneven plank floor, his mouth gagged, his hands and feet bound behind him.

Wolf Shadow rose and unlocked the outside door. Two Indian braves, wearing the same paint and Huron clothing as Wolf Shadow, slipped silently into the room. The first warrior, a lean Shawnee named Spear Thrower, handed Wolf Shadow a loaded musket.

The second man, Two Crows, leaned close to Wolf

Shadow and whispered. "We found Zeke in the barn. He'll not interfere."

"You didn't have to kill him, did you?" Wolf Shadow asked. He'd given orders that none of the whites at Clough's trading post should be hurt unnecessarily.

Two Crows shook his head and grinned. "No, we just scared him half to death." He tapped the big skinning knife stuck in his belt. "He took one look at me, dropped his knife, and ran."

"Good," Shadow replied. Motioning to his companions to remain where they were, he pushed aside the deerskin curtain and moved silently into the store.

The trading post was laid out like a letter T. The main section of the building was two cabins built end to end. One was the original structure, the actual store; the second was the public room where Clough sold food and drink and sometimes took money from travelers to let them sleep on the floor. Both the store and the public room had doors on the front leading outside. The storeroom had a door leading to Clough's living quarters at the back, as well as the entrance to the public room.

Shadow could hear Jacob Clough's voice plainly from the lean-to rooms in the back. Jacob was cursing his Ojibwa woman.

Three more disguised braves waited outside the storeroom door. Heavily armed and hooded, they moved into the trading post as soon as Shadow lifted the iron bar across the door. It was pitch-black, but he didn't need light to identify his fellow tribesmen—he knew the scent and walk of each Shawnee warrior as he knew the lines on the palms of his own hands.

Yellow Elk would be first. He was the oldest, a seasoned warrior whose black hair bore threads of gray. He always placed himself in the greatest danger, to prove to the younger men that he was as vigorous as he used to be. Close on Yellow Elk's heels was He-Who-Runs. Shadow recognized the short, quick breaths He-Who-Runs took when he was courting danger. And the solid bulk behind them would be Fat Boy, the half Delaware. Broad and muscular, slow to anger and slower of speech, Fat Boy was one of the bravest men Wolf Shadow had ever known. When he walked, Fat Boy planted each foot as though it were an oak that would grow in that spot for a hundred years.

"Harrison!" Jacob Clough called. "Where the hell are you?" Wolf Shadow whirled as he heard the white trader coming. "Didn't I—"

Shadow leveled the musket at Jacob's midsection, and the white man groaned aloud.

"Don't shoot," he cried. "Don't shoot me, for God's sake. I'm your friend. I've done nothing wrong. Your chiefs have given me the right to trade here."

The two warriors from the public room moved into position behind Jacob Clough. Wolf Shadow acknowledged them with a nod. "See if the woman is alone," he ordered in the Iroquois language. The men obeyed without hesitation.

"I've no quarrel with the Huron," the trader insisted shrilly. Shadow backed him slowly into the public room as He-Who-Runs and Yellow Elk began to search the store for muskets and powder and shot.

"You sell whiskey to Indians," Wolf Shadow accused in broken English. The sound of breaking wood came from the store.

"Here guns!" Fat Boy called.

"You can't steal my guns!" Jacob protested.

"You break white man's law, sell whiskey," Shadow said. He raised the muzzle of the musket until it brushed Jacob's long nose. "No whiskey.

Whiskey bad for Indian. Make Indian crazy. Indian drunk on firewater—you cheat him.''

"I ain't cheated no Hurons. Ask anybody.'' Jacob was breathing hard, and sweat ran off his fear-contorted face in thick drops.

Wolf Shadow prodded him in the throat with the musket and motioned toward the door. ''Go.''

As they walked out into the snow, Wolf Shadow could hear the crackle of burning logs. Behind the trading post was an old one-room cabin, half-sunken into the hillside. Jacob used it as a place to keep his stock of whiskey. The cabin door hung open at a crazy angle, and inside, one of Shadow's men was systematically smashing the liquor barrels and jugs.

"What have you done?'' the trader cried. ''You've ruined me!''

"Look and remember,'' Wolf Shadow said harshly in Iroquois. He switched back to broken English. ''This time we burn firewater, steal guns. You sell whiskey again—you die. Your scalp dry over Huron fire.'' Shadow glanced over his shoulder. Yellow Elk and He-Who-Runs were strapping a bundle of muskets onto Jacob's gray mare.

Fat Boy appeared at Shadow's shoulder and held out a black leather box. The Shawnee warrior opened it. Inside lay an array of gleaming knives, saws, scissors, probes, and other unfamiliar steel items. The silk-lined box had been cleverly constructed so that every square inch was filled. The spaces between the instruments were packed with needles, rolls of silk thread, tiny glass bottles, and even smaller round, wooden containers.

Wolf Shadow touched the surface of a small box. There were slits cut into the surface, and from each hole protruded a razor sharp blade. He turned blazing eyes on his white captive. ''What is?'' he demanded.

"For bloodletting,'' the trader stammered. ''It's

a surgeon's kit . . . nothing of value to you. Instruments for English doctor. Bad medicine for Indian. Very bad."

Wolf Shadow nodded and closed the case, then motioning for Fat Boy to add it to the loot being loaded onto the horses. He turned back to Jacob. "Remember,"he repeated. "Next time, wolves chew your bones." He uttered a short yell, waved to his companions, and then loped off into the trees.

Jacob stared after them through the falling snow. "You've ruined me," he cried. "Damn you! Thieving Indian bastards!"

From the open doorway, Abequa, his Ojibwa wife watched. Jacob's back was to her as he cursed and shook his fist after the raiding party. He didn't see her smile.

Chapter 2

Wolf Shadow led his men back through the
falling snow to a cave an hour's march from
the trading post. There, two half-grown Shawnee
boys waited anxiously beside a small fire for the war
party's return. When Shadow gave the repeated
hoot of a great horned owl—the signal that all was
well—the boys ran out of the cave smiling.

Despite the narrow, hidden entrance, the shelter
was high and deep enough to bring the two horses
inside, out of the bitter weather. The boys led the
animals into the back of the cave and gave them water while the men settled around the fire pit and
began to cut off chunks of hot roasted venison. The
silence that the warriors had maintained since they'd
left Jacob Clough's was broken, and the Shawnee
men began to laugh and talk all at once as they removed their Huron disguises.

Spear Thrower slapped He-Who-Runs on the back
and began to tell him an elaborate yarn about the
fight Jacob Clough's hired man had put up in the
barn. The men pretended not to notice young Snowshoe, Yellow Elk's son, who had finished his chores
and moved close to the men to listen to the story.
The second boy, Beaver Tooth, joined the group as
well.

"Pay Spear Thrower no mind," Two Crows chided. "There wasn't any fight. The white coward ran like a startled doe when he saw Spear Thrower's face. He's probably still running, for all I know. Maybe he'll run all the way back to the Great Salt Sea."

He-Who-Runs winked at Yellow Elk. "Nothing strange about that. Lots of people run away when they see Spear Thrower's face. His wife says he's so ugly she wouldn't put up with him if he wasn't such a good hunter."

"Hunter, nothing," Spear Thrower insisted. "Lover! I'm such a great lover, she knows she'd never find anyone who could please her like I do."

"Well, if we're going to talk about pleasing women . . ." Yellow Elk put in.

"Watch what you say in front of your son," Two Crows warned. "He'll tell his mother, and you'll be in big trouble."

Snowshoe, a muscular boy of fourteen with light skin and chestnut-brown hair, reddened and stared at the ground. His father clapped him on the shoulder and laughed. "I wasn't going to say anything that would anger your mother," Yellow Elk assured him. "I was only going to remind Fat Boy of the time . . ."

Wolf Shadow let the voices of his comrades recede in his mind until they were mere whispers. Crouching by the edge of the fire pit, he warmed his hands as he stared into the hypnotic flames. He'd already stripped off the whiskey-sodden clothes and scrubbed the hated Huron markings from his face and arms with handfuls of snow until his skin tingled; now he was in the process of purifying his thoughts.

Crossing the border between this real world and the spirit realm was not as difficult for Wolf Shadow as it was for other men. He was a moon dancer—

what the white men called a medicine man. He knew
the secrets of healing, not only the ailments of the
physical body, but of the mind as well. But he was
not just an ordinary shaman; he was more powerful
than that. He was called a great shaman.

According to Shawnee tradition, a great shaman,
one who possessed extraordinary powers, was born
into the tribe only once every hundred years—at a
time when his people needed him most. This special man, with one moccasined foot in the spirit
world and one planted firmly in this world, was
expected to be a diplomat and political adviser to
the chiefs, as well as a counselor to individual
members of the tribe. His was a life of service to
his people. The task required such dedication that
there was no room in the shaman's life for personal
ambition or selfish desire.

Wolf Shadow folded his arms across his bare chest
and exhaled softly. His mind was still troubled—so
much so that he could not concentrate on his med-
itation. His jaw tightened imperceptibly as he gazed
into the red-gold flames.

They reminded him of the white woman's hair.

A rush of impatience caused his frame to tense.
He could almost hear the scornful mocking of his
boyhood teacher, Red Smoke. *Wooden head! Control
of others begins with control of self.* By force of will
alone, Wolf Shadow compelled his muscles to relax,
the coursing of his blood to slow.

Yellow Elk pushed a chunk of meat into Wolf Shadow's hand. "Eat," the older man urged with a grin.
"There's a time for dreaming and a time for filling
one's stomach."

Obediently, Wolf Shadow took a bite of the juicy
meat, but the battle still raged in the dark corners of
his mind. He was trying to decide if he should do
something about the white woman. He chewed
slowly. Considering the welfare of an enemy woman

was a grave fault for a dedicated shaman. It had been many years since his personal concerns had interfered with his duty.

He should have been relaxing with the others . . .

The mission had gone well. Jacob Clough's stock of firewater had been destroyed, and the trader had been badly frightened. No lives, red or white, had been lost. And, lastly, valuable guns had been taken for the Shawnee cause.

His plan had been executed without a single mishap . . .

He paused and wiped the corners of his mouth, carefully washing his hands in the bowl of clean water provided by one of the boys.

The raid had been perfect—except for the woman.

Wolf Shadow took another bite of the venison. The succulent meat seemed tasteless. By the Great Circle of Life, why did that pale-skinned woman plague him so? He bit down hard and winced as he caught the back edge of his tongue between his teeth.

Could she be a witch? he wondered. Then he saw the humor of his own apprehension, and the corners of his mouth turned up in a smile. He was becoming as superstitious as an old grandmother.

He sniffed. If the one they called Fiona was an enchantress, she had the most shapely legs he'd ever seen on a witch. Although her skin was so pale it freckled and her hair was an unnatural shade of red, she was young and strangely attractive. Wolf Shadow stared into the fire and let the memory of the woman materialize in his mind's eye.

His sensual lips tightened. No Shawnee man could consider such a woman handsome, he decided. True, she was small and well-proportioned, and she walked with inborn grace, as an Indian woman should, but there the similarities ended. Fiona's eyes were round instead of slanted, and no woman who possessed eyes of that strange color

could be called beautiful. Proper women had eyes
as black as a crow's wing. While Fiona's were the
shade of a sprouting oak leaf. Her chin was pointed
instead of round. Her nose was too thin, and it
turned up slightly at the end. By Shawnee stan-
dards, the white woman must be considered ill-
favored.

Instantly he rejected the label. The need for
honesty in thought and action had been drummed
into his being since he was a barefoot toddler. He
could not call such a female, not even an enemy
squaw, plain. No, he decided, green eyes and hair
like beaten copper did not make a woman plain—
they made her unique.

It was a puzzle. He'd been taught that Wishemenetoo, the Great Good Spirit, had created all women
alike. Yet no woman Wolf Shadow had ever known
was exactly like another; no willow tree was the
same . . . no snowflake. His dark sloe eyes caught
the gleam of the flames, and his smile widened.
Snowflakes caught the moonlight and glistened in
the air like quartz crystals. He wondered if Fiona's
hair would shine in the sunlight.

Someone threw a blanket around his shoulders.

"Look at him," Spear Thrower remarked. "His
spirit walks the treetops and leaves his body to
freeze." His laugh was deep and genuine. "The
greatest shaman the Shawnee have ever known, and
without us to watch out for him, he'd catch his
death."

Wolf Shadow opened his eyes and fixed Spear
Thrower with a smoldering gaze. "Be careful how
you speak of great magic workers," he said softly.
"One day I might come out of a trance too fast and
turn you into a bat."

Spear Thrower countered the threat with an ob-
scene remark, and Wolf Shadow laughed and threw
his arm around his friend.

The good-natured bantering echoed through the cave until the fire died to coals, and the men began to doze. Wolf Shadow remained alert, despite the guard posted outside. His mind was still too busy for sleep.

He glanced around the darkened cave and smiled. It was true what Spear Thrower had said—his friends did look after him. The Shawnee braves who had made up this raiding party were the most courageous of his people, the greatest trackers and the fiercest fighters; they were the best of the best. Most had been his friends since he was a boy. They trusted him, and they believed in him without fearing his powers, as many others did. They accepted his dream of uniting the Shawnee and Delaware tribes to halt the advance of the white men. But even these friends did not realize the extent of the threat the light-skinned Europeans posed to the Indian way of life.

If the white men could not be stopped, they would swallow up the Shawnee land, bite by bite. They would drink the clear, sweet water and leave only fouled mud in their wake. They would not cease their relentless gobbling of the Creator's blessings until the red man was only a memory in his own land.

Wolf Shadow had devoted his life to the struggle. Nothing else mattered . . . certainly not his own safety. If it came to that, he would sacrifice himself and his comrades to save the Shawnee race.

A branch snapped in the heat of the coals, and fiery red-orange sparks spewed upward into the velvet blackness of the cave. Like glowing bits of stars . . . stars as red and vibrant as the white woman's hair.

With a sigh, Wolf Shadow leaned over and shook Yellow Elk and whispered instructions into his ear. Then he rose to his feet. From a bundle, he took fringed leggings of elk hide, sewn with the fur inside, stepped into them and knotted the ties at his belt. Over his feet he drew knee-high winter moccasins of otter skin, boots so waterproof and warm that he would not feel the bite of the snow.

Yellow Elk helped him to don the necklace of mountain lion claws and the armbands of copper that fit tightly over his heavily muscled biceps. Then the older warrior adjusted the wolfskin cape—the badge of the shaman's office—over Wolf Shadow's broad shoulders and wrapped it tightly at his waist with leather bands to keep out the wind. The wolf's head with glittering mica eyes and bared teeth settled into place over Wolf Shadow's hair and forehead, as tightly as a second skin.

Yellow Elk stood back and grinned, but Wolf Shadow could not miss the hint of awe in his friend's eyes. "Even the ghosts will fear you tonight," Yellow Elk joked. His Adam's apple bobbed in his tanned throat, and his voice became husky with truth. "I know I'd not want to meet you in the woods. You look more spirit than man—that's certain."

Wolf Shadow bared his teeth in the hint of a smile and nodded his thanks. Then, slinging a musket over one shoulder, he moved out into the softly falling snow as silently as a night spirit.

Fiona O'Neal was more terrified than she'd ever been in her life.

She had been afraid when she was ten years old . . . when her mother had died in childbed and left her alone and destitute in the slums of Galway. She'd traveled for days along the stony roads of Ireland, a hungry, ragged urchin, searching for a grandfather she'd never met . . . a grandfather who'd cursed the day she was born.

Years later, she'd felt sickening doubts of fear

when she'd sold herself into slavery and sailed away from her homeland to an unknown future in America. She'd trembled with anguish and dismay when her indenture had been sold to Jacob Clough and she realized that he meant to take her into the trackless wilderness.

But she'd never known the panic she felt now at the mercy of these men.

She'd regained consciousness to find that she was tied across a mule, being carried God-knows-where by Nigel and Karl. It was pitch-black and snowing. Her feet were so cold they felt like lumps of ice, and her tears froze on her cheeks. The sharp spine of the mule cut into her stomach and made her nauseous—a condition hardly aided by the stench of Nigel's improperly cured buckskins.

"Untie my hands," she demanded. "If I must ride this poor creature, at least let me sit it upright—not dangling over the side like a slab of fat pork."

"The bloody bitch is awake," Karl snarled.

Nigel laughed coarsely. "I told ye she were."

They argued then, over whether to untie her or not. In the end Nigel won out, and he stopped the animals and cut her loose. He yanked her against him and slobbered over her face, and he squeezed her breasts roughly when he lifted her back up on the mule, this time in a sitting position. Now, at least, she didn't want to throw up every time the animal took a step.

She knew what would come when they stopped for the night. No girl-child could grow up on the waterfront of Galway without seeing and hearing what men did to women . . . without learning the shameful names of lust.

She'd been eight when a British soldier had exposed himself to her and offered her a silver penny to rub his shaft. She hadn't learned to speak English yet, but she wasn't too young to guess his meaning.

An Irish street girl without a father knows when to run, or she doesn't live long enough to shed a woman's monthly blood.

The swirling snow had drifted hock deep on the mules, and the icy wind was from the north and rising. The cold cut through the trade blanket and chilled Fiona until her teeth chattered. She fingered the amulet she wore around her neck and prayed the two trappers would go on riding through the shadowy forest forever.

Taking her own life would be a mortal sin, but she'd risk losing her soul to keep these human animals from possessing her body . . . from touching her with their hot, dirty hands. She would kill them both or herself, she vowed.

She clutched the charm and willed herself away from this frozen wilderness. If she clamped her eyes shut and held her breath, she could almost smell the heady fragrance of blue peat smoke and see it rising straight up to heaven from the clusters of white-washed cottages along the shore of Galway Bay.

The amulet was all she had left of home. She'd worn the heavy necklace since she was a babe. Her mother had said the ancient piece was solid gold, a gift from her father, and no matter how hungry they'd been, her mother had never sold it to buy food. For fear that someone would steal the precious antique, her mother had painted it black. *Black for the curse it carries*, Eileen O'Neal had said many a time. *Black for the evil that would take you far from home and kin, and pure sweet yellow gold within. Gold, my darlin', gold for the shining blessing.*

Fiona drew in a long, shuddering breath. Her mother's voice had been low and husky and full of authority; it was a voice that never failed to turn men's heads and make even the gentry pay heed. Fiona could hear Eileen's lilting tone now if she listened hard enough.

The amulet was a gift from your lordly father to you when you were but hours old . . . Her mother had repeated the story so many times that Fiona could recall it word for word. . . . *A birthing gift fit for a princess. I cried when first I laid eyes upon the shining glory of the Eye of Mist. "Hardly fit for the likes of our daughter," your father replied, all proud and filled with the joy of seeing you so fat and fair. "I'll see her wed to a prince when she's grown," he promised. As God is my witness, little one, those were his very words. He said the amulet had been handed down in your Scottish grandmother's family for time out of time. "Whosoever possesses the Eye of Mist shall be cursed and blessed," so the legend goes. "The curse is that you will be taken from your family and friends to a far-off land. The blessing is that you will be granted one wish. Whatever you ask you shall have—even unto the power of life and death."*

"Unto the power of life and death," Fiona murmured. She opened her eyes and stared into the swirling snow. If she believed in such nonsense as magic necklaces, she'd use the amulet now to strike Karl and Nigel stone dead. Or . . . She thought wistfully of the columbine that had trailed over the wall at the bottom of her grandfather's yard. Or she'd use the Eye of Mist to turn back time and wish herself a child again in James Patrick O'Neal's parlor. No, she decided, not her grandfather's parlor—his office. She'd spent her happiest hours there, watching him tend his patients, holding and sterilizing his instruments and studying his medical books.

Dour and short-tempered, James Patrick O'Neal had reluctantly given her a home after her mother, Eileen—his only child—had died. He'd never forgiven Eileen for giving birth to Fiona out of wedlock.

Or me for being born, Fiona thought painfully. But he gave her an education few boys in Ireland could boast of. He taught her much of what he'd learned in medical school and in forty years of practice as a physician. He gave her a calling, a purpose in life.

Fiona didn't have to guess what her grandfather would say about the mess she'd gotten herself into. *Any fool who'd indenture himself like a cart horse and go off to the Colonies deserves anything they get.* If she'd used common sense and stayed in Ireland . . .

If she'd stayed in Ireland, she might well have ended up hanging from a rope.

Since the days of Cromwell, the English hand of conquest lay heavy on her Catholic homeland. The Black Night, her people called it. The penal laws enacted by William III forbade the education of Catholic children and closed the schools. Even parents who could afford it were not permitted to send their children abroad to be educated. Catholics had no vote and were barred from holding public office or from attending university. Many priests had been imprisoned or put to death, and all religious orders were exiled from Ireland. Thousands of acres of privately owned land had been confiscated, and inheritance rights had been severely restricted.

Hundreds of starving people walked the roads begging for work. Once her grandfather died and his house and belongings were confiscated, she'd had nowhere to go, and no way to support herself. A woman alone in Ireland—without family or money—became a thief, sold her body to strangers, or died alone in a ditch.

Instead, Fiona had chosen to begin a new life in America. And she'd ended up facing rape and murder at the hands of these men . . .

The terror and hardship of the bitter night were beginning to take their toll. Fiona had ceased to shiver, and her eyelids felt weighted with lead. She'd never been exposed to such harsh weather in Ireland, but she remembered reading the symptoms of patients who had. She knew that she had to remain alert and that she must keep the blood circulating in her hands and feet.

She tried to wiggle her toes and realized with a sinking feeling that her legs were numb from the knees down. Her fingers were stiff with cold, but she'd folded her arms across her chest under the blanket, and tucked her hands under her armpits.

It was snowing so hard now that she couldn't see Karl or Nigel. The rump of Nigel's mule was a moving white mound just beyond her own mount's flicking ears. She didn't know where Karl was—if he was riding behind her or ahead. If she was last in line, she wondered if she could just rein in her mule and stop. How long would it take before the trappers missed her?

Would she just sit on her mule in the middle of this endless woods until she and the animal froze to death? And if they did, would it be an easier death than what awaited her at the end of the journey?

Quitter!

Fiona's eyes snapped open, and she stared around her, expecting to see James Patrick O'Neal's scowling face materialize out of the darkness. Grandfather's dead, she told herself firmly. If I'm hearing his voice, it's only my mind playing tricks on me.

Quitter. It was her grandfather's voice, all right. *Weak stock on your father's side. What more can I expect of an Englishman's bastard?*

"Scot," Fiona murmured through cold, cracked lips. "He wasn't English—he was a Scot."

Same thing. A gentleman. Her grandfather's withering sarcasm cut deep, as it always had. *Weak stock, weak blood. Any farmer knows interbreeding makes worthless livestock. No O'Neal was ever a quitter. Your mother had more gumption than you when she was half your age.*

Nigel's harsh voice intruded on Fiona's dreaming. "Hold yer blathering tongue, slut."

''He was a Scot,'' she repeated stubbornly, barely loud enough for her own ears to hear.

Her grandsire had always forced her into the position of defending her father . . . defending a man she hated. It wasn't fair, but it was James Patrick O'Neal's way, and nothing short of God or the devil would change it.

Whenever the dusty Latin texts were too hard for her, or she couldn't figure out the handwritten recipe for mixing a medicinal formula, her grandfather would goad her to try again and to keep trying until she succeeded. He never laid a hand on her in anger. But if she sickened at the sight of bedsores on a dying man, or blanched at the cries of a woman giving birth, he would taunt her until she found the strength to face what appalled her.

''I guess you made me tough, Grandfather,'' Fiona whispered into the wind, ''but it never made me love you.''

The mule stopped short, and Fiona fell forward over the animal's neck, barely catching herself from tumbling into the snow.

''We're here,'' Karl said. ''Get down offen thet mule.''

Seconds later, before Fiona could force her stiffened limbs to obey, he cuffed her sharply alongside the head. The blow brought her fully awake. She slid her leg over the mule's back and kicked free of the stirrup, then let herself drop. Her knees folded under her, and she landed facedown on the ground, under the animal's belly.

Excruciating pain shot through her as pins and needles of sensation seized both feet. She bit her lip to keep from crying out, crawled from under the mule, and used the saddle leathers to pull herself up to a standing position.

Nigel's hand clamped over Fiona's shoulder, and he dragged her several yards to a crude log structure. "Home sweet home," he said, throwing his shoulder against the door and dragging her inside.

She shuddered and shrank away from him. He smelled worse inside out of the wind, and the stink turned her stomach.

Nigel caught her chin cruelly between his fingers. "No need to be so standoffish," he said salaciously. "Before spring comes, we're gonna get to know each other real well."

"I'll kill you if you touch me," she threatened.

He laughed. "Once ye see what I got, ye won't be backin' off, ye'll be beggin' fer it."

"Rot in hell," she retorted.

His fingers dug into Fiona's face, and he shoved her roughly away from him. "That's what my last woman said," he taunted her, "and she ended up as wolf bait."

White-hot anger drove back the smothering fear as Fiona sank to her knees on the dirt floor and tried to think clearly. Nigel and Karl believed she was helpless. Well and good, let the English bastards think so! She was no longer bound hand and foot, and both trappers carried weapons.

If only she could just stall their sexual assault long enough to get her hands on a gun . . .

Chapter 3

Fiona rubbed her ankles, trying to restore the flow of blood to her feet. The pain was still severe, but hurting was better than feeling nothing.

It was no warmer inside the cabin, but at least the wind had stopped. The earth beneath her was damp and smelled of stale rodent droppings and mold. Ahead and to her left, she could hear Karl swearing, but it was too black in the hut to see her own hand.

Suddenly a spark flared, followed by another, and she realized Karl was trying to start a fire. She heard one of the animals bray and glanced over her shoulder toward the open door, where the white wall of falling snow was broken by the outline of a mule.

Nigel led the animals inside, one by one, and tied them along a wall. Karl's fire had caught, and he soon had a small blaze starting in a crude mud and stick fireplace. Fiona was drawn to the flames.

"Let the woman tend the fire," Nigel said. "She can cook us up some vittles."

"I ain't lettin' her near no damned fire," Karl replied. "She near burned me t' death." He leered at Fiona and rubbed his crotch. "Don't think I fergot what ye done t' me, bitch. I'm gettin' first turn at ye."

"Food first, then futterin'," Nigel snapped. "I

don't know 'bout you, Karl, but I needs my strength fer what I got in mind.''

Her cheeks burning with shame, Fiona forced herself up onto her tingling feet and shook the snow off her blanket. She knew what kind of men these were; she'd seen them in the back alleys of Galway and Dublin and Philadelphia. They were like hungry dogs—if she showed her fear, they'd be on her in seconds.

Stiffening her spine, she folded the scarlet woolen blanket and glanced around the drafty hovel with contempt. "This be where you live?"

Nigel grunted, then grinned. "Sassy, ain't she, Karl. I likes 'em with spirit. I likes a woman what bites and scratches.''

Fiona suppressed a shudder. She was light-headed with terror. This couldn't be happening to her. She put her hands behind her back and clenched her fists until her nails cut into the palms of her hands. These filthy men, this terrible place, surpassed belief.

At home in Ireland, she'd seen horrible poverty in the slums. And later, after she'd gone to live with her grandfather, she'd traveled with him to tend the sick in isolated country cottages. Many times, they'd spent the night waiting for a baby to be born, or for a critically ill patient to either get better or die. She'd shared a single room with a dozen crying children, and occasionally a goat or a litter of pigs. Never had she seen living quarters as vile as this.

Mule droppings littered the floor on one side of the windowless cabin; the other half of the room was empty except for a table made of uneven logs and a wide sleeping pallet of moth-eaten skins. As Fiona stared around the hut in disgust, Nigel dropped a bundle on the pallet and two rats ran out. Instantly Nigel brought his boot heel down on one rodent's head and kept stomping until the squealing stopped. The second rat escaped through a gap in the outer wall.

"Don't squash him too bad," Karl shouted. "He looks fat. Might be a mite tastier than that salt pork ye bought down to Jacob's." Karl turned toward Fiona, and she saw the raw, blistered flesh on his burned face and smelled the stink of singed hair. "Nigel's partial t' roast rat, ain't ye Nigel?"

His one-eyed partner kicked the pallet a few more times. When no more rats fled from the bed, he said to Karl, "What I'm partial to is fresh woman. Maybe we'll jest play a hand o' cards to see who has her first."

A moan rose in Fiona's throat, and she stifled it with a fist over her mouth. Nigel's musket leaned against the wall next to the door. She wouldn't give up hope yet. Trembling, she picked up a rusty iron spider. "I can cook pork or rat," she said flatly, wiping the inside of the frying pan with the corner of her skirt. "Makes no difference to me." She swallowed hard. "Have you got onions and potatoes in those saddlebags?"

"Sit down and shut up," Karl told her. "Ye get any closer t' this fire, an' I'll cut ye so bad yer own mother wouldn't look at ye."

"Cards, or dice," Nigel offered. "You was always lucky at dice."

Karl frowned and touched his ruined face. "No need t' play," he said. "I get her first. I said it, an' I stand by it."

Fiona gasped as Nigel's hand flashed to his boot top and came up holding a fourteen-inch skinning knife. "Take yer chances like a man, Karl, or wait yer turn."

She began to move toward the door.

"Sit, bitch," Karl ordered.

Fiona crouched where she was. Gooseflesh rose

on her arms, and her mouth tasted of ashes. She clutched her amulet and mouthed a silent prayer.

"Dice." Karl grinned. "Winner keeps her all night."

"The hell you say," Nigel began. "I—" He broke off as the howl of a wolf sounded only a few yards from the cabin. The mules stiffened and began to pull at their ropes, their eyes rolling in fear.

Karl exhaled loudly. "Jeezus!"

The bone-chilling cry came again, closer yet, and Fiona hugged herself and eyed the sagging wooden door. The mules were snorting now and pawing the dirt floor. Their ears were laid back flat on their heads.

Suddenly there was a scratching on the far wall. "Damned wolves! I'll give 'em something to chew on." Karl grabbed his musket and fired through the logs. The mules went wild, kicking and braying. One broke loose, reared up, and lashed out with its hind feet.

Fiona heard a dull plopping noise from the hearth. The fire hissed and sputtered and nearly went out as a great chunk of snow fell into the center. Another wolf howled, and Fiona jumped up and ran to grab the halters of the three mules that were still tied. She hadn't gone a full stride when something heavy struck the outside of the door.

Sweat was pouring down Karl's face. "It ain't natural," he said, reloading the musket. "I never knowed wolves to act so."

Nigel's hands were shaking as he yanked a pistol from his belt, poured powder into the frizzen, and pulled the trigger, sending a lead ball through the board door.

The dun-colored mule Fiona was reaching for snapped its rope and began pitching around the room, hooves flying. Fiona shielded her head with her arm and backed against the wall as the rest of the mules broke free.

A second lump of snow fell down the chimney, plunging the cabin into almost total darkness. Then, without warning, the door was wrenched open. Fiona screamed as she saw a huge wolf standing upright in the doorway. The beast's eyes and teeth caught the last flicker of the dying fire.

Karl's musket roared. An instant later another shot echoed through the room. Fiona stared in disbelief as Karl groaned, clutched his chest, and fell backward against the hearth. Nigel gave a wild cry and dashed, skinning knife in hand, toward the terrible apparition in the doorway. The dun mule bolted for the opening and collided with the hulking trapper. Nigel went down beneath the animal's hooves. The wolf ducked aside, and the mule escaped into the night, followed by the other frightened animals.

Suddenly the room seemed to be encased in silence . . . a quiet so deep that Fiona could hear her own blood pounding in her ears. The air was thick with the acrid smell of black powder. Frozen with fear, she stared at the open doorway. A dark, furry shape materialized out of the falling snow, and a thousand years of Irish civilization dropped away . . . leaving Fiona with the superstitious dread of the unknown. Every tale of spectral ghost and banshee that she had ever heard rose to haunt her. Her hair stood up on the back of her neck, and her throat constricted so tightly that she couldn't breathe.

She heard the crunch of paws on the snow-covered door sill and found her voice. "Get thee gone, creature of the night," she cried in Gaelic. "In the name of Mary and her blessed Son—get thee gone!"

The answer came softly in accented English—a man's voice, as deep and rich as the earth beneath the snow. "Trust me."

She drew in a ragged breath, not certain of what she'd heard. "If ye be not of God's children, I bid thee go," she pronounced, this time in English.

"Peace to you, woman. I mean you no harm."

Fiona struggled with her own sanity. Her eyes saw a wolf that walked upright and fired a gun; her ears heard the concerned voice of a cultured gentleman. "Be ye Lucifer?" she demanded. Hadn't her mother warned her that the devil's tongue was as sweet as new-made honey? "Or one of his demons?"

The wolf-man laughed—a tone so human and merry that she nearly smiled herself. Her mind told her what she was seeing and hearing was impossible; her heart told her she had nothing to fear from the figure outlined against the snow.

"Stay where you are," he commanded. "I promise I won't hurt you."

He moved past her in the darkness, so silently that she sensed rather than heard his passing. The wind blowing through the open door was cold, and her teeth began to chatter. A scraping sound came from the direction of the hearth, and she knew that the wolf-man had lifted Karl's body and was dragging it away.

A man moaned in pain—Nigel, Fiona decided, judging from the location of the groans. She waited, motionless, not knowing if she should flee into the storm or stay where she was.

Flint and steel struck together, and a spark lit the darkness for a heartbeat. Fiona watched as another spark flared, followed by a fiery glow. She closed her eyes against the light, and when she opened them again, she saw that the wolf-man was crouched and breathing life into an infant flame.

A minute passed. The creature fed the fire bits of dry tinder until it blazed up, and his face was revealed in the flickering light.

"You're a man," Fiona said.

"Just a man," he replied. "Come and warm yourself." He added twigs to the red-orange flames, then rose and went to close the door.

She retrieved her blanket, wrapped it around her shoulders, and went to the hearth. She dropped to her knees and held out her hands to warm them, her back on the wolf-man. "Do you have a name?" she asked. Her voice sounded oddly thin to her own ears.

"Men call me Wolf Shadow." He returned to stand behind her.

She twisted to look up at him over her shoulder. "And women, what do they call you?"

He laughed again, and she saw straight white teeth and a strong nose below the wolf's head mask. "I have not noticed that they call me often," he replied. He dropped to a squatting position beside her. "Don't be afraid," he said, his voice becoming serious once more. "I came for you. I came to take you from this place."

Fiona's breathing slowed to near normal. She licked her dry lips and looked for the first time at Karl's grotesquely twisted body. He lay on his back. The front of his shirt bore a round hole surrounded by a dark red stain. "You killed him," she said woodenly.

"Yes," Wolf Shadow admitted, "I did. But he needed killing."

"I think the other man, Nigel, is still alive."

Wolf Shadow touched her cheek with a bronzed hand. To her surprise, she didn't recoil from him. She should have been afraid, but she wasn't.

His almond-shaped eyes were so dark brown that they seemed carved of wet, shining ebony. Fiona held her breath and stared into their bottomless depths, then realized with a start that he was no stranger. "You . . ." she murmured. "You were . . . I saw you at Jacob Clough's trading post." She shook her head as memories of the drunken Indian returned full force. The Huron had met her gaze, and for an instant she had felt his compassion at her plight. "It was you, wasn't it?"

He nodded, almost imperceptibly.

She sniffed. His scent was clean and wholly male. There was no trace of liquor on him, nor any smell of unwashed flesh. Even the musky odor of the wolf-hide was not unpleasant. Fiona sucked in a deep breath. How had the wolf-man transformed himself from a drunken Huron to . . . to . . . She smiled as she realized she still didn't know who or what he was. "Who are you?" she asked.

"You see me," he answered cryptically.

"You are an Indian."

"It pleases your kind to call me so."

"And what do you call yourself?"

He nodded approval, as though she was a bright pupil. "I am of the Western True People, the Shawnee."

"You're not a Huron—not one of the Iroquois?"

"I am not."

"Then why did you come to Jacob's and pretend—"

He silenced her with a gentle motion. "Later, perhaps. As you say, the one near the door lives. Build up the fire, and I will see if I can help him."

"I'm an apothecary," she offered, "and I know the healing arts."

"The bearded one abused you—yet you would tend his wounds?"

Fiona stood up. "I was taught to help the sick and wounded, not to judge them."

His dark eyes caressed her with approval. "I think you are wise, Fiona of the Flaming Torch." He smiled. "For an Englishwoman."

She shook her head. "I be no Sassenach. I'm Irish." She rubbed a hand across her face. This must be a nightmare—it could not really be happening. How could she stand here calmly and have a discussion with a wild Indian who dressed like a beast and spoke like a barrister? Cautiously, she stepped around Wolf Shadow and went to kneel beside Nigel.

The trapper lay on his back. A gash on his forehead was bleeding badly, and one arm was clearly broken. Fiona could see another wound just above his left knee. Nigel's buckskin trousers had been torn, and the flesh was cut to the bone.

Fiona lifted the injured arm, feeling the extent of the break with gentle fingers.

"Stop the bleeding first," Wolf Shadow said.

Her heart thudded wildly. She'd not heard him walk across the room, not seen him move from his position at the fire. Was it possible that he was a demon after all? She swallowed the lump in her throat as a prickly sensation ran down her spine. "Mother Mary protect me," she whispered under her breath.

The Indian knelt by Nigel's head and placed a handful of cobwebs on the swelling gash. "Bring snow," he ordered. "We will pack the arm and leg to slow the bleeding."

Fiona shook her head. "No," she argued. "The bad blood must flow freely to cleanse the—"

"Do as I say, woman."

She raised her eyes, and her gaze collided with his. The force of will was overwhelming, and her chest seemed suddenly tight.

Wolf Shadow had taken off the wolf's head cape, and she could see that he was a light-skinned man in his prime. One muscular arm and sinewy shoulder were exposed through his hide wrap. A beaten copper armband encircled his bicep, and around his powerful neck hung a string of animal claws. His hawklike nose jutted between craggy cheekbones, and his compelling eyes glittered beneath brows as dark and sleek as a raven's plumage. His upper lip was firm and thin; the lower one gave a hint of controlled sensuality. Thick, midnight-black hair was brushed back from a high, broad forehead to fall loosely around his shoulders.

He was beautiful . . . and terrible .. and she was afraid.

Old Scat won't come for you with cloven hooves and lashing tail, her mother had warned. *He'll come in the guise of a handsome man with a silver tongue and hands like silk.*

Fiona wondered what that copper-gold skin would feel like if she touched it. The thought made her cheeks go hot and her nipples tingle against her coarse linen shift.

"Oh!" She gasped, clasping her hands together to keep them from trembling. The heat from her cheeks raced through her blood to cause the strangest sensation in the pit of her stomach.

What was wrong with her that she let this pagan savage affect her this way? Hadn't she just seen him kill a man without the slightest remorse? Her mouth went dry. An hour ago she'd been in danger of rape and murder by the human beasts who lay on the cabin floor. Now she was safe from them, but her fate rested in the hands of a native barbarian. If Christian men could use her so cruelly, what could she expect from a wolf-man?

She had heard stories of Indian atrocities . . . of scalping and mutilation . . . of cannibalism. He'd told her he had come for her. Why would he do such a thing?

"The snow," Wolf Shadow repeated, taking hold of her arm. "We must hurry before he awakens."

His touch burned through her woolen sleeve. She pulled away, confused and more than a little frightened. As she glanced down at Nigel, the physician in her noted that the cobwebs had done the trick. The heavy bleeding from the cut on the trapper's head had almost stopped.

Wolf Shadow regarded her expectantly, and she hurried toward the door. He began to cut away the buckskin around Nigel's injured leg.

By the time Fiona had packed Nigel's wounds with snow and heated more snow to make water, Wolf Shadow had pressed the trapper's arm bone into place and bound it with cloth from Karl's shirt-sleeve. Fiona watched with approval as the Indian cut bark from the inside of the logs to use as splints. Then he tied Nigel's ankles together and fastened his uninjured arm tightly against his waist.

"The wound on his head is not deep enough to kill him," Wolf Shadow said. "He will be dizzy for a few days, but it will heal."

"It should be stitched," Fiona insisted. "If I had a needle and thread . . ." She sighed. It was use-less. There was nothing in the crude cabin that would serve to sew up the gash.

"To sew the edges together would make a bad scar," Wolf Shadow said. "The cobwebs stopped the bleeding, and the snow cleaned the wound. I have bandaged it. For such as this one . . ." He nudged Nigel with a moccasined toe. "We have done enough for him."

Wolf Shadow had dragged Karl's body to the far corner of the cabin, closed the trapper's eyes, and covered him with a deerskin. Fiona rolled a fur and put it under Nigel's head, then tucked hides around him to keep him from freezing. Nigel was semicon-scious and alternately cursing and moaning.

Fiona was so tired she could hardly keep her eyes open. She felt light-headed, and her stomach growled from hunger. She couldn't remember when she'd eaten last . . . was it just this morning?

She washed her hands and face in some of the

warm water and wrapped the blanket around her. There was no chair, and the only bench had been destroyed by the mules, so she sat as close to the fire as she could and leaned sleepily against the hearth. Her eyes seemed to have sand in them; the more she rubbed them, the more they stung.

"Sleep," the Indian said, coming to stand beside her. "I will keep watch."

"And who will keep watch on you?" she asked with more courage than she felt. The weariness dragged on her muscles and spirit. She covered her face with her hands. "I'm sorry," she said. "You've done me no harm. It's just that . . ." Tears welled up and blurred her vision. "If you mean to ravish and murder me, could you do it and get it over with?"

He chuckled and sat down, legs crossed. He held out his big hands to the warmth of the flames. "For a wise woman, you do not listen well. I mean you no harm."

She closed her eyes and heard the wind howling around the cabin. "What will happen to the mules? Will the wolves eat them?"

"Mules are tough."

"But . . ." Her eyes snapped open. "You were the wolves, weren't you? You made the howling?"

He shrugged.

"And the snow . . . the snow that fell down the chimney and put out the fire . . . You did that too."

He smiled, and she saw that his teeth were as white as sun-bleached clamshells. Good teeth were rare in men or women. It had never occurred to her that savages might have teeth so straight and white. She closed her eyes again to think of what she wanted to ask him, and when she opened them again, it was morning.

Nigel's swearing woke her. Her neck and back were so stiff, she felt as though she'd slept in an oyster barrel. Absently, Fiona rolled her head to ease the soreness, then suddenly the memory of what had happened the night before flooded over her. She came to her feet and glanced around the room. The wolf's head cape lay folded on the table. The Indian was nowhere in sight.

"Damn you to hell, bitch, let me loose," Nigel demanded. He raised his head and strained against his bonds. "Let me loose before thet Injun comes back and scalps us both."

As she stood there, not knowing what to do or say, the door opened. Outside, the storm had passed, and the sun sparkled off the new snow. Wolf Shadow stood in the doorway, one of the mules behind him.

"I found this one," he said. "The others are long gone." He knotted the mule's rope to the door latch and entered the room. Slung over his shoulder was his musket. The mule moved sideways, and Fiona saw that the animal was loaded with several packs.

Wolf Shadow crossed to the table and picked up his wolf's head cape, and Karl's pistol and powder and shot bag. He tucked the pistol in his belt and pulled the cape over his head and shoulders. "It is time we left," he said to Fiona. He held out a bronzed hand to her.

"Are you out of your mind?" Nigel screamed at Fiona.

Wolf Shadow glanced down at Nigel. "I will place a knife on the hearth. You should be able to cut yourself loose in time. I'm leaving you enough supplies to live on until your wounds heal."

"You murderin' bastard," Nigel yelled.

Wolf Shadow raised his eyes to Fiona's. "Come," he said softly. "Trust me, Irish Fiona."

She took a deep breath and looked at white man on the floor. Devil or savage, the wolf-man had treated her better than Nigel. Hesitantly, she took one step toward Wolf Shadow and then another.

"Your scalp will be hanging from an Injun lodge-pole," Nigel warned.

Fiona took another step and put her trembling hand in Wolf Shadow's. "Be you Beelzebub himself, I'd sooner put myself in your care than his," she said, indicating the bearlike trapper.

The wolf-man smiled. He tucked his arm in hers as smoothly as any highborn gentleman and led her out into the bright, cold morning. He lifted her up onto the dun mule between the packs, and Nigel's and Karl's muskets, then tucked the scarlet blanket around her. Taking the mule's reins, Wolf Shadow led them off into the thick woods.

Fiona squared her shoulders and stared straight ahead . . . never once looking back. "Better Beelze-bub himself," she murmured softly. And her heart leaped in her breast as she remembered the unspo-ken promises in the depths of his dark eyes.

Chapter 4

For a long time the wolf-man led the mule silently through the stillness of the snow-bound wilderness. Giant trees reared from the forest floor to tower overhead in majestic grandeur, trees so thick and tall that they seemed to Fiona to be relics from the ancient days of the legendary Irish hero, Conn of the Hundred Battles. Sunlight filtered through the dry leaves and intertwined branches to glisten off the pristine carpet of white, drifted snow.

The glare hurt Fiona's eyes and made her squint against the brightness. The air was so cold and pure that she could taste the bite of evergreen with every breath she drew. Her nostrils and tongue tingled with the scent and flavor of pine and cedar. Her head felt light, yet she continued to inhale the clean air deeply, letting the untainted forest purge her body and mind of the terror she had experienced in the trappers' cabin.

Reason returned. Fiona fingered her amulet and murmured her mother's words under her breath. *Any wish . . . unto the power of life and death.* She sighed, wondering if the charm had saved her. She hadn't wished . . . not aloud, anyway. Did it matter?

The slightest sound escaped her throat, and her

eyes opened wide as the wolf-man stopped and turned to stare at her. Her body stiffened, and her hands clutched the mule's cropped mane. For an instant, the Indian's gaze locked with hers; she felt her cheeks grow hot and lowered her eyes. His immobile expression softened, and he smiled at her. Without speaking, he turned again and began to lead the mule forward.

Ripples of fear ran up and down her spine. She caught her lower lip between her teeth and sucked on it thoughtfully. In her joy to be shut of Karl and Nigel, she hadn't fully considered what danger she might be in now. Her skin prickled, and she felt the hair rise on the back of her neck. How could she have been so foolish as to feel safe with this savage? She was still a captive . . . a prisoner of a man who wore the skin and claws of a wild beast.

"Am I?" she asked, unwittingly voicing her apprehension aloud. Her words seemed to echo in the hushed forest, and the mule gave a start and plunged ahead a few steps. The man never altered his stride.

"Are you what?" he asked softly.

Again, Fiona was struck by the precision of his speech. Where had he learned the King's English? Shouldn't a savage—even one who could communicate in a civilized tongue—sound like a barbarian? "Am I your prisoner?" This time, her tone was controlled. The mule flicked its long ears, but it didn't shy.

The Indian made no answer.

She wondered if he'd heard her. "I've no money," she continued, "and no rich kin to pay my ransom. It would be an act of Christian charity to let me . . ." Her words caught in her throat as she realized her mistake. He wasn't a Christian. Fiona knotted her fingers into the mule's bristly mane and swallowed the lump in her throat. "An act of human kindness," she finished lamely.

Her captor purposefully turned left at a pine tree which looked to Fiona like every other pine tree and led the mule up a slight incline.

"I think it's only fair that you tell me what you mean to do with me," Fiona insisted with a sudden rush of bravado. "By Christ's tears, if I'm to be murdered, I need to make my peace with God."

"If I'd meant you harm, I'd have left you with your own kind." He didn't bother to look back at her, but his tone conveyed his annoyance.

"How do you speak English so well?" she demanded.

"How do you?"

Fiona felt her cheeks grow hot. It wasn't anger she'd heard in his voice, it was amusement. In his own subtle way, he was laughing at her. "It's not the same thing," she insisted. "I'm . . . I'm . . ."

He glanced back over his shoulder at her. "You are Irish, not English. You have made this very clear to me. The English and the Irish have been enemies for time out of time. Is this not so?" His dark eyes sparkled with intelligence, and she shivered under their scrutiny.

"Yes."

"If you have learned the tongue of your enemy, then why shouldn't I?"

"But you speak the King's English better than I do," she protested. "At least your speech is more formal than my own." She raised her chin a notch. "Sure and it's unnatural."

"Like a talking crow?" he flung back.

"No, but . . ." She drew in a deep breath as her thoughts tumbled wildly. Her tongue felt clumsy—somehow detached from her brain. She'd always been known for her quick wit, for the ability to give better than she got. *A witch's tongue in an angel's face*, her grandsire had said.

Damn, but this wolf-man would try the patience of a saint! She glared at him, then felt her will weakening under the sensual impact of his sloe-eyed stare. Half-naked native or not, he was a great broth of a man.

If it weren't for his slanting almond-shaped eyes and the granite ridges of his high sweeping cheekbones, this wolf-man could have stepped into a public house in Galway and been served a pint of beer without raising a single eyebrow in the room. His bronzed skin was no darker than that of many an Irish fisherman, and if he was tall and broad with muscles that rippled beneath his deerhide clothing, she had seen one or two men in Dublin that were near his size and beauty.

Aye, she mused. Dress him properly and cut his hair, and a woman could find little fault in his looks.

Wolf Shadow broke into her reverie. "Men say I have a gift for understanding the words of strangers. I know the language of the Iroquois, the French, and the Cherokee."

By Mary's veil, he was still laughing at her, she realized. His eyes danced with mirth even though his craggy features remained immobile. Fiona's temper bubbled up, smothering her fear and curiosity. "You're avoiding my questions," she snapped. He played games with words. Even when he talked, he told her nothing she wanted to know. "What do you mean to do with me?"

He shook his head, and a smile played across his lips. "You are bold for a white woman, but your manners are as bad as those of your men. Did your father teach you nothing at his knee? Is it not customary among the Irish to offer thanks to one who has saved your life?"

"I do . . . I mean . . . A gentleman would not ask for thanks," she sputtered. "And no, my father taught me nothing." Bitterness turned her tone to ice. "He didn't stay long enough." She scowled. "I'm grateful for your help, of course, but I—"

"Wolf Shadow is no gentleman," he corrected. "The word is from *gentle*. I am a warrior of the Shawnee and a shaman—a maker of spirit medicine. No one who knows Wolf Shadow would call him gentle." He folded his arms over his chest, and his lips formed into a thin line. His eyes grew hard. "It is not Wolf Shadow who is the problem, Irish Fiona. It is you who are the problem."

She stiffened. "If you will just take me to the nearest white settlement," she began, "I would—"

He uttered a low sound of regret that needed no interpretation. "No. I cannot."

"Why not?" A rush of dread spilled over her. He *did* mean to hold her as his prisoner! She was no better off now than she had been with Nigel and Karl. "Why can't you?" she cried. "You don't have to take me all the way—just show me the right direction. You have to let me go! I'll be nothing but trouble to you—I can promise you that!"

"You are already trouble for me."

Tears threatened, and she blinked them away. "I've done nothing to you! Why won't you let me go?"

"Where, Irish? Where should I take you?"

"Philadelphia—Annapolis." She wracked her mind for the names of American towns. "Boston. I don't know. Anywhere. Any English settlement will do."

"Ah." He lowered his arms and nodded slowly. "I see. I am to return you to the English."

"Yes. Of course." She leaned forward, knotting her small hands into fists. "I have nothing to pay you with now, but later—when I earn money—I can give you a reward.''

''And if I take you back to the English, you will be free?''

''Yes. Well, not exactly, but—''

Wolf Shadow seized the mule's bridle, moving so quickly that he startled Fiona into crying out. ''Do not lie to me, woman! Never lie to me.''

His eyes were like glowing coals. Gooseflesh rose on Fiona's arms as his angry gaze scorched her bare skin. ''I'm not lying,'' she protested.

''Jacob Clough sold you to the white trappers, but they did not take your indenture papers. You belong to Nigel or to Jacob. You are not free. You are a bondwoman.'' Wolf Shadow let go of the bridle, turned away, and began to lead the animal through the woods again.

''Yes, but—''

He kept his eyes on the forest ahead. ''This indenture makes you a slave. Yes or no?''

She wilted under his attack. ''I'm not a slave,'' she argued. ''It's not—''

''A Shawnee woman is a free woman. No man tells her to come or go, to give her body or not. I will take you to the Shawnee. There you will see what freedom is, Irishwoman. There you will know the difference between the Shawnee world and the white.''

''I don't want to go with you,'' she insisted, leaning forward over the mule's bony withers. ''If you take me south—to the Chesapeake—no one there would know I was indentured. I could change my name. Start a new life.''

Wolf Shadow quickened his pace, and the mule broke into a trot. ''The English law will follow you,'' he insisted. ''Jacob Clough will declare you a runaway. You cannot hide your hair or your face. You say that you know medicine. How many red-haired women apothecaries are there? The law may not find you in the turning of a moon, or in a season, but they will find you, Irish Fiona." He stopped and whirled on her. "They will take you back to Jacob Clough in chains, and he will give you to a man like Nigel again. Is that what you want?"

"You can't hold me against my will! I'll take my chances with—"

The mule suddenly threw up its head and snorted. It opened its mouth to bray, but Wolf Shadow caught the animal's nose and mouth between his broad hands. He clamped down hard, cutting off the mule's breath. Eyes rolling, the mule struggled to get free, throwing itself back on its haunches.

Fiona tumbled off into the snow, gasping as she got a mouthful. She scrambled up to see Wolf Shadow drawing his knife along the mule's throat. Covering her mouth to keep from screaming, she watched, horrified as great gouts of crimson sprayed the white snow. The animal's front legs buckled, and it went down, eyes already starting to glaze over.

"Why?" she managed. "Why did you—"

Wolf Shadow silenced her with a dire glance. The bloody knife flashed again, cutting free the guns and a pack containing powder and shot. "Come!" he ordered, extending a hand stained red with gore.

Fiona shook her head. Her knees felt as though they were made of water. Her lips formed the word no, but no sound came from her throat.

His fingers clamped around her wrist, and he brought his face so close to hers that Fiona could feel the heat of his breath on her cheek. "Run or die," he whispered harshly, pulling away her red blanket and tossing it into a snowdrift.

She ran.

Her feet flew over the crusting snow as they sped

downhill away from the dead mule. Leaping over
fallen logs and ducking under branches, they fled
through the still forest. Wolf Shadow never loosened his grip on her wrist as they ran. Despite the
weight of the guns and pack he carried, Fiona could
barely keep pace with him.

Run or die. Run or die. His words thudded in her
head like the ring of a blacksmith's hammer on a
steel anvil. Heart pounding, she ran until her side
cramped, until she thought her lungs would burst.
Her breaths came in rasping gasps, and no matter
how hard she tried, she was lagging farther and farther behind.

Without warning, Wolf Shadow stopped. Too exhausted to think of the consequences, Fiona dropped
to her knees and sucked in deep gulps of air. He let
go of her wrist, and she stared up at him in confusion. Why had he changed from the hero who had
rescued her to a madman? Why had he butchered
the mule and started this mad dash through an endless forest? She had seen nothing, heard nothing that
could cause him to take leave of his senses!

"Stay where you are," he ordered. "Don't
move."

She watched as he began to step backward in his
own tracks, retracing their path for a hundred feet
or more. Then he seized an overhanging cedar
branch and pulled himself up into the tree. Aston-
ished, Fiona waited, not daring to move from her
spot.

There was a slight dusting of snow as Wolf
Shadow made his way up into the cedar, and then
the movement of the boughs showed him coming
down. He lowered himself feetfirst from a branch
and dropped to the ground. As he came toward her,
Fiona could see that he had left the pack and one of
the muskets behind in the tree.

He approached, and she noticed that he was still

carefully walking in his own footprints. When he reached her, he offered his hand. It had been wiped free of blood. "Come. We must go."

"Why?" she dared.

He took her hand and pulled her to her feet. "Can you run?"

She swallowed hard and nodded. "I can run."

They started at a lope and steadily increased their speed, always downhill. This time, when Fiona's legs began to fail her, Wolf Shadow caught her around the waist and slung her over his shoulder.

He ran, carrying her, for what seemed to be another mile before the ground dropped away into a sluggish, ice-encrusted marshy area. There he slowed to a walk, carefully stepping on the patches of frozen ground.

"Put me down," she insisted. She pushed away from him, but a heavily muscled arm pinned her to his shoulder with such force that it squeezed the breath from her lungs.

Beyond the shrub willows were more rocks, and below that a rushing creek about six yards wide. Her captor didn't hesitate; he broke through the ice on the shore and waded into the frigid water. He turned right and walked upstream, still balancing her on his shoulder. The water was up to his thighs, and Fiona shuddered at the thought of the cold he must be feeling.

"Where are you taking me?" she asked. "Why are—"

"Quiet."

His hair hung across her face. She drew in his unique musky scent with every breath—not an unpleasant smell, but totally alien, like nothing she had ever known. "Put me down, please," she whispered. "I can walk." Even as she said it, she knew she lied. She couldn't walk in this icy water. No human could.

"Must I bind your mouth?" he demanded. "Do not speak."

The stream grew ever rockier. The sound of the rushing water filled her head, making her even colder. Once, he slipped, nearly plunging them both under. Against her will, she clung tightly to him. Then, without warning, he lowered her into the stream. She gasped in shock as the water closed over her feet and legs, weighing on her heavy woolen skirts.

"Hurry," he said, pulling her toward what looked like an impenetrable wall of wind-sculpted ice. Teeth chattering, she forced her feet to obey, stumbling over the slippery rocks. He led her within an arm's length of the ice barrier, then turned right and pointed out a gap between solid rock and what she now realized was a frozen waterfall. Catching her around the waist, he pushed her into the narrow space. It was too low to stand. She crouched, her back against the cold stone, the curtain of glistening ice only inches from her face.

"Make a sound and you will die," he whispered. "Wait for me, and pray to your Christian God." He removed his wolfskin cloak and tucked it around her, then slid one of his two remaining muskets along the wall at her back. "Trust me, Irish." His features softened, and he gave her a quick smile before vanishing from sight.

Fiona wasn't certain if it was a smile of comfort or of madness. Shaking with cold, she clutched the hide around her freezing body. She could see nothing but the gleam of distorted light filtering through the ice, hear nothing but the rush of the stream. Her hiding place seemed more like a tomb than a place of refuge, and she was too frightened to pray.

Without Fiona's weight, Wolf Shadow retraced his path downstream swiftly. He had frightened the woman badly; he knew it, but he'd had no time to try and assuage that fear. At the same time that the mule had caught the scent of horses on the wind, he'd heard a faint whinny and smelled them himself. Not one horse, but several. Horses meant white men, and more than two whites—where none should be—meant trouble. He regretted having to take the life of the mule, but in another instant the beast's braying would have betrayed their position. Fiona hadn't understood the danger.

Wolf Shadow exhaled sharply. He was thinking of the woman again instead of concentrating on keeping them alive. By the sacred breath of Wishemenetoo! What was she doing to him?

Why had he left his friends to rescue a white woman anyway? She would bring him nothing but trouble—even she realized it. Involving himself with her endangered his mission. How was he to convince the Shawnee and Delaware to band together and reject the white civilization if he brought an Irish woman to the People's land?

And she had not even the decency to be grateful for being rescued.

Wolf Shadow knew what Irish Fiona thought of him. He had seen the truth in her eyes. It was the same look that all whites gave him. Even in England . . . even when he'd dressed in their clothes and eaten at their tables, even when he'd bested them at their own games . . . they still thought of him as an animal—a crafty one to be certain, but still a wild beast.

He knew how a wolf must feel when a human stares into its eyes.

Men ruled the world now, but the old tales told of a time when animals had ruled. Wolf Shadow wondered if they would ever rule again. If they did, it would be because Wishemenetoo judged men and found them unworthy.

What was there about white-skinned men that made them so arrogant? If they stepped on a piece of land, they claimed it as their own. If they drank water from a spring, they built fences to keep other men and animals from drinking. If they entered a forest, they felt compelled to cut down the trees and burn them.

The land that Wishemenetoo had given to the red man was vast. There would have been room for the strangers to raise their families, game and fish and water enough to share. The Lenni-Lenape, those the white men called the Delaware, had welcomed the first Englishmen to their shores. Now they held the land along the salt sea in an iron fist, and the only red men there were the old and the dead.

Year by year, the English and the French moved steadily west, eating up the tribal hunting grounds, building their roads and towns, killing the red men with their diseases and their liquor. The white men burned the People's cornfields and desecrated their sacred places. They murdered copper-skinned babies and made whores of the women. The bounties on Indian scalps were higher than the bounties on wolves.

With the fragmentation of the tribes, the Shawnee were becoming weak, unable to defend themselves from their hereditary enemies in the Iroquois League—the Seneca, the Mohawk, the Cayuga, the Oneida, the Onondaga, and the Tuscarora. Hemmed in by the Iroquois and the French to the north and the English to the east and south, the Shawnee and their Delaware cousins were being pushed westward. Soon their backs would be to the great river. Beyond lay the prairies, the home of fierce tribes who would defend their land to the death. The Shawnee must regain their power by allying themselves with the Delaware and the other Algonquian-speaking nations. They must unite and hold this ground against all white men. It was his mission to weld them together, and he must do it if it cost him his life.

With the future of the Shawnee at stake, with time so short and chances of success so slim, he could not afford to consider the fate of one Irishwoman . . . to put her welfare before the good of so many of his own people.

All he had to do was abandon her. Alone in the forest, he would be as hard to catch as his totem, the gray wolf.

Using the overhanging branches of a hemlock, he swept his tracks to hide them, then left the stream and climbed up on the bank. He was so cold that he could hardly feel his flesh below the knees. Gritting his teeth, he stomped in place to restore the flow of his blood. He blew on his fingers to warm them, then crouched to replace the damp powder in the musket with dry. A waterproof bag around his neck kept a precious store of the fine black powder needed to fill the frizzen pan that would fire the gun.

Wolf Shadow cautiously parted the boughs of the hemlock and scrutinized the forest. There was no sign of movement, and no bird sound. An absence of friendly noise screamed danger as loudly as the squawk of a crow. He waited.

The Seneca warriors came over the crest of the hill like a pack of hunting hounds, bending to touch his tracks, sniffing the trail and crying out to the men on horseback behind them. The Frenchman Roquette, the hair buyer, spurred his gray stallion through the trees. Four more white men, three in uniforms and one in buckskins, rode hot after him.

Wolf Shadow smiled thinly. Roquette. He'd not been wrong when he'd slain the mule or run like a frightened buck with Irish Fiona over his shoulder.

His inner voice had saved him again. So many times . . . yet each time that his instincts proved right he felt as though a gift had been bestowed upon him. "Thank you, Wolf Spirit," he murmured under his breath.

If Roquette's Seneca caught them, he would be dead and the woman would be used by the Frenchman and his dogs. Whether she was dead or alive, Roquette would find value in her. Alive, she would bring a high price from any lonely white trapper, and when her soul departed her broken body, Roquette would demand a ransom from the English settlers. When they paid, they would receive only a corpse. He had done it before.

The English might offer a bounty on Indian scalps, but Roquette took the game one step further: he paid hard silver to the Indians for English scalps. So long as he could keep the Indians and the English at each other's throats, he kept the path open for the French to seize the Ohio Country.

Wolf Shadow raised his musket and took careful aim at the Frenchman on the gray horse. Much good would be done for red man and white if he sent a lead ball through Roquette's heart. He sighed. It was not a shaman's way. His was the path of persuasion and reason. As foul as Roquette was, as great a stain on the face of the land, still, he was not as important as the task of uniting the Shawnee. If Wolf Shadow killed Roquette now, he would die at the hands of the Seneca warriors. He would die, and Irish Fiona would be left helpless.

Wolf Shadow clenched his hands around the musket. He was not afraid to die, but he was afraid for the woman.

He forced himself to remain motionless and watched as the first Seneca brave reached the far side of the creek. The painted warrior twisted around and cupped both hands to his mouth, letting out a chilling whoop that rang through the snow-locked forest.

Chapter 5

Wolf Shadow waited and watched as the Seneca spread out along the stream searching for the spot where he and the woman had left the water. One man passed within a musket length of the hemlock, so close that Wolf Shadow could see that the enemy brave bore a ghastly scar down one side of his face. The spot where his left eye should have been was a twisted knot of flesh, and the empty cavity was painted yellow.

Ah, Wolf Shadow mused. The Seneca has but one eye. Any novice shaman should be able to cloud the other eye. He held his breath, concentrating on the ring of power that surrounded him, a power that drew strength from the grandfather hemlock. Weave a web to dull the Seneca's mind, Inu-msi-ila-fewanu, he prayed silently. Wrap me in a cloak of invisibility.

The Seneca stopped and glanced toward the hemlock. He took a step toward the overhanging boughs. Wolf Shadow tightened his finger on his musket trigger.

Suddenly the disfigured warrior slipped and fell headfirst into the icy creek. Sputtering and gasping, he struggled to his feet. The Seneca's yellow and black paint smeared and ran down his chin, to the delight of his companions downstream. They howled with laughter, calling out crude insults, while Scarface shook the water from his musket and emptied the useless powder in the stream.

Muttering with anger, the Seneca climbed onto the icy bank a few feet upstream from Wolf Shadow's hiding place and proceeded to reload his musket.

Roquette reined in his stallion at the creek bank and stood in his stirrups, glancing up and down the stream. "Find them, you devil-spawned bastards," he shouted in French. "How far can they be?" He switched to badly accented Iroquois. "I want that woman," he cried. "Find them before nightfall, and I'll pay double for the scalp of the Shawnee brave."

Involuntarily, Wolf Shadow glanced down at his water-soaked moccasins. They had identified him as Shawnee by the marks of his footwear. Each tribe constructed their moccasins differently, and the Shawnee had learned the fine art from their Delaware cousins. He wondered if it had been a mistake to change from the Huron moccasins he'd worn earlier at Jacob Clough's.

Scarface waded back into the water and started upstream, studying the streambank. A second Seneca moved along the eastern side of the creek doing the same. The place where Wolf Shadow had left the woman was upstream and around a bend, out of sight.

Stay where you are, the shaman urged in his thoughts. Don't move, don't even breathe.

In her ice prison, Fiona was shivering so hard she couldn't keep her teeth from chattering. The sound of the Seneca war cry echoed in her head long after it had ceased to reverberate through the forest. She didn't know if the terrible sound had been made by a man or an animal. If it had been human, had it come from the wolf-man, or from whatever he thought was chasing them?

She rubbed her hands together to try and warm them, wondering if the Shawnee had left her here to die. How long was she expected to wait? When night fell, she knew she wouldn't survive the cold. Her feet had lost all feeling, and she was so thirsty she'd even licked at the ice. It hadn't quenched her thirst, just made her colder.

She slipped stiffened fingers up to touch her amulet. The charm seemed as frigid as the ice. So much for magic, she thought hopelessly. If she'd had the sense God gave a goose, she'd have tried to barter the golden necklace for passage to America, or she would have tried to buy her own indenture when the apothecary died in Philadelphia.

But selling the amulet had never seemed an option. Her mother had seen them both go hungry without parting with the Eye of Mist. She'd made Fiona promise to keep the necklace—no matter what.

Her mother had treasured the amulet because it had been a gift to Fiona from her father, and because it made real his promise to care for Fiona and "see her wed to a prince" when she was grown. It was Eileen O'Neal's hope, one she wouldn't let go of . . . even on her deathbed. So long as Fiona wore the necklace, Eileen could imagine that her Scottish lord would come back for them both. Eileen had never stopped loving him, and she'd tried desperately to instill that love for her father in Fiona's heart.

Fiona rocked back and forth, setting her teeth against the chill that crept through her blood. Love hadn't made her keep the Eye of Mist . . . not love, and not the foolish notion of magic. She'd kept it out of hate—hate for the man who'd taken his pleasure on a trusting woman and ruined her life.

For a woman to bear a child out of wedlock in Ireland was the ultimate disgrace. Eileen's adultery reflected on the honor of her family and every other decent woman. The pain that most troubled Eileen was what she had done to her own child. So long as Fiona lived, she would bear the shame of illegitimacy; not even Holy Church could lift the scarlet stain of bastardy. The torture of that sentence had turned her mother's face old before her time and streaked her lovely auburn tresses with gray.

But Fiona didn't hate her father for her birth. She hated him for abandoning her and her mother. She hated him so much that she'd vowed to kill him if she ever laid eyes on him, and she'd kept the amulet in memory of that hate.

Giving up and dying here in this godforsaken forest would mean leaving that promise of revenge against her father unfulfilled. She'd be damned if she'd let him best her again!

Anger lent Fiona strength to fight the cold. "I'll not stay here and freeze to death," she muttered in her native Gaelic. "And I'll not be dictated to by a madman who thinks he's a wolf. I'll—"

"Yong wee!"

Fiona's head snapped toward the source of the guttural cry, and she stared into the face of a shrieking demon. Her eyes widened in horror as she smelled the rank scent of bear and saw the jagged scar that deformed the Indian's painted features into something less than human. His mouth gaped open, gleaming with teeth filed to jagged points. One empty eye socket was dyed yellow, and the single eye staring back at her was as black and merciless as hell's deepest pit.

"Yong wee!" the savage shrieked again as he dragged her roughly from her hiding place and raised a stone tomahawk over her head.

Fiona fell to her knees in the frigid water, and the shock forced her into action. A submerged rock gouged her left shin, but she barely felt the pain as she drove her head upward to butt her attacker in the belly with all the strength she could muster. He gasped and slipped backward into the stream. Fiona flung herself on top of him, kneed him in the groin, and pushed his head underwater.

The Seneca knocked her aside with one powerful blow. He came up sputtering, his terrible face contorted with rage, and swung his tomahawk at her.

Time seemed to stand still for Fiona. She held her breath and waited for the fierce warrior to deliver what she knew would be her death blow. Her right hand dug frantically in the icy stream for a rock to defend herself with; but even as her fingers closed around the pitted surface, reason told her it was too late.

"Yah te a!"

Another harsh male voice penetrated Fiona's terror. The axe smashed down, coming so close it grazed her hair. She screamed, then struggled to her feet, her skirts weighed down with water. Her heart thudded wildly as she stared up at the second Seneca warrior.

He seemed as fearsome as the first, despite having both eyes in his head. He was thick and muscular, with dark skin and a fierce expression. His hair was roached and dyed to an unnatural red color, and his face was streaked with warpaint. His features contorted as he argued loudly with the first Indian and gestured.

One Eye turned his back to them both and gave a heated reply. Fiona couldn't understand a word of their exchange, but it was plain from the way the newcomer kept shaking his musket at her that she was the object of their disagreement. She began to back away from them, one step at a time, trying not to lose her balance on the slippery streambed.

Suddenly Wolf Shadow loomed up behind the second warrior. Fiona tried not to let her expression reveal the tiny hope that flared within her.

Wolf Shadow wrapped a bare arm around the red-roached brave's neck. Muscles bulged as he tightened his grip. The Seneca struggled for only seconds, then stiffened. His eyes went wide and his mouth opened. Wolf Shadow released him, and he slowly crumbled forward. Fiona saw the bloody knife wounds in the Seneca's back just before his startled face hit the water.

Wolf Shadow was already lunging toward the one-eyed man, swinging his musket like a club. The scarred Seneca whirled, saw Wolf Shadow, and let out a guttural cry. He blocked the musket with his axe, staggering back under the force of the blow.

Fiona blinked as a knife appeared in the Seneca's free hand. "Shoot him!" she cried to Wolf Shadow.

The one-eyed warrior slashed out with the knife. Wolf Shadow dodged the thrust and swung the musket again. Suddenly remembering the fist-sized rock in her hand, Fiona flung it with all her might, striking the Seneca full in the mouth.

Wolf Shadow leaped on top of the Seneca, and the two went down locked in mortal combat. Over and over they rolled in the water. Fiona shuddered as sunlight gleamed on the Seneca's knife blade. She reached down into the stream for another rock and lifted it high, waiting for a chance to throw it at the painted warrior without hitting Wolf Shadow.

Blood ran down Wolf Shadow's arm, but he paid it no heed. Inch by inch, he forced the Seneca's head back until water covered his face. Fiona caught a glimpse of the brave's fear-filled eyes, and pity knifed through her as the man struggled wildly.

"Stop!" she cried. "He's drowning." Bubbles rose to the water's surface. The man had nearly stopped kicking, but still, Wolf Shadow held the barrel of his musket across the Seneca's throat. "Let him up," Fiona insisted. "You're murdering him."

Wolf Shadow gave no sign that he heard her.

"Stop it!" Fiona pounded his back with her fists. "Let him up before he drowns."

A minute passed, seeming to Fiona like hours. Finally the wolf-man released the pressure on the musket and stood up. The Seneca's head remained submerged; his moccasined feet bobbed in the running water.

"Murderer," she accused. She turned toward the bank, stumbling, shivering. She felt suddenly exhausted.

Wolf Shadow pulled the scarfaced man from the water and dragged him to the place where he'd hidden her beneath the falls. He removed his wolfskin cloak and his second musket, and shoved the body of the dead warrior upright in the cavity. Then he recovered the body of the brave he'd slain with a knife and placed him beside the first man. Lastly he took a corner of the wolfskin, a section from which dangled a claw, and, using the Seneca's own blood, imprinted the pawprint of a wolf on each dead man's forehead.

Horrified by the barbaric act, Fiona shuddered and covered her face with her hands. How had she forgotten that Wolf Shadow was an uncivilized savage? Now he'd reminded her by murdering two men before her eyes and then defacing their corpses. "You didn't . . . didn't have . . . to . . ." Her speech sounded strangely slurred. She was cold—so cold.

"Irishwoman, can you walk?"

Fiona lowered her hands and looked into Wolf Shadow's face. "Don't . . . touch me," she warned

him. "Don't . . ." She blinked her eyes and swayed.
The earth seemed to open before her, and she cried
out softly as she tumbled into a black void.

The odors of wet wool and roasting meat teased
Fiona's consciousness. She moaned and snuggled
deeper in the soft, warm furs. The sound of a rich
male voice singing seemed to come from far away.
She couldn't understand the words, and the repetitive rise and fall of the melody was totally alien. Yet
in some subtle way it soothed her. The chanting surrounded her, wrapped her in a protective cloak, and
made her feel safe and loved.

She sighed as the tension drained from her muscles. She felt as though she were cradled on a warm
blanket of clouds. The cold . . . the fear . . . the confusion . . . all were fading memories. She moistened
her lips with her tongue and tried to open her eyes.
Her lids seemed to be made of lead; they were too
heavy. She lifted a hand and let it fall. It brushed
against bare skin. Questions rose in her mind, but
forming them was too difficult. Asking them would
be impossible.

Gentle fingers ran through her hair.

The chanting was closer now . . . it was all around
her. The timbre of the voice brought tears to her
eyes. The pull of sleep was intoxicating. By sheer
will Fiona struggled to stay awake. And lost.

A warm hand caressed her naked back.

She exhaled softly and snuggled her face against
a broad male chest. Her eyes snapped open, and she
gave a little cry of alarm.

"Hush, Irish. You are safe here," Wolf Shadow
murmured.

She pushed frantically away, tangling her legs
with his long ones. "Oh!" Fiona rose to her knees
and stared at him in shock.

He lay inches away, stretched out on their shared bearskin, his left hand casually supporting his head, one knee slightly flexed. She swallowed hard. Wolf Shadow was stark naked, his skin glistening in the flickering light.

Fiona's mouth went dry as her gaze dropped from his dark, hypnotic eyes to the wide expanse of his powerful shoulders. Muscles bulged beneath the silken skin of his broad chest, accented by the copper bands that encircled his massive biceps. His torso was long and lean, his belly flat, his hips smooth and sinewy.

Here and there the faded scars of old wounds cut the surface of his golden skin, but they did not detract from his male beauty . . . they made his physique even more breathtaking. Her eyes widened as she took in the bloodred tattoo of an animal's pawprint on his muscular left thigh. Her eyes rose to meet his. In that fathomless, amused scrutiny she read an unmistakable challenge, a dare she could not let pass.

Trembling, she forced herself to look at his naked body again. Her cheeks grew hot, and a curious tingling began in the pit of her stomach as she stared at his hairless chest and the smooth, bronze planes of his waist and loins. She had never seen a man with such an absence of hair on his body, but the sparse nest of dark hair above his manhood seemed as natural as the length and fullness of his erect shaft. She couldn't tear her eyes away until she heard his soft chuckle.

Fiona gasped, realizing that she was as unclad as he was. Quickly she pulled the tanned hide up to cover her nakedness. Fear and confusion filled her, and the fingers of her right hand knotted in a thick, silky animal pelt as memories of what had happened at the stream came flooding back. She shrank away from him, knowing that there was no place to run—that she was at the wolf-man's mercy. "Who are you?" she managed weakly. "What are you?"

He chuckled. "You asked me that before."

His words were slow and reassuring—the same tone he had used with the mule when it became bogged in the snow, she thought. But he'd cut the mule's throat, suddenly and brutally and without reason. As he'd killed the two Indians. Murdered them and defaced their bodies . . .

"You've nothing to fear from me," Wolf Shadow repeated. "This cave is a secret place. They won't find us here."

Fiona couldn't stop trembling. How could he lie there as naked as the day he was born and talk to her so calmly? The firelight reflected in the depths of his coal-black eyes. Was it compassion she read there, or madness? "You . . . you drowned that man," she began. "You murdered him . . . and now . . ." Her voice trailed away under the force of his gaze.

The thought that she had looked on his nakedness curled in the back of her mind. Not only had she looked, but she had taken pleasure in the sight of his terrible beauty. She forced the damning thoughts away. She couldn't face them now. She stiffened. "Now do you mean to rape me?"

"Pah." He rose and stalked to the far side of the fire. "I expected more of you, Irish." Anger made his speech hard and clipped. "You were cold unto death. I warmed your body with my own—nothing more."

"You expect me to believe that?"

"Your clothes were wet—as were mine. I'm not such a fool as to try and dry your thick English clothes with my skin."

"How . . . how dare you?" Her words sounded

idiotic as they fell from her lips. He didn't expect
her to believe he'd stripped her naked and lain with
her for her health's sake, did he? How could he think
she would be so gullible?

He shrugged. He snatched up his drying loincloth
and wrapped it around his hips, covering his geni-
tals. "We did not join." His gaze raked her insolently. "If I had shared pleasures with you, Irish
Fiona, you'd not have had to ask. You would know
you had been loved by a man."

"And that—" She pointed to the bulge in his loincloth. "Do you take me for a lackwit? I know when
a man is . . . is sexually excited. You meant to take
advantage of me. You—"

"Cease your caterwauling, woman. I am not made
of stone. You are soft, and your scent is sweet. If
my body reacts as any man's would, I am not to
blame."

"You shame me," she cried.

"You shame yourself." He picked up her damp
shift and threw it across the fire at her. "Cover yourself if it makes you feel safer. But do not blame me
if you die of lung fever."

"I never get sick. I won't get sick now," she flung
back defiantly.

"Then what happened to you on the stream
bank?"

"It was the cold. No one could stand in that icy
water without suffering a chill—no human could. I
don't know about demons. Are you a warlock that
you don't feel as other men do?"

"I thought we were just discussing my human
feelings." He turned away from her and donned a
sleeveless vest. "Cold water is nothing to me. It is
the practice of my people to bathe summer and winter. Even Shawnee children break ice to swim."

Fiona jerked the shift over her head, then wrapped

herself again in the tawny fur. As angry as she was with Wolf Shadow, she still craved the heat of his fire. Keeping her eyes on him, she wiggled her bare toes closer to the coals. She couldn't see a thing beyond the circle of firelight, so she assumed it was night.

She still felt weak and drowsy. Saint Bridget be thanked that she'd awakened when she had—before he'd had his way with her. Her hand clutched the fur at her throat, and for the first time since she could remember, she didn't feel the familiar weight of the Eye of Mist. Frantically, she searched for it. "My necklace," she cried. "Where's my necklace? I must have—"

"Calm yourself," Wolf Shadow soothed. "What you seek is here and safe. It is not the Shawnee way to speak of *mesawmi*, the spirit medicine of another, but I am a shaman, and what is forbidden some is different for me. When you shook with cold and would not wake, I feared the power had departed your amulet."

"Where is it? Give it back to me," she demanded.

He nodded and walked to the shadows. "I never meant to keep it from you." He returned at once with a tightly woven bark basket, no larger than a man's fist. Taking a forked stick from the edge of the fire, he secured the necklace without touching it and passed it over the flames to her.

Fiona grasped her amulet in surprise. It was no longer covered with black paint. Instead the beauty of the ancient goldwork gleamed as though it were newly forged from the artist's hand. "Oh." The charm seemed to pulse with life in her hand. She slipped it around her neck. "Thank you," she whispered. "I . . ." She fingered the necklace, her heart thudding. "You had no right to take it in the first place," she reminded him.

"Perhaps," he replied, "but it was wrong to cover it so. Spirit medicine needs the light of the sun and the touch of your flesh. You dull the power when you hide it from the Creator."

"My mother painted the necklace to keep it from being stolen by some man."

He pursed his lips and nodded. "Perhaps you were right. I know little of Irish magic."

"It isn't magic."

"No?"

"No. I'm no witch. I don't deal in such evil."

"Spirit medicine is never evil. It can only bring protection to the wearer—protection and good."

"I'm a Christian—a Catholic. Don't talk to me of heresy."

He settled down on the far side of the fire, legs crossed, arms folded across his chest. "Heresy? You wear the amulet, Irish Fiona, not I."

"It's only a keepsake. Something my mother gave me."

His eyes narrowed suspiciously. "Your tongue speaks one thing, but your eyes say another. Did I not warn you about lying to me?"

"My mother and my father," she hurried to say. "It was important to my mother that I wear it— always."

"And your father?"

"He's nothing to me. If I wear what came from him, it's to remind me that I'm going to kill him if I ever lay eyes on him."

Wolf Shadow steepled his hands and idly rubbed his forehead with his joined fingers. "So . . . You call me murderer when I kill those who would kill us, yet you seek the life of the man who gave you life."

"You don't understand. The two things have nothing in common. What's between me and my father is none of your business. He killed my mother and he abandoned us both. He deserves to die. What you did—back at the stream—was unforgivable. That man you drowned—he was helpless. You could have let him live."

He shook his head. "A Seneca is never helpless. If I left him alive, he would come after us. He'd seen you. Once Roquette knew that there was a white woman to be had, he would follow us with his Seneca dogs until we were hunted to ground."

"I don't know what you're talking about. Who is Roquette? I didn't hear any dogs. All I saw were two Indians, and you killed them both. You desecrated their bodies."

"Roquette is a Frenchman, and the Seneca war cries you heard were the baying of his hounds."

"You expect me to believe you?"

"You must believe me. Our spirit paths have crossed. It may not be what you or I wish, but your future is linked with mine."

"You can't hold me against my will," she said fervently. "Take me back to my own kind—please. I don't belong here." She couldn't be here. By Mary's robe, if she stayed a day longer God alone knew what she might do. Thoughts of his virile male body loomed in the shadows of her mind. She didn't know if she was more afraid of him or of herself.

She'd never been tempted by the sins of the flesh—she'd believed she never would be. Hadn't her mother's weakness for a man brought her to disgrace and an early death? Fiona had vowed she'd never make the same mistake. She'd sworn on a sacred relic of Saint Anne, promising to keep herself pure and to dedicate her life to the art of medicine.

Wolf Shadow poked at the glowing coals with a branch, then raised his gaze to hers. "What you and I want means nothing, Irish Fiona. The trail the spirits have planned for us is already blazed in the stars.''

''There is no *us*,'' she protested, pulling the soft fur blanket tighter around her as fear again chilled her blood. ''There is not and never can be an *us*.''

May Inu-msi-ila-fe-wanu will it to be so,'' he murmured. ''For I want to be free of you as much as you want to be free of me.''

Chapter 6

For three days they remained hidden in the cave while snow fell outside, blanketing the forest and meadows, and making further pursuit impossible. They were the most disturbing three days Fiona had ever known.

Wolf Shadow was unlike any man she had come in contact with—so much so that dealing with him stretched the limits of her patience. He was a superstitious savage, a man who could murder in cold blood and walk away without any sign of pity or regret. Yet he was also an intelligent human being who showed the compassion of a priest and courtly manners that would not disgrace a prince of Europe.

She was desperately afraid of him. Every instinct told her that trusting him would be a fatal mistake; yet she wanted to believe him when he told her that he meant her no harm. She was repelled by his utter barbarity, yet drawn by the sensual magnetism of his magnificent animal body and the memory of his touch.

His wolf's mask image haunted her dreams.

Sleep should have brought her peace, but it did not. Instead, when she was so exhausted that she could no longer keep her eyes open, she found herself drawn over and over into the same disturbing dream.

She was lying on a bed of moss beside a stream. There was a willow tree overhead, and the scent of heather was heavy in the air.

She removed her dress and stockings and petticoats, and waded barefoot into the stream. She was laughing and looking down in the water.

Then the wolf's mask appeared beneath the surface. She dipped her hands to touch it, and a golden man rose from the depths. A naked man, so beautiful of form that she cried out with joy to see him.

He stood within arm's length, and sparkling drops of water rolled down his golden-bronze skin, falling like liquid diamonds into the stream.

His eyes watched her from behind the mask, and although he didn't speak, she knew he wanted her to let down her hair. Slowly, she took out the pins and dropped them into the water, and her unbound tresses fell loose around her waist.

He nodded, and she knew that he wanted her to remove her shift and stand before him naked.

She did.

The golden man held out a hand, palm up and fingers spread. As though in a trance, she raised her hand to press against his. Thumb to thumb, and fingers to fingers.

His touch was intoxicating. Like strong wine.

He laughed, and the sound thrilled her. One by one, he flexed his fingers, moving ever so slightly against hers. Rubbing. Caressing. Sending a molten heat rising in her body. Igniting an unfamiliar yearning . . . a desire so strong and deep that she knew she would die if she couldn't fulfill it.

And then, suddenly, the golden man began to sink in the water. She kept her hand pressed against his, trying to keep him from vanishing. Trying desperately to hold him. But she couldn't.

He was gone. Except for the wolf's mask beneath the surface. She could see it, but no matter how she tried, it was too deep to reach.

She cried out in disappointment and woke. And in the brief passage of time between dream and reality, the wolf's mask floated just out of reach before her.

With full consciousness came confusion and shame. Fiona drew up her knees and wrapped her arms around them, trying to ignore the throbbing in her loins and the tingling in her breasts.

The memory of the golden man's touch haunted her waking hours.

She was astute enough to know that Wolf Shadow was the erotic man in her dream, and that realization was so disturbing as to be almost mind shattering. Lust for a man, even a dream lover, was an emotion that Fiona had never before experienced.

She had never trusted men, and she had built up a lifetime of defenses against them.

Since she was a child, men had told her that she was beautiful—that she had hair like a sunset over Galway Bay and the come-hither eyes of a fallen angel. But experience had been a good teacher. She'd seen her once-exquisite mother change from a vibrant young woman to a gaunt, hollow-eyed jade. And when the sparkle vanished from her eyes and the quickness from her step, when her cheeks ceased to glow with youth and her body thickened from poor diet and ill use, the men stopped giving compliments and gifts. Instead, they called her hard names and tumbled her against the walls in dirty alleys.

Men used women. Men fed women lies and took pleasure on their bodies. A woman had no defense save her own wit and the strength of her own hands and spirit.

Fiona's mother hadn't learned the lesson. Eileen

had never ceased to believe in the unkept promises
Fiona's father had made to her. She'd harbored no
hate for her own father who'd driven her from his
house, or the lover who'd cast her and her child
away like useless chaff. A part of Eileen had remained innocent, even when she couldn't feed herself on the coin she received from delivering the
babies of prostitutes. Even when she was forced to
accept the protection of one man after another to
survive.

Understanding Wolf Shadow and defending herself against him would have been easier for Fiona if
she could have hated him as she had hated the two
white trappers. Evil men like Nigel and Karl were
devil-spawned, but she knew what they wanted—
she had seen many of them in her lifetime. She could
fight them with her brains and her hands. But she
had no emotional weapons against Wolf Shadow,
and she couldn't hate him. He had showed her
kindness. He had cared for and protected her.

Weakness in men she could understand. Her
grandfather, for all his bristly exterior, had been
weak. He'd driven away a daughter he loved for
fear of idle gossip, and he'd denied his Catholic religion and pretended to be a Protestant in order to
study and practice medicine. Fiona had cared for her
grandfather, but she had never forgiven him his
weaknesses of character.

She was not foolish enough to believe that there
were no good men. For the most part, the priests
she had known had been genuinely good. And one
of the British soldiers her mother had lived with had
been a decent man. He'd fed them and provided a
snug room and stout clothing during one bitter winter—before he'd been shipped back to his wife and
children in Wales. Fiona didn't doubt that some men
treated their families with respect and compassion.

But those men were few and far apart. She had more faith in her ability to care for herself, to control her own life, than to put her future in a man's hands.

Certainly, she would never willingly place herself in the power of a man who thought he was a wolf. It was unthinkable.

As if he'd heard her unspoken thoughts, Wolf Shadow called to her, tearing Fiona from her troubled reflections.

"Come, Irish. Eat. The meat and bread will be cold." He rose from where he was crouched beside the fire pit and held out a bark plate of food. "I am not known for my cooking," he said, "but I did manage to roast the venison without burning it."

His hand brushed hers as she took the food, and she started like a frightened doe. Shivers ran up and down her spine; her fingers throbbed as though she had been burned. Trembling, she retreated to her own nest of furs on the far side of the fire from his bedrobes. Her hunger had vanished . . . replaced by a breathless confusion.

She peered at him from under half-closed lids, afraid that he would make another move toward her, afraid that he would not.

It was the first time he'd touched her since she'd awakened naked in the cave to find them both wrapped in the same bearskin. He had returned her clothes to her as soon as they were dry, and he had taken care to keep his loins covered since then. He had behaved toward her with respect and compassion, but try as she might, she couldn't blot out the memory of his long, muscular body next to hers. Or of his smooth bronze skin . . . skin that shone even now in the flickering firelight.

She closed her eyes to block out his image, but her mind betrayed her. What would it be like to be kissed by a man like Wolf Shadow . . . to unleash that untamed might in a frenzy of sensual passion? The recklessness of her thoughts terrified her, and she clutched the bark plate so tightly that the wood cut into her fingers.

What was wrong with her? Was she bewitched for certain? Mother Mary help her! She had never known a man—she was a virgin. How could she have such sinful lusts?

Fiona swallowed the knot rising in her throat and tried to breathe naturally. Moisture gathered in the hollow between her breasts and trickled down in beads of warm perspiration. Waves of dizziness assailed her. Abruptly she dropped the plate, rose, and wrapped a lynx skin around her shoulders as a shawl.

She crossed to the cave entrance and scooped up a double handful of fluffy snow. Thrusting her face into it, she welcomed the numbing cold, letting it shock her back to reality.

I'm a captive of this man as much as I was of Nigel and Karl. I need to use my wits to stay alive and to escape as soon as I can. Any unnatural thoughts I might have are only the results of what I've been through. I need to remember who I am, and who and what he is. Wolf Shadow is an Indian, and I'm white. He's my enemy, and I must never forget it.

"Fiona."

"What?" She whirled and faced him, pulling the lynx skin tightly around her for protection.

"The wind bites. Don't linger there. Eat all you can and try to sleep," Wolf Shadow advised. "Tonight there is no moon. As soon as it is dark, we'll leave for my sister's village."

"By night?" She returned to the far side of the fire, still unable to look directly into his eyes. Her heart beat a tattoo against her chest. "What about wolves?" She'd heard their howling in the dark-

ness, and it brought back memories of the night Wolf
Shadow had stormed the trappers' cabin. "I've no
wish to be devoured by a wolf."

"The Iroquois—the Seneca are a part of the Iroquois League—do not hunt at night." He smiled
thinly. "They are afraid of ghosts." He finished the
last bite of his portion of venison and licked the tips
of his fingers clean. It was not necessary to tell Fiona
that he had given the enemy reason to fear the supernatural.

He'd left the cave the past two nights while she
was sleeping and harried Roquette and his allies.
He'd killed a Seneca sentry and marked his body
with the bloody print that was his signature. A second warrior he'd overpowered and left alive, being
content with merely scarring the brave's chest with
a wolf's teeth. That man had been barely more than
a boy and too young to be guilty of the heinous acts
that most of Roquette's men had committed against
the Shawnee.

"I said wolves—not Iroquois," Fiona reminded
him.

Her face was pale against the dark cave wall, and
he longed to crush her against his chest and taste
the warm sweetness of her mouth. His heart leaped
within him as he remembered the feel of her cradled
against his shoulder. He should have thought her
ugly—this woman of his white enemies. Instead, he
found her fair skin with its smattering of freckles
intriguing. He wanted to touch her cheek . . . to cup
her firm, round breasts in his hand. He wanted to
smell the unique woman-scent of her and taste the
honey of her woman's cleft.

His hand still tingled from her touch. He could
not stop his eyes from following her.

Wolf Shadow had always found night-black hair
beautiful. In his years in England, he'd never con-

sidered the blond-haired women attractive, and the redheads were nothing to turn his head. But Fiona's hair caught the flame of the campfire at night and the glory of the sun by day.

She was trouble, and he wanted to be as far away from her as possible. She was his enemy. They shared nothing—not religion, not native language or customs, not even friendship. She feared him, and he wasn't certain she wouldn't try to kill him if his back was turned. He could never let down his guard enough to trust her.

There was no room in his life for a woman. There could never be room for a white-skinned woman.

Yet he desired her with every breath he took. She haunted his dreams. She shadowed his every waking thought.

"I said nothing about Indians. I'm afraid of wolves."

Her soft English with its lilting Irish accent touched a chord deep within him. He wondered how his name would sound on her lips in a moment of shared ecstasy.

Shaking off the disturbing thoughts, he tried to look at her dispassionately, as though she were his cousin or the wife of one of his friends. Without longing. Without wishing for what could never be. "Four-legged wolves will not harm us." His voice sounded harsher than he meant it to. "They are my totem animals," he explained, "my spiritual brothers." He clasped his hands together. "Besides, the wolves of the forest are not hunters of men. The deer have more to fear from them than you do."

He would take her to his village and give her over to the care of his sister, Willow. Once he was back with his own people, he could focus on the importance of his mission. He could depend on Willow to do what was best for Fiona and to make her welcome among the Shawnee.

"You've given me little reason to trust what you say." Her tone was accusing.

He knew that she had been disgusted when he'd shoved the Seneca's bodies into her ice cave and placed the wolf prints on them. How could he explain that he had done those things to instill fear and superstition into the hearts of the Seneca? Legends of a half man, half wolf passed from tribe to tribe, and helped to protect his people.

The Shawnee were outnumbered, beset by enemies on all sides. The Iroquois were as plentiful as acorns in a forest. If he had to resort to trickery to defeat his enemies, so be it. Once the Seneca were dead, it did not harm their souls if he used their bodies as a weapon against their own kind.

He was a shaman, and the first rule of his profession was silence. He'd been taught secrecy from the first day he had crawled from the sweat lodge into the keeping of the wily old medicine man, Red Smoke. If Fiona thought he was cruel—if she believed he was a madman—then she must do so. He could not break lifelong habits to suit the tender feelings of a white woman.

He went to the back of the cave and took down the surgeon's box his warriors had carried from the trader's storeroom. He took it to the fire and lifted the lid.

"That's mine!" Fiona cried. "I brought it with me from Ireland." She slammed the lid and grabbed the box, holding it protectively against her chest.

He chuckled. This shy quail chick could be bold enough in defense of something she considered her property. "Prove that it's yours," he dared.

She backed away and put the fire between them. Ignoring him, she opened the kit and scrutinized the contents.

"You need not worry. I haven't stolen anything."

"You stole it from Jacob Clough, didn't you?"

He chuckled again. "Hurons. Thieves, the lot of them. A drunken Huron stole the box from the trader's. If it's yours and not Clough's, give me proof."

"There. There's proof," she declared, pointing out the initials stamped on the lid. "JPO. James Patrick O'Neal. My grandfather. The surgeon's instruments were his, and I inherited them when he died. They're mine."

"Very well," Wolf Shadow agreed mildly. "If they're yours, they're yours. And you can thank that drunken Huron that they aren't still sitting in Clough's store. Wrap *your* physician's box in a deerskin and I will carry it to the Shawnee camp for you. It's going to be a long walk."

"I carried this case from Ireland. I can carry it a little farther."

With a shrug, he turned away and began to prepare his own belongings for the journey. Let her carry the box if she wished—she'd give it over soon enough. She was strong for a woman; it was clear to him that she'd not led an idle life. But walking in snow took great energy. She'd be lucky if she could stay on her feet for the twelve-hour march, let alone support a heavy burden. "Must you make everything difficult?" he asked, without looking at her. "I would be your friend, Fiona."

"If you want to be my friend, take me to the English," she flung back.

"You are a bird that knows but one song."

"I'm not a bird—I'm a woman. You've no right to hold me. I've done nothing to you or your people."

He let her angry words slide off him like melting snow off the cave overhang. He could not let her go. He could never live with himself if she ended up in the hands of Jacob Clough again. I should have killed him when I had the chance, he thought. Perhaps the only answer now would be to find Jacob and Fiona's indenture papers and destroy them both. Then he could let her go back to the English.

Killing Jacob in cold blood would be an evil—different from killing the Seneca. The question was, would killing Jacob be worse than keeping Fiona a prisoner among the Shawnee? It was a dilemma he would have to consider. For now, he would keep Fiona safe . . . and if she was unhappy, she had only herself to blame.

The sun was high overhead when they arrived at the Shawnee Indian village the following day. Fiona was so weary she could hardly lift one foot in front of the other, but she'd not fallen behind, and she had carried her grandfather's instrument case every step of the way.

The camp lay in a bend beside a river, sheltered from the winter winds by wooded hills and so hidden that she hadn't realized they were within miles of a human settlement until she heard the barking of dogs.

Wolf Shadow cupped his hands around his mouth and gave a series of cries that sounded to Fiona much like the gobbling of a turkey. Immediately the call was repeated from the right, and then again—directly overhead.

The branches parted, and Fiona was startled to see a boy's round face staring down at her. He shouted a greeting, and Wolf Shadow grinned and returned the salute. ''That's Beaver Tooth,'' he told Fiona. He spoke briefly to the boy in Algonquian, the Shawnee language, then translated for Fiona. ''He was with us on the raid on Jacob Clough's. He wants to know if your hair is real or a wig.''

Fiona looked back at the spot where she'd seen Beaver Tooth's curious face, but the boy had vanished. "Why did he want to know that? Is he planing on scalping me?"

"You're safe enough," Wolf Shadow replied solemnly. "I told him it was dyed that color." He pointed. "The camp is just ahead, beyond that cedar grove."

"Do I look like a doxy, that I'd dye my hair?" she demanded. "Why did you lie to him, and why was he hiding in a tree?"

Wolf Shadow laughed. "I cannot say for certain that you don't dye your hair. In London I saw an Englishwoman on the stage with hair so yellow it would hurt your eyes. I do not think she was born with that color hair. The boy was—"

"You were in London?" she interrupted. "You went to the playhouses in—"

"It is rude to talk when I am answering your questions," he reprimanded her. "Beaver Tooth is a sentry. He's supposed to see us without being seen. These are dangerous times. A village without guards soon becomes a village of the dead."

"But what about England? How did you—"

He silenced her with a motion of his hand.

Just in front of them, an older warrior with gray streaking his black braids stepped from behind a tree, a musket cradled in the crook of his arm. He nodded to Wolf Shadow, and the shaman smiled and spoke to him in his own tongue. The warrior stared suspiciously at Fiona.

She offered a weak smile and clutched her instrument box against her chest. "Good day to you, sir," she mumbled. The brave ignored her.

Wolf Shadow took her arm. "This is Yellow Elk," he explained. "He's a good friend."

"He doesn't look friendly," she answered in a low voice.

"No. He hates whites."

"That's a comforting thought."

Wolf Shadow tilted his head toward her and arched one eyebrow wryly. "Yellow Elk has good reason. The English soldiers killed his mother." His dark eyes held her captive. "And what reception would you think I'd get in Philadelphia? This is Shawnee land, Irish. Many will resent you for being here." He continued on, talking to Yellow Elk as they walked. Not knowing what else to do, Fiona followed them.

London, she thought. He said he'd been in London. Was it possible he was telling the truth? It would explain his knowledge of the language, but . . . She hurried to keep up with Wolf Shadow's long strides. As much as she resented him, he was her only protector among the hostiles. If he deserted her, what would she do?

Barking dogs and shouting children ran toward them as they neared the camp. Fiona counted several dozen bark huts and one larger structure with log uprights along the walls. There didn't seem to be any formal arrangement of the shelters, but the paths between them were swept free of litter and pounded hard from use.

Women and old people spilled from the huts, surrounding them, all talking at once in Algonquian and pointing at Fiona. There were a few warriors visible around the village, but they continued with what they had been doing, pretending not to notice the commotion. Fiona stopped a few feet behind Wolf Shadow and waited, trying not to reveal how frightened she was.

In spite of her apprehension, she was unable to stifle her physician's curiosity. The Shawnee villagers had the same light coppery skin as Wolf Shadow, and all were well-formed in face and body. The babies were plump and bright-eyed; the chattering children seemed free of the eye infections she'd seen so often in the slums of Irish towns. The women were small and pretty, all with black hair and eyes as dark as coal.

Several women shouted at Wolf Shadow; one shook her fist angrily at Fiona. He answered them calmly in their own language, all the while maintaining his good-natured expression. She couldn't understand a word, but heard her name mentioned several times.

A small dun-colored dog yapped at her heels, and from the corner of her eye, she saw a tom turkey—tail spread and feathers puffed out—stomping the ground in tight circles, moving ever nearer. She took another step closer to Wolf Shadow just as a boy darted out of the crowd and yanked her hair—hard.

Fiona whirled on him. "Stop that!" she admonished. "It hurts, and . . . and it's rude, very rude."

The child's mouth opened, and he began to howl. Tears rolled down his cheeks as a gray-haired woman lunged forward and yanked him to safety.

Wolf Shadow put an arm around Fiona's shoulder. "Don't be afraid," he said. "No one will harm you."

The gray-haired woman glared at her, but Fiona noticed two other women whispering behind their hands. One looked pointedly at the older squaw and the weeping child, and giggled.

"I'm not afraid," Fiona said. Surely he didn't expect her to let herself be abused by a naughty child.

A tall, graceful woman in a beaded dress ducked out of the large bark house and walked quickly toward Wolf Shadow with an expression of relief and delight. He hugged her affectionately and turned to introduce her to Fiona. "This is my sister, Tandee—in your language, Willow." He motioned. "Willow, this is Fiona. Willow speaks English," he explained.

"She'll make you welcome. You'll stay in her wigwam for the time being."

Willow's exquisite features hardened, and she replied in a quick burst of words. He answered in Algonquian; she frowned and shook her head no. It was plain to Fiona that Willow had no intention of welcoming her into her home.

"Take her back where she come from," a sensual young woman with an infant on her back called in heavily accented English. "We no want her here. She make trouble." She pushed her way to the front of the group. Shell earrings dangled from her ears, and more shells were laced in her loose, flowing hair. "I, Shell Woman, say you no belong here."

The other women began to speak in Algonquian. Yellow Elk shrugged and moved away from Wolf Shadow toward the long house. The dun-colored dog continued to bark annoyingly at Fiona.

Wolf Shadow exhaled slowly and straightened his shoulders. "Fiona is our guest," he told his sister. "I expect you to treat her as such." He scowled at the grumbling women and spoke sharply in his own language.

"I not bite my tongue!" Shell Woman retorted hotly. "Is she prisoner? If prisoner, give her to me. I will find work for her."

"Enough," Wolf Shadow said, his patience clearly at an end. "You shame me. If the guest of your shaman is not welcome here, then I am not welcome."

Spots of color appeared on Willow's cheeks. Her irritation lingered for a few seconds more before she nodded and looked directly into Fiona's eyes.

"Honored guest," Willow said formally in soft, distinct English, "come, please, with me. I would offer to you food and fire."

Fiona shook her head. "No."

Wolf Shadow shot her a withering glance.

She stiffened. "No. If I am a prisoner, you must

do with me as you will. If I am an honored guest, I'll not enter a house where I'm not truly welcome."

A titter of amusement rose from the gathered women. Wolf Shadow glared at Fiona, then turned his biting gaze on his sister. "You behave like children, both of you," he said.

Suddenly the tension was broken by a man's loud voice. A brave appeared from one of the huts on the far side of the village. He shouted and waved to Wolf Shadow. Shadow signaled that he'd heard.

"That is Spear Thrower," he explained. "His wife, Sage, is in pain. Go with my sister. She'll look after you." He walked swiftly toward Spear Thrower's wigwam without waiting for a reply.

"Wait, I'll come with you," Fiona offered.

"No." Willow shook her head. "No. My brother has no time for you now. Sage is with child. She has pain since the night, but it be no . . . not time for child to be born. It is—" she struggled for the English words—"too early for born." She held up six fingers. "This many turnings of moon."

"Premature labor," Fiona said, nodding her understanding. "But I may be able to help. I'm a trained apothecary, and my grandfather was a physician-surgeon. I studied under him, and I have delivered many babies."

Willow looked unconvinced. "Sage be Shawnee woman. I no think she want white medicine."

"If the life of her unborn child is in danger, I've got to try to help her whether she wants me or not."

"No," Willow insisted. "Wolf Shadow is shaman—great medicine man. You go where he say no, he have great anger."

Fiona turned her back on Willow and hurried after Wolf Shadow. White skin or red, it didn't matter. Surely labor was the same in all women. She knew medicine, and if she could use her superior European knowledge to prevent a miscarriage, she must try, no matter what opposition she had to face from primitive superstition.

No one attempted to stop her as she crossed the open area, and Fiona's resolve stiffened as she neared the sick woman's hut. She was needed here, and if Wolf Shadow tried to prevent her from practicing her healing arts, he'd soon have a taste of Irish temper.

Chapter 7

Fiona pushed aside the hanging deerskin door and entered the wigwam. It took a few seconds for her eyes to adjust to the dim light, but when they did, she saw that the single room was crowded with people—all glaring at her. Even a wailing toddler quieted in mid-scream and gazed at her with astonishment.

Fiona flushed under the obviously hostile attention, took a deep breath, and drew herself up to her full height. "I . . . I'm a doctor," she explained, trying to convey professional dignity. "A . . . a medicine woman."

The wigwam was high in the center with sloping sides made of bark panels. A knee-high platform of logs, about three feet high and covered with animal skins, ran around the interior walls. There was no furniture, not even a single chair. The floor was dirt, pounded hard and swept bare. Four adults and several children were seated on skin rugs around a glowing fire. Bundles, baskets, and an assortment of items Fiona didn't recognize hung from the roof supports and were piled on the platform to the right of the fire pit. The smoky hut smelled of tobacco, herbs, and wet fur.

Wolf Shadow was crouched to the left of the fire

pit beside the patient. His welcome was no warmer than that of the others. "You have no business here," he said harshly.

Ignoring him, Fiona moved toward the woman in labor. She lay on the low platform on a bed of furs, eyes closed, round face contorted with pain. "Don't be frightened, I've come to help you," Fiona began.

"Don't touch her." Wolf Shadow took hold of Fiona's arm. "This is no place for you."

An old woman shook her fist and muttered something that Fiona knew could only be unpleasant. A swell of distrustful murmuring rose from those around the fire. The baby began to cry again.

"Please," Fiona entreated. "I've tended many cases like this. If you'll only let me look at her." She clutched her medicine case and looked up into Wolf Shadow's irate face. "I have herbs here that—"

A muscular brave leaped up from beyond the fire and handed the weeping toddler to the old woman. "You go," he ordered, motioning with his hand. "Leave my house. You have no welcome here."

"I can help," she insisted. "Are you the husband? Spear . . . Spear Thrower?" He nodded. "I know about such things. I can use white medicine to help Sage."

Wolf Shadow made a sound of impatience and propelled her toward the doorway. "Outside."

Her face flamed as she heard the Shawnee shouting approval. "You don't understand," she protested. "I—"

He shoved her through the door and followed her out into the cold air. "Are you stupid that you can't understand a simple order?"

She twisted out of his grasp, her temper flaring. "Are you such a fool that you don't see I only want to help? I'm trained for such cases."

A muscle twitched along his tight jawline. "And naturally," he replied sarcastically, "European knowledge of such matters is superior to the primitive customs of savages.''

"You said it. I didn't.'' She balanced the heavy physician's case on one hip and glared at him with stubborn righteousness.

"Pah!'' Wolf Shadow spat on the ground.

"My grandfather earned his medical degree at one of the finest universities. I studied under him for years. Will you let that woman lose her baby—maybe die because you're too arrogant to consider I might know more about the complications of childbirth than you do?''

His features hardened. "I am a shaman—a moon dancer,'' he explained with rigid patience. "I have studied medicine since I was six winters old. The suffering of women is not unknown to me, Irish Fiona.'' He glanced around at the curious villagers, drawn near by the heated words exchanged between their shaman and the red-haired white woman. "Have you all nothing to do?'' he demanded.

The onlookers scattered, pointedly turning their attention to other matters. Willow walked toward Wolf Shadow, an amused expression on her face, and spoke to him in Algonquian. "I knew when I laid eyes on her that she would be trouble, brother. Why, when you finally decide to cause woman trouble, must it be with an Englishwoman?''

"I have need of a sweat house,'' he replied in English, ignoring her sarcasm. "Fiona says she is wise in the ways of *Englishmanake* medicine. She claims to be a healer in her own land. She says I will not let her treat Sage out of arrogant pride.''

Willow shrugged and continued to speak in the Indian tongue. "Only you can know if that's true, brother.'' She turned an appraising look on Fiona, and the amusement faded from her brown eyes. "Sage and Spear Thrower trust you,'' she murmured. "If their unborn child is lost, they will not blame you. But . . .'' She left the rest unspoken.

Wolf Shadow looked at Fiona. ''I will accept your assistance, since you are so certain of your abilities. But you must understand, if the child dies . . . if Sage dies, the Shawnee will blame you. You are the enemy. If you do nothing, no one will blame you, but if you treat Sage and she becomes worse—''

''If I don't try to help her, I'll blame myself,'' Fiona said. It was unnerving to be able to understand only half of what was being said between Wolf Shadow and Willow. She knew Willow disliked her, and she was certain that whatever the Indian woman was saying about her wasn't flattering.

''So be it,'' Shadow replied. ''You will do as I say, Irish Fiona. You will break no taboos.'' He glanced back at his sister. ''I'll need the sweat lodge.''

''It's already prepared,'' she answered, still speaking Algonquian. ''Yellow Elk knew you would want to cleanse yourself from the raid before you touched a patient.''

''Once I am purified, see that she''—he inclined his head in Fiona's direction—''does the same. Give her clean clothing and paint her face in the manner of a first degree initiate.''

''And if she refuses?'' Willow asked.

''Then prevent her from coming near Sage's wigwam.''

''You want your otterskin bag? And the powdered root of moccasin flower?''

He nodded. ''I have a fresh batch—in the reed basket hanging over my turtleshell drum. Look for a small clay bowl with three yellow slashes on the lid. And painted trillium—the white blossoms, not the red. They are in the same basket, but the bowl has a wooden lid marked with a white star.'' He glanced back at Fiona and spoke to her in English. ''Go with my sister. She will prepare you to enter

Sage's lodge. Do exactly as she says, or I'll never let you within an arrow's flight of another of my patients."

In less than an hour, Fiona stood shivering at the entrance of Sage's wigwam. In the elapsed time, she'd been stripped naked and shoved into a dark hole in the ground, baked and steamed, then dragged into an icy river and scrubbed dry by Willow and three other women. Despite her protests, they'd painted her still stinging cheeks with yellow stripes and braided her hair into a single plait. They'd refused to return her confiscated clothes and shoes, replacing them instead with a shapeless deerskin dress and high, soft moccasins.

She'd not slept in two days, but her fatigue had vanished. Excitement and fear sent tingling sensations to every inch of her body. She hoped Sage hadn't gotten worse since she'd last seen her, and she desperately hoped that after all her bold talk, she'd be able to help the woman.

Two Shawnee women stood outside the hut, one on either side of the doorway. They were chanting in Algonquian and shaking painted gourd rattles decorated with white feathers. Neither woman seemed to see Fiona, but since they made no attempt to stop her, she touched her amulet once for luck, stooped, and entered the wigwam.

Again, she had to pause to let her eyes become accustomed to the dim light. This time the room was empty except for the patient and a tall figure in a wolfskin. The fire was built up higher, so that the interior of the wigwam was comfortably warm. Fiona's medicine case stood on the sleeping platform at Sage's feet.

Fiona noticed an odor of cedar in the air . . . cedar and something else she couldn't identify. She looked at Wolf Shadow for permission. "Is it all right if I touch her now?"

He nodded and stepped back into the shadows. "Of course. Now you're purified."

"That's what you call it. I call it torture." She shuddered as she remembered the shock of the cold river water after the intense heat of the sweat lodge. "I prefer my bathwater heated, thank you," she quipped.

He chuckled softly.

Cautiously, Fiona approached the sick woman. Her eyes were open, and beads of sweat stood out on her forehead. She flinched when Fiona first touched her arm, but gradually as Fiona ran her fingers over her and murmured words of sympathy, Sage relaxed.

"She speaks no English," Wolf Shadow said, "but I can tell you some of what you need to know. She was in good health until she slipped on the riverbank. This is her second child. The first is nearly two winters—two years," he corrected, "old. Actually, he was born in the month you call June so he is about twenty months old. Usually Shawnee women have their children farther apart, but Sage's mother died last winter, and she was hoping for a girl-child to continue her mother's clan line."

Fiona concentrated on the feel of Sage's swollen womb as she experienced another light contraction. Fiona wanted to question Wolf Shadow about his last statement—that Shawnee women usually have children more than twenty months apart. Surely he couldn't mean they used some form of birth control. The only sure method would be to refrain from having sexual relations—but would savages understand and be able to carry out such a plan? She forced herself to stop conjecturing and concentrate on her patient. There would be plenty of time to ask him later.

Fiona's grandfather had always said that asking too many questions was counterproductive in a physician. It was her weakness, and she admitted it. She'd always demanded to know why. "Some things you do because it is the way they've always been done," he used to shout at her.

She struggled to clear her mind of everything but helping Sage. "Often, women have false labor," she said aloud, unconsciously imitating her grandfather's bedside manner, "but if this has been going on since last night, then . . . Do you know if she's had any bleeding?"

Wolf Shadow held out a woman's loincloth to show the stains. "Not enough to dislodge the child," he said.

"No great loss of blood, good. Has she passed water?"

"Of normal amount and composition."

Fiona laid her ear to the patient's belly to listen for the infant's heartbeat and was rewarded by a strong rolling movement. She smiled and covered the mother. "The baby is alive."

"Yes," Wolf Shadow agreed, "she is."

"You can't know it's a girl."

"It's a girl."

Fiona uttered a sound of disbelief. "No one can tell such a thing until a child is born." She'd heard the old wives' tales for predicting the sex of a baby, and the superstitious claptrap for conceiving a boy rather than a girl. All of it was nonsense. She opened her grandfather's case and scanned the contents. Her grandfather had owned several valuable dispensatories and a classic text on midwifery, but they'd all been sold with his estate. She'd have to rely on her memory for exact dosages of medication.

"I gave her a tea of moccasin flower and trillium. Her contractions were harder, but they've eased, and they're coming farther apart."

Fiona bit back the reply that sprang to her lips. What would James Patrick O'Neal say if he could see her standing in an Indian hut in America, discussing midwifery with a savage in a wolf suit? The answer to that question was too outrageous to consider. Instead, she removed a blue bottle labeled *Balsam of Life*, and the box device for bleeding patients.

Unconsciously, she nibbled her lower lip. Nettle tea might help; her grandfather had favored that with a little honey and powdered ginseng. "It will be all right," she said, uncovering Sage's arm. "Don't be afraid." Fiona hoped the confidence in her tone would make up for her inability to communicate in the Shawnee language. "I'll need a bowl of some kind," she said to Wolf Shadow.

The shaman's hand fell heavily on Fiona's shoulder. "What do you think you're doing?"

"Bleeding her. All patients with—"

"No." He took the bleeding-box from her hand. "Sage needs her strength. There is no need for that."

"Bleeding is the accepted—"

"Not among the Shawnee. We consider such treatment barbaric." He picked up the blue bottle, uncorked it, and sniffed.

"Don't do that," Fiona protested. "It's . . ."

Wolf Shadow tasted the potion and grimaced. "Pah. It's nothing more than raw spirits." With a flick of his hand, he upended the container and poured the contents into the fire. The flames sputtered and flared up. "I allow no spirits in this village," he said firmly. "They are the curse of my people. And yours," he added. "They fog the brain and turn men and women into animals. What else do you have in that demon case?"

"Keep your hands off my case," she said, trying not to alarm the patient. "Do you know what you've done with your meddling? That's all the balsam of life I have. It cost two gold guineas."

"What else did you intend to give her? Powdered unicorn horn?"

Fiona gritted her teeth. "Nettle tea and ginseng."

"The tea won't hurt her. She's eaten nothing since she began having the pains, and she needs all the liquid she can take." He motioned toward the fire. "The water in that pot is clean and hot. You can steep your nettle tea in one of those gourds."

Fiona prepared the medicinal drink in seething silence. When it was ready, Wolf Shadow took it from her, tasted it, then carried it to the patient. Sage drank it slowly and lay back on her bed of furs. It was obvious to Fiona that Sage was still uncomfortable and badly frightened of her.

"What now?" Fiona asked. She wondered if she'd be allowed to remain with the patient, or if Wolf Shadow would send her away again for another session in the sweat house.

"Now we wait," he said. "Sit over there, beyond the fire, and don't speak. Not a word, do you understand?"

She obeyed him without answering. The warmth of the small room was beginning to make her sleepy again, but she forced herself to remain alert as Wolf Shadow began to sing in a deep, rich timbre. From a pouch at his waist, he produced a drum no larger than the palm of her hand. The sound of the drum was soft and muffled, almost an echo of his chanting.

A rainbow of colors radiated out from the fire. Fiona blinked. Had Wolf Shadow thrown something into the flames? She hadn't seen his hands move in that direction, but he was dancing now, a half step, half shuffle in time to the drum.

Clouds of blue smoke swirled up from the fire pit, drowning the rainbow hues. Fiona smiled, thinking Wolf Shadow could have made a fortune selling magic tonic from the back of a peddler's wagon. The colors in the fire were a trick obviously, but how did he make them?

Fiona's eyelids closed. Immediately she opened them again. Was she dreaming? The walls of the hut seemed to have vanished. All around her were trees. But . . . She shook her head to clear her senses. The trees were covered with green leaves—the bright green of early summer. The air was filled with the scent of honeysuckle and clover and . . . and wild strawberries. She opened her mouth to cry out, and then remembered the shaman's warning.

She pinched the inside of her elbow hard—hard enough to wake herself from a dream—but the forest didn't vanish. To her left she could see a rolling meadow, and beyond that a river. Wolf Shadow was still singing, but now she could hear birdsong as well. It was unnerving—impossible.

She shut her eyes tight and opened them again. Now there was no wigwam at all, just towering trees so high and broad, only patches of blue sky were visible through the treetops. She tried to focus on the beech leaves floating around her. She reached out to catch one in her fingers.

This can't be, she cried inwardly. It's a hoax—a charlatan's trick. But if the trees aren't real, why does the leaf taste and smell like . . .

The clouds rose again from the fire pit, and Fiona knew no more until she felt the motion of being carried. The air around her was cold, and when she opened her eyes yet again, she saw the heavens ablaze with stars.

"Put me down," she said. "I—"

"Shhh, go back to sleep," Wolf Shadow soothed. "You're tired."

"No." She began to struggle, and he lowered her to her feet. She looked up into the velvet-black heavens. The stars looked close enough to touch. They'd never seemed this bright in Ireland. The snow-covered ground was bitter cold through her moccasins; it crunched under her feet. "It's still . . . night," she stammered. Flashes of memory returned, memories too confused to be real. "Sage? What of Sage?"

He steadied her with his arm. "She's sleeping. The pains have stopped, and her family is with her. We can rest now."

"Where are you taking me?"

"To my wigwam. You said you wouldn't go to Willow's wigwam, and everyone else in the village is asleep."

She stepped away from him, shivering in the raw night air. The cold was so intense it hurt her teeth. "I'm not going anywhere with you," she argued. "You drugged me."

"You know that's not true."

She looked back toward Sage's wigwam. "Either drugs or witchcraft. What happened in there . . ." She exhaled slowly, and her breath made puffs of steam in the air. "It . . . it was unnatural."

"I performed a healing ceremony, nothing more."

"I saw . . ." Fiona shook her head, unwilling to put into words what she had seen . . . what she had smelled. "You *are* a warlock," she accused. Butterflies danced in the pit of her stomach. She knew it wasn't fear that caused the strange sensation; it was something else.

He chuckled. "No, I'm not. What evil I do, I do with my hands like any other man. I value my soul as much as you do, Irish. I practice no black arts."

"Then how . . ." The cold bit through the leather dress. Fiona was shivering so hard that she could barely speak, but it wasn't the bitter air that made her tremble. It was the power, the magnetism, of this man.

"You can't stay here, little one. You'll freeze." He took off his wolf's cape and draped it protectively around her, fur side in. His fingers caressed her bare arm, and she flinched. "I've sworn to you that I'll do you no harm."

She looked up into his face. Moonlight reflected off his cheekbones, outlined his craggy features, and glittered back at her from his luminous, almond-shaped eyes. He stood there as solid as a granite outcropping, muscles taut, bare-chested in the cold winter wind. Completely alien.

She took a hesitant step toward him. His smoldering gaze sent giddiness through her. She took another step, and her heart skipped a beat as he crushed her against him and covered her mouth with his own.

The heat of his body permeated her as she pressed ever closer, savoring the sweet taste of his lips. How could their lips fit so perfectly together? she wondered . . . as though they had always been one. The heady scent of his clean male virility filled her head and turned her knees weak. Breathless, she clung to him, offering no protest when he swept her off her feet and began to carry her again.

Fiona let her head fall back into the crook of his arm and instinctively parted her lips. To her surprise and sudden joy, his warm, wet tongue filled her mouth. "Ohhh," she murmured. Her eyes dilated with pleasure. The texture of his tongue against hers was a delight, and she returned the favor without hesitation. She threaded her fingers through his night-black hair and pulled him closer, unwilling for the wonderful sensations to end.

Wolf Shadow ducked to enter the doorway to his own wigwam, and Fiona felt the warmth of the fire in the snug dwelling. He sank to his knees and lowered her carefully onto a bearskin rug. "Fiona, I—" he began, but she held out her arms to him, and he left his thought unfinished.

The intensity of his searing kiss shocked her. Her

last shreds of fear were washed away by the delicious sensations that thrilled her and made her hungry for more. The tip of his tongue flicked sparks of liquid fire along her upper lip, teasing the corners of her mouth. She sighed and snuggled back against the thick fur, no longer trying to understand what was happening, no longer caring why.

As Wolf Shadow leaned over her, his hair brushed across her cheek like a curtain of ebony silk. His deep voice whispered her name, making her tremble with wanting him. His tender mouth trailed hot, moist kisses down her throat and nuzzled aside her amulet to kiss the sensitive flesh beneath.

Fiona caught his beautiful face between her hands and lifted it so that she could look into his dark eyes. Her pulse quickened as their gazes locked, and she realized instantly that he shared the burning fever that threatened to consume her with desire.

Flushing under his passionate gaze, she moistened her lips and tilted her head to kiss him again. This time, when he thrust his tongue into her willing mouth, she sucked on it, drawing him deep into her . . . reveling in the sensual feel of his hard, stabbing tongue against hers.

Wolf Shadow moaned with desire and ran a hand over the curves of her breasts. Fiona made a small sound of delight as her nipples hardened to tight buds of aching torment. She arched her body against his, wanting to feel the weight and length of him pressed against her, wanting something she dared not give name to.

Her mind whirled. She felt as though she were standing on the edge of a cliff with only air and sea beneath her. One step and she would go over the precipice. One step more and . . . She had been kissed before, but no man had ever caused her to feel such sweet, hot hunger . . . such throbbing, incandescent longing. What madness was this? she wondered. Or had everything that had happened in her life been madness and this was the only sanity?

"I want to look at you," he whispered. "Look, my Irish Fiona . . . nothing more."

Her throat constricted. *Stop. Stop before it's too late,* her inner voice cried. *Will you be like your mother and give yourself to a man without marriage?* But when she opened her mouth to speak, she answered, "Yes."

He took hold of the hem of her deerskin dress and slid it up her hips. Trembling, she leaned forward to help him pull it over her head. Suddenly shy, Fiona covered her bare breasts with her arms. Her cheeks burned, but when she dared to look at him, he was smiling back at her.

"Only look," he said huskily. "For I think that you have never been with a man."

"No . . . never."

Tears clouded her vision as he took her hands in his and pulled them away from her breasts. Waves of heat flushed her body, but she found the strength to raise her head and meet his scalding gaze.

"Beautiful," he murmured. "You are the most beautiful woman I've ever seen." Her braid had come undone, and he lifted a lock of her hair to his lips and kissed the red-gold strands. "I've thought of you like this so often . . . since you lay in my arms in the cave . . . I was afraid I'd dreamed you . . . but you're real."

Tears welled up again in her eyes, and emotion choked her so she couldn't speak. She swayed as his hungry stare caressed the curve of her hips and lingered intimately on her triangle of bright russet curls. Soundlessly, her lips formed his name, and she reached out to him.

"I never chose you, Irish Fiona," he whispered huskily. "The spirits chose you for me." Slowly, he rose on his knees and pulled a red woolen trade blanket from his sleeping platform. He drew in one long, shuddering breath and covered her. "You are untouched, my Irish *equiwa*. As much as I want you, I . . . I can't."

"But . . . but . . ." She pushed up on one elbow, her eyes wide with confusion. "You don't want me?"

He stood and wrapped his wolfskin around his shoulders. "Sleep, Fiona. Tomorrow we will talk of this. If I don't go now, we will do something we may both regret."

She stared after him in shocked silence as he pushed aside the deerskin and ducked out through the entrance, leaving Fiona alone with her doubts and tears.

Chapter 8

"**F**ee-on-nah?"

Fiona opened her eyes to see Willow bending over her. "Oh," she gasped, pulling the blanket up to her chin. Light was streaming through the open doorway, and Fiona could hear children's voices outside the wigwam.

"Have no fear, Fee-on-nah. Willow no come for harm you. See, me . . . I . . . bring you English dress." She held out Fiona's own shoes and clothing.

Glancing around first to make certain that they were alone in the hut, Fiona hastily donned her own things. During the night someone had washed them; they were clean and smelled of mint. "Thank you," she said awkwardly. She wondered what Wolf Shadow had told his sister about her, and if Willow suspected she and Wolf Shadow had been intimate. "Is . . . is he—"

"This one's brother not here."

Fiona suddenly remembered her patient. "Sage? Is she all right?" To her relief, Fiona noted that her grandfather's precious surgical case lay at the feet of the bearskin where she'd been sleeping. Last night, she'd completely forgotten it and left it in the sick woman's wigwam.

Willow nodded. "Sage good, no have pain. My brother talks with council." She frowned. "White woman bad for him. No marry you." She shook her head vehemently.

"Marry me?" Startled by the outlandish notion, Fiona widened her eyes in astonishment. "God forbid!" She bent to buckle her shoe. The leather was slightly damp, but her woolen socks were dry. "I don't know where you'd get such an idea. I have no intention of marrying any man, and if I did, it wouldn't be a Shawnee. Your brother's safe from me," she answered firmly. She kept her face averted so that Willow couldn't see her eyes. Memories of what she had allowed Wolf Shadow to do flooded over her, and she was deeply ashamed. She should have rebuffed him when he had first kissed her, but she hadn't. She'd welcomed his mouth . . . his hands on her . . . She'd touched him and returned hot caress for caress.

Gooseflesh rose on her arms as she replayed the scene of their fervent lovemaking in her mind. Merciful Mary! Thank the Lady that Wolf Shadow wasn't here this morning—she could never have faced him. "All I want is . . . is to return to my own people," she said.

Fiona knew she had led Wolf Shadow on. She'd offered herself to him like a common whore, and he'd rejected her. He'd turned away in . . . In what? Disgust? Fiona's stomach churned. How could she have been so weak? Before, she'd held every man at bay. She'd fought tooth and nail to protect her maidenhood. What was there about this wolf-man that had cut through her defenses like a scythe through ripe wheat?

She'd wanted all of him. She still did.

Tears of shame and anger filled her eyes, and she dashed them away. "Your brother saved me," she continued, trying to maintain her shattered composure. "I'm grateful, but I never asked to be brought here. And I never asked to be his wife." She glanced up into his sister's disbelieving face and unconsciously fingered her golden amulet. "I'd . . . I'd sooner be dead," she lied.

Willow's exotic features were expressionless. She inclined her head slightly and settled down on the rug. "We talk, Fee-on-nah."

"Fiona," she corrected.

"Fiona." This time, she pronounced her name with only the slightest accent. The Indian woman sighed heavily and produced a wooden bowl of corn pudding and flat corn patties. "Eat," she instructed. She sat silently while Fiona nibbled the Indian bread and tasted the pudding.

"It's . . . it's very good," Fiona said. Suddenly she was starving. She ate every spoonful of the honey-sweetened porridge and devoured the bread to the last crumb. "Thank you."

Willow held out a gourd full of clear river water. Gratefully, Fiona accepted it and quenched her thirst. Then the two women sat in silence, watching each other.

Willow broke the standoff. "My brother . . . my brother not like other men," she began.

"No, he's not," Fiona agreed. "He's a good man, but I've never met anyone quite like him."

Willow shook her head. "No . . . not that he be Shawnee with red skin, and you know only white man. Wolf Shadow not same as Indian man either." She struck her breast lightly with the back of her hand. "Here, in *ki-te-hi* . . ." She struggled for the English word. "Heart." She motioned with her hand. "In your tongue, I not talk good," Willow apologized. "No can—"

"Go on," Fiona urged. "I understand you perfectly. You're saying that your brother is different from other men in his heart."

The Indian woman shook her head impatiently. "Not just heart." She touched her forehead with a slim finger. "Wolf Shadow in head and heart is different. He is shaman—great shaman—born to save Shawnee people. Since time he is child, he be teached—"

"Taught," Fiona supplied gently.

"He be taught," Willow continued. "He taught all Shawnee spirit medicine, healing medicine. But . . ." She raised an index finger. "Not enough. He must be taught *Englishmanake* ways. Elders send him to Philadelphia, to white school-of-church. He taught speak English, taught write, read books of white man. Wolf Shadow no like, come back Shawnee. Council say he is ready. Red Smoke, Shawnee teacher. Red Smoke great medicine man, great moon dancer, greatest all tribes. Red Smoke say Wolf Shadow not ready. He make two winters learn more shaman way of Shawnee, then must go again to white school-of-church."

"But he told me he'd been to England," Fiona said. "Across the ocean."

Willow nodded. "So. Wolf Shadow again go white school-of-church. *Englishmanake* John Parker want make English man of God. John Parker is . . . is priest. No." She shook her head. "Not priest."

"Minister?"

"So. Min-ister. John Parker want make my brother Wolf Shadow minister—want make him like son. Take him away across salt water to land of Scot."

"Scotland?"

Again, the Indian woman nodded. "Scotland. France. England. John Parker great chief in own land, much rich. Buy teacher for Wolf Shadow, many teacher. My brother learn ride horse, wear white clothes, shoot gun, fight with long knife." Willow paused for breath and held up four fingers. "So many winters he be gone. Shawnee fear he no come back. Fear he be eaten by English ways. Willow no afraid. Wolf Shadow promise sister he return, promise Red Smoke he return."

"Four years he was gone," Fiona urged, wanting to hear the rest of the story.

Willow nodded. "So. Four years." A smile lit her eyes. "My brother return to his people. Now he is more . . . more different. Eyes." She pointed to her own eyes. "Eyes wise. He learns much of English, learns how many English, learns he must stop English or they no stop until every Shawnee dead. English want our land, he say." An expression of dread passed across Willow's comely face. "Wolf Shadow says English and French fight over our mother the earth. He say they be greedy children." She took hold of Fiona's hand and gripped it tightly. "He say if they can not have the toy, they will crush underfoot." Willow's long, feathery lashes fluttered, and her eyes grew wide with apprehension. "Is so, Fiona? Do your people wish to crush us underfoot? Do they want our land?"

Fiona felt her initial dislike for Wolf Shadow's sister fade. Willow was a good woman. She loved her brother and her tribe, and it was only natural that she'd be resentful of a white-skinned enemy captive. Fiona leaned forward and covered Willow's slim hand with her own pale one. "It's not an easy question you ask me. I am not English, I'm Irish. The English are my enemies too."

Willow's dark eyes narrowed. "You look English to this one."

"And you look Iroquois to me," Fiona replied. "But you aren't, are you?"

"Pah!" Willow puckered her face in disgust and pulled away. "Iroquois. Drinkers of blood." She shook her head. "No Iroquois. Iroquois very bad, like English devil. Iroquois cut flesh from prisoner.

Eat. Willow not Iroquois—better dead than Iroquois.''

Fiona nodded and moved closer to the fire. A cold February wind whipped around the wigwam and tore at the deerskin flap with icy fingers. Fiona pulled the red blanket around her shoulders and glanced around the hut.

Wolf Shadow had said that this was his wigwam, and it was obvious to Fiona that no woman lived here. There were just as many baskets and bundles hanging overhead from the arched wooden frame as she had seen in Sage's wigwam, but most of the wall space was taken up with weapons and carved wooden masks. What looked like the stuffed body of an otter was hanging to the right of the doorway, and several pairs of men's moccasins lay in a heap on the fur rug underneath. A low platform of logs covered with skins ran halfway around the hut, but it was so piled up that no one could have slept on it. The hut wasn't dirty—the only smells were herbs, tobacco, and furs. Instead, Fiona decided, the shaman's wigwam was untidy, much as her grandfather's house had been when she first went to live with him.

"My brother live here by lone," Willow said, as if reading Fiona's thoughts. "No time for wife. Many Shawnee *equiwa*—squaw—follow him with their eyes. He be brave warrior, great hunter." The Indian woman spread her hands, palms up. "He belong to Shawnee. No belong self. No time for wife."

"What does a shaman do—other than heal the sick?"

Willow's voice dropped to a hushed whisper. "Spirits." She motioned toward the sky. "Eyes not see all. Ears not hear all. Hands not touch all. Life is mystery, so?"

"Yes," Fiona agreed. "Life is a mystery."

"Shaman speak with spirit, listen spirit, touch

spirit. Shaman know magic.'' She paused. ''My brother, Wolf Shadow, he comes to save the Shawnee.'' She held up both hands, fingers spread wide, then knotted them into tight fists. ''Shawnee, Delaware, Menominee, Ojibwa. Like fingers on hand. Small, weak.'' She raised her clenched fists. ''My brother make us together—strong. My brother stop English, stop French.''

''He wants to unite your tribes so that they can stand against the Europeans—against the English and French.''

''So.'' Willow nodded. ''This be our hunting ground. Here we stand or die.'' She exhaled softly. ''You not answer question. You believe English want Shawnee land?''

''Yes,'' Fiona said. ''I do. They wanted my land, Ireland. We were small, and once fierce warriors, but the English were many. They came with weapons and many ships. Now my country is a conquered land, where children are forbidden to speak their own tongue or worship God as our grandfathers did.''

''Mmm.'' Willow crossed her arms over her breasts and rocked back and forth in an ancient gesture of mourning. ''Why is this?'' she asked finally. ''The Shawnee do not cross the salt sea in canoes to take English land. They not cut down English trees or build walls around English rivers. Why, Fiona? Why English come here?''

''England is an island,'' Fiona explained. ''A land surrounded by water. It's small, with too many people. The English are farmers; they must have more land or they will starve. So they take their ships to other lands and drive out the people.''

''Greedy, like crows.''

''Yes, but smart, Willow, very smart. I don't believe Wolf Shadow will be able to stop them from coming.''

"Wolf Shadow smart."

"The Irish were smart. Sometimes smart isn't enough. Now my people must learn to live under English rule. It may be that the Shawnee will have to learn new ways too."

"You know much about these English."

Fiona watched as a log flared up and a yellow-orange flame devoured the small sticks Willow added to the fire. "My father was English . . . Scot, really . . . but they are much the same—cousins."

"As the Delaware and Shawnee be cousins."

"Aye, I suppose."

"You loved this English father."

Fiona's head snapped up. "I hate him. He used my mother and abandoned her—abandoned me. If I ever find him, I mean to kill him."

"He must be very bad, this father—as cruel as Seneca."

"My mother died because of him."

"So . . ." Willow poked the glowing coals with a green branch. "I think I do not hate you, Irish *equiwa*. I think I see why my brother not hate you." She sighed. "But you still make trouble for Wolf Shadow. He say to Shawnee, take nothing of English but steel and gun and black powder. Follow old ways of grandfathers. Turn back on English ways."

"I told you, all I want is to return to the English settlements."

"I see my brother's eye on you. I see your eye on my brother. You not see him as enemy. You see him as man."

"That's true," Fiona admitted. "I do see him as a man, but we are not meant for each other. I have my own customs, my own religion. There can never be anything between us. It's better if I go away quickly, before . . . before . . ." She trailed off, unable to put her fears into words. It was the truth.

Wolf Shadow had shown what he'd thought of her when he'd left the wigwam last night. She must get away before she shamed herself any further.

"You mean these words, Fiona?"

"Yes, of course I mean them."

"Good. This one, Willow, help you go."

Fiona sighed. "Wolf Shadow won't—"

"You have brother?"

"No, but—"

"Brother not always know right. You leave is right. Willow help Fiona go back to English. When Fiona gone, Wolf Shadow understand."

"You'll really help me escape?" Her mouth felt suddenly dry. "It won't put you in danger, will it?" Fiona remembered Wolf Shadow's terrible anger against the Seneca. She wouldn't willingly unleash that temper on anyone. "He wouldn't—"

"Pah." Willow shrugged. "This one be sister. What he do? Shout. Make anger, then think. It better you go. Tonight." She stood up. "Come to my wigwam. This one say is better, Shawnee people no talk-talk behind hand about shaman and red-haired Englishwoman." She looked into Fiona's face. "You have trust Willow?"

Fiona nodded. "Yes, I have trust. As you say, this is the best for us both. Once I'm gone, Wolf Shadow will understand that." Pushing back her doubts, she straightened her shoulders and followed Willow out into the cold, bright morning.

The next few hours were pleasant ones for Fiona. Willow's earlier frosty attitude had completely vanished, and she guided Fiona around the Shawnee town, introducing her to friends and relatives. Fiona's patient, Sage, welcomed both women into her wigwam and shyly offered Fiona a bracelet of delicate blue shells as payment for her healing.

"For thank help," Sage murmured softly. "No

pain." She made a rocking gesture with her arms. "Ba-bee make kick. Is good." Her round face crinkled with joy.

"Yes," Fiona agreed. "It's very good. But you must take care. Do no lifting, and get lots of sleep. I will cherish your gift."

Willow translated, and Fiona was rewarded with a huge smile from her patient. Sage said something in rapid-fire Algonquian, and Willow nodded. "She says you have magic hands—hands of healer."

Sage motioned toward a deerskin rug and invited Fiona to sit down.

The three women sat around Sage's fire pit and communicated with a mixture of English, Shawnee, and hand signals. Their grateful hostess offered them bowls of delicious hot turkey broth, which they enjoyed while Sage's adorable toddler played peek-a-boo with Fiona.

"This wouldn't be the turkey that nearly attacked me when your shaman brought me to the village?" Fiona asked.

Willow covered her mouth with her hand and giggled. "No. *Pa-la-wah* is . . ." She spread her fingers and searched for the elusive English word. "No eat. Play . . . feed. Is . . . friend bird?"

"A pet," Fiona supplied. The Indian women nodded vigorously and giggled again, as though the thought that someone would eat that particular turkey was ridiculous.

Fiona turned the beautiful bracelet on her wrist, thinking how mistaken she'd been to call these people barbarians. As they'd toured the camp earlier, she'd seen several old people, so feeble they could hardly walk. Each one was clean and warmly dressed, obviously well cared for; all were treated with the utmost respect.

Fiona had also held a child with shriveled legs and a blind stare in her milky sloe eyes. The girl was so badly handicapped that she was unable to feed herself and had to be tended like an infant. Still, her mother had taken the trouble to braid beads into her crow-black hair and adorn the child with a necklace of copper bells and an intricately sewn headband. High beaver moccasins with a quillwork design of exquisite red and blue birds covered the little girl's twisted feet.

Fiona smiled as she remembered those birds. Beautiful bright colored shoes for a child who could never see the colors. The moccasins had cost her mother many hours of tedious labor. Yet the birds were not wasted; they proclaimed to all who could see that here was a child who was dearly loved.

As a physician, Fiona knew how hard it was to keep such a child alive. It required more than a mother's devotion. Someone had hunted meat for this child, had trapped the beaver to make her moccasins and skinned the deer to make her dress. Some man—a father, an uncle, a grandfather—had protected mother and child from wild beasts and enemies. Such concern for a child who could never be of use to the tribe proved to Fiona that the Shawnee were a people of great compassion.

In Europe such afflicted children were usually allowed to die at birth. Fiona had heard of crippled and blind infants being sold for use in begging, and she'd seen their poor little bodies abandoned in alleys and on roadsides.

"That child," she said, breaking into Willow's conversation with Sage. "The little blind girl . . ."

"Ah-lahk-wah?" Willow smiled. "Star."

"I didn't know that Indians allowed such babies to live."

Willow's eyes grew large in disbelief. Quickly she translated for Sage, and the pregnant woman gasped. "Who say such evil?" Willow demanded. "Shawnee love Star. Love all child. Child is . . . is gift of Great Spirit. Child no belong mother, father. Child belong Wishemenetoo. Child loan to mother . . . loan to father. Must love. English no love such child?''

"Yes, some mothers and fathers do," Fiona answered, "but still it is hard for some to care for such a crippled child."

"Star no born of Acohqua, her mother. Star born of Delaware woman. Woman die when Star born. Acohqua, Singing Kettle, take baby for self. Love Star."

"Singing Kettle adopted the child?" Fiona wasn't certain she'd understood. Was it possible that the Shawnee woman had willingly accepted the burden of such a child?

Sage and Willow both nodded fervently. " 'Dopt," Willow agreed. "Delaware woman—we no say name of dead—friend. Singing Willow promise friend she care for Star."

"Aiyee." Sage pulled her own healthy baby boy into her lap. "Acohqua love Ah-lahk-wah."

Fiona sighed. "Acohqua must be—" She broke off as a cold draft touched her neck. She turned to see Wolf Shadow standing just inside the wigwam. Startled, she blinked, not certain he'd still be there when she looked again. How had he entered the hut barely an arm's length away from her without making a sound?

"I would speak with Fiona," he said abruptly.

"She stay my wigwam," Willow informed him. "Is better. Village no whisper behind hand."

He stared down at Fiona. For an instant their eyes met, and she was nearly overwhelmed with a rush of longing to be held in his arms again . . . to taste his skin . . . to feel his hands on her body. If only there was some way, she thought. Some way to close the gap that divided their worlds. Then he crushed those fragile yearnings with a scowl so stony that Fiona shrank back as though he had struck her.

"Yes. It is better," he said in frigid tones. "I don't have the time to watch after a white woman." Wolf Shadow turned his attention to his sister. "A messenger has arrived from Wanishish-eyun. Ross Campbell will bring an English delegate from the Maryland Colony to the High Council meeting. Ross Campbell promises his Delaware cousins will also come and listen." He glanced back at Fiona. "It may be that Ross Campbell can find a solution to your problem. He is only half white, and he has always been a trusted friend to the Shawnee. After the council meets, I will speak to him of you. If anyone can get your indenture without bloodshed, it will be this man."

"When is this meeting?" Fiona asked.

Willow made a sound of derision. "My brother try call chiefs many moons. Some say yes they will. But they no come. Some . . ." She shrugged. "Matiassu—"

"I will deal with Matiassu in my own way," Wolf Shadow insisted.

Willow laid one palm over the other and slid her hands apart in a sign for an abrupt ending. "Matiassu must die," she said. "You kill, then call council."

"Shawnee does not kill Shawnee," her brother chided.

Willow sniffed. "I think Matiassu now more Seneca than Shawnee. He forgets his people. Forgets our laws. You kill him before he kill you."

"If I must kill Shawnee to unite the People, then I'm a bad shaman and not worthy of the title. I'm going with He-Who-Runs and Two Crows to Tuk-o-see-yah's village. Moonfeather is there. It may be that with the aid of the peace woman I can convince Tuk-o-see-yah to host the High Council meeting."

He flashed his sister a smile. "Not only is Tuk-o-see-yah one of the most respected of the Shawnee chiefs, he's also Matiassu's grandfather."

Willow stood up. "You're certain Moonfeather will help?" she asked in Algonquian. "Our peace woman has a white husband, and her daughter is half white. What makes you certain she'd back an alliance that may have to fight the English?"

"Her heart is Shawnee," he answered in English. "She will side with us."

"I don't understand," Fiona said. "Who is this Moonfeather, and what is a peace woman?"

Willow seemed surprised. *"Englishmanake* no have peace woman?"

"No." Fiona reluctantly looked at Wolf Shadow for an explanation.

"Among the Shawnee are born certain women, usually descended from the same family line," he said. "From childhood they are trained in the skills of healing with herbs." He raised a dark eyebrow. "This is complicated. Are you certain you want to hear it?"

Fiona stiffened. "I asked you, didn't I?"

"A peace woman may have certain powers over the supernatural that ordinary women do not. She is born for the honor, but it takes many years for her true ability to develop. She must be wise and unselfish. She must put the good of the Shawnee people—all the people—above her own desires. Once a peace woman is recognized by the elders, she may act as a judge to settle domestic disputes. She can perform secret women's ceremonies as well as those having to do with the family. She can name newborn children and marry couples as well as offer prayers for the dead."

"But that be not her great service," Willow said. "She is first a peace woman. She say, 'Go to war,' warriors take up tomahawk. She say, 'Stop war,' men fight no more." Willow's eyes flashed with pride. "Life comes from woman, not man. Only woman say, 'Stop war.' "

"This Moonfeather can stop men from killing each other?" Fiona asked in disbelief.

Wolf Shadow shrugged. "In theory. The council may decide to attack an enemy, but if a peace woman opposes the war, there probably won't be one. There are many stories told around our campfires of battles ended by such women."

"And you think this one, this Moonfeather, will help you convince the chiefs to unite the Shawnee?"

"I do."

"You're going to this Tuk-o-see-yah's village?" she said. "Is it far?"

"Not far." He turned away, toward the entrance, then stopped and looked back at her. "Trust my sister. She'll look out for you." Before she could answer, he had ducked through the deerskin and was gone.

"Wishemenetoo protect him," Willow murmured. Sage echoed the sentiment in her own tongue.

Fiona stared after him, wondering what she should do. He'd said it was possible this Ross Campbell could help her get free from Jacob Clough. If she waited . . .

"Tonight," Willow said in English. Fiona glanced back at her, and Willow nodded. "Tonight," the Indian woman repeated. "You go now, before too late."

Fiona drew in a deep breath. Willow was right. It would be best if she took this chance. Who knew if and when another opportunity to escape would present itself? She couldn't depend on Wolf Shadow or his promises. He'd made it clear what he thought of her.

"Aye," she murmured, "tonight." She'd never

depended on a man before. Anything she'd gotten out of life, she'd gotten by making her own decisions and taking her own chances.

A pang of regret surfaced in the back of her mind, but she ruthlessly pushed it away. She had to go, and go quickly, before she made a bigger fool of herself . . . before she became more deeply involved with a man who would never love her. "Before it's too late," she echoed, but she knew in her heart that it was already too late. No matter how much time or distance she put between them, she would never forget Wolf Shadow or cease to yearn for the sound of his voice . . . or the feel of his arms around her.

Chapter 9

The frail birchbark canoe danced across the sparkling surface of the river, moving faster than Fiona had dreamed possible. Along the banks, the winter-barren trees seemed to fly past as the two Shawnee raised and lowered their paddles in unison, digging deep into the clear cold water and driving the canoe along. They'd not slackened their pace since the early hours of darkness the night before.

Willow had led Fiona to the river and pointed to the broad, muscular warrior in the stern of the canoe as she pushed the boat out into the current. "Fat Boy speak English some. Good man—brave. You not be afraid." The warrior's round face was inscrutable; he'd not changed his expression or said a single word to Fiona since she'd climbed into the boat.

The other member of her escort party was the village sentry, the boy Wolf Shadow had called Beaver Tooth—the one who'd asked the shaman if she was wearing a red wig. Beaver Tooth was friendlier than Fat Boy, but the youth spoke no English. The most he could do was to turn and smile at her every hour or so.

Willow had promised that these two men would guide her safely to a white settlement. She'd explained that both were close friends of Wolf Shadow, but that they agreed with Willow that the shaman would be far better off if Fiona returned to her own people.

It was now midmorning, and Fiona wasn't certain if she could go much longer without relieving herself. She shifted nervously and pulled her blanket closer around her shoulders. Her toes and ears were numb with cold, and her bottom was sore. She was used to discomfort, but she hoped she wouldn't shame herself by wetting her shift in front of these men. Stubbornly, she set her teeth together. Hell could freeze over before she'd beg these stoic savages to stop and let her go in search of a private spot.

About a quarter of an hour passed. The only movement on the river, other than the swift-moving canoe, was a swooping hawk. Then, abruptly, the waterway made a sharp bend to the left around an outcropping of gray rock. Just beyond the hulking stone barrier, Beaver Tooth lifted his paddle and laid the dripping blade on the bow of the canoe. Almost in unison, Fat Boy steered the boat up onto a sandbar.

"We stop," the hulking warrior rumbled.

Beaver Tooth sprang out of the canoe and pulled it up on the yellow sand. Grinning, he offered Fiona his hand and assisted her ashore. The canoe was so light she was able to climb out, surgical case in hand, without even wetting her leather shoes.

Waving her on into the trees ahead, the youth helped Fat Boy lift the canoe and carry it up the slight incline. Fiona watched as they concealed the boat with fallen branches and returned to the sandbar to erase their tracks. Not waiting to ask permission, she took the opportunity to hurry ahead into the woods and ease her kidneys. When she returned, Beaver Tooth and Fat Boy were waiting for her. Between them, they carried everything that had been in the canoe.

Fat Boy led the way up a narrow trail, heavily marked with deer tracks. Fiona followed them a few hundred yards to a sheltered spot beside the rocky outcrop that had jutted into the river. In just minutes, the men fashioned a tiny hut of green saplings with a deerhide cover. Beaver Tooth spread another hide on the leaf-covered ground inside and motioned from Fiona to the completed structure. She glanced at Fat Boy to be certain of Beaver Tooth's meaning.

"You," he replied in flat, almost mechanical English. "You eat, sleep." He pointed up at the sky with a square, thick finger. "You . . . wigwam. Night come, we go." He imitated paddling the canoe with his massive arms.

The youth unrolled a skin bag and offered Fiona corncakes and a bark container. She removed the lid and stared at the lumpy gray-brown contents. Beaver Tooth took a pinch between his fingertips and put it in his mouth.

"Eat," Fat Boy instructed her. "Pemmican. Good."

Fiona swallowed hard and shook her head. "No, no thank you," she stammered, wondering what the god-awful mess was. "Bread is fine, thank you. I'm not really very hungry."

"No," Fat Boy said, opening a similar box and beginning to chew the lumpy mixture with gusto. "Is meat, berry. Good. Make strong."

Tentatively, Fiona tasted the pemmican. It was strange, but not unpleasant. She crunched a dried berry between her teeth and slowly began to eat. By the time she'd finished half of her meal, the boy had returned from the river with a gourd of water. She finished in silence and crawled into the miniature wigwam, taking her medical box with her. Covering herself with a blanket, she curled into a ball. She was certain she was too apprehensive to sleep, but the rich food and warmth soon made her drowsy.

When she opened her eyes again, it was so dark she couldn't see her hand in front of her face. She held her breath and listened, trying to remember where she was. Cautiously, she pushed aside the skin and peered out into the misty blackness. The night air was damp against her cheeks; the wind had been replaced by a creeping fog. The waxing moon was hidden by masses of thick clouds.

Where were Beaver Tooth and Fat Boy? Had they deserted her? Had they treated her with such kindness merely to lull her into trusting them so that they could leave her alone in the wilderness? "Beaver Tooth?" she called softly. "Is anyone there?"

A twig snapped, and Fiona froze. Thoughts of ferocious beasts sent shivers down her spine. She held her breath and listened. There was no sound but the pulsing of her own blood in her ears.

She reached up to touch her amulet. The gold necklace felt hot against her fingertips, and she began to tremble. Twice before she'd received the same impression from her charm, and both times she'd been in great danger.

Saint Anne, protect me, she prayed silently. Her fingers felt clumsy as she fumbled for the latch on her surgical kit. It seemed to take forever to lift the lid and grope for the handle of her largest scalpel. "Whoever's out there, I warn you—I'm armed," she called out in Gaelic. As soon as the bold words left her lips, she realized how foolish it was to threaten the unknown in a language they couldn't possibly understand. She repeated her challenge in English.

An unearthly cry—like a dying woman's scream—

sounded from the forest, then reverberated from tree to tree through the thick fog.

The hair on Fiona's neck raised, and she caught her lower lip between her teeth and bit down until she tasted blood. She crouched in terror, not daring to move a muscle.

The horrible shriek came again, closer this time. Waves of dizziness threatened Fiona's consciousness. Nothing of this earth could make such a sound.

Banshee . . . banshee, whispered the mocking voice in her brain. *The undead make such an outcry.*

Fiona bit her injured lip harder.

Run! Run! the voice urged. *Run for your life . . . or your immortal soul.*

But an older instinct for survival bade her remain motionless. She stared into the mist, suddenly aware of a huge golden form moving toward her on stealthy clawed feet. She blinked; once, twice. Her breath caught in her throat as the head and body of a huge cat materialized from the fog. An acrid scent of musk and rotten meat assailed her nostrils; simultaneously she heard a deep, rumbling growl. A lion!

"Meshepeshe!" A familiar human voice rang out from the far side of the campsite.

Fiona's heart thudded wildly. It was Wolf Shadow. She didn't understand where he'd come from or what he was saying, but she would know that deep, rich timbre in the pits of hell. "I'm here," she answered. Relief flooded over her. He'd come to rescue her again. She didn't know how he'd managed it, but her faith in him was so great that she didn't question it.

"Shhh, don't move a muscle, Fiona. Stay where you are, and don't make a sound."

Fiona couldn't tear her gaze from the monstrous apparition. She heard Wolf Shadow, but he was out of her line of vision, beyond the big cat; his fog-distorted voice seemed to come from far away. Was she dreaming him, or was the stalking beast in front of her a nightmare?

"*Meshepeshe*," he repeated, entreating the cat to turn toward him. "Come, *meshepeshe*." He called the cougar with soft, sweet words of endearment, like a suitor calling his beloved.

Fiona watched as the big cat's eyes caught a flicker of light from the fog-shrouded moon and glowed green in the darkness. For an instant, the mountain lion crouched low to the earth, its long ropelike tail swaying back and forth. Then it lifted its massive yellow head and snarled, exposing long white fangs.

Fiona clutched her amulet with one hand and the scalpel with the other as her mind went blank. She stared into the face of death.

The cougar sprang.

Uttering a growl as fierce as that of the animal, Wolf Shadow dashed toward the cat.

The mountain lion twisted in mid-air, touched the ground with a single hind paw, and launched itself onto Wolf Shadow. They slammed into the earth with a loud thud and rolled over and over, man and screaming cat indistinguishable in the blinding fog.

Fiona scrambled out of the shelter and flung herself across the clearing, scalpel in hand. She'd not gone three feet when a musket roared inches from her face. Her ears ringing from the explosion, Fiona staggered back into the arms of a man.

Startled, she screamed and slashed out at him with her scalpel. The surgical instrument struck something soft, and she heard a man's groan of pain before iron fingers closed around her wrist. She struggled wildly, trying to get free, but he tightened his grip until the scalpel dropped from her numbed fingers.

"Be still," a gruff voice ordered. Fiona ducked her head and butted it into her captor's chin. He released her wrist, and she ran to where the dead cougar and Wolf Shadow lay. Trying to hold back the tears, she went down on her knees and reached for Wolf Shadow, crying his name over and over in her terror.

Her hands encountered fur and teeth. "Don't be dead," she pleaded. "Please, please, don't be dead." Frantically, she tugged at the heavy head of the cougar. Hot blood soaked her bodice and skirts. "Wolf Shadow," she murmured. She would not let him die like this . . . die to save her.

Fiona was vaguely aware of men around her in the fog. She heard the strange syllables of their Indian language, felt their dark-skinned hands on her as they tried to pull her away.

Her physician's mind knew that her efforts were futile. Frail human flesh was defenseless against raw animal fury. All her life, Fiona had been a practical woman. She had known that the minute the shaman turned the cat's attack from her to himself, he was a dead man. She knew, and yet she continued to struggle with the mountain lion's carcass. Until she found no pulse—until she laid her cheek against Wolf Shadow's lips and found no breath of life—she couldn't rest.

A torch flared behind her, illuminating Wolf Shadow's bloodstained face. He lay still . . . so still . . . as still as death. Sobbing, she crawled to him and cradled his head in her lap. "Shhh, shhh," she whispered, not knowing or caring what nonsense fell from her lips. "It will be all right." She wiped away the blood on his face with the hem of her skirt.

Wolf Shadow's face, for all the crimson gore, was unmarked by the cougar's teeth or claws. Fiona touched his lips with her fingertips and grimaced when she found them motionless. "Mother Mary help him," she whispered as she continued her examination, feeling for the pulse in his throat. Fiona gave a strangled sound of joy. Wolf Shadow had a pulse; it was thready and slow, but blood still coursed in his veins.

"Enough woman." A strange brave's face scowled into hers. He gripped her shoulders and yanked her to her feet. "What use has a white woman for a Shawnee moon dancer?" he demanded. His gruff voice was heavily accented and full of authority.

"He's mine," she replied instinctively. She glanced from the stern warrior to the man lying sprawled beneath the cougar. "I'm a doctor. You must let me help him." The brave shoved her back away from Wolf Shadow, and she noticed that blood trickled from his right forearm.

"You lie, Englishwoman," the Indian retorted. He raised his muscular arm and sucked at the wound, then spat the blood on the ground. "The shaman, Wolf Shadow, has no woman. If he had a woman, she would not be white." He smiled coldly into her face. "I, Matiassu, great war chief of the Shawnee, claim you as a spoil of war."

"No!" Fiona glared back at him. "I'm not lying. I belong to Wolf Shadow. He captured me from the English." And then—inexplicably—she said the only thing that came into her head. "We are husband and wife."

"Liar." The man struck her shoulder with the flat of his hand and knocked her backward.

Her head hit the trunk of a tree, but she never felt the pain. "I am," she shouted, repeating the lie with brazen audacity. "I am the wife of the shaman, Wolf Shadow."

Fiona's words penetrated Wolf Shadow's agony and echoed in his head. *I am the wife of the shaman,*

Wolf Shadow. He groaned and opened his eyes. "Do you think the two of you could stop arguing long enough to get this cougar off me?" he said in Algonquian.

Several Shawnee braves grabbed the cat's legs and dragged it aside. Wolf Shadow drew in ragged lungfuls of air and tried to ignore the pain in his ribs, arm, and thigh.

Fiona ran to him and knelt beside him. "By Mary's robe," she murmured, "you've lost enough blood to drown an ordinary man." Her gentle hands ran over the gaping wound in his thigh. "I'll have to sew this at once," she said matter-of-factly.

Wolf Shadow looked up at her and wondered if he'd only dreamed the words he'd heard her say.

Matiassu moved to stand over him. "So, shaman," he said in their native tongue, "you have less command over the animals than men believe you do."

"Over cougars at least," Wolf Shadow replied hoarsely. Fiona was checking his ribs, and he felt the crunch of broken bones grating against each other. He gritted his teeth against the pain and fought an increasing nausea. "Who shot the cat?"

"I did," Matiassu said. "You owe me a life."

"So." Wolf Shadow nodded slightly. "I owe you a life." He noted that Matiassu had taken to wearing his hair in the Seneca style, shaved except for a scalp lock, rather than long as he had in the past. He also observed that the musket Matiassu held loosely in the crook of his arm was a new one of French design.

"I'll not let you forget," the war chief answered.

"I didn't think you would."

"This English squaw claims to be your wife," Matiassu continued in rapid Algonquian. "Is she?"

Wolf Shadow let his eyelids drift shut. It was true.

He had heard Fiona say the words. His eyes snapped open, and he fixed his gaze on the flame-haired woman. "This is my wife," he said softly in English. "I am her husband."

Fiona shivered in the torchlight. Wolf Shadow saw the apprehension in her eyes.

"I ask you again, shaman." Matiassu's English was accented with French. "Is she your woman?"

"Fiona is my wife," Wolf Shadow repeated firmly.

The war chief switched back to his own language. "She claimed to be yours, but I didn't believe it. I'd not heard that you'd taken a white woman to your sleeping mat." He arched a thick eyebrow. "You have spoken overmuch of rejecting all things English. Can it be that the 'chosen one' speaks of one trail and follows another? I think you give us much to discuss around the campfire."

Fiona glanced up at Matiassu. "I need to fetch my box. His wounds must be sewn before he can be moved. He's lost a terrible amount of blood."

Matiassu motioned to one of the watching braves. In less than a minute, the case was produced. "Here." He tossed Fiona's scalpel to the ground beside her. "You should be more careful with your toys, Englishwoman."

Hastily she grabbed it and tucked it into its proper place in the kit. "I need the light," she said. A warrior held the torch closer, and she took a needle and silk thread from the box.

Wolf Shadow struggled to sit up. Fresh blood spilled from scratches on his arms and chest, and the pain from his ribs was almost unbearable. "No," he said, waving her back. "You're not going to sew me up yet." Panting, he leaned on one elbow and held out a hand to Matiassu. "I need your knife," he said, switching from English to Algonquian, "or I need you to find mine. I used it on the cat."

Matiassu spoke to one of his companions, and the man handed over the knife. "Here," he said, wiping the blade on his fringed legging. He regarded the bone handle with its silver inlay for a moment, then offered it to the shaman. "A good knife. It would be a shame to lose it."

Fiona looked from one man to the other. "I have to do this right now—"

"No," Wolf Shadow said. "Not yet." He passed the knife to her. "Hold the blade in the flame until it is red-hot."

"Why? What are you—"

"Do as I say, woman."

Matiassu snickered. "Perhaps this *is* your wife," he said in taunting Algonquian.

Wolf Shadow thrust the hilt into the war chief's hand. "Heat it," he said.

Matiassu smiled. "And for this service, may I claim another life?"

"One, I think, is sufficient."

"Speak English," Fiona said. "I can't understand either one of you." She threaded the silk through the eye of the steel needle.

"I must burn the wound on my leg," Wolf Shadow explained to Fiona. "When I've done that, you may treat my injuries as you please."

"Burn it? But there's no need," she protested. "I can—"

He seized her wrist with a grip too strong for a dying man. "You will do as I say," he instructed. "Exactly as I say. If you don't, I'll have you tied to a tree." Several of the watching braves laughed, and Wolf Shadow turned a scowling countenance on them. "Where is Beaver Tooth? Where is Fat Boy?" he demanded. "They were with her."

"I've not seen either of them," Matiassu said mildly in his own tongue. "Have you, Ohshosh? Wahpetee? Any of you?"

"Not I."

"Nor me."

"I've not seen either of them since the Corn Dance last fall," Wahpetee answered smoothly.

"Perhaps they wandered into the forest and became lost," a young brave named Horse's Tail offered sarcastically.

"They are both good men," Wolf Shadow said quietly. "They are both my blood brothers. It would be a pity if harm came to them, for if it did, I would have to find those responsible and seek revenge."

"Brave talk for a man who cannot even stand," Matiassu pronounced. He held out Wolf Shadow's knife—the blade glowed a dull red.

"No," Fiona said. "Don't . . ."

Wolf Shadow held the knife in his hand and took a deep breath. Then, before Fiona could stop him, he laid the hot steel against the gaping wound on his thigh. Smoke and the smell of burning flesh filled the air.

Wolf Shadow fell back on the frozen ground, the knife still clutched in his hand. Sweat poured over him as he fought waves of blackness.

"Not enough," Matiassu said. "The wound is long. You will have to burn it again if you want to escape death from claw poison."

Fiona leaned over him. She was weeping, and her tears fell onto his face. "Give me the knife," she whispered.

"The . . . the wound," Wolf Shadow managed between clenched teeth. "It must . . . be . . ."

"Give me the knife," she repeated. "If it must be done, I'll do it."

He released the knife and concentrated on the flame, knowing that the flame must purify the wound. He let his mind conjure up a single star against a night-black sky. And when the searing pain came again, he embraced it and soared upward with the agony . . . becoming one with the fiery star and letting it cleanse his soul.

Chapter 10

Fiona straightened her shoulders and shielded her face from the whirlwind of twigs and dried leaves borne on the raw March wind. Ducking her head, she covered her hair with her shawl and hurried through the crude camp to the spring a few hundred feet away.

A Seneca sentry, one of Matiassu's allies, stared insolently at her as she passed, but Fiona ignored him. If she'd learned anything in the ten days since Wolf Shadow was attacked by the cougar and they'd both been held prisoner in Matiassu's camp, it was that captured women held a different position among Indians than among Europeans. She still feared for her life, but she was almost certain she wouldn't be subjected to torture or rape. That assurance gave her the courage to walk within arm's length of the scarred Iroquois, who wore a necklace of dried human fingers dangling around his neck, without quaking in her boots.

"Traditionally, our people do not commit rape as the English do," Wolf Shadow had explained to her, in an attempt to soothe her fear. "A man who shares the pleasures of the sleeping mat with a woman gives her power over him—both physically and spiritually. Thus, an angry woman could curse a man;

she could cause him to lose his sexual prowess. She could even ruin his luck in battle or hunting. No Shawnee would trade everything he holds dear for the sake of a brief physical encounter."

"But I've heard stories—" she'd argued, unwilling to believe his assurances so easily.

"Our women tell their children tales of English soldiers who steal babies and roast them over fires for dinner. Our women believe these tales as your women believe the stories of sexual atrocities. I can speak only for the traditional Shawnee and the Delaware. Evil and foolish men will doubtless take on the habits of the Europeans in time, and then Indian women will be as much at risk from Indian men as the white women are from their men. But for now I can promise you—even among Matiassu's renegades, your scalp is much more in danger than your maidenhood."

"I'm certain that should make me sleep better at night," she'd answered wryly. And in some strange way, it had.

Wolf Shadow's wounds were healing faster than she would have believed possible. The life-threatening gash on his thigh, seared shut by the hot steel, hadn't even become septic. The other teeth and claw marks had caused fever and a great deal of pain, but careful nursing had prevented the infections from turning gangrenous. There was nothing she could do for his cracked ribs but bind him tightly and wait for the bones to knit.

"It's no more than you deserve," he'd chided her. "You must tend me, since it was your fault that you ran away and I had to come after you and be nearly eaten by a lion."

She'd been shocked that he wasn't angry with her for trying to escape.

"If I thought I was being held prisoner, I would

do the same," Wolf Shadow had explained. "I blame Willow more than I blame you. She betrayed me."

"And I didn't?" she'd asked hesitantly.

"A little, but you made up for it when you told Matiassu that I was your husband."

No matter how many times she had asked, Wolf Shadow had refused to tell her how he had tracked her down the river and found her. "I am a powerful shaman," he'd teased. "I can't tell a white woman all my secrets."

When she reached the ice-crusted spring, Fiona crouched and washed her face and hands in the cold running water before cupping her fingers together and drinking. The spring was sweet, the clear water almost intoxicating. At the base of the crumbling rocks, directly beneath the continuous flow of bubbling water, green shoots had sprouted. Every time she came to fetch water, it seemed the plants had doubled in size. The bright green drew her gaze and filled her heart with hope of winter's end.

Finally, Fiona filled the water skin directly from the flow. Wolf Shadow insisted that she use only the purest water to heat for bathing his wounds. When Fiona slung the rawhide strap over her shoulder and straightened under the weight of the heavy container, it banged awkwardly against her hip and spilled water over her tattered skirt.

She paid the spreading dampness no more attention than she paid the sullen Seneca brave. Instead, she concentrated on her language lesson for the day. To help pass the time, Wolf Shadow had begun to teach her Algonquian. "*Jai-nai-hah*—brother; *don-nii-na*—sister; *elene*—man; *equiwa* . . . or *squaw-o-wah*—woman; *keep* . . . no, *keeqa*—wife." A triumphant smile spread over Fiona's face. "Brother, sister, man, woman, wife." She knew them all perfectly. Just let Wolf Shadow try and tease her today. She hoped she'd never have to learn another word of

Algonquian as she'd learned *meshepeshe*—panther.
The big cat had been close enough to give her nightmares for the rest of her life.

Serves you right, you devil's spawn, she thought.
A beast so vicious deserved to end up as a rug on
Matiassu's floor.

The war chief had claimed the cat's skin. He'd
stripped the bloody carcass and carried it back here
to stretch on a frame for tanning. She hadn't cared
what happened to the thing—her only concern had
been Wolf Shadow's life.

With her head high, Fiona began her walk back to
the hut where Wolf Shadow lay. Matiassu's camp
was totally different from the Shawnee village where
Wolf Shadow had taken her earlier. Here there were
only a few women and no children at all. The wigwams were smaller and covered with skins rather
than bark. This was a war leader's band, not a group
related by family. Matiassu's followers were gathered from different villages, even different tribes, including the Seneca. Fiona estimated the number of
warriors in the camp to be about three score—a for-
midable fighting group according to Wolf Shadow.

Despite her lack of understanding of their customs
and language, Fiona had learned a great deal about
her captor in the past week. Matiassu was a Shawnee, as were most of his men. But the big war chief
didn't share Wolf Shadow's dream of uniting the
Shawnee and other Algonquian tribes against the
Europeans. He had his own ideas and his own political ambitions.

Matiassu wanted the Shawnee and Delaware to
become part of the Iroquois League of Nations. He
actively sought the favor of powerful Seneca and
Mohawk chieftains, and he made no apologies for
his ties with the Frenchman Roquette.

As Fiona neared the hide-covered shelter she
shared with Wolf Shadow, she heard the war chief's

raspy voice raised in anger. He was speaking Algonquian, but there was no doubt in her mind that he
and Wolf Shadow had disagreed violently again.

She ducked inside the shadowy hut and busied
herself with heating water over the fire pit. Wolf
Shadow lay against the far wall, propped up on a
wooden back rest; Matiassu paced back and forth,
gesturing wildly. He paused long enough to throw
Fiona a withering glance, then continued his tirade.

"The Iroquois have proved they can stand against
the English," Matiassu said hotly. "The Iroquois are
powerful. They've said time and time again that
they'd welcome us, and together we'd form an Indian alliance no European might could challenge."

Wolf Shadow shook his head. "The Iroquois and
the Shawnee are bitter enemies. If we join with
them, they will swallow us whole. Our children will
learn Iroquois ways, and our women will dance to
the beat of Iroquois drums."

"Better Iroquois than English."

"And are the French any more to be trusted than
the English?" Wolf Shadow demanded. "Would you
have us smoke the pipe of friendship with Roquette,
the Scalp Buyer?"

"Roquette is what he is. When he is no longer
useful to us, we'll destroy him." Matiassu made a
quick chopping motion with his right hand. "Until
then, I'll take his fine French muskets and his steel
hatchets."

Wolf Shadow glanced at Fiona, then back at the
war chief. "The French want our land as much as
the English," he stated in Algonquian. "One is as
dangerous as the other."

"Roquette says they are only interested in fur
trade—beaver pelts bring a high price across the
sea."

"And you'd believe Roquette's word—the word

of a man who steals our women and sells them to the French as whores?"

Matiassu's hawk face darkened with anger. "I believe nothing, only what I see with my own eyes. I see the English cutting the earth with iron plows; I see them bringing their white-skinned wives and children to live on Shawnee land. I don't see the French doing these things. Only French men come, trappers and Jesus talkers. If they want to trade trinkets and weapons for beaverskins, so be it. There are more beaver in our streams than fine French muskets."

"You don't care that Roquette and the other traders give our men firewater and cheat them in trade when they're too drunk to stand, let alone bargain."

"Pah!" Matiassu spat on the floor. "You're a moon dancer—a holy man. What do you know of men's desires? The taste of whiskey is as intriguing as the taste of a woman's honey. You should try it sometime."

"I've tasted both."

Matiassu laughed. "So, the great shaman boasts that he's only human after all." He threw Fiona such a piercing look that she flushed and averted her face. "Human enough to lie, eh? I don't believe she's your wife. I think you're both lying to keep me from selling her to Roquette."

Wolf Shadow's heavy-lidded eyes reflected flickers of flame from the fire pit. He shifted and raised himself on one elbow. "When have you known me to lie, Matiassu?" he asked softly. "Fiona is a free woman. You heard her declare before witnesses that she was my wife, and you heard me say it was so. You know the law as well as I do."

"I know the law." Matiassu swallowed and beads of perspiration appeared on his broad forehead. "If a man and woman declare before witnesses that they are man and wife, the union is as binding as a formal one." His big hands knotted into clenched fists. "You tricked me," he insisted. "She wasn't your wife . . ."

Wolf Shadow smiled thinly. "Perhaps, and perhaps not. You'll never know, will you?"

"And if I take her anyway? If I kill you where you lay and sell her to the Frenchman?"

"I'll come back from the dead and haunt you. I'll rob your soul and leave you to wander the earth without form or rest for all eternity."

Wolf Shadow's face seemed to acquire a translucent glow, and Fiona gazed at him in sudden apprehension. Had he taken a turn for the worse? She started to go to him, but he stilled her with a slight wave of his hand.

"I have the power to do those things," Wolf Shadow continued in his own tongue. "You know I can . . . and you know that I would. Touch Fiona at your immortal peril."

Abruptly Fiona's stomach felt queasy, and she was aware of how warm it was in the small wigwam. She knew they were talking about her—she'd heard Wolf Shadow speak her name. For the first time in hours, she remembered the lie she'd told about being his wife.

Matiassu drew back as if he'd been struck by an invisible fist. His coal-black eyes dilated in fear; his features took on a pasty hue. Muttering under his breath, he whirled around and rushed out of the shelter.

"He is a dangerous man," Wolf Shadow said in English, when the war chief was far enough away so that he could no longer hear. "He's still threatening to sell you to Roquette."

"Will he?" Fiona's heart skipped a beat.

"I won't let him, Irish."

She rose and brought him a cup of water. "How

can you stop him? You've barely strength enough
to walk."

"He's afraid of me."

Fiona glanced back nervously toward the entranceway. "I don't think he's afraid of anyone."

Wolf Shadow chuckled softly. "I threatened to
steal his soul if he touched you."

Fiona shuddered and made the sign against the
evil eye. "Don't say such wicked things. You'll have
me thinking you're a warlock after all."

"You've known all along that I'm a shaman."

She shrugged. "Aye, a shaman, you say. There's
others would say you dabble in black magic."

"Magic is magic, *keeqa*. There is no black or white,
only intent to do good or evil."

She nibbled at her lower lip. "I don't like such
talk, I tell you. If you keep it up, I'll—" Her green
eyes hardened to jade as she realized what he'd
called her. "I'm not your wife."

Wolf Shadow's amused gaze raked over her, searing through her clothes, burning her skin with cold
fire. "But you are, Fiona. And you'll not see the day
when I can't protect my wife from a man like—"

"I'm not," she protested. "I only said that to—"

He seized her shoulders and pulled her to him,
covering her soft mouth with his hard one. Startled,
she struggled to free herself from his embrace.

He held her as easily as if his arms were made of
steel. All the while, his firm lips pressed against
hers, demanding, challenging.

Fiona's cries of protest grew weaker as her own
senses betrayed her. The clean, sweet taste of his
mouth, the earthy, man-scent of him, sent her mind
reeling. Her knees went weak, and her muscles
turned to liquid. A curious, hot fluttering began in
the pit of her stomach and spiraled upward, con-
stricting her chest so much that it was hard to
breathe.

The hot, wet tip of Wolf Shadow's tongue teased her lower lip, while the hand that no longer held her shoulder captive crept around to rub small, delicious circles on her back.

Desire flooded through her, and she kissed him with a fierce yearning that drove everything from her mind but the sweet, wild sensations of his fiery caress. His hands were moving over her body, touching her in intimate ways no man had ever done before. Small sounds of pleasure escaped her throat, and she heard his breathing quicken to match her own.

"Sweet *equiwa*," he murmured. He reached out and pulled the rawhide thong from her hair, running his fingers through the heavy mass of her red-gold tresses and letting them fall free around her shoulders. "You are my wife," he insisted. "And I will never let you go."

She opened her mouth to argue, and he kissed her again. The feeling was so wonderful that she couldn't think straight. She wanted to tell him that this was no place for such behavior. They weren't alone—Matiassu could return at any moment. She wanted to argue that it was broad daylight, and no decent woman would engage in such lustful behavior. Instead, she welcomed his deepening kisses and thrilled to his whispered love words in her ear.

Tremors of passion rocked her as Wolf Shadow pulled her full length against him and cupped the fullness of her breast through her thin woolen bodice. She took his face between her hands and let her fingers run over the smooth bronzed skin . . . let them trace the outline of his craggy brows and tangle in his long, night-black hair.

His tongue filled her mouth, and her heart beat faster. She clung to him, forgetting where she was, forgetting all danger. Forgetting everything but the magic of this moment.

Fiona slipped her hand under his deerskin vest and ran her tremulous fingers over his hard-muscled chest. She touched the edge of a bandage and parted his vest to kiss his salt-tinged skin. "You taste like the sea," she whispered, then doubts rose to trouble her. Was she behaving like a common jade? She raised her head to look into his deep-set, liquid eyes. "Is it wrong to kiss you like this?" she asked. "I've never done anything like—"

"*Ki-te-hi* . . . my heart . . . my sweeting. Kiss me anywhere you like." His deep voice was husky with tenderness. "I want you to touch me and kiss me . . . as I kiss you." He slid his hand down her hip and lower until he could reach beneath her skirts. "I love you," he murmured. "I've never known anyone like you, my Irish Fiona, and I never will."

"We shouldn't be doing . . ." She sighed with pleasure as Wolf Shadow ran his warm hand possessively up her leg, sending shivers of delight to the tips of her toes. Unable to remain motionless, she squirmed against him. Her breasts felt tight and swollen; her nipples throbbed with a restless aching.

"Yes, we should," he said. He lowered his head and nuzzled against her breasts. "I want to taste you," he murmured. "I want to taste your sweet, rosy buds." He pressed his lips to her throat, and her stomach knotted as she imagined his lips, his tongue on her hard, aching nipples.

"Please," she whispered, not certain if she was begging him to stop or continue. The pressure of his stroking fingers under her shift was making her giddy; she felt an unfamiliar wetness between her loins. "Please . . ."

Somehow her bodice had come untied. Between kisses he slid it over her head. His tongue darted out, flicking, teasing the rise of her breasts at the neckline of her linen shift. She leaned closer, and one strap slipped off her shoulder.

"Fiona," he said hoarsely, "my Fiona." Gently, he trailed feather-light kisses across the taut skin of her breasts, and she moaned softly. His hot, wet tongue brushed her swollen nipple, sending threads of molten fire spilling through her veins.

"Ohhh!" she cried.

His breath was warm on her naked flesh as he circled her rosy areola with his moist tongue and drew her nipple into his mouth. Fiona dug her nails into his shoulders as eddies of desire rocked her; shamelessly, she pushed aside her shift to offer her other breast.

The throbbing spread like wildfire down through her chest to the pit of her stomach. Wolf Shadow moaned and pressed full length against her as his seeking fingers delved into her secret place. "You will like being a wife," he murmured. "You are a woman born for joy."

She arched back to give him access to her breasts again, and the rising flames within her fanned hotter and hotter until suddenly, without warning, it seemed the earth rocked, and she was tumbling through a bottomless void of exploding stars. She cried out, and then fell back limply in his arms.

Fiona's breath came in gasps as though she'd been running. "What . . ." she stammered. "I . . . What . . ."

He chuckled softly and brushed his lips against hers in a tender kiss. "A taste of that joy, my *ki-te-hi.*"

She hid her face in his shoulder as a rosy tint infused her features. "I'm sorry . . ." she began in bewilderment. "I . . . I didn't . . ."

"You have much to learn of love, Irish," he teased, planting warm kisses in her unbound hair. "I shall teach you, but some lessons . . ." He chuckled again. "Some are best left until I regain all my strength."

Mortified, Fiona clamped her eyes shut and tried to regain her composure. What had she done? How could she have let him touch her in places she scarcely touched herself? Had Wolf Shadow bewitched her to make her behave so wantonly?

Her fingers went to the golden amulet around her neck. Could it be the curse of her necklace that had brought her to this? Could the magic . . . No, it was impossible.

Shaking off her foolish superstitious notions, she pulled away from him and opened her eyes. He was staring at her with such devotion that she flushed to the roots of her hair. No, she decided firmly, what had happened between them was not sorcery. It was the most natural of human urges—the most powerful after the need for survival. She wanted Wolf Shadow to hold her and touch her in the ways no unmarried woman had any right to be touched.

But he said that she was his wife . . .

Fiona took a deep breath and rose to her feet. She wasn't his wife—she could never be. He was a heathen, and she was a Christian, a Catholic. The only marriage that could ever be binding between them would be a union blessed by a priest of the Church.

She turned her back to him. What was she thinking of? How had the thought of marriage between them ever arisen? True, she had said the words to Matiassu, but she'd not meant them. It was only a ploy to save herself from a fate worse than . . .

Fiona's eyes clouded with tears, and she blinked them away. She folded her arms over her chest and turned back to him. He was smiling at her with a tender expression that would have touched the heart of a stone gargoyle.

"You have nothing to be ashamed of, Fiona.

You're innocent of such things between a man and a woman, I know, but—''

"I cannot be your wife."

His eyes narrowed. "Is it the color of my skin that troubles you?"

Fiona shook her head. "No, Wolf Shadow, I think the color of your skin is beautiful . . . 'Tis not that."

"Then what? Say what you will, we are husband and wife, according to the laws of my people. You declared twice before witnesses that you were my wife. That makes us married."

"And according to the laws of my people, we're not."

He sat up and began to rise, but she waved him back. "No, don't. If you stand, you may tear loose my stitches."

"It's time." He stood and steadied himself with one hand on a sapling used for framework in the shelter. "I don't care what gods you worship, Irish. If you and I suit each other, what does it matter? You may teach our children anything you please, and I shall teach them Shawnee ways."

"I am a Catholic. Do you understand what that means?"

He nodded. "I think so."

"Would you be willing to forsake your . . . your Indian gods to become a Christian? Would you accept my Catholic faith as your own?"

His features hardened. "My gods, as you call them, are doubtless the same as yours. There is one Creator of all, Fiona. We may use different names, and we may speak to Him in different languages, but there can be only one."

"I cannot marry you if you won't become a Catholic."

"You already have."

"I haven't. I'm not your wife and . . ." The words seemed to stick in her throat. Why was it so hard to make him understand? "Your people . . . the Shawnee are totally different from anything I've ever known. This isn't my world. I don't belong here."

He took hold of her shoulders. "Look into your heart, woman," he urged. "There is no way we could meet; yet we did. I should hate you for the color of your skin—I should find you ugly. Instead . . ." He leaned forward and brushed her forehead with his lips. "Instead, I find you the most desirable woman I've ever known." He pulled her against him and wrapped his arms tightly around her. "We were destined to be together, you and I." He stroked her hair gently. "Do as you will, Fiona. Fight, scream, kick . . . If it is written in the stars, then we will be together." He released her and stepped back, wincing slightly against the pain of his wounds. "It was you who said you were my wife."

"You know why I did that," she protested. "It was only to keep Matiassu from doing something horrible to me."

"So." He looked pensive. "You would be my wife if I became a Catholic?"

"I . . . I don't know. Maybe." She covered her face with her hands. "So much has happened to me so quickly. I'm confused and . . ." She dropped her hands. "I think I would marry you. There's no logic to it. It would be madness but . . . I think I would."

"And if I refuse to take your religion as my own?"

"There could be no marriage. Any children we had would be bastards, born in shame." A lump rose in her throat. "As I was," she murmured softly. "I could never bring a babe of mine into the world to be the same."

"Ask anything else, Fiona. This thing I cannot do. I am a shaman of the people. I cannot turn my back on the way of my mother, and her mother, and her mother before her. I cannot turn my back on Wishemenetoo."

"Then we have our answer, don't we? Take me to this Ross Campbell and ask him to help me. It's best for us both if I return to my own kind."

"I will not hold you against your will, Fiona, but if you do this thing, if you leave me, you will regret it for the rest of your life."

"Maybe I will," she admitted, "but it's what I have to do." Turning away from him, she ducked through the entranceway.

Outside, she stopped and looked around. The camp was strangely deserted. Several of the shelters were stripped of their hide coverings. Only skeletons of peeled saplings remained. There was not a voice sound to be heard, only the *rat-ta-tat-tat* of a woodpecker in a tree across the clearing. "Wolf Shadow," she called. "Wolf Shadow, come out here."

"Where is everyone?" she asked him when he joined her. "Where have they gone?"

He glanced around and smiled thinly. "It seems that Matiassu no longer cares for our company," he said. "He's taken his followers and gone."

"Without a sound?"

"Yes, my innocent, without a sound. The Shawnee do not crash through the forest like Englishmen driving ale wagons. My camp is larger than this one, and we can move as quickly and as silently as if we need to."

Unconsciously, she moved nearer to him. "What do we do now?"

"Now I will try to find Beaver Tooth and Fat Boy, and I will take you with me to Tuk-o-see-yah's camp. If it isn't too late, I'll try to complete the mission I was on before you ran away."

"Maybe Beaver Tooth and Fat Boy just left me and went back to camp."

Wolf Shadow shook his head. "No, I don't think so. Willow told me that they'd promised to deliver you safely to a white settlement. I'm afraid Matiassu did something to them.''

''Killed them?''

''So. And if he has . . .'' His forehead creased in a frown. ''If Matiassu has killed Shawnee, then he has crossed a boundary that cannot be recrossed. Shawnee does not kill Shawnee. It is the greatest of all evils.''

''And if he did kill them?''

''Then it is my duty to see that Matiassu pays the price. And the price will be very high . . . very high indeed.''

Chapter 11

Two weeks later, Fiona followed Wolf Shadow and his sister, Willow, into Tuk-o-see-yah's large camp. Dozens of bark-covered wigwams, nearly identical to those in Wolf Shadow's village, were clustered at the edge of a river surrounded by virgin forest. There seemed to be about twice as many houses here, but it was difficult for Fiona to judge because some were built in the shadows of the trees. In the center of the village was a large clearing of hard-packed earth.

Wolf Shadow, Fiona, and Willow were accompanied by Yellow Elk, Two Crows, and a dozen other warriors as well as several women, all dressed in their finest clothing. Wolf Shadow had explained to Fiona that Yellow Elk was the acting chief of the Alwameke Shawnee.

"He was elected by the council of elders after the death of our last chief, Yellow Elk's older brother. He must serve for two years before he is a full chief, but even then, a majority village council vote can remove him from office."

Yellow Elk walked ahead of the Alwameke in haughty splendor. The graying chief wore beaded, white buckskin leggings and a copper breastplate that Fiona could have sworn was part of an antique

Spanish suit of armor. Yellow Elk's hair was plaited
into two long braids and intertwined with dozens of
elk teeth. He carried no weapons other than the
knife at his waist, but his son Snowshoe and another warrior kept pace beside him. Each of them
was heavily armed with a musket, tomahawk, and
flintlock pistol.

The shaman's attire was even more awe-inspiring.
If Fiona had created a savage witch doctor from her
wildest imagination, nothing could have equaled
Wolf Shadow's barbaric regalia.

Head high and dark eyes smoldering beneath the
fierce wolf's head cape, Wolf Shadow strode along
with the fluid grace of a Persian prince. Mica chips
that had been stitched into the beast's eye sockets
glittered in the bright sunlight. The shaman was
taller than most of his companions, and his broad,
muscular chest was bare except for a silver gorget
and a string of puma claws.

High quill-worked moccasins covered his muscular calves, reaching up over hard, sinewy thighs to
brush the fringes of his white leather loincloth. His
hair was loose and long, hanging over his shoulders
and down his chest in glossy ripples. Earrings of
panther teeth and eagle plumage dangled from his
ears.

Fiona could not help the thrill in her breast as she
watched him make his entrance into the Shawnee
village. By Mary's robe, he was a heathen savage.
But devil take her soul if Fiona had ever seen a man
to match him.

Tuk-o-see-yah's people flocked out to welcome
them. Men waved and shouted; women called ex-
citedly, and dogs and children ran in circles around
the visitors. Dogs barked, babies cried and squealed,
and four older women began to dance and chant to
the accompaniment of a drum.

Fiona pushed back her shawl to get a better view

of the encampment. She wore a borrowed deerskin dress of Willow's with her own shawl over her head to cover her hair. "Not to hide the fact that you are white," Willow had advised, "but to prevent too many questions when we first arrive at Tuk-o-see-yah's camp. Many Shawnee have light skin, but none have hair like a forest fire."

Their stately procession faltered as a gray-haired matron hugged Yellow Elk, and some of the warriors dropped out of place to greet friends and relatives. Willow waved to a round-faced, heavyset woman. "Amookas!" she called. "Amookas." Willow tugged at Fiona's sleeve. "That my cousin," she explained. "Butterfly Woman—Amookas." The woman grinned and shouted something, and Willow glanced at Fiona. "Will you be all right?" she asked. "I—"

"No, no, I'll be fine. Go see your cousin," Fiona said quickly. Willow had gone out of her way to be kind since Wolf Shadow had brought her back to the village, and she'd even suffered verbal abuse from her brother for her part in Fiona's escape attempt. Fiona didn't want to do anything to cause Willow further problems. "Go ahead," she urged. Willow hurried to embrace the smiling Amookas.

Fiona understood enough Algonquian now to make out some of what was being said. Two small boys peered curiously from the doorway of a round bark-covered wigwam. "Look," the bigger one cried. "It is the shaman."

"It's Wolf Shadow," a handsome boy in his early teens declared.

An old man leaned on a staff and called the traditional greeting in a loud voice. *"Ili kleheleche?"* Do you draw breath yet?

Fiona smiled, proud of her ability to understand, and certain what Wolf Shadow's reply would be.

"In truth, Grandfather, I do," the shaman returned. "And do you draw breath?" The old man's reply was beyond her comprehension, but it drew laughter from the women around him.

"*Ntschu!*" Two Crows lifted his musket in salute. Fiona smiled again as she caught the Algonquian word for *friend*.

More Indians joined the group around them, and it grew too noisy for Fiona to make out anything more. A second drummer joined the first, and other women and children began to dance with the four matrons. A dog yapped and, from somewhere beyond the wigwams, Fiona heard a horse whinny.

Suddenly she felt uneasy . . . a feeling her mother had always described as a goose walking over her grave. Snapping her head around, Fiona looked directly into the eyes of a white man wearing buckskins and a red knit cap.

"Mam'zelle," he said, touching his hat. His loose-lipped smile and knowing gaze made her feel dirty.

Fiona averted her eyes and quickened her step, narrowing the distance between her and Wolf Shadow. When she glanced back a minute later, Redcap was gone.

Wolf Shadow stopped and Fiona almost bumped into him. His attention was fixed on a slender, petite Indian woman emerging from a wigwam.

"Wolf Shadow. Welcome," she said in soft, bell-like Algonquian. Her heart-shaped face creased in a smile that made her large eyes shine like stars. A lovely child, a smaller version of the exquisite woman, appeared at her side.

The little girl noticed Fiona and smiled at her. To Fiona's surprise, the Indian child's eyes were a bright, clear blue.

"Nibeeshu Meekwon," Wolf Shadow said. "Greetings to the illustrious peace woman," he continued in English. "There's someone I want you to meet. Fiona." He turned back and took her arm.

"This is Fiona," he explained. "She is my wife. Fiona, this is the peace woman I told you about, Nibeeshu Meekwon—Moonfeather, in English."

The child's eyes grew wide, and she covered her mouth with her hand. Moonfeather's expression remained serene. She nodded slightly and gestured toward the wigwam.

"It's good to see you," Wolf Shadow said, leading Fiona toward the hut. "Is Ross Campbell here?"

"Nay. He was, but he had to return to Wanishisheyun." She glanced at Fiona and smiled. "Fort Campbell, the English call it. His wife, Anne, is with child and she isn't strong." Moonfeather stood aside for Wolf Shadow and Fiona to enter the wigwam, then she and the child joined them inside. "Cameron Stewart is here, though. He says he'll take word of our alliance, do we make one, to the Maryland and Virginia governors."

Fiona couldn't keep her eyes off the Shawnee peace woman. The beautiful Indian's English was as plain as her own, but Moonfeather spoke with a decidedly Scottish accent.

Moonfeather motioned Fiona to a place on the women's side of the fire. "Ye honor my house," she said sincerely. Then she spoke rapidly in Algonquian to Wolf Shadow. "An Englishwoman?" she demanded. "What are you thinking of?"

"Your husband's skin is white," the shaman answered mildly.

"Ptahh! I'm not the one who's been telling the tribes to cast out the Europeans. I'm only a peace woman—and a woman whose father came from across the sea." Moonfeather shook her head. "You're out of your mind, Shadow. You're moon sick. When the tribal leaders learn that you've taken a white wife, they'll laugh behind their hands. This is no time for you to grow woodenheaded over a woman—not if you want the vote to go your way."

Wolf Shadow shrugged. "I didn't plan Fiona—she just happened. Now that she's mine, I'll not give her up, and if the people won't accept her . . ."

"You're risking all you've worked for these many years," the peace woman warned. "Tuk-o-see-yah seems inclined to listen, despite his grandson Matiassu. He's here, you know. He arrived last night with his warriors."

"I didn't suppose he'd miss it. Roquette too?" Moonfeather nodded. "May the ground sink under his feet and his seed wither," Wolf Shadow swore. "As for Fiona, I love her and I believe she loves me. I was hoping someone would adopt her. It would be easier if she became a Shawnee."

Moonfeather sniffed. "And that someone wouldn't be me, would it?" she asked suspiciously. She shook her head. "It wouldn't be the first time you tried to drag me into one of your games." She rolled her eyes and mocked him softly. "Oh, illustrious shaman."

He refused to take offense. "We've been friends for a long time."

"Aye, we have," she answered, returning to her accented English. "I be your friend, and I shall be yours, too, Fiona, do ye wish me to be."

"I'd like that," Fiona replied. The conversation had been too difficult for her to follow, but she'd heard the word *wife*, and she suspected she had been at least part of the subject. "Wolf Shadow believes that he's my husband, but he's mistaken. We were hoping that this Ross . . . Ross Campbell could help me return to the English settlements."

"If ye truly want to return, I may be able to help you," Moonfeather said. "I was once far from my home and badly in need of a friend." She looked across the wigwam at the little girl. "This is my daughter, Cami Sh'Kotai. She speaks English well enough—for all she prefers the tongue of the People."

"Hello, Cami," Fiona said. "I'm glad to meet you."

The child regarded Fiona solemnly. "Are you really the shaman's wife?" she asked shyly.

"No," Fiona replied.

"Yes, she is," Wolf Shadow said at the same time. He crossed his arms over his chest. "You've grown into a fine young woman, Cami, since I've last seen you. I hope you do your mother proud."

"Thank you, shaman," Cami murmured.

"Does she study hard?" Wolf Shadow asked Moonfeather.

"She does."

"I try, shaman," the child added.

"Good, you'll make a fine peace woman yourself one day and you—" Wolf Shadow paused and stared at Cami's left ear. "What's that?" The child looked puzzled as he drew closer. "What's that in your ear?" he asked seriously. Reaching out, the shaman appeared to produce a string of shell beads from behind Cami's ear. "Whatever are you doing with these?" he demanded.

The little girl giggled with delight.

"Is this a new fashion, Moonfeather?" he asked her mother. He dangled the pink shells in front of Cami's nose with one hand while the other hand plucked a pair of matching earrings from under her chin.

Fiona joined the laughter. Wolf Shadow's sleight-of-hand was so skillful, she'd not seen the earrings until they appeared as if by magic between his fingers.

"Thank you, shaman," the child said, slipping the necklace over her head. "They have beautiful."

"Aye, they *are* beautiful," Moonfeather corrected gently. "And now, Cami, I think it's time you sought out your grandsire's company. Tell him that Wolf Shadow has arrived, and we'll all meet later at the council fire.'' The child nodded, thanked Wolf Shadow again, and left the wigwam.

''She's a daughter to be proud of,'' Wolf Shadow said.

''Aye, so lovely her father fears for her safety,'' Moonfeather replied thoughtfully. ''Sometimes I wonder what kind of world she'll inherit. Looking at her, it's hard for me to remember that most of the blood that flows through her is *Englishmanake.*''

Wolf Shadow smiled. ''You need have no fear on that account. Her soul is Shawnee. She's very like you.''

''And verra like her father.''

''I didn't know you did magic tricks,'' Fiona put in. ''You're good. You could easily make your fortune in London.''

''Aye,'' Moonfeather agreed, ''he could, couldn't he? There was one old faker that sold water of life in front of Saint Paul's—''

''You know Saint Paul's? You've been to London?'' Fiona asked. It was difficult for her to believe that here in the wilds of America were *two* natives who both spoke wonderful English and had traveled across the sea to London. She'd only been there once, when she was fourteen. Her grandfather had taken her with him when he went to London to purchase medical supplies.

Moonfeather laughed. ''Aye, I've been there. 'Tis a long story indeed, but one ye might enjoy if we're ever snowed in long enough to hear it.'' She sobered. ''I've been to England. I spent more time there than I care to remember. Cami's father is English.''

''Is he here?'' Fiona asked, then instantly regretted her rash tongue. She had no business interrogating this gracious woman about her personal life.

Doubtless, her child was born out of wedlock and the rascally father was far away. Fiona averted her eyes and felt the cursed heat rise in her face again. Ever since she was a child, blushing had been her bane. Her red hair and fair complexion assured that she couldn't tell a lie or even see one hound sniff another's backside without flushing crimson as a beet—revealing her most private thoughts for all the world to see. "I'm sorry," she murmured apologetically. "It was rude of me to ask."

Moonfeather laughed again—a merry sound like water bubbling over a rocky streambed. "Nay, do not apologize to me. Living with an English husband for ten years has taught me that the Shawnee and the Europeans have quite different ideas about what is proper and what is not. I be not so easily offended as once I was."

She poured cider from a small cask into a pewter tankard and handed it to Fiona. "Drink," she said. "Make yourself at home. This wigwam has been prepared for our mighty shaman and his . . . his family." She poured a second tankard for Wolf Shadow. "My English husband has a plantation near the Chesapeake in Maryland. We made a bargain many years ago, my flaxen-haired *Englishmanake* and this one . . . a bargain copied from Greek mythology. For half the year, I live with him, and for half the year, I remain with the Shawnee." She spread her small hands expressively. "My Brandon has suffered in the bargain, I fear, for when the times are difficult for the Shawnee, I am needed here."

Fiona glanced around the large hut, realizing for the first time how luxurious it was. Not only was there a copper kettle on an iron grate over the fire, but there were woolen blankets hanging on the walls and stacked on the sleeping platforms. There was even a wooden chair—the folding kind carried by the military for use by their officers. She regarded

Moonfeather with new respect, surprised at the status she must have with these people to be able to show her guests such hospitality.

"Willow and I are not on the best of terms at the moment," Wolf Shadow said. "She told me she would be staying with your aunt, Amookas, but Fiona and I will be very comfortable here. Thank you."

Fiona couldn't help grimacing. "If you think to have me cook for you," she said, "you'll be disappointed. I've no skill whatsoever in that direction."

Moonfeather smiled. "Nay, there's no need.'Tis considered an honor among the women to see who can prepare the best dishes for a visiting shaman. You'll have more than enough to eat, I promise ye."

"I should go and see Tuk-o-see-yah. If you'd keep Fiona company—"

"Go on," Moonfeather urged. "He has need of your services. He broke a back tooth eating his newest wife's walnut bread, and he's been in pain for two days. I offered to pull it for him, but he wouldn't let me touch it—you know how he is about his teeth." She glanced at Fiona. "Our esteemed chief has seen many winters, and he prizes each tooth in his head. I suspect he's afraid of the pain, but . . ." She chuckled. "Tuk-o-see-yah survived an Iroquois gauntlet without making a sound, and he cut a French bullet out of his own leg. How can a woman accuse such a brave man of being frightened of having a tooth pulled?"

"Would he let me see him?" Fiona asked. "I have a special instrument in my kit for tooth drawing."

"She is a medicine woman, this Irish of mine," Wolf Shadow explained. "She's skillful—for an English *equiwa*."

"I have a lot of experience at pulling teeth," she assured them, "and I could give him laudanum for the pain."

Wolf Shadow moved toward the entrance. "I'll ask him." He winked at Moonfeather. "I'd certainly let her pull my tooth, if I needed one out—wouldn't you, peace woman?"

"Go on with ye," the Indian woman said, waving toward the doorway. "Tuk-o-see-yah's feelings will be hurt if you don't pay your respects at once. I'm certain Roquette and Matiassu are there."

Wolf Shadow frowned. "Two of my friends—Beaver Tooth and Fat Boy—have vanished. Matiassu says they left his camp alive . . ."

Moonfeather laid a hand on his arm. "It wouldn't be the first time Matiassu has been accused of the death of a fellow Shawnee. My uncle still believes he killed my cousin."

"We sent out scouts to search for them. No trace . . . no trail and no bodies."

"You know the old Shawnee saying about luck," Moonfeather said.

"Even the luck of the wisest fox runs out in time," he supplied. "If I find out Matiassu was responsible for harming them, I'll—"

Moonfeather stopped him with a finger to her lips. "Nay, dinna speak promises I might have to try to prevent. My way be not violence, shaman. Some things it's best I dinna ken."

"Stay here, Fiona," Wolf Shadow said, glancing toward her. "I won't be long. When I come back, I'll show you—"

"Tell the chief I would be happy to look at his tooth," Fiona reminded him. "I can even give him laudanum first, if he wants."

"All right, I will." Wolf Shadow left the wigwam, and the deerskin hanging fell behind him.

Moonfeather turned to Fiona. "I have English tea, if ye'd like some."

"For sure?" Fiona's mouth watered at the thought. "I'd love it."

"No milk, I'm afraid, but I can offer you sugar."

Fiona sighed with contentment as she watched the petite Indian woman measure tea leaves into a pot. Fiona hadn't tasted tea since she'd left Philadelphia, and then only rarely. Tea was expensive, and not something served regularly to bondwomen.

"I've known Wolf Shadow since I was a wee bairn," Moonfeather began. "He's a good man, but he can be exasperating at times." When the tea had steeped, she took Fiona's pewter mug, rinsed it, and poured her tea. She continued talking, making Fiona feel at ease.

Despite her usual reticence, Fiona found herself telling Moonfeather how Wolf Shadow had saved her from the white trappers, and why he kept saying that they were married. "I said he was my husband to keep Matiassu from selling me to the French. It's no true marriage—it can never be, no matter what he says. We are of different worlds, Wolf Shadow and I."

"Ye ken his mission?" Moonfeather asked.

Fiona nodded. "He's told me that he wants to form an Indian nation to stand against the Europeans."

"Then ye see why the two of ye canna be together." The dark-haired woman sighed. "Wolf Shadow has always put the good of his people ahead of his own needs. Ye are wise to see that having a white wife would hurt his cause."

"I do care for him," Fiona admitted. *You love him,* her inner voice cried. *You love him more than you have ever loved another human being.* "But I want no husband, red or white. Loving a man brought my mother sorrow."

Moonfeather raised her head and stared directly into Fiona's eyes for a long minute. "We have much in common, perhaps more than ye ken."

Fiona's throat constricted. What was it about this

woman that made her feel as though they had known each other for a lifetime? "Will you help me?" she implored.

"I—" Moonfeather broke off as the door cover was pushed aside and the shaman's form appeared in the opening. "Wolf Shadow . . ."

"Fiona." He motioned to her. "Bring your box, and come with me. Tuk-o-see-yah says he'll try your white medicine. He let me take a look, and half the tooth's broken off at the gum line."

Fiona got to her feet and picked up her box, casting a final glance at Moonfeather. "Thank you for your kindness," she said sincerely.

"We'll talk again later."

"We'd be best not to keep Tuk-o-see-yah waiting," Wolf Shadow said. Fiona nodded and followed him outside and through the camp to the chief's wigwam.

Fiona couldn't suppress a smile when they left Tuk-o-see-yah's hut an hour later. The tooth pulling had gone off without a hitch, and the elderly chief was sound asleep, snoring loudly. With luck, he'd sleep the afternoon away, and when he woke, his pain would be gone. Wolf Shadow had insisted that she pack the chief's empty socket with powdered charcoal from white cedar, once the bleeding from the extraction had slowed, but otherwise the shaman had let her treat the patient by herself.

"You have good hands," he said, as they made their way back across the camp. "People trust you."

"Despite my skin color?"

His eyes narrowed. "You could heal Shawnee if you stayed with us. Does it matter to you if a hurt child is red or white?"

"Can you never leave it alone?" she snapped. God knows she wanted to stay with him . . . wanted to feel his arms around her every night and see his face when she opened her eyes in the morning. But experience had taught her that a woman who listened to her heart instead of her head was a fool.

There were too many odds against them. If she lived with him out of wedlock—without a Christian marriage—she'd never know peace, and she'd dread the coming of children that should be every woman's blessing. And if real war broke out between the English and the Shawnee, they would be on opposite sides.

He touched her hair. "Your words burn as brightly as your hair," he said, "but you fight a battle you cannot win. We were born to be together."

She stepped away from him. "You promised you would help me return to my own people. Was it a lie?"

His face paled beneath his coppery tan. "No man would call me a liar and live."

Hot anger made her lash back at him. "Is that a threat? Kill me, then! But, by God, if you don't, I'll get free of you!"

"Fiona O'Neal!"

Fiona whirled toward the sound of her name. A dozen rough-looking white men armed with muskets strode toward her. Among them was the red-capped man she'd seen staring at her earlier . . . and the fur trader, Jacob Clough! "Jacob." The word came out a whisper. She took another step backward as steel bands seemed to constrict her chest. Jacob, here? Fear washed through her, and she clutched her surgical kit tightly. Had he come to take her back to the fur trapper?

The tall, sleek man on Jacob's right, obviously the leader of the group, wore a tailored red and white French military jacket and buckskin leggings with dark grace. His yellow-blond hair hung loose to his shoulders, and his small, pale eyes scrutinized her insolently from beneath a high jutting forehead. A neatly cut yellow beard covered his chin, and part of a thin scar ran upward to crease his bottom lip.

A lion, Fiona thought crazily. He looks like a lion.

"Woman?" he rasped. "Are you Fiona O'Neal?" His gravelly voice bore a heavy French accent.

"That's her, right enough," Clough said. He spat on the ground at Fiona's feet. "Thought ye'd find yerself a red buck and run outa yer lawful indenture, didn't ye?" He reached out to grab her arm, but she jerked away from him.

"Touch my wife and you're a dead man," Wolf Shadow said quietly.

Fiona's heart pounded against her chest. Her mouth went dry, and the tension in the air was so sharp she could taste it. From the corner of her eye, she saw Matiassu move into the clearing. Most of the Indian braves crowding around were his men, she realized with sudden dread.

"Are you Fiona O'Neal?" the yellow-haired lion man repeated.

"Yes, I am, but—"

Wolf Shadow stepped protectively in front of Fiona. "My wife is none of your concern, Roquette." Fiona shivered at the deadly warning in his soft tone.

"Ah, the shaman, isn't it?" Roquette sneered.

Jacob Clough grinned, exposing rotting teeth. One of the other white men guffawed.

Roquette nodded, and Jacob Clough lowered his musket until the muzzle pointed at the center of Wolf Shadow's chest. "It's you who must stand aside, shaman," the Frenchman said. "She's my property. Bought and paid for."

Wolf Shadow met the Frenchman's gaze without blinking. "Fiona is a free woman."

"Afraid not, medicine man." Roquette reached into the inner pocket of his coat and produced a folded parchment. "I just bought her indenture from her rightful owner, Jacob Clough. I paid hard silver for her, and I intend to take possession here and now."

"No . . ." Fiona murmured to Wolf Shadow. "Don't risk your life for me. I'll go with him."

"Give her to Roquette," Matiassu called in English, pushing his way through the crowd. "You've no need to steal a white woman. If you want a wife to warm your blankets, I'll give you mine."

"Get out of the way, shaman," the Frenchman said, "or suffer the consequences." He glanced at Clough, and the trader eased back the hammer on his musket.

"You must take her over my body," Wolf Shadow replied.

"No!" Fiona cried. "I won't—"

"Have it your way," Roquette snarled. "Shoot him."

Fiona screamed as Jacob Clough pulled the trigger.

Chapter 12

W olf Shadow twisted and threw himself over
Fiona, knocking her to the ground, as the explosion deafened the onlookers. Instinctively, the
Shadow covered his head with his hands as fragments of wood and steel rained down around them.

"*Merde*," Roquette exclaimed.

Someone was screaming—crying out for his
mother in French. Another throat emitted strangled,
choking moans and then ceased to make any noise
at all. For long seconds there was only the sound of
one man's agony, then Shawnee and whites broke
into pandemonium.

Wolf Shadow rose and pulled Fiona up with him,
turning her face against his chest so that she couldn't
see. She was sobbing, and he soothed her with his
touch rather than with words.

A few yards away, Jacob Clough lay sprawled on
his side, his mangled face mercifully turned to the
blood-soaked earth. The remains of his shattered
musket, the barrel twisted and gaping, lay beside
him. A haze of blue-gray smoke hung over his
shocked companions, including the Frenchman in
the red cap who continued to howl and clutch his
throat.

"Sorcier," muttered the white trapper bending over him.

Roquette trembled with anger as he fingered the bloody gouge running down his right cheek. "You're a dead man, shaman," he said.

Wolf Shadow nodded imperceptibly. "But not today, and not by your hand."

Angry grumbling rose from Roquette's crew. The Shawnee crowded around, staring at the dead man and the ruined musket. "He tried to shoot the shaman, and Wolf Shadow witched him," an old woman cried.

"Wolf Shadow killed the white man without touching him," a gaunt brave agreed.

Yellow Elk and Two Crows, both heavily armed, pushed their way through the throng to Wolf Shadow's side. "Are you all right?" Two Crows asked.

"Take care of my wife," Shadow instructed his friends in their own tongue. "Fiona," he said, switching to English. "Go with Yellow Elk. You'll be safe with them, I promise."

Fiona's green eyes were dazed, her face smudged with dirt. "What happened?"

"Jacob Clough's musket blew up when he tried to fire. Go on with Yellow Elk." Shadow gently pushed her away, fighting the urge to wipe her dirty face. "Take her," he repeated.

"She's not going anywhere," Roquette protested as Yellow Elk led Fiona away. "She's still my property."

"What's wrong with all of you?" Matiassu demanded brusquely of the crowd. "The trader's gun exploded. It was an accident—something that could happen to anyone who was careless with the black powder. There's no sorcery here. Give the woman to Roquette, I say."

Instantly, there were answering cries of "No! No! The spirits have spoken."

"They tried to murder our shaman! Kill them all!" a hothead shouted in Algonquian.

"Kill Roquette! Kill the Hair Buyer!" a youth urged.

Wolf Shadow held up his hand. "There will be no killing. We have come to talk, not dip our spears in the blood of whites. Since when do the Shawnee murder their guests?"

A wrinkled old crone shook her bony fist. "Roquette deserves to die!"

As the villagers' mood turned ugly, the Frenchmen gathered in a knot, back to back, weapons ready. The red-capped man still crouched on his haunches, rocking, trying to stem the flow of blood from his wounds.

Pity for the injured man tugged at Wolf Shadow's conscience. His physician's mind was already gauging the extent of blood loss. "I say we will not harm these men so long as they do not fire on us," the shaman said. "Matiassu is right. Jacob Clough died because of his own foolishness." His fiery gaze raked the crowd, lingering on the faces of the agitators. "You know what I think of Roquette. But what we do here in council is more important than Roquette's death. He has come to talk in peace, and he can go in peace."

"So says your shaman." Moonfeather came to stand in front of Roquette. Her clear voice carried through the hushed crowd. "So also says your peace woman." She glanced at Roquette and pinched her nose in a gesture that told the Shawnee what she thought of the Frenchman. Then, she clasped her hands together and nodded to Wolf Shadow in respect. "You have all seen what happened here today. Matiassu says that Jacob Clough died of carelessness. I agree. Jacob Clough lived a fool and he died a fool. He tried to meet Wolf Shadow's magic with powder and shot."

Cheers rose from the onlookers. Even Matiassu's Seneca nodded agreement with the peace woman's words.

"Each man and each woman must decide what happened and why," Moonfeather continued. "It is the Shawnee way." She smiled faintly. "But there can be no doubt who Wishemenetoo favors."

Loud cries of "Whoo! Whoo!" and "Ay! Ay!" signaled the group's support for her words.

The peace woman waited until they were quiet before completing her speech. "The woman, Fiona, is a free woman," Moonfeather declared. "She is wife to our shaman—to our mighty moon dancer—Wolf Shadow! So say I, Nibeeshu Meekwon, Leah Moonfeather Stewart of the Wolf Clan."

The resounding answer of a hundred throats echoed approval. Wolf Shadow threw one final glance of contempt at the French renegade and his followers, and strode away to find Fiona.

Yellow Elk and Two Crows escorted Fiona through the large camp to a European-style military tent of gray canvas. Several white men in buckskins squatted before a fire near the entrance; they stood as the three approached, and Yellow Elk spoke to one of them in the Indian tongue. Fiona waited, casting apprehensive glances back the way they had come.

She hoped Wolf Shadow wasn't in danger for her sake. She didn't know who these white men were, or why Yellow Elk had brought her here. Suspicion that Wolf Shadow had betrayed her and was handing her over to the French after all rose in her mind, but she pushed the thought away. He wouldn't do that; she knew he wouldn't. Impatiently, she tapped her foot.

Yellow Elk and the frontiersman seemed to come to some agreement, and the shaggy blond yanked off his fur hat and nodded respectfully to Fiona.

"Timothy O'Brian at yer service, ma'am. Best ye go inside. Ye'll be safe there—as safe as any of us be," he added wryly.

He walked toward the tent. "Come along, ma'am. Sure'n ye'll be safe wi' Mr. Stewart—his lordship, the Earl of Dunnkell, to give him his proper due. But ye needn't worry. Cameron Stewart's a fine gentleman and a regular chap. He don't hold by no fancy titles out here in the woods. If ye'll bide here fer the blink of an eye, I'll tell Mr. Stewart a lady has come to visit." He flashed a charming grin and ducked inside the tent.

Homesickness filled Fiona at the sound of Timothy O'Brian's Irish accent. She wondered how such a good Irish lad had ever ended up in this wilderness.

Timothy was back in a minute, still shyly twisting his coonskin cap between his big fists, telling her that Cameron Stewart would be pleased to receive her. They exchanged smiles again before Fiona hesitantly entered the tent. She stopped inside and gave her attention to the elegantly dressed middle-aged man seated at a folding desk. Immediately he rose, replaced his writing quill in the ink bottle, and smiled graciously at her.

"Good afternoon, mistress," he said, coming forward. "I'm Cameron Stewart, Earl of Dunnkell. How may I be of service to you?" His words were softly polite, but he was staring at her as though she had two heads.

Fiona flushed under his intense scrutiny, swallowed back her nervousness, and matched him stare for stare, taking in the powdered wig, the spotless woolen coat and breeches, the crisp white shirt and shiny boots. He was in his fifties, she guessed, but his handsome face was only slightly lined, and he still had straight white teeth. His blue eyes were faded, shrewd but kindly, and his square chin bore a tiny scar—doubtless from some long-ago fencing accident. Cameron Stewart's shoulders filled the elegant coat, and his hands were tanned and lean—not lily-white as those of most of his class. And in his cultured tone she detected a trace of the Highlands.

"Sir." She nodded, but offered him no curtsy. This was America—was it not? In Ireland, she'd have had to give way on the street and bow her head. Not here. Not if it cost her her life. She'd shown all the forced servility to powdered lordlings she ever intended to.

"Please." He waved her to a chair. "Forgive me for staring at you, but you startled me. You look very like someone I knew a long time ago."

"We've not met, sir," she said coolly.

"No . . ." He shook his head. "I'd remember such a lovely face if I'd seen it before. 'Tis fey . . . just an old man's silly notion that you remind me of a lady I knew long ago. You're Irish, are you not?"

"Aye." She was oddly reluctant to give him her name. He'd find out soon enough that she was nothing but a runaway bondwoman.

He chuckled. "The woman I knew . . . she was Irish, too."

"We do count women among our kind."

Cameron Stewart shook his head again. "It's the weather, I fear—and the circumstances. I meant no discourtesy. It's just that . . . you do look so very like her."

"If your acquaintance had red hair, there is no mystery. I'm told often that we all look alike."

"Nay." A charming smile spread across his handsome face. "I have never seen two women who I thought looked so alike . . . until today. Your eyes are quite an unusual shade of green, you know."

"It wasn't my idea to seek shelter with you," she

said, her anger flaring. "If I disturb you, there's no need for me to remain."

"I have offended you."

Fiona felt instantly ashamed. What was wrong with her, to be so churlish to a gentleman who'd offered her only kindness? He hadn't even demanded her name. "You haven't offended me. I have no complaint," she said, calming. "But it's been my experience as an Irishwoman, Lord Dunnkell, that the English, especially those of your class, have done little to warrant friendly feelings between us."

"I do not use my title in Indian country. My given name is Cameron Stewart. And I'm a Scot, not an Englishman." His husky voice took on an edge of polished steel.

Fiona couldn't help but feel amused. So, she thought, the lordly Cameron Stewart is a Scot, and he does have a temper hidden beneath that smooth exterior. Her estimate of him rose several notches.

"This is America," he continued. "Whatever political disagreements exist between our people might best be left beyond the sea. If the Irish have reason to complain, so do the Scots. But I'm a practical man, and I see no sense in raking up old coals. Like it or not, *we* have an English king." He raised one auburn brow. "Or German, if one wishes to be exact."

Fiona looked down at her beaded moccasins peeking out from under her patched and ragged skirt. Stewart was obviously a rich and powerful man; what must he think of her—a white woman here among the Indians? She peered up at him through her lashes. He was treating her like an equal. Surely he didn't believe she was quality? "I am naught but a plain woman of no significance," she said with some heat. "You've no need to—"

Stewart laughed. "The wife of Wolf Shadow?" He pursed his lips and shook his head once more. "Fie, m'lady. Being wife to the great moon dancer places you as high in Ohio Country as one can go.''

Her green eyes sparked flecks of hot gold. Was Stewart taunting her, amusing himself at her expense? "I'm not his wife," she protested.

"But you are his . . ." Stewart searched for a gentle word. "The shaman believes you to be his wife."

Fiona pursed her lips and nodded.

"That complicates things a great deal," he said. "I've explicit instructions from Governor Calvert of Maryland not to offend Wolf Shadow or the Shawnee in any way. Many lives may depend on our working out a peace treaty with these tribes."

"I can tell ye I ain't bound by no sech folderol," Timothy O'Brian declared.

Both Fiona and Stewart regarded the frontiersman in surprise. They'd been so engrossed in their conversation, neither had noticed him enter the tent.

"Beggin' yer pardon fer stickin' my oar in yer affairs, ma'am, but as we're both Irish, I figure we're kin. Ye say this heathen's not your husband?"

"I have no husband," she stated firmly. "I never had one and I never intend to."

"There ye have it, yer lordship. No white woman should be abandoned to the Injuns just 'cause ye can't afford to offend a painted medicine man." Timothy's tone became heated. "Could ye rest easy back on the Tidewater if a child of yourn was left at the mercy of these savages?"

Stewart's expression hardened. "The Shawnee are different from whites, but they're not savages. If ye believe otherwise, you're more a fool than I judged you, O'Brian."

"No insult meant to your daughter Lady Kentington, sir. You know we count her different than these others, but—"

Stewart's eyes grew cold. "My daughter Leah, Lady Kentington, is Shawnee. I'll not have her or her people insulted. I'll not have her children insulted.''

"I spoke without thinkin'," O'Brian apologized.

"That tongue may be your undoing," Stewart warned. He glanced at Fiona. "Sometimes he forgets who pays his wages."

"Aye, true enough," Timothy admitted, "but on that I was plain from the first. My da left the green fields o' Kerry so his boyos would none o' them have to hold their tongues for no gentleman. I am who I am and what I am, and iffen ye don't like it, well, to hell and gone wi' ye, sir. No offense meant."

Stewart laughed. "And none taken."

"The Indians have treated me well," Fiona admitted.

Stewart fixed her with a piercing gaze. "Damn if you don't look enough like her to be . . ." An expression of loss flickered over his features. "That was a long time ago. A man's memory fades as he grows older, they say." His gaze locked with hers. "Do you wish to leave here and return to the English settlements?"

"Yes . . . at least, I think so," Fiona said, and was surprised to realize that she wasn't certain. What was wrong with her? Of course she wanted to go back to her own kind . . . didn't she?

"I'll help you, naturally," Stewart went on. "I could do no less. But it won't be easy. I'll have to convince Wolf Shadow to allow you to go with us. Perhaps my daughter can be of help." He folded his arms across his chest and looked thoughtful. Timothy cleared his throat loudly. "Oh, did you want something in particular, O'Brian?" Stewart asked. "Or did you just come in to interrupt my conversation with the lady?"

Fiona looked from one man to the other. Something was very odd here. In all her days, she'd never known a hired man to speak so boldly to a lord without being punished severely, and she'd never known a gentleman so much at ease with common folk. Either Cameron Stewart was not what he seemed, or the rules she'd lived by all her life had suddenly been changed.

"I wanted somethin'," the frontiersman answered plainly. He offered his left hand, palm up, for inspection. Fiona noticed an angry red swelling at the base of his thumb. "Got a thorn in m' hand. Yellow Elk said the lady was a physician o' sorts."

"Yes, I am," Fiona replied. "Would you like me to take a look at it?"

"Yes, ma'am. I dug some at it with my skinnin' knife, but that only seemed t' make it smart worse. Damned thorn's workin' in, 'stead of out."

Fiona glanced back at Stewart. "Do you have any objection, sir, if I treat him in here?"

"Go ahead, by all means. That hand looks bad. You should have said something sooner. I'd have gotten Leah to see to it."

Fiona opened her surgeon's kit and removed the tweezers. Her curiosity was aroused. Who was the mysterious Lady Kentington? She'd seen no sign of an Englishwoman since she'd arrived in the village. "This isn't bad," she said, tilting Timothy's hand to get a better look at the swelling. His fingers were short and thick, his palm square and solid. "It's gone in deep, but I'll have it out for you in a second."

"S'all right, miss. I don't half mind havin' ye hold me hand."

He grinned down at her. "Too bad your wife isn't here to do this for you," she said lightly. "Any woman with a sewing needle could tend to it."

"Miz O'Brian is passed on, God rest 'er soul," Timothy said, crossing himself with his other hand. "I'm a widow man, miss." He flinched as she dug deeper. "Ouch."

"There." She produced the black tip of a thorn. "Now, just let me put some—"

"Naw." Timothy jerked his hand free and rubbed it against his buckskin breeches. " 'Twill be right as rain now."

The sound of raised voices came from outside the tent, and one of the white men Fiona had seen earlier poked his head inside. "Mr. Stewart, the shaman is here to claim his woman."

Wolf Shadow appeared in the doorway. "Cameron." He nodded a greeting to the Scotsman. "Fiona."

Cameron Stewart frowned. "Fiona? Your name is Fiona?" For a brief instant, Fiona saw a look of pain on his face. Then it was gone as quickly as it had come. "I thought—"

"She has no business here," Wolf Shadow said. "Thank you for keeping her safe for me."

O'Brian stiffened. "She stays with us."

Stewart lifted his hand. "She claims she's not your wife. She's asked for my help in returning her to her own people."

Wolf Shadow's eyes narrowed. "You are a good man, Cameron, and Ross Campbell speaks for you. I will forgive your breach of manners in interfering in a private matter between husband and wife."

The air between the two men seemed to crackle with tension. "I can't let you hold her captive against her will," Stewart said softly. "If there's a question of payment, I'm willing to pay a ransom—" He broke off abruptly as a cannon exploded somewhere in the village, not far away.

At the sound of the big gun firing the men dashed outside. Fiona grabbed her medical case and followed close on their heels, nearly bumping into a slim, handsome Indian boy who was standing close to the tent entrance and carrying a musket taller than he was.

"Kitate?" Stewart said to the boy. "What's happening?"

A second explosion resounded from the far side of the encampment. Fiona looked in that direction and saw blue-gray smoke drifting up above the wigwams.

"It is nothing," the boy replied in precise English. "Roquette's French. They show off small cannon."

"Impressing the masses, eh?" Stewart said.

Wolf Shadow shrugged. "Some will be impressed. Matiassu has many followers." He moved to Fiona's side and took her arm. "This is Moonfeather's son, Kitate. He'll take you back to our wigwam."

"Not against her will," Stewart repeated.

Wolf Shadow's jawline hardened, and Fiona saw a corded muscle flex on his neck.

"No trouble," she said, "please. I'll go with him."

Cameron Stewart's worried gaze met hers. "Are ye certain? I'll help you if you want me to."

"No. I'll go," she replied.

"We'll discuss this later," Stewart said to Wolf Shadow. "I can't allow you to keep a subject of the English king against her will."

Wolf Shadow nodded. "I will see you later, after the council meets. When we have finished our business . . ." He squeezed Fiona's arm lightly. "Kitate will keep you safe."

The boy turned and walked away, and Fiona followed. After a few yards, she stopped and looked back. Wolf Shadow was watching her, and the expression in his eyes made her knees go weak.

He loves me, she thought. He really loves me.

She opened her mouth to speak to him, then closed it and continued behind Kitate. Cameron Stewart would aid her if she wanted him to. For weeks, she'd prayed for a way out of Wolf Shadow's hands. Now that way looked clear.

Her stomach turned over.

No man had ever looked at her like that before . . .

Damn you for being a lovestruck simpleton, she told herself. No woman in her right mind would choose to remain with savages. If she stayed, she risked her immortal soul . . . and the soul of any children she might bring into the world. But if she left him . . . Oh, Heavenly Mother. If she left him, would she ever again know the sweet sensation of such a man's adoration?

Chapter 13

All afternoon and into the evening more Indians continued to arrive at Tuk-o-see-yah's village. Fiona was joined in Moonfeather's wigwam by the peace woman, Wolf Shadow's sister Willow, Cami, and the older matron Amookas. Kitate remained on guard outside the entrance.

"He grows, this son of yours," Willow said to Moonfeather. She spoke in English, out of regard for Fiona.

Cami, Moonfeather's nine-year-old daughter, covered her mouth with her hand and giggled softly. "My brother thinks he is a man."

"Soon he will be," Moonfeather said. "Don't tease him. Wait until you're thirteen; you'll find it isn't so easy." She continued brushing her daughter's long, straight black hair with slow, rhythmic strokes.

Fiona noticed how the peace woman's eyes glowed when they looked down at the child and how carefully she ran the brush through Cami's tresses. Swallowing a lump in her throat, Fiona remembered her own mother and how much she missed her. It was obvious that this little girl was greatly loved, not only by her mother, but also by the other women present.

Amookas made a soothing sound that conveyed her agreement without words. Her strong work-worn hands patted out corncakes, one after another, and laid them on a flat rock to bake in front of the fire. "Like a son to me, Kitate," she said in her softly slurred English. "Almost he fill empty place in this one's heart." She patted her ample breast with the back of her right hand. "Empty left by a son who no longer walks this earth."

Cami glanced at Fiona. "Matiassu killed Auntie's son—Niipan's twin brother—when I was a baby," she explained. "He tried to kill me too. I have a scar on my neck where an arrow hit my cradleboard."

Moonfeather began to braid the child's hair. "Matiassu was tried and found not guilty by the council," she reminded her daughter. "We cannot say he murdered my cousin, Amookas's son."

"Ptahh." Amookas slapped a corncake on the rock with such force that it split in two. "If Tuk-o-see-yah not good man, good chief—if many feeble old men not stay on council—Matiassu pay for his evil."

"It be long ago, Aunt." Moonfeather's Scots burr was thick with sorrow as she added another stick to the fire. "I loved my cousin dearly, but council word be law, and the Shawnee live by law. If Matiassu escaped punishment for the death of my cousin, it was written in the stars. He will answer for his deeds in time."

"Aiyee, she speaks true," Willow agreed. "The spirits have long memories."

Fiona felt a twinge of guilt as she remembered Wolf Shadow's missing friends, Beaver Tooth and Fat Boy. If the men were dead, as the shaman believed, she knew she must share the blame. If they had died needlessly, it had been because they were helping her escape. "Wolf Shadow thinks this Matiassu caused the disappearance of two men from his village," she said. "They were good to me. I keep hoping they'll show up safe."

"No . . ." Willow shook her head. "My brother would know if they be alive. He knows Matiassu kill them. Proof he not have. Proof he *must* have to accuse Matiassu before council."

"Enough sad talk," Moonfeather said, securing Cami's braids with white leather ties. "We ha' reason to rejoice. Our families are going to be joined by blood." She smiled at Fiona. "My cousin Niipan weds Willow this night."

Willow blushed. "It be time. Too long I sleep alone."

"She's been a widow for six years," Cami whispered to Fiona. "Since her husband and baby died of measles."

"You're going to be married? That's wonderful news," Fiona said. "Why didn't you tell me?"

Cami giggled again. "She didn't know it. Auntie Amookas arranged the match today. She called her son, Niipan, and Willow together and told them they were wasting time. They liked each other, and they were both lonely, and they should be having babies."

"Cami!" Moonfeather chided. "Hold your tongue. Is this how I've taught you to show respect for your elders?" The admonition was followed by a hug. "Ye chatter like a jay, child."

"But Auntie did," Cami insisted. "I heard her."

Willow blushed. "You not tell everything you know."

"Atchh." Old Amookas beamed. "Child say only truth. Too long you and my son watch each other with deer eyes. He be shy of women. You shy of men. Good people good for each other, this one say." She turned her bright black eyes on Fiona. "Two daughter I find this night."

Moonfeather took a deep breath and caught Fiona's

hand. Fiona realized that everyone was looking at her instead of at the bride-to-be. "Amookas has agreed to become your mother in tonight's ceremony," Moonfeather said. "She will adopt ye into the Shawnee tribe."

"Adopt me?" Fiona said in bewilderment. "But why?"

"Wolf Shadow ask," Amookas replied. "Stop Roquette take you. You Shawnee, bond of paper mean nothing. Less than nothing."

"A Shawnee woman is free," Cami said. "Not even Roquette would dare touch one of us."

"Not openly," Moonfeather finished for her. "We know he has kidnapped our women, and bought and sold them. But Tuk-o-see-yah and the council would never turn ye over to him. They will protect ye as if ye be born one of us."

Confused, Fiona looked from one bronzed face to the other. Moonfeather had offered her nothing but kindness. But what was she getting herself into?

"It's for your own protection, nothing more," Moonfeather said in her lilting tones. "It nay will keep you from leaving us, if that's what you want." She squeezed Fiona's hand. "Trust me. I wouldn't do anything to hurt ye. Wolf Shadow asked me to adopt ye, but be better to come from Auntie. I be Wolf Clan. Now, you will be Wolf too—we will be sisters, thee and me."

"And Wolf Shadow?" Fiona asked. "What . . . what clan is he?"

Willow shrugged. "He is Wolf, but he is all clans. A shaman must be blood kin to all clans."

"What is law for most people is different for a moon dancer," Moonfeather said. "Don't try to understand our ways all at once—it takes a lifetime. Suffice it to say that you and I and Willow will be sisters."

"And you will be my aunt," Cami put in. She

laughed again. "If my mother adopted you, we'd be sisters."

Moonfeather held Fiona's gaze with her own. "Will you let us do that for you, make you a Shawnee woman?"

"Do I have to give up my faith?"

"No. Adoption has nothing to do with religion. Among the Shawnee, all children come from God. They are His—only loaned to us. We adopt each other's little ones as a natural part of life. And over the generations, we have learned to adopt adults as well. Family love is the greatest of all ties. We offer you this gift out of love, Fiona—nothing more."

"Then I accept with thanks."

"Usually an adoption, like a wedding, takes place in full view of the tribe. But tonight, Wolf Shadow fears that Roquette and Matiassu would use you as an excuse to delay the council meeting and to cause strife among the council members. Since adoption is a women's matter, we will do it here. Once you are Shawnee, they can offer no more protest."

"Niipan and I want same," Willow said. "Blessing of peace woman only."

"You deserve feast," Amookas said. "Much eat, much dance. Be happy."

"We will be happy," Willow answered. "But this one rather be alone with new husband than dance."

"So." Amookas gave in gracefully. "We dance at birth of papoose."

Willow blushed harder, and Cami giggled.

"Auntie," Moonfeather said, "would you harvest maize before the first planting?" And even Fiona joined in the answering laughter.

Willow's wedding was as simple as she had requested. Her bridegroom entered the wigwam a few moments later, followed by three other Shawnee women. He sat beside Willow while Moonfeather spoke briefly in Algonquian. Then Amookas offered her new daughter-in-law a freshly baked corn-cake. Willow broke the bread and offered half to Niipan. Everyone watched in silence as they ate the cake, then shared a gourd of water.

Next, Cami shyly unfolded a red woolen blanket and handed it to the bride. Willow draped the blanket over her shoulders, leaned close to her groom, and allowed him to pull the blanket over both their heads. Immediately there were exclamations of congratulations from the witnesses. Amid warm laughter and hand clapping, the two newlyweds ducked out of the wigwam and vanished into the darkness.

Now it was Fiona's turn. To her shock, she found herself stripped naked before the gathered women. Cami offered her a container of warm water and whispered to her that she should wash her face and hands in it. Speaking softly in the Indian tongue, Moonfeather dipped her fingers in the water and sprinkled it over Fiona's bare breasts and thighs. As Amookas took hold of Fiona's arms and turned her around, Fiona heard Moonfeather give a small sound of surprise.

Fiona glanced into the peace woman's eyes and saw that she was staring at Fiona's amulet. Quickly Fiona covered it with her hand. A look of confusion crossed Moonfeather's smooth face, and she reached out as if to touch the necklace.

Fiona shrank back. "It's mine," she stammered. "My mother gave it to me." Why was the Shawnee peace woman so alarmed by the sight of her necklace? And why did the gold suddenly feel so hot against her skin? A strange prickling ran down Fiona's spine, and she felt light-headed. It's too warm in here, she thought. There are too many people.

"Where did you get it?" Moonfeather demanded. Fiona took another step back, brushing against the bark-covered wall with her bare shoulder. "I've always had it," she answered. The charm was so hot now, it seemed to scorch her fingers. She took a deep breath and then another, trying to clear her head.

Amookas began to sing, and Moonfeather backed away at the sound of her aunt's voice. But she continued to watch Fiona from the shadows.

Embarrassed, Fiona remembered her indecent state of undress and tried to shield her nakedness from the chattering women. Then, to her relief, Amookas stepped forward and handed her a white deerskin dress. Quickly Fiona pulled it over her head.

Moonfeather gave Amookas a brush, and the older woman began to brush out Fiona's hair. The peace woman never took her eyes off Fiona's necklace. Someone passed a soft beaded headband to Amookas, and she slid it over Fiona's unbound hair. One by one, the women came forward and offered gifts of jewelry: strings of beads, earrings, a beaded medallion collar, and shell ornaments to adorn Fiona's hair. Amookas thanked each woman formally and fastened the jewelry on Fiona.

Finally Amookas clasped Fiona's hand in hers and lifted it over the fire. She spoke first in Algonquian and then in halting English. "This be my child," she said. "This my daughter. Her name shall be . . ." Amookas stared at Moonfeather expectantly.

"Her name shall be Weeshob-izzi Chobeka Equiwa, Sweet Medicine Woman, and all of the Wolf Clan shall call her sister."

There were cries of "Whoo, whoo" from the women. Still talking among themselves, they touched her, one after another, and filed out of the wigwam. Cami followed them, carefully balancing the water container.

"So," Amookas declared. "Is done. We make

good Shawnee squaw, you. Tell Roquette, go rot."
Then she kissed Fiona's cheek and followed the others outside. Now only Moonfeather remained.

Fiona looked down at her hands. They were trembling. "Why . . . why did you stare at my necklace like that?"

The peace woman shook her head. "Nay, this be not the time. We must gather around the campfire." She offered Fiona a faint smile. "Leave your medicine box here. Don't worry, it will be safe. The Shawnee do not steal from each other."

"I want an answer."

"And I've given ye all the answer I intend to . . . for now." Ignoring Fiona's protests, she led her outside to a place near the center of the encampment where Tuk-o-see-yah's Shawnee had gathered.

Dozens of Indian men, women, and children were seated on the ground around a hard-packed open area. In the center, a fire blazed in a wide stone-lined pit. The crowd shifted to allow Moonfeather and Fiona passage to the inner circle. "Sit here," Moonfeather said, indicating an empty spot on a deerskin rug between two giggling girls and an elderly woman. "I have duties to perform, but you'll be safe here. Roquette and his people are on the far side."

The only light came from the campfire; the rest of the village was dark. Thick clouds hung low in the sky, keeping the moon from brightening the night. The air was cool and damp. Fiona was glad that the deerskin was beneath her and that she was close enough to the fire to feel some of its heat. She settled herself, cross-legged as the others around her were sitting, and waited to see what would happen.

The deep, resounding boom of a log drum came from the far side of the circle, and the crowd hushed. Another drum joined the first. *BOOM . . . boom-boom-boom. BOOM . . . boom-boom-boom.* The two drums beat as one, but the second gave off a higher pitch.

For long minutes, there was nothing but the rhythm of the drums. Then faintly, as if from a great distance, came a muffled rattle. A log cracked in the center fire pit, crashing down into the coals and sending a spray of fiery sparks upward into the misty night sky.

Fiona became caught up in the spell of the drums, waiting . . . waiting. When the rattle and the drums were joined by the high piercing notes of an eagle bone flute, she smiled. The music was strange, different from any sound she had ever heard, yet she could not stop tears from gathering in her eyes.

From the corner of her vision came a woman, stepping gracefully, weaving in and out of an imaginary ribbon that circled the fire. The dancer's face was shadowed by a blanket, but when she came close enough, Fiona saw that it was Moonfeather. Fiona's necklace was tucked under the neckline of her deerskin dress, but it seemed to her as though the peace woman's dark gaze lingered on the amulet. A shiver ran through Fiona, and involuntarily she covered the charm with her hand. Again Fiona felt a burning sensation from the Eye of Mist, and the hair on her arms prickled.

Three times Moonfeather's stately shuffle brought her past the place where Fiona sat, and each time Fiona was certain that she felt a reaction from the ancient amulet. As Fiona tensed for the peace woman's fourth pass, she realized that Moonfeather's place had been taken by a slim male figure.

Kitate. In each hand, the boy carried a turtleshell rattle. His chest was covered by a breastplate of linked elk bones, and his braided hair was held in place with a band of gleaming copper. Feathers trailed behind him, sewn to his high elkskin moccasins and dangling from the back of his copper headband.

The tempo quickened. Kitate's steps became faster and more intricate. He bent low to the ground, then straightened in time to the drums and leaned back until his hawk feathers brushed the hard-packed earth. More drums and rattles sounded from different spots around the circle. As the boy danced and danced, the fire collapsed in on itself until the blaze became an orange glow surrounded by mist.

"Drink."

Fiona started as a strange woman tapped her shoulder.

"Drink." The squaw held out a wooden bowl.

"No." Fiona shook her head. "I don't wish—"

"Drink."

Fiona saw that other bowls were being passed. Reluctantly, she sipped the pale liquid. It was sweet and tasted faintly of sarsaparilla. When she tried to hand the bowl back, the woman urged her to take more. Fiona drank again, and the woman retrieved the bowl and moved on.

The drums stopped.

A deep sigh, almost as strong as a sudden wind before a thunderstorm, rolled across the assembly. Then there was only silence . . . a silence so deep and profound that Fiona was certain she could hear the throb of her own blood pulsing through her veins.

From the east, from a great distance, came the eerie howl of a gray wolf. Fiona's breath caught in her throat as primeval fear choked her.

Another wolf answered from the west, this one closer, the cry louder. Then a third howled from the north, and finally a fourth sounded to the south. The chilling notes died, then rose again in unison— all four wolves howling together.

A small child whimpered; a woman soothed her.

The village dogs began to snarl, raising their hackles and baring their teeth as they heard the challenge of their ancient enemies.

The wolves became silent; the dogs barked and whined, then ceased their clamor. Stillness gripped the air as fog locked the village in a timeless trance.

Suddenly there was a puff of smoke, and the fire flared anew. A tall, caped figure appeared in the haze. Two sets of eyes gleamed, and Fiona stifled a cry of surprise, then realized it was Wolf Shadow in his wolf's headdress and cloak.

The drums began again, and he danced. Round and round in the firelight, he moved. Beneath the wolfskin, he wore only moccasins and a breechcloth, and his copper-hued body glistened with oil.

Fiona leaned forward, her gaze fixed on his swaying, graceful form. He seemed larger than life, even more magnificent in his pagan glory. His black hair flowed behind him like a river of ebony silk, and his eyes glowed with an inner fire, as fierce and wild as any forest wolf.

The shaman's movements were astonishing. No European dancer could flow with the drumbeats as Wolf Shadow did. His body bent and twisted; he leaped into the air and spun with the agility of an animal. And as Fiona watched, it seemed to her that he did become one with his wolf totem.

She blinked. There, in the air above the flames, she saw—or thought she saw—a real wolf. Motionless, he crouched, head up, jaws open to reveal savage teeth. Then a spear flew across the fire pit, piercing the image. As suddenly as the wolf had come, it was gone.

Fiona pinched her arm, wondering if she was dreaming. Had she truly seen a wolf? Had she partaken of a drug that dulled her senses or caused her to imagine what wasn't there?

Wolf Shadow paused and turned. He flung out

one superbly muscled arm, and the fire sparked yellow and green. A heavy smoke rose above the fire pit, and from the smoke a wolf appeared once more. That wolf was joined by another, and then another, until it seemed a pack of ghostly beasts ran in silence above their heads.

The shaman extended his other arm, and the vision vanished in a shower of blue stars. Wolf Shadow's voice broke the stillness as he spoke first in Algonquian, and then again in English. "The one shall fall," he intoned, "no matter how strong or how valiant. But the wolf pack knows no master. So shall the Shawnee and Delaware know no master if we unite as one."

There was a general outcry from the audience. People were getting to their feet as the drums began again, pounding out a different rhythm. Painted braves entered the circle and began to dance. Fiona tried to follow Wolf Shadow with her eyes, but he was lost in the chanting, richly clad dancers. A woman stepped in front of Fiona and Fiona got to her feet. She looked around for someone she knew, then decided to try and find Moonfeather's wigwam again.

She'd not gone more than a few yards from the crowd when a strong hand closed over her shoulder. She spun around to stare into the stern face of Cameron Stewart.

"Come with me, girl," he said. "I'd have answers to some questions."

She tried to pull away from him, but he held her firmly. "Let go of me!" she insisted.

"You'll talk here or in my tent," Stewart said. "I want to know who you are. I won't hurt you, but I must know."

"You've no right to lay hands on me."

He took hold of her other shoulder and pulled her

to within inches of his face. "What's your name? Your whole name?" he asked suspiciously.

"Fiona O'Neal."

"Moonfeather told me you have something that once belonged to me."

Fiona struggled against him, but the muscles under Stewart's white lawn shirt were as hard as rock. "Let go of me! I'm no thief."

"I didn't say you were." Before Fiona could stop him, Stewart released her left shoulder and reached beneath the neckline of her deerskin dress to bring forth her amulet.

"Don't touch that! It's mine!" Drawing back her free hand, she balled up her fist and struck the older man squarely on the chin. She followed the blow with a kick to Stewart's knee, then twisted and tried to run. Despite his surprise at the unexpected attack, he caught her and yanked her against him.

"Not so fast." His breathing was coming hard, and his features had become tinged with an ashen pallor. "Please . . ." he managed. "I'm sorry. I didn't mean to be so rough with ye. But I have to know. Where did you get this necklace?"

Hot tears rolled down Fiona's cheeks. "My mother gave it to me," she cried, "and before that it came from a cowardly son of Satan who called himself my father."

Stewart released her and staggered back. The imprint of her knuckles was visible on his chin. "That amulet was my mother's. I gave it to my infant daughter, Fiona, on the day she was born," he whispered hoarsely. "What was your mother's name?"

Fiona stared up at him in disbelief. "Eileen O'Neal."

"Your grandsire's?"

"James Patrick O'Neal."

"On what day were you born?"

She backed away. "Saint Anne's feast day."

Stewart drew his hand across his forehead. "An impostor could know those things. Are you an impostor? Have ye tracked me here to America to claim the real Fiona O'Neal's inheritance?"

"God rot your greedy bowels! What makes you think I'd want to soil myself with your money? If you are my father, I want nothing of you but to see you burn in hell!"

She trembled with the force of her white-hot anger. "Are you that man, Cameron Stewart? Are you the fine gentleman, the married man who lured an honest Catholic girl to his bed, got his bastard on her, and then abandoned her?" Fiona balled her hands into tight fists. Her head throbbed as though it were clenched in an iron vise. "She died mourning you—did you know that? But she wouldn't tell me your name. Not even on her deathbed. She had that much pride, did Eileen O'Neal. She'd not have any daughter of hers run after a Sassenach begging for scraps."

"Your grandfather swore to me on his father's soul that both of you were dead. He showed me a fresh grave and said you and Eileen were buried there."

"Liar! She waited for you . . . waited until he threw her out of the house. All the village saw her shame."

"One woman . . . an old woman, Maire Shaughnessy, told me not to believe your grandfather. She said your mother was alive. She said she'd seen her leave the house at night with something wrapped in her shawl. I searched for her for two years. I offered rewards in every county."

"You didn't hunt hard enough."

"I tried, Fiona. I did. I loved her . . . I loved you."

"I'd sooner believe gold guineas grow on plum trees."

"Maire Shaughnessy was old and senile. After two years without finding a trace, I began to think she'd imagined seeing Eileen run past her door."

"You didn't find us because you never tried."

"In God's name, Fiona—"

"Don't blaspheme before me. I despise you. I've hated you since I was old enough to dodge rocks and know what bastard meant."

Cameron Stewart took a step closer. "You've family you don't know about. Not just me but—"

"I'd sooner claim kinship with a spider!"

"Give me a chance to make up the lost years, child. I can take you out of here, give you anything you—"

"No!" She shook her head. "I want nothing from you—nothing." Behind him in the shadows, she saw Wolf Shadow striding toward them. "My home is here now," she cried, flinging herself into the shaman's strong arms. "This is my husband." She buried her face in Wolf Shadow's broad chest. "My husband," she sobbed. "Forever and ever."

His arms tightened around her. "Forever?"

"Aye," she agreed. "Forever."

Chapter 14

Minutes later, Fiona was in Wolf Shadow's arms again—in the privacy of Moonfeather's wigwam—regretting every impulsive word she'd said.

What have I done? she cried inwardly.

Instantly, her mother's favorite saying echoed in her head. *Out of the frying pan and into the fire.*

Saint Anne, preserve me, Fiona prayed. My sharp tongue has done for me now.

It wasn't the insults that she'd hurled at Cameron Stewart, or even the fact that she'd punched him in the face, that plagued her. If he was in truth her father, and it looked mightily like he was, he deserved every bitter accusation, and worse. No, she'd take nothing from him—no sops to soothe his guilty conscience. Eileen O'Neal had given her daughter pride, if nothing else.

I'd sooner die unshriven than take his charity, she vowed. No, those weren't the words that pushed her over the edge and into the coals. It was the promise she'd given Wolf Shadow that would be her downfall.

He is my husband, she'd shouted for all to hear. And when Wolf Shadow had asked her if she truly meant to stay with him forever, she'd repeated the rash statement.

Forever . . .

Doubts crowded her mind. She was Irish, blood and bone. How could she ever be Shawnee? Would she ever be able to look into the eyes of this man who held her with such tenderness and not see a savage? Could she abandon her own religion, endanger her immortal soul and that of her future children?

Wolf Shadow's lips touched hers again, and she sighed deeply. She felt safer here than she'd ever felt in her life. But would it be enough? Could she stop thinking long enough to simply exist?

"Your body is here," he murmured in his deep, husky way, "but your soul flies." The tip of his damp tongue caressed her bottom lip. "I would have all of you, little wife."

He raised himself on one elbow, and his loose dark hair brushed against her cheek. "I will send Stewart away if you wish."

Wolf Shadow was naked except for his loincloth, and she wore only the fringed deerskin garment. Without corset or petticoats, she felt as undressed as he was. He was pressed against her in an intimate manner, so intimate that it was hard for her to think straight. "Why?" She wrenched the painful question from her deepest sorrow. "Why did he come here?"

Wolf Shadow toyed with her amulet. "Some things are beyond understanding. But this I can tell you: it was no accident. The world is wide. To meet here in this time and place . . ." He shrugged. "It is easier to turn the wind than to change what is written there."

"I don't want him to be my father. I hate my father. He was a monster."

"And Cameron Stewart is no monster."

"No." Her half-whispered reply was full of pain.

"Even good men sometimes do great evil."

"He abandoned my mother. He left her to . . ."
Fiona shook her head. "The things I saw . . . the
things she had to do to keep us alive . . ." She
turned her grief-stricken face up to him. "All my life
I've wanted to kill him. God help me, I think I still
do."

"Shall I kill him for you? Shall I bring you his
scalp stretched on a willow hoop?"

"No!" Fiona's stomach turned over. "Don't say
such a horrible thing."

Wolf Shadow chuckled. "I think your hate is less
deeply rooted than you know." Eddies of warmth
flooded through her as his strong fingers traced her
collarbone and the hollow of her throat.

"Murder is a mortal sin. I could kill him in anger,
but I could never ask you to do it."

"And if I did it for love of you?"

She shivered. "I could never forgive you."

He moved his warm hand slowly up the side of
her neck and into her hair. The act was soothing,
and Fiona felt herself slipping into a heady, languid
state. Unconsciously, she moistened her lips and let
her eyes drift almost closed.

"You are so wise, my Sweet Medicine Woman,
and yet so foolish. You are too full of love to hate."
He leaned down and kissed her lightly on the forehead.

Fiona felt strangely weak, and the thought that
she might be drugged surfaced in the back of her
mind. She stared up at him. "What was in that
drink?" she demanded. "What I saw . . . or thought
I saw . . ."

His soft laughter was like an evening breeze across
a field of heather. "No, Irish. What you saw and
what you feel now are real, not illusion. I will not
tell you that a moon dancer does not eat or drink of

plants that open doorways to other worlds. Of that, it is forbidden for me to talk. But I can tell you that you were given nothing more than honey water and sassafras.''

She clasped her hand around his wrist so tightly that she could feel the strong pulse of his blood. ''But I saw a wolf . . . wolves.''

''Then for you . . .'' He lifted a lock of her hair and kissed it. ''For you,'' he murmured, ''the wolves were there.''

Fiona felt his free hand on her midriff; the heat of his callused palm burned through her thin deerskin dress, and she gasped in surprise as tremors of pleasure radiated outward from his touch. She drew in a deep, shuddering breath. ''It was a trick,'' she argued. ''I know the wolves in the air were only—''

He silenced her protests with a kiss. His mouth covered hers with exquisite sensitivity. Her heartbeat quickened as, once again, she was overwhelmed with the virile scent and taste of him.

It seemed the most natural thing in the world for her lips to part and his tongue to play provocatively across the roof of her mouth. She arched against him, and his hand slid up to cup her breast.

''You ask more questions on the sleeping mat than any other woman I've ever known,'' he teased when the kiss ended.

She clung to him, letting the sweet, unfamiliar sensations drown her doubts until nothing mattered but this moment. The overpowering presence of his naked body, the warmth of the fire and furs were intoxicating. Her mind whirled, and words spilled out that she never meant to say. ''Have there been many women?''

''I have not asked you, Irish Fiona. What you did before you were mine means nothing.'' His fingers splayed across her thigh.

"I've never been with a man . . . not like this."
She swallowed again, and tiny fingers of fear and
anticipation played over the surface of her skin. Tonight she would not content him with touches and
kisses. She had run from Stewart into Wolf Shadow's arms, and in doing so she'd given up the
right to protest his possession of her body. She
knew it, and her ingrained sense of honesty would
demand nothing less. She owed Wolf Shadow
much. She owed him, and she always paid her
debts.

It's not just payment, her inner voice cried. *You want
him. You want to know what it would feel like to have
his power fill you . . . to be truly a woman.*

Her conscience spoke the truth. But knowing it
was true did nothing to quell the feeling that she
was standing on the edge of the cliffs of Ireland.
One step and she would fall into nothingness.
And if she fell, she was afraid she'd never stop
falling.

He cupped her face in his hand and lowered his
mouth to hers. His breath was sweet, his lips firm.
This time his kiss demanded more of her, and when
his tongue filled her mouth, she sucked on it gently
. . . savoring the velvet texture as his fingers closed
around her swollen nipple.

She moaned as the exquisite sensations intensi-
fied, and she became suddenly aware of a moist heat
in her loins.

"What passes between a man and a woman causes
pain for a woman, the first time," Wolf Shadow
murmured. "The pain is quick and quickly forgotten. You will never suffer it again."

"What happened . . . before . . . when you . . ."
Waves of heat suffused her skin as she remembered
the intimacy she'd permitted, and she shut her eyes
tightly. He'd touched . . . no, more than touched.

He'd teased her to spasms of carnal ecstasy. Even now, she was too embarrassed to speak of it. "Between my legs," she whispered shyly. "You . . ." She felt his burning gaze and forced herself to look into those luminous dark eyes.

"Giving and receiving pleasure is a thing of beauty between two people who love," he said. "There can be no shame." His hand closed over hers, and he guided it down to press against his own hot, swollen sex. "I want you to touch me," he continued, "as I touch you."

She gasped in shock. At some point, he'd removed his loincloth. Wolf Shadow was stark naked.

For a long moment, fear gripped her. She was no cloistered nun; she'd seen unclothed men before. She'd touched their limp members and washed them with a physician's professional aloofness. When she was a child, she'd been backed against a wall by a drunken sailor in full sexual arousal.

But she was a child no longer.

Curiosity overcame fear. Trembling, she let her fingers run the length of his tumescent member. Wolf Shadow didn't move, but she heard his sudden, sharp intake of breath.

Big, she thought. He's too big. Anything this large could never . . . Her own breathing grew tight as she stroked the contours of his silken rod. Instinctively, she caressed the taut, inner skin and the swollen head. He gasped again.

"You learn quickly," he said.

"I have a good teacher."

She ran her hands up his flat stomach and over the sinewy muscles of his chest, letting her fingertips linger on his nipples, teasing them until they swelled to hot nubs. Wolf Shadow's chest was smooth and hairless, totally different from those of most of the Irishmen she'd seen. She marveled at the softness of his coppery skin, satin over marble. For there was nothing soft beneath his skin—his muscles were like coiled steel springs. She liked the feel of him.

"What's fair is fair," he said hoarsely. She made no protest when he pulled her loose dress over her head and tossed it away. He kissed her again, and the aching in her loins returned, stronger and more incessant.

He rolled onto his back, and somehow she was astride him, her damp nether curls pressed against the heat of his hard, taut belly. He found her breast with his mouth, and she cried aloud as he took her nipple between his warm, demanding lips.

She wanted more.

She rubbed against him as he caressed her breasts and suckled them. His need became stronger . . . his body arched beneath hers, and he moaned deep in his throat. His handsome face became sheened with moisture.

Fiona's desire flared as she pressed closer, wanting to be part of him . . . letting the fevered hunger carry her nearer to the edge of that precipice.

His fingers brushed her woman's folds and slipped inside. She was wet and hot, and she needed . . . she needed . . . "I want you," she whispered. "I want . . ."

He lifted her and pressed her back against the heaped furs. His mouth plundered hers while his fingers teased her breasts until she thought she would go mad with the wanting.

He knelt between her legs, and she opened for him.

His huge, pulsing member pressed against her wetness.

"Only this once it will hurt," he murmured. "And never again."

He plunged into her, past the thin barrier that

barred his way, filling her with his swollen need. She cried aloud at the sensation.

He withdrew and dove again, then lay still as she came to grips with the fullness. He moved yet again, slowly, finding a rhythm. Her discomfort faded, then was gone as she caught his excitement. Her mouth found his, and his kiss gave her courage.

He thrust into her with long, hard strokes, and the fires in her loins flared again, until she forgot the pain and concentrated on the giving and taking.

Something was very close . . . She didn't know what, but she could almost reach . . . "Ohhh," she cried. "Ohhh." She had done it. She'd stepped into that empty space. She tumbled through a rainbow of color.

He clasped her to him and whispered her name. She felt his own shuddering release.

They lay listening to the sound of their own breathing with her head tucked into the hollow of his arm and their hair tangled together.

He broke the silence. "Did I hurt you?"

"Only a little."

"I could wait no longer. I'm sorry, Fiona. I'd never willingly give you pain."

She averted her eyes. "What . . . what happened afterward, I liked that."

"I know why you came into my arms tonight. You ran from Cameron to me. Was I wrong to make you mine, Fiona? Was it wrong to accept your promise to stay with me forever, when I knew that your words were uttered in a moment of panic?" His voice was raspy with choked emotion.

She waited, unable to answer.

"My little wife." He held her as though she were made of priceless crystal . . . as though she might suddenly shatter in his hands. "If I did . . . if I did, it's because I have never loved another woman as I love you. And I swear to you, I will never love another.''

''If I die before you do?''

''A wolf mates for life.''

She sighed, and the contentment that enfolded her was sweeter than the joy she'd known only a few minutes before. ''I don't regret my promise, Wolf Shadow,'' she murmured. ''I did run from Cameron, but I ran to you. It feels right to be here in your arms. It feels very right.''

I think I love him, she thought. It's not possible, but I really think I do. Does it matter why I promised to stay with him and be his wife? If I do truly love him, how can it matter if I said the words before I thought about them?

Wolf Shadow . . . my great, beautiful broth of a man.

She ran her fingertips along his smooth jawline. Did he ever shave? she wondered. In all the time she'd known him, she'd never seen him do so. Was it possible he had no facial hair at all?

''You aren't sorry?'' he whispered in her ear.

''No, I'm not. I am your wife, and you are my husband.''

''And if I love more than you do . . . does it matter?''

She snuggled against him. ''I'm happy,'' she said sincerely. ''I'm happy, and I want to be here in your arms. Is that enough?''

He kissed her tenderly. ''It's more than I hoped for.''

She closed her eyes and listened to the strong, regular throb of his heart. For long minutes they didn't speak, then he broke the silence.

''If I could, I would hold you like this forever, *dahquel-e-mah*.''

''What does that mean?''

He chuckled. *"Dah-quel-e-mah* . . . my love."

"Dah-quell-ma."

"Close enough." Gently, he kissed the corners of her mouth and her eyelids. "I never thought I could feel like this about any woman, let alone a white woman. You've taught me much, Fiona."

"We come from different worlds."

"From this night on, there is only our one world." He brushed her lips with his.

"You must teach me your language."

"There is much I want to teach you."

She smiled up at him in the firelight. He was so real . . . so warm . . . so solid. Was it possible she could find happiness with this great, shining barbarian? Joy bubbled up inside her as she remembered the feeling of being one with him. "Am I a good student?" she teased.

His sloe eyes narrowed. "You may need more instruction . . . much more instruction," he said with a solemn expression.

"Soon?" she dared. They laughed together, and she thought that the melody of their mingled laughter was worth more than all the gold in England.

All too soon, he sat up and covered her tenderly with a blanket. "I must return to the great campfire," he said. "Talk will go on all night. I must be there to speak for the Shawnee League."

"You have to leave me?"

He sighed. "I do. But before I go, there is something you should know."

Fiona toyed with a strand of his hair, wrapping it around her index finger.

"If Cameron Stewart is your father, you should know that you are not his only daughter."

Her eyes widened. She hadn't thought of that . . . not really. She'd known her father had a wife in England, of course, but she'd never thought of having half brothers or sisters. "He has children by his English wife?"

"There is an English daughter that I know of, but there is one closer. Moonfeather, the peace woman, is his daughter."

Fiona sat bolt upright. "Moonfeather? But that can't be." It was too much to accept.

"She has an amulet like yours," Wolf Shadow said. "A gift from Stewart when she was a child. I've seen it."

"She can't be my sister." Fiona caught her amulet and squeezed it tight. How was it possible? How could they find each other here in the wilderness, thousands of miles from the land of her birth? "Why didn't you say anything about her necklace if you'd seen it?" she demanded.

He shook his head. "Among the Shawnee, an amulet is spirit medicine. We do not speak of such things. They are too holy for words."

Fiona sat up, heedless of the blanket as it fell away, leaving her naked before his steady gaze. Moonfeather had noticed her golden amulet; she'd behaved strangely when she'd seen it during the adoption ceremony. "She knew . . . She knew and said nothing."

"Moonfeather told Stewart, and then she told me." Wolf Shadow took hold of her arms and pulled her close to kiss her. "I love you," he said when they broke apart, breathless. "I love you, and I will protect you always, from my people as well as yours."

"I don't want anything from him," she said, looking from Wolf Shadow into the darkness. The old ache filled her chest, and her mouth grew dry. "I hate him," she whispered. "I want nothing of his."

Wolf Shadow hugged her one last time, then turned to begin dressing. "He will try to persuade you to go back to Annapolis with him. He is a lord among his people, very rich, very powerful.''

"I don't give a tinker's damn how rich he is." She shook her head. "Never. I won't go a single step with him." She closed her eyes, and her dying mother's face rose before her. "He wasn't my father when I needed one—he's nothing to me now."

Wolf Shadow pulled on a moccasin. "Your pain is deep. Sometimes a wound must be opened to let out the poison before it can heal. Do not let your bitterness toward your father taint the tie that can exist between you and Moonfeather."

"She doesn't want me to be with you."

"No."

"She says that I will harm your alliance, that some people will refuse to listen to what you say because I'm white."

He settled his wolf's cape around his shoulders. "You are mine, Fiona. Nothing and no one can change that."

"But if you . . . if your plan fails . . . Will you blame me?"

He snapped his head toward her, and the wolf's mica eyes glittered wickedly in the firelight. "You are Shawnee. You are my wife. I will never give you up."

"But if it came to a choice?" She rose on her knees and extended a hand to him. "If it was your people or me?"

"My life, in this world and the next, is yours."

"That's no answer."

"I will have both." His deep voice rang with authority. "I will have you and the alliance." He moved toward the entranceway. "You are safe here. Yellow Elk and Kitate stand guard outside."

"Outside?" Fiona's cheeks grew hot. "They've been there all along? They knew what we were . . . Oh."

He chuckled. "They keep watch over my beloved wife. What she does with her husband in the privacy of their lodge . . ." He shrugged. "Who knows?"

"I'm sure they have good imaginations."

"Sleep, Fiona. I'll be back as soon as I can."

The deerskin flap swung down behind him, and Fiona picked up her Shawnee dress and pulled it over her head. Glancing around the wigwam, she realized that this was her first home as a married woman.

Married. Am I, she wondered, or am I no wiser than my mother? Have I traded everything for a man's arms around me, for his sweet promises?

She sunk to her knees beside the fire pit and stared into the glowing coals. Ireland, her homeland, seemed so far away. Was it only two years since she'd picked bluebells in the fields outside Dublin? Two years . . . or two hundred years?

"I always swore I'd never marry," she murmured. "And now . . ."

But could there be a marriage without a priest?

The voice of her conscience rose hotly. *For a Catholic there can be no marriage not blessed by Holy Church.*

What if she conceived a child from this night's pleasure? Not only born without a name, but born with copper skin and eyes like a fallen angel . . . What was it they called them? Half-breed. Her child—a half-breed bastard.

Fiona hugged herself tightly and rocked back and forth. Wolf Shadow said he loved her. He'd promised to keep her safe. In his powerful arms she'd felt protected. Could he be different from other men? Could she trust him?

And if she could trust him, could she ever make a life for herself and her children among these savage tribes? Could she cast away her old life? Her Catholic faith . . .

She dashed away her tears. "This is my wedding night," she murmured stubbornly. "I will be happy . . . I will."

Chapter 15

It was not Wolf Shadow but Moonfeather who woke Fiona in late morning. "Sister," the peace woman called softly in English. "Sister, be ye awake?"

Fiona sat up and rubbed her eyes. By the time she was thinking clearly, Moonfeather was striking a flint to rekindle the fire.

"Ye must learn to tend your own fire," Moonfeather admonished gently. "It be bad luck to let a fire pit grow cold while someone is living in the wigwam." She offered a tentative smile. "Nay verra bad luck for such a newly made Shawnee *equiwa*, I be certain." She motioned toward a bowl of cornmeal mush. "I've brought ye breakfast."

Fiona took a deep breath. "Wolf Shadow says you claim to be my half sister. Prove it."

Moonfeather added cedar shavings to the feeble sparks and blew on them. When they flared, she fed the new flame with dry twigs. Not until a strong blaze took hold of branches as thick as her thumb did she meet Fiona's demanding gaze. "Cameron Stewart—our father—says the Irish are all fire and spit." She dusted off her hands with a quick motion and reached inside the neckline of her fringed shirt to pull forth a golden amulet nearly identical to Fiona's.

Goose bumps rose on Fiona's arms as her eyes took in what her mind refused to accept. Her fingers clutched her own amulet. She knew every incised line, every curve in the pattern.

The Shawnee peace woman held out her own keepsake, and Fiona took it with trembling hands. Fiona's teeth chattered as she brought the two pieces together. Her breath came in uneven gasps as her mind fought to accept the unacceptable.

"They be not exactly alike," Moonfeather said. "Mine is shaped like an arrowhead without the stem. Yours is rectangular and contains half of the Eye."

Fiona swallowed hard. The two sections fit together perfectly, the ancient pattern gleaming as brightly as the day it had been completed by some artist whose bones had turned to dust centuries before Saint Patrick set foot on Ireland's green shore. "He . . . he has the rest? Your . . . our f-father." The word was alien to her, almost too difficult to say. "Cameron Stewart," she went on in a rush. "Does he have the rest of the necklace?"

"Aye." Moonfeather chuckled. "Nay, not really. He did have it. I saw it whole when I was a bairn. He cut my piece away with a wee dirk. 'Twas held with golden wire, ye see. There are four sections that make up the necklace. He had it from his mother, and she from hers—back into the mists of time. 'Tis called the Eye of Mist, did ye ken that?"

Fiona's senses reeled, and once more she was seized with the feeling that this was all some dream. How could this stately Indian woman be her sister? Fiona glanced down at her own fair, freckled arm. Moonfeather's skin was the color of clover honey, and her beautiful, almond eyes as black as the stones on Galway's shore. "He abandoned my mother," said Fiona.

"He says not."

"He's a liar."

Moonfeather reached for her amulet. "Nay, sister. Cameron Stewart, the Earl of Dunnkell, is many things, but he doesna lie. He swore to me that he loved your mother dearly. He says you are the very image of her."

"In looks, perhaps. But I'm not the fool for a man's honey-coated words that she was. Did he tell you he loved your mother too?"

"I know he did. My earliest memories are of them laughing together. There was love in my parents' home."

"It seems he finds loving women easy."

Moonfeather nodded. "Aye," she said with a faint smile, "but if a man has a weakness, I can think of worse."

Fiona held the two pieces of the charm together. The gold seemed to give off a strange tingling; the sensation of heat had returned, stronger than ever. It seemed to her as if the necklace was a living thing, pulsing with life—keeping time with the beat of her own heart.

"Ye feel the power, don't ye?" Moonfeather said.

Reluctantly, Fiona surrendered her sister's part of the Eye of Mist. "I'm so confused I don't know what to think," she admitted. "Next I'll be seeing leprechauns." Her green eyes darkened. "I do know that I hate my father," she said. "I've hated him all my life."

"Aye," her sister replied, putting her necklace over her head and tucking it back inside her shirt. "For many years I thought I hated him too. He left my mother when I was five. But hate destroys the hater. 'Tis a nasty growth that eats inside ye, 'til your eyes canna see the beauty of the world."

"Stewart's lucky I don't find a gun and shoot him."

"Fash ye, little sister, ye be as fierce as any Seneca." She motioned toward the bowl of mush. "Eat. An empty stomach in the morning only makes one cross as a badger."

Realizing that she was starving, Fiona accepted the invitation and began to eat. The porridge seemed flat without salt or sugar, but it was hot and filling.

"We are truly sisters," Moonfeather said. "Sisters of clan as well as blood. Ye should know something more—we nay be alone. Cameron Stewart is a lusty man. We have another—"

"An English sister. Yes, Wolf Shadow told me. But an unexpected father and a Shawnee sister are quite enough for one week. It's a lot to accept, and I've no love for the English. She and I would take one look at each other and both run like hell the other way."

Moonfeather looked amused. "She has a name, this English sister of ours. 'Tis—"

"I don't want to know," Fiona insisted. "I don't care who she is. She's rich, and English, and far away. I don't give a tinker's damn for her. I wish her no bad cess, but she's nothing to me. A stranger. Best it stay that way."

"And me?"

Fiona licked the last of the mush off the wooden spoon. "You're bossy, and you talk funny for an Indian."

Moonfeather laughed, a sound like tinkling bells. "Aye, I'll grant ye that. My husband says so often."

"But I think I like you anyway."

"And I think I like ye, for all your ill manners."

Fiona's temper flared. "What's wrong with my manners?"

" 'Tis nay your fault, younger sister. Ye were nay born Shawnee. Among our people, 'tis verra wrong to interrupt another, and rude to show disrespect to an elder sister."

"You're angry with me because of Wolf Shadow, aren't you?" Fiona set the bowl on a flat rock and stood up. "You don't want me to be with him."

"I want what is best for my people," Moonfeather replied, "and for Wolf Shadow and for you—although I be certain ye willna believe that." She got to her feet. "The council is over. Roquette and his men left before dawn. Already many of the tribes are breaking camp."

"What did the council decide? Are they going to form the alliance as Wolf Shadow wants?"

Moonfeather laughed. "Ye dinna ken the Shawnee and Delaware at all. This was not a council to decide; this was a council to decide about deciding." She folded her arms across her chest and shrugged. "Who can say what our people will do? Each man and woman will return home and talk to his own clan. In a few months, the tribes will elect representatives to meet at a real High Council fire. Then we shall see what comes of all this."

"I do care for him, you know," Fiona admitted. "Wolf Shadow . . . I do care for him deeply."

"Aye, I see that ye do." Moonfeather grew serious. "Our shaman be different from other men. If ye betray him—ever—he willna forgive ye. He is the light of the Shawnee. If ye hurt him or my people, I willna forgive ye either." She hesitated. "Cameron . . . our father wishes to see ye before he returns to Annapolis. Can ye not find it in your heart to speak with him?"

"We have nothing to say to each other."

"He searched for your mother. He offered a great reward."

"So he says."

"Whose word do you believe?"

"My mother lies in a pauper's grave. What words can mend that?"

" 'Twas your grandsire's sin. He swore you both were dead when Cameron came to fetch ye to England."

"Lies on top of lies."

" 'Tis old anger speaking through your mouth, sister. Think on it, and you'll realize truth when ye hear it. Cameron was wed to an Englishwoman. He went home to England to make a place for your mother. When he came back, ye both were lost to him."

"You weren't there. You know only what he tells you," Fiona flung back.

"Nay, Irish, 'tis the Eye of Mist that shaped your fate. Ye know the legend, do ye not? Ye know the blessing and the curse we who possess the amulets carry with us?"

"Superstition. Old wives tales."

"Do ye ken the legend?"

"Yes . . . yes, my mother told me. She said that the curse is that you will be taken from your family and friends to a far-off land."

"Have ye not been taken to that land, Fiona?"

"I don't believe a word of it," she lied.

"And the blessing?"

Fiona shook her head. "More nonsense."

"Nay, not nonsense, but magic." Moonfeather's dark eyes reflected the flickering flames of the campfire. "The blessing is that ye will be granted one wish." Her voice took on a hushed tone. "Whatever ye ask ye shall have—even unto the power of life and death. Remember that, sister. Brand those words into your heart. Never forget. For the day will come when ye will need that blessing. It did for me, and I swear to ye that the amulet possesses a power far beyond anything ye can imagine."

Fiona frowned. "I'm a physician. I believe in what I can see and touch."

"The Eye of Mist came to ye from your Scottish grandmother. She believed, and the part of you that is from her believes. Deny it all ye please. Ye ha' kept the amulet safe all your life. Ye didna sell it, not when ye were sore in need. Ye ken the power, little sister, even if ye willna admit so to yourself. 'Tis the Eye of Mist that has brought us together, 'tis the Eye of Mist that gave us back a father we thought lost."

"To hell with him, I say," Fiona muttered between clenched teeth.

Moonfeather made a clicking noise with her tongue. "So be it. But ye are verra young yet. In time, ye may think differently." She clasped her hands together. "I have a favor to ask of ye—no, nothing to do with Cameron. It is Kitate, my son . . . your nephew. It is the time of his manhood ceremony, and Wolf Shadow is his guide. My son follows the shaman trail."

"But I thought your husband was English," Fiona said. "He doesn't care that his son studies such pagan practices?"

"Kitate is the son of my first husband, not Cami's father," Moonfeather explained. "Kitate is Shawnee through and through." For a moment her composure vanished, and Fiona saw only the face of an anxious mother. "I trust Wolf Shadow, of course, but Kitate is my only son. The manhood trials are dangerous, and he is, after all, only thirteen."

"What do you want me to do?"

"Wolf Shadow will take you away for a while into the mountains to be alone. It is our way. You are newly husband and wife, and it is only right that you have time together. But when my son comes, show him a woman's kindness. He's a good boy.

He's honest and brave. If you give him a chance, you'll see what a special man he can be.''

"He's hardly spoken a word to me.''

Moonfeather nodded. "Aye. That is why I ask your patience with him. He is a boy. He idolizes Wolf Shadow, and he fears you will keep him from his mission.''

"You want me to befriend him?''

"If ye can. If ye can't, just don't make an enemy of him.''

"I'll do my best to keep the peace between us.'' Fiona promised.

"Thank you.'' Moonfeather turned toward the doorway.

Timothy O'Brian appeared. "Mistress Fiona. I'd speak to you. Fergive my bargin' in so, but—''

"Ye shouldn't be here,'' Moonfeather warned. '' 'Tis dangerous.'' She glanced back at Fiona.

"No, it's all right,'' she said. "I treated Timothy's hand. I'll see him.''

Moonfeather looked unconvinced. '' 'Tis not good, his being here. Wolf Shadow will—''

"I said he can stay,'' Fiona replied.

Moonfeather shrugged. "As ye will, sister. I bid ye farewell. Until we meet again.'' With a nod, she hurried out of the wigwam.

"I mean t' cause ye no harm,'' O'Brian said. He looked around the hut and lowered his voice. "If ye want to escape, I'm yer man. Hell take 'em all, if I'll leave a colleen here among these savages.''

"It's not like that,'' Fiona said. "I'm not a prisoner.''

"Ye can't be wife to such as him,'' the Irishman said. "Ye're a white woman.''

"Wolf Shadow is a good man.''

"He's an Injun.''

"Thank you for your concern, but I don't need—''

"Cameron Stewart will help ye, do ye but ask 'im. He swings a lot of weight back in the Colony. I doubt even these heathens would want to go agin' him."

Fiona shook her head. "No. I want nothing from Stewart."

O'Brian took hold of her arm. "Think about what ye're doin'. I seen white women after they been with the savages a few years. Ye'll have half-breed babes hangin' on ye. Ye'll be old afore yer time."

"These people have treated me decently," she said. "I can practice medicine here. It's all I've ever wanted out of life."

"Ye could practice yer healin' at Bennett Springs. They's not enough of us t' call a town, 'bout a dozen families. We ain't never had no doctor. Ye think on it, miss. We're plain folk, but ye'd be welcome. Every summer a priest comes t' say real Mass, to bless the dead and christen young'uns."

"I've a husband here among the Shawnee."

"Ye could have a husband at Bennett Springs. White women is scarce as hens' teeth, west of the Chesapeake. A real husband." O'Brian pulled her close. "I'd stand afore the priest wi' ye, Miss Fiona. And I'd never throw up t' ye what ye done before ye slipped my ring on yer finger. I've got a boy needs a mother, and I'd do right by ye."

"It's an honor, you asking," Fiona said, "but I—"

"Think on it, miss," he said, releasing her and stepping back. "I'll be comin' again for the council fire in the summer. Do ye change yer mind, Timothy O'Brian's yer man. And the offer stands whether ye're breedin' or not."

Fiona exhaled softly. "You're a good man, Timothy O'Brian, and if I didn't already have a husband, I might just take you up on that."

He reached into a leather bag hanging from his belt and removed a small flintlock pistol, along with shot and a powder container. "I want ye t' have this," he said. "Keep it near ye. Have ye ever fired a pistol?" She nodded. "It may save yer life in this wilderness."

Fiona accepted the weapon. "Thank you, and thank you for the offer of your protection."

His ruddy face showed his struggle for the right words. " 'Twas not made out of pity, Miss Fiona. Best ye know that. Ye're kind and clean, and ye're Irish. I like the way ye walk and the way ye hold her chin, proud-like and scared o' nothin' and nobody. We could make it—ye and me. Ye think on it."

Outside the wigwam a horse whinnied, and Fiona heard Cameron Stewart's voice. She brushed past Timothy O'Brian and ducked outside.

Her father sat astride a prancing bay gelding, his back straight, his eyes fixed on Wolf Shadow. "I mean to speak with her. I'll have that much," Cameron insisted.

Wolf Shadow stood inches from the nervous horse, his features impassive. "My wife is a free woman," he replied. "If she doesn't want to see you, she doesn't have to."

The shaman's fierce gaze never left Cameron's face, but Fiona knew he saw her come out of the wigwam, and she knew he saw O'Brian follow. "It's all right," she said, walking to stand at Wolf Shadow's side. She drew herself up to her full height and stared at her father. "I've nothing more to say to you, sir."

"I was there when you were born," Cameron said. "I wanted to call a midwife, but Eileen begged me not to. I caught you with my own hands, and I cut you from your mother. I loved Eileen," he declared softly, "and I loved you. I promised her I'd marry you to a prince when you were grown." He saluted Wolf Shadow with a faint nod. "You've found your own prince, daughter, and I wish you happiness with him."

"Good day to you, Lord Dunnkell," she answered haughtily. "God speed your journey away from here."

Cameron's eyes filled. "God go with you, daughter," he replied huskily. "May we meet again soon under better circumstances."

O'Brian swung up on his own horse and murmured farewell to Fiona, and they both wheeled their mounts and rode across the camp to the rest of their party.

Wolf Shadow glanced down at her. "I meant what I said. You are a free woman. If you want to go with them, I'll not raise a hand to prevent you from leaving."

"No." She shook her head. "No, I gave you my word, and I'll be after keeping it. Where you go, I shall go, and your people shall be my people."

He put an arm around her shoulder and gazed down at her. He didn't speak, but he didn't need to. Fiona read his heart's message in his dark, liquid eyes.

They slept that night under the open sky, with pine boughs for a mattress and a thousand glittering stars for a roof. Twice they made love, and twice more Fiona was transported beyond the bounds of time and space into a realm of physical and mental abandon.

Wolf Shadow was a tender lover, patiently leading her step by step to shared ecstasy, always keeping his fiery passion in check, waiting for her to find fulfillment before he reached his own powerful climax.

Afterward they laughed together and bathed naked in the icy water of the river. He led her, teeth chattering, from the riverbank and wrapped her in a furry bearskin until her cheeks glowed with warmth and joy.

"You are my gift, Irish Fiona," he murmured. "You are the one person I have searched the earth to find. I will never let you go."

She laughed and snuggled against him. "You told me I could go," she reminded him. "You said I was a free woman."

"That was the voice of the shaman," he answered. "He has to be fair. My inner wolf spirit knows nothing but his mate. You're mine, and I'll rip apart any man or beast who tries to take you from me."

"And me? What of me?" she'd teased, secretly thrilled by his savage threats. "If I willingly ran away? Would you rip me limb from limb and devour me?"

He took her small hand in his and laid it over his heart. "Never," he promised. "Never will I harm you, my *lehelecheu* . . . my breath. Sooner would I cut out my own heart."

"*Lehelecheu* . . . my breath," she repeated, thinking how poetic the endearment was. She lay close to him, her cheek against his broad chest, and listened in utter contentment to the steady rise and fall of his breathing. She fit against him perfectly, like a kidskin glove fits a hand, and for the first time in her life she felt content.

Each day's travel took them farther from the Shawnee camp and deeper into a wilderness that Wolf Shadow said was uninhabited. It seemed to Fiona that the trees were larger here, the grass a more vivid green, and the sky a richer blue.

In the early morning, when the grass was heavy with dew and crystalline drops hung like diamonds from the wild grape vines, Wolf Shadow showed Fiona where to find heartweed and moccasin flower and rattlesnake root. He taught her the names and uses of the downy yellow and bird's foot violet, and he explained how to make a clear syrup of wood sorrel for stanching blood and curing mouth ulcers. "Used carefully in tea, the Delaware believe it is a strong aphrodisiac," he added with a twinkle in his eye. "When I am old and can no longer satisfy you, you can add it to my morning mush and save our marriage."

She laughed and twirled around like a giddy girl, filling her lap with purple violets and musing of a time when they might grow old and gray together. Teasingly, she braided a wreath of flowers and hung it around his neck. And he pressed her back into the sweet spring grass and covered his mouth with hers, and they made hot, fervid love in the bright sunlight amid the rising scent of violets.

Fiona's days were full of laughter and her nights were full of passion; and if the sound of Stewart's plea for forgiveness sometimes crept into her mind, it was a faint plea, and one easily pushed aside. Her father's proud, anguished face contorted with pain as she'd last seen him was not so easy to forget. Her answer was to wipe Ireland and Fiona O'Neal from her mind—to become Sweet Medicine Woman, a Shawnee squaw alone in the forest with her lover.

Sweet Medicine Woman had no past, only a future. She had no need to worry about whether her marriage was a true one; she had only to drink her overfilling cup of happiness and revel in the strong arms of her husband.

Each morning Fiona would open her eyes and stare into Wolf Shadow's face. Until she saw him looking back at her with love, until she smelled his clean, minty breath and felt his lips on hers, she was afraid it was all a dream. She was desperately afraid she would wake under the eaves of Jacob Clough's dank cabin and find that her life lay in ashes once more.

But the days piled upon one another until they became weeks, and she lost track of how many mornings they had laughed and whispered love words into each other's ears. Each dawn began with his smile, and each night ended with the feel of his arms around her until Fiona O'Neal and her sadness seemed almost another woman, long dead and buried. She was happy—truly happy—so long as she closed her mind to everything that had happened before Wolf Shadow had taught her to love.

Chapter 16

Orange ribbons of light spilled across the eastern sky as Fiona followed Wolf Shadow along a faint deer trail in the early mist of a fresh May dawn. Around them, the forest was coming to life. From a pine bough overhead, Fiona heard the incessant scratching of a gray squirrel, seconds before it scampered out on a swaying limb and chattered angrily at her.

"*An ee-wah*," she said, pointing up at him.

Wolf Shadow nodded. "*An eek wah* . . . squirrel. Your Shawnee is improving."

She repeated the word, trying to imitate his pronunciation exactly, although she'd heard no difference at all between what she'd said and what he'd said.

He motioned her to a halt and pointed at a pattern of vee-shaped track in the damp earth. "*P'sek see.*" He held up two fingers. "They passed here only a short time ago."

Deer. She knew the word. She'd watched him skin and dress a yearling buck only a few days before. They'd enjoyed the rich meat, then salted the rest and hung it high in a tree to keep scavengers away until they could finish it.

The Shawnee wasted nothing of the animals they

hunted. The deerhide would be sewn for clothing or used as a blanket; the horn became eating utensils, fish hooks, and ornaments. The hooves were boiled down to make glue to hold arrowheads tightly on their shafts. Even the brain was put to use in tanning the hide.

"There is a sacred bond between hunter and hunted," Wolf Shadow had explained when he'd burned tobacco to appease the dead buck's spirit. "From the death of the deer, I take life. I eat of his flesh, and when I die, my flesh will return to the earth. Grass will grow over my grave, and the deer will eat." He'd said a prayer for the deer's soul, and danced in celebration. "Life is a circle, my Fiona—a circle of life." The first piece of roasted venison had been consigned to the flames in an offering. "So long as we take only what we need, the Great Spirit will provide for us. But if I scorn the deer, if I insult his spirit, if I am greedy and shoot too many, the deer will vanish from this place and I will know hunger."

He'd caught her hand, and they'd danced together in the moonlight, keeping step to the cadences of the silvery night, intoxicated by the pulse of life through their veins.

He'll make a savage of me yet, Fiona mused now as she stepped carefully over the deer's spoor. For some strange reason, she was reluctant to disturb the perfect pattern of the tracks with her own passing. Or perhaps . . . She smiled. Perhaps the Irish are not so far from being barbarians themselves. Or mystics . . .

What was it Wolf Shadow had said about life being a pattern? No . . . not a pattern, but an intricate dance. "We are but dancers in a great celebration," he had said. "The earth is our dance floor . . . the spirits watchers. If we miss a step, or break the pattern, we cause the spirits pain."

Fiona glanced up at Wolf Shadow, striding ahead

of her with feline grace, and shivers of pride made her want to shout out her joy in the morning hush.

His back was as straight as a surveyor's line, his tightly muscled buttocks and hard thighs a sight to set a woman's blood racing. His narrow loincloth covered only a finger's width of waist and little more between his cheeks.

If ever a man was made to wear so little, he was that man, she thought. It was all she could do to keep from running to catch up with him and cupping one of those lean buttocks in her hand. Just looking at him made her feel as if butterflies were tumbling inside her.

I'm shameless, she decided without the slightest guilt. A wanton born. She moistened her lips and smiled as she remembered their passionate love-making the night before.

Nothing had prepared her for a man like Wolf Shadow. No one had ever told her there were so many ways for a man and woman to pleasure each other. She was an able pupil, but it seemed to her that before she could perfect one new position or delight, he revealed a new one.

Fiona laughed out loud, and he glanced over his shoulder and smiled at her. "Do you like my sister's gift?" he asked.

She looked down at her fringed skirt and blushed. Her legs were nearly as unclothed as his—the doe-skin fringes barely covered her thighs. And her vest . . . Holy Saint Anne! The residents of Dublin would be scandalized. Her sleeveless white vest dipped low at the neckline and stopped inches beneath her breasts. Three rawhide laces held the garment to-gether, but she knew Wolf Shadow could catch glimpses of her breasts when she moved.

"At home I would be put in the stocks for dress-ing like a whore," she answered. "But I must admit, it's cool, and I've never felt so free."

Free . . . She did feel free. Without petticoats to smother her legs and drag her down, she found she could walk all day without tiring. The soft spring breezes tickled her bare midriff, and the sun tanned her legs. "Next you'll have me wearing eagle feathers and bear claws," she teased.

"A woman doesn't wear eagle feathers—at least most women don't," he replied. "Eagle feathers must be earned."

Just then a sharp-shinned hawk screeched and dove down through the canopy of interlaced foliage and plunged between the trees in pursuit of an unseen victim. Wolf Shadow stopped short and stared after the bird, then murmured something in Algonquian.

"What's wrong?" Fiona asked. "It's just a hawk."

He nodded, but something in his bearing made her certain that the bird's appearance troubled him. They continued on their way in silence until they reached a small clearing where Wolf Shadow had pointed out a lightning-killed beech tree a few days earlier.

"There's a beehive in there. I'll steal you some honey to sweeten your mint tea," he had promised.

Since they'd left Moonfeather's village a month ago, they'd survived on wild game and spring greens. What little cornmeal and beans they'd brought with them had been used up, and Fiona longed for bread and jam and a cup of real tea. Last night they'd dined on grilled trout and wild strawberries. Wolf Shadow had done the cooking. What skill she possessed lay in baking scones or preparing a hearty soup. Making edible meals over an open campfire was beyond her ability.

Before they'd left their campsite this morning, Wolf Shadow had rubbed his chest and face with the crushed leaves of fleabane. "In fall, I'd smoke the bees," he'd explained, "but they are weak after winter. We need only a little honey, so I'll depend on my charm to steal it without getting stung."

Fiona settled onto the grass and watched with apprehension as he approached the hollow tree. He'd assured her that he could take a few combs of honey without being attacked by the bees, but it was difficult to believe.

When he was within three yards of the tree, he began to sing, a slow, deep, repetitive strain. He continued moving toward the hive, but he moved so slowly that Fiona had to stare to be certain he hadn't frozen in place.

Minutes passed. The hot, bright morning sun warmed her, and she stretched out on her stomach in the thick new clover. Birdsong and the hum of bees filled the air. Fiona noticed the bees all around her, sipping nectar from the clover blossoms and circling overhead. She leaned her chin on her hands and let her eyes close, enjoying the warmth of the earth and the sweet smell of the air.

Without meaning to, she drifted off to sleep.

Something warm and wet dripped onto the center of Fiona's lower back. "Oh," she murmured, then felt the same sensation in the hollow behind her left knee. "What—"

Wolf Shadow's deep laughter rumbled close to her ear. He seized her and rolled her over in the soft grass. When he kissed her, his mouth was sweet with the taste of wild honey.

"What are you doing?"

His sticky fingers fumbled with the laces on her vest. "I promised you honey," he said.

She giggled and threaded her fingers through his thick hair. She loved his hair. She never tired of touching it, of brushing it down his back or feeling it slide over her skin. "Did you get it?" she asked.

He kissed her again, answering the question without words.

"Shut your eyes," he ordered.

She did.

He parted her vest, and she giggled again as she felt the warm drops on her bare breasts.

"What are you doing?" She touched the sticky spot and brought her index finger to her mouth. "You're dripping honey on me," she squealed.

"Mmm." His tongue was warmer than the honey.

"Oh . . ." She opened her eyes.

"No," he commanded. "You must keep them shut. This is an important part of the bee tree ceremony." She laughed again. "This is very serious," he insisted. "I am the shaman. You're only the assistant. You must obey my instructions without question."

She opened one eye a crack.

"No peeking."

His tongue traced her lower lip; then he gently sucked her upper lip. His breathing deepened as he took her in his arms and trailed damp, hot kisses down her neck to the hollow between her breasts.

Joy curled in Fiona's stomach and sent sweet sensations to her knees. "Ummm," she murmured, keeping her eyes tightly shut. "I hear and obey your words, oh, great shaman."

Chuckling, he slipped her vest off one shoulder and then the other, leaving her bare to the sun's rays. "The great shaman has a beautiful assistant," he murmured, "with skin as white as dew and breasts like mountain peaks." He laid her back in the grass and stretched out beside her.

Fiona giggled as she felt more honey drip over her breasts and belly. She was acutely aware of a growing warmth in her loins that had nothing to do with the sun and everything to do with this great husband of hers doing delicious things to her body.

His lips found her nipple, and she gasped. "Ohhh
. . . that's nice," she whispered.

"Very nice," he agreed. His fingers were sticky
with honey as he brushed her other nipple lightly,
then teased it to a hard, erect peak with the pad of
his thumb. A warm tingling flowed down her breast
and caused an urgent throb between her thighs.

She ran her hand along the curves of his sinewy
shoulder, thrilling to the feel of his hard, corded
muscles rippling beneath his copper skin. Then she
moaned with pleasure and gripped him, her nails
digging into his flesh, as he suckled her swollen nipple until it ached with sweet fire. "Oh, don't stop,"
she murmured. "Keep doing what you're doing."

He kissed her other breast in the same ardent way,
and her desire flared as he slipped a hand under her
skirt. "And shall I keep on doing this too?" he demanded.

She made a tiny sound in her throat as he used
both hands to undo her belt and slide her skirt down
over her bare legs. "Wolf Shadow . . ."

"Shhh," he said. "It's all part of the ceremony."

His soft chuckle sent excitement down her spine.
She wore nothing but her woman's loincloth and
moccasins. In seconds he'd removed them as well
and tossed them aside.

His hands were everywhere on her body . . .
moving over her . . . touching . . . caressing . . .
teasing.

Fiona's chest felt tight and her head giddy. She
knew that she should protest. What decent woman
would let a man strip her stark naked in a meadow
in broad daylight? But she didn't want him to stop.
She wanted him to go on touching her . . . and she
wanted to touch him in return. "Is this allowed?"
she asked mischievously as she slid her fingers down
his chest. "May a shaman's assistant do this?"

"It's imperative," he assured her, capturing her hand in his and moving it lower. "And so is this."

She shivered with delight as she touched the proof of his desire, then laughed as she felt more warm drops on her belly and thighs. "Stop . . ." she protested, opening her eyes, but they both knew she was enjoying the game as much as he was.

He pressed his body against her and wrapped his long, muscular legs around hers. His dark hair swept over her cheek as he nuzzled her neck and planted warm, damp kisses behind her ear.

She trembled with desire. "Wolf Shadow," she whispered, "I do love you." Taking his chin in her hands, she raised his face. His ebony eyes were heavy-lidded with passion.

"And I love you, my Fiona."

She traced the line of his cheekbone with a fingertip. How beautiful he is, she thought. When Eve first opened her eyes in the Garden of Eden, Adam must have looked like this.

Desire shook his body. "Sweet Medicine Woman," he whispered huskily.

She moistened her lips. "Kiss me," she begged.

This time his kiss was no longer playful, but hard and demanding. His tongue filled her mouth, and his powerful arms crushed her against him. She met his passion with her own fire, giving him kiss for kiss and touch for touch.

"The most important part of the ceremony," he managed, between long, hot, deep kisses, "is that every drop of honey must be licked off."

"No matter where it is?" she asked.

"No matter where."

She arched against him, reveling in the tumescent length of him, thrilling in anticipation to what she knew must come. "Even . . ." She whispered into his ear.

"Most importantly there," he replied, "lest the spirit of the bees be offended."

She flung herself back in the warm, soft grass, neck arched and breasts heaving. Her skin was flushed, her breathing deep and quick, her pulse pounding.

He straddled her with his knees and leaned over her, pressing his huge, swollen, pulsating sex against her bare thigh.

Fiona breathed deeply of the scented air and let her hands caress his chest and shoulders. I love him, she thought. He's right . . . We were born to be together like this.

His mouth was doing wonderful things to her throat; his strong hands were hot against her skin. His hips undulated against hers until the heat built within her so that she moaned with desire. She raised sticky fingertips to his chest and smeared him with the sweet. It seemed to be the most natural act in the world to taste the honey . . . to flick her tongue against his smooth skin and feel the contour of his hardening nipples against her lips.

He tasted of honey, and salt, and man.

Excitement raced through Fiona, and she exhaled softly. Her body was trembling beneath his; her mind was aflame with wanting him . . . with wanting to be a part of him. She arched against him, willing herself to release the past, letting her heart carry her beyond all barriers, opening herself to this man.

His burning shaft brushed the entrance to her sex, and the earth seemed to move beneath her. "I want to fill you with my love," he rasped. "I want to go deep, deeper than I've ever gone."

"Yes. Yes," she urged.

She fastened her teeth on his skin and nipped him. She felt like laughing and crying at the same time. Her soul seemed to have taken flight. She was tumbling through time and space in glorious excitement. He pulled away, and her eyes snapped open. She raised her arms to him.

"The ceremony," he whispered. "The ceremony must be complete."

The warm drops of honey seared the skin of her belly like molten lead. She threw back her head and writhed against the thick grass in wanton abandon.

He lowered his head and licked the honey, one drop at a time. Tremors rocked her body. She spread her legs wider and dug her nails into his shoulders. Her breath came in jagged gulps; perspiration covered her body in a thin sheen.

He squeezed the handful of honeycomb over the russet triangle of her nether curls, and she sobbed with anticipation. His hot, wet mouth pressed against her.

"Please . . ." she panted. "Please . . . no more. I need you . . . I need you . . . inside me."

"Shall I fill you, little wife?" he asked, and his tongue laved her love-swollen mound.

"Now . . . now."

The warm honey dripped between the folds of her wet opening. "Every drop," he said softly, "lest we anger the spirit of the bees."

She closed her eyes and gave herself up to the sweet, wild passion of their love.

The sun stood two hours past noon when Fiona raised her face from the hollow of his shoulder and listened. What was that sound?

It came again. A faint shuffling. A squeal, and then a grunt, almost like that of a piglet.

Puzzled, she looked around. The meadow seemed quiet, much as it had been before she and Wolf Shadow had begun to make love. The breeze had shifted slightly; now it blew from the west rather than from the northwest. The steady drone of the bees remained, along with the occasional song of a bird.

She exhaled softly, deciding the strange sound had been nothing more than her imagination. Then the squeal came again from the edge of the woods. Fiona sat bolt upright and stared.

Waddling out of the trees came a small buff-colored ball of fur. Two beady eyes and a little black nose tilted up toward the sky. Then the tiny creature opened its red mouth and bawled like a human baby.

Wolf Shadow's body went taut, then he came to his feet beside her in slow motion. *"Ne nipauwi. Don't move,"* he ordered. "Stay perfectly still."

"What—" she began.

He silenced her with a fierce glance.

Confused, she looked back at the furry animal. Was it a fat puppy? What could possibly make Wolf Shadow react so violently to such a harmless animal?

"Bear cub," he whispered. His musket and war club lay a few feet away, between them and the bear. Even his knife had been discarded when he'd taken off his loincloth. "Whatever you do, don't move," he repeated. "If the sow charges, lay flat on the ground. Don't run, and try not to move, even if she attacks you." Slowly, he inched his way toward the weapons.

Fiona's gaze scanned the shadowy forest. What he'd said made sense. If this was a baby bear, there must be a mother nearby. But where was she? And why didn't Wolf Shadow want her to run away?

The cub paused in its innocent ramble to bat at a yellow butterfly. The butterfly flew away; the cub scrambled after it, tripped over a rotten branch, and did a somersault. Despite Fiona's fear, it was all she could do not to laugh.

The cub bawled, its cry a cross between that of a

calf and a puppy. The answer came from the woods on the far side of the clearing, a rumbling bellow that made gooseflesh rise on Fiona's arms. She caught her breath and waited, watching for a shape to materialize from the shadows of the trees.

When the nightmare became real, Fiona's mouth went dry. A scream rose in her throat, but she stifled it by sheer will. The bear lumbered out into the meadow from the north; the cub was at the south side of the clearing. Fiona didn't need Wolf Shadow to point out the danger. They were between the mother bear and the cub.

The old sow rose on her hind legs, her huge front paws waving in the air. She was as big as a full-grown bull. Her hair was black, but the years had streaked her with gray and given her a ragged look. One ear was missing, the other flattened against her gnarled head. Her mouth gaped open, and Fiona could see the rows of ivory teeth surrounding a bloodred tongue.

The mother bear snarled again, and the baby gave an answering whine. The sow sniffed the air and swayed back and forth, seemingly scanning the meadow for her lost youngster. Beyond her, Fiona saw a second cub scramble up a pine tree.

Wolf Shadow slid the musket into Fiona's hands. "It's primed and ready," he whispered, "but don't shoot. Whatever you do, don't move, and don't pull the trigger."

The she-bear roared again.

"Look at her eyes," he said. "She's nearly blind."

Fiona caught a whiff of rotten meat and dried blood; the smell made her stomach turn over with nausea. It's the bear I smell, she thought. The taste of fear was acrid in her mouth, and she strained to breathe.

The bear cub bawled and started toward the sow. The most direct route would take it over Fiona's lap.

Then the cub sniffed the air and stopped short, puzzled by the strange scent of man.

The she-bear dropped to all fours and came toward them. Wolf Shadow stepped in front of Fiona. "Stay still," he reminded her. Slowly he moved to the right, three feet, then four.

"No," Fiona cried. "What are you doing?"

The bear grunted and reared up again. Her deep roar seemed to shake the earth. Saliva dripped from her open maw, and her yellowed claws gleamed like daggers in the sunlight. Her head snaked out as her cataract-clouded eyes spied Wolf Shadow.

The bear looked from the man to the spot where she could hear her cub on the far side of the clearing. She tottered, then fell forward on all fours. Her muscles tensed, and she rolled the skin back from her muzzle like a snarling dog.

"*Sehe*," he ordered.

Fiona gave a faint moan. Did he think he could tell a bear hush and it would? Was he mad?

Naked, with empty hands, he moved toward the angry sow. "*Sehe, nee ke yah.* Be still, mother." He brought his palms together and then spread them before him. "*Penno wullih.* Look yonder."

The sow growled a terrible challenge.

"Peace to you, mother," he continued in the Shawnee tongue. "I come not to harm you, but to share your meadow."

Fiona stood and lifted the heavy musket, aiming it at the bear. The bear took a dozen running steps toward Wolf Shadow, and she forced back the hammer with shaking hands.

Wolf Shadow stood motionless. "Be at peace," he continued in Algonquian. "We mean you no harm. I have gathered honey. Take it as a peace offering."

A Shawnee war whoop split the air. Fiona spun around to see a slim, bronze figure, bow in hand, streak toward the buff bear cub. With another howl, the boy slapped his bow on the cub's back. The little creature let out a cry and barreled across the meadow toward the mother. The boy struck the cub again, and the terrified animal sped past Fiona and Wolf Shadow, ducked under the mother, and ran squealing into the woods behind her.

The mother bear gave one final snarl, turned, and loped after her cub. Too shocked to move, Fiona stood where she was until Wolf Shadow took the musket from her clenched hands and pulled her against him.

Fiona began to weep as he patted her back. "*Sehe, sehe,*" he soothed. "It's all right."

Sobbing, she clung to him. "I thought . . . I thought . . ." she managed, then broke down in tears again.

Kitate came to stand grinning beside them.

"I suppose you think you saved us," the shaman said in English. "Another moment, and I'd have convinced her to leave."

Kitate nodded. "Yes, I'm sure she would have, right after she had had your head for dinner."

"Why didn't you just shoot the damned bear with the gun?" Fiona demanded, wiping her eyes with the back of her hands. Suddenly she realized that she was standing in front of Kitate as naked as the day she was born. Her face flamed as she ran to where her skirt and vest lay, turned her back, and dressed as quickly as she could.

Kitate kept grinning.

"I was teaching Sweet Medicine Woman how to steal honey," Wolf Shadow explained as he donned his moccasins and loincloth.

"I see," the boy said, grinning even wider.

Fiona fumbled with the ties on her vest. They were sticky with honey, as was the front of her fringed skirt. She avoided Kitate's gaze as she searched the grass for her woman's loincloth. Wolf Shadow found it and tossed it to her. She noticed that he seemed as pleased with himself as her nephew did.

"Why didn't you shoot the damned bear?" she asked again.

"She was a grandmother bear with children. I thought I could convince her to leave us alone."

"You tried to talk a mountain lion out of attacking and that didn't work. What in God's name made you think you could do it with a bear?"

He shrugged. "I've done it before. The magic just doesn't go well when you're around."

"She's probably a witch," Kitate put in.

"I'm not a witch," Fiona protested. "No sane man would try to face down a bear."

"No white man maybe," Kitate said, "but mother's husband, Brandon, did once, and he's English. I think ye be right, Aunt. No sane man would."

"I'm a great shaman," Wolf Shadow declared. "I know the medicine to speak to bears."

"Maybe this bear spoke only Iroquois," Fiona said.

Wolf Shadow grinned at her. "The bear didn't eat us, did she?"

"No," Fiona admitted. "But it was Kitate who saved us, not you."

"Don't be so sure," Wolf Shadow replied. "How do you know my magic didn't call the boy?"

Chapter 17

It was early June. Fiona counted the weeks again in her head, unable to believe her own reckoning. But it was true. The days here, deep in the wilderness of the Ohio country, seemed to flow together and spill over the rocks of her consciousness like a clear mountain stream.

Could it have been so long ago that she'd first set foot on American soil? Could it have been so many weeks since she'd last seen the man who claimed to be her father?

Fiona sighed heavily and clasped her amulet. Wolf Shadow never ceased to plague her about Cameron Stewart. *Forgive him,* he told her. *Listen to what your father says. Hatred eats at the heart of the one who hates, not the object of the bitterness.* "Damned if I will," she muttered. "He betrayed and abandoned my mother and me. He didn't want me when I was a babe. What does he want with me now?"

She propped her chin on her palms and leaned forward, supported by her elbows. She was lying on her belly on a hillside, her gaze on an eagle trap in the valley below. Wolf Shadow was hidden in the trees, somewhere not far from the trap, while Kitate crouched in the earthen pit waiting for an eagle to take the bait.

"This is insane," she'd protested when Wolf Shadow had explained what was involved in capturing a live eagle. "Kitate's only a boy. An eagle could put out his eye with one swipe of its claws."

"To be a man, he must capture the king of the sky," Wolf Shadow had replied.

"He's not a man."

"He will be."

"You'd risk a boy's safety to satisfy a primitive ritual?"

"It has always been done so."

He was so stubborn. When she disagreed with him, Wolf Shadow would listen politely, then do what he wanted to do from the start.

And they did disagree. Often. So often that Fiona sometimes wondered at the rationality of her decision to be his wife.

She would never understand him and his Indian ways. She would always be a stranger looking on.

Except when he drew her into his arms and kissed her. Except when he sang to her or played a love song on a bone flute. Except when she lay in his arms at night, and he pointed out the scattered stars in the sky and told her stories about the shapes he saw there: the Hunter, the Bear, the Star Maiden, and others.

She trusted him as she had never trusted another living man. Yet she didn't trust him completely. She couldn't.

"Damn. Damn. Damn," she uttered in exasperation. What had he done to her? She'd given herself up to him body and soul. And she loved it. At least most of the time.

Kitate had brought news of angry grumblings in the Indian camp. "Many are suspicious of Fiona," he'd told Wolf Shadow when he thought she was asleep. "My mother says that the chances of a Shawnee alliance are farther away than ever. Even

Tuk-o-see-yah questions your allegiance to the Shawnee. He asks how you can expect us to put away all English things when you take a flame-haired Irishwoman to wife.''

Wolf Shadow had not answered Kitate. He had gone away from the campfire and not returned until morning. And when she had tried to discuss the issue with him, he'd brushed her off with a careless shrug of his broad, bronzed shoulders.

"You are my wife. So long as we walk the earth."

"But I won't come between you and your dream," she'd insisted. "It means too much to you."

"I will have both—you and the alliance."

He had refused to speak of it again.

The hard barrel of her flintlock pistol dug into her hip, and Fiona shifted her position, removing the weapon from the carrying pouch Wolf Shadow had sewn for her and laying it in the grass. She'd kept the pistol near her ever since the bear incident. Wolf Shadow had taught her how to load and fire the gun, and had insisted she practice her aim. She was no expert shot yet, but she could handle the weapon safely and hit anything the size of a man at twenty feet.

A high-pitched *kleek-eek-eek-eek* sounded from overhead, and Fiona scanned the cloudless blue sky for sight of an eagle. She saw nothing.

It had taken the boy two days to dig the pit and weave a covering of branches to cover the top. Wolf Shadow had instructed him, but he hadn't helped, and he'd refused to let Fiona give any assistance. "Kitate must do this thing himself," he'd explained. "It is our custom."

Last night Wolf Shadow had told her of the final test of manhood Kitate must pass, and it had turned her blood cold.

For several years, the boy had been studying under Wolf Shadow. He'd been chosen to become a

shaman as Wolf Shadow had been chosen when he
was young. Today the boy must capture an eagle
alive. He must remove one feather from each wing
and then set the bird free. One feather would go to
his mother on the night of his naming ceremony;
the second would be Kitate's—an outward symbol
of his bravery. Capturing the eagle would give him
the right to sit in the men's council, to join war parties, and to take a wife when he came of age.

"He has already purified himself and fasted for
five days in a high place. He has already had a sacred vision and been chosen by an animal totem.
Kitate must show that he is worthy to become a
Shawnee warrior. He must prove his courage and
his dedication to me, his teacher. I have set him a
task that women will sing of in the winters to come,"
Wolf Shadow had told her. "He must go alone and
unarmed to a Seneca camp and steal one of their
wooden false faces—a ceremonial mask."

"You're out of your mind," she'd flung back.
"You can't! That's crazy. You'll get the boy killed
for nothing."

"And for everything."

"What do you want with this false face?" she'd
demanded.

"I don't want it. The mask isn't important. We'll
send it back to the Seneca after Kitate's naming ceremony."

"Then why have him risk his life for it?"

"Because it is our way." His dark eyes had lit with
mischief. "Be glad I didn't order him to bring back
a live Iroquois shaman. It's what my master demanded of me when I was his age."

Fiona shielded her eyes from the bright sunlight
and peered down at the eagle trap again. How could
she face Moonfeather and tell her that she'd let Wolf
Shadow send her only son on such a useless ven-

ture? How could she herself ever forgive him for such reckless disregard of a boy's life?

Kleek-eek-eek-eek. The piercing screech cut the still air again. This time Fiona saw a black spot in the sky almost directly overhead. Was it an eagle? Had the trap really worked?

"I bait the trap with a dead rabbit," Kitate had explained, "and I call him with prayer."

"I don't believe you'll catch an eagle in that thing," Fiona had said. Now she wasn't so certain.

There were two holes in the woven top of the pit, holes large enough for Kitate's hands to fit through. When the eagle landed on the mat and tried to steal the rabbit, the lad would try to seize the bird's legs. It had seemed a mad plan—outrageous—until Fiona had heard of the scheme to send Kitate to steal the mask. Now the eagle trap seemed merely stupid, hardly worth fighting over.

Fiona rose to her feet, trying to focus in the glaring light. The spot had become the outline of a bird, diving down at a tremendous speed. Fiona's pulse quickened with excitement as she waited to see if the eagle really would land on the trap.

"Where is the shaman, woman?"

A man's harsh voice startled her, and she whirled around to see Matiassu standing only a few feet away. Horrified, she looked past him to see if he was accompanied by his warriors. She saw no sign of them. "What are you doing here?" she cried. He wore no warpaint, but he carried a musket in his hands, and a steel tomahawk and knife hung from his belt.

Scowling, he took a step toward her. "Where is he?" The eagle shrieked again, and Matiassu looked down at the valley floor and spied the bird struggling on the roof of the trap. "Ah, the shaman hunts eagle," the Shawnee war chief said.

"No," she answered. "I mean . . . yes." Why was

he here? He meant them no good, she was sure of that. Fear made her wary. She took a deep breath and tried to look composed. "Are you here to kidnap me again?" she demanded.

"No. I come to bring a message." He reached out to grab her, and she spun away and darted to the spot where her pistol lay hidden in the tall grass. Matiassu lunged after her, but she was too quick for him.

She hit the ground, scooped up the flintlock, cocked it, and turned it on him. "Drop your musket," she said.

His face paled in surprise. He stopped, barely an arm's length away, his dark eyes dilated in surprise and anger.

"I said put it down," she repeated.

"You won't shoot me, woman."

"Move one muscle and, by the sweet blood of Christ, I'll blow a hole in you that no shaman magic can patch," she threatened. She held the heavy weapon in both hands. "The musket. Throw it away from you."

"Has the weeping woman become a fierce badger?" he mocked. "You be too soft to kill a man."

"Try me." For what seemed an eternity to Fiona, he glared at her. She glared back, unwilling to give him an inch.

Then, with a rough laugh, Matiassu cast the musket to the grass. "So," he said grudgingly, "perhaps you be a badger."

Unwilling to press her luck, Fiona opened her mouth and screamed as loud as she could.

Wolf Shadow came running.

She knew that he'd arrived when Matiassu shifted his grim scrutiny from her to an object beyond her back, and his expression changed.

"Matiassu."

Warm relief surged through Fiona as she heard Wolf Shadow's voice. Still, she kept the muzzle of the flintlock aimed at the center of the war chief's naked chest.

Wolf Shadow came to stand at her side. "It's all right," he said. "You can lower the gun. He's alone."

"We don't know that," she said.

"I know."

Matiassu raised an open palm. "Greetings, moon dancer."

Wolf Shadow nodded. "Why are you here?"

"I come to bring you a warning." Matiassu switched from English to Algonquian.

"You?"

Matiassu smiled thinly. "We are enemies, you and me. It is good for a man to have strong enemies. They make a warrior great."

"If you are my enemy, then why are you here, and why should I believe anything you say?" Wolf Shadow asked in English.

"Roquette is angry with you," the war chief continued in the Indian tongue. "He knows you stir the Shawnee against him and against his French brothers. He has placed a bounty on your head and on that of your badger woman. One hundred louis d'or for your head and stones, another fifty for the woman—alive. He wants her for his sleeping mat."

Wolf Shadow switched to Algonquian. "And you have come to warn me . . . out of love."

Matiassu laughed. "Between you and me there is no love. Between us is only that which will end in death. But when I kill you, shaman, it will not be for the Frenchman's gold, it will be because you are a dangerous man and need destroying." He slapped his chest. "I am Matiassu. I do not kill for hire. I kill for pleasure."

"As you murdered my friends, Beaver Tooth and Fat Boy?"

Matiassu smiled. "Do their scalps hang from my belt? Do I look like a man who would slay unsuspecting Shawnee brothers?" He shook his head. "Prove that I have harmed them or cease making accusations." He turned away, then stopped and looked back. "When I have killed you, shaman, I will not give your red-haired woman to Roquette—at least not until I tire of her." He raised a clenched fist in salute, then spun on his heel and strode off toward the forest.

Fiona stood trembling as she watched him go. "What did he want?"

"He came to tell me that the French have put a bounty on our heads."

"Why?"

"With me dead, Roquette believes the council will vote against the alliance . . . the way he wants them to."

"But why would Matiassu come to tell you?"

"Because he is my enemy, and because he is Shawnee."

"That doesn't make any sense. He's evil."

"Even wicked men have honor."

She stepped closer to him, aimed the pistol at the ground, and eased the hammer down carefully to keep it from firing. "What are you going to do?"

"Kitate caught his eagle. I'll help him get his feathers without injuring the bird, and you can tend Kitate's scratches so that they will not turn to poison."

"But Roquette? What will you do about Roquette?"

Wolf Shadow looked thoughtful. "At dawn tomorrow Kitate will leave on his mission, and we will start back to Tuk-o-see-yah's village. It is closer than my own home. If Seneca dogs hunt us, you will be safer among the Shawnee with your sister Moon-feather.''

Fiona's throat constricted. "I'm afraid of Matiassu. I don't trust him.''

He put his arms around her and pulled her against him. "Neither do I,'' he admitted, "but he's done us a favor. I owe him, and I must pay him that favor before I send him across the river to join his ancestors.''

"You mean to kill him?''

"And take his scalp.''

"You can't. That's horrible. It's barbaric.''

"He killed either Beaver Tooth or Fat Boy, or both of them. He hacked the scalp locks from their heads while they still breathed.''

She pressed her cheek against his bare chest and closed her eyes. "How can you be certain?''

"I just am.''

"But even if he did, you don't have to be his judge. Let someone else—''

"I am the moon dancer. I am the judge. I will lift his hair and divide his scalp lock between the mothers of my dead friends in token of my judgment.''

Nausea rose in Fiona's throat. She pulled away from him in horror. "No. You couldn't. It's not civilized. If you do that . . . if you do such a terrible, savage thing, I won't stay with you. I couldn't stay with you anymore.''

His bronze features hardened; his eyes glittered like black ice. "You would have killed him if he'd tried to take your weapon from you. True?''

Fiona shuddered, remembering the smell of Matiassu's body and the malevolence in his gaze when she'd held him at bay. "To save my life . . . or yours,'' she admitted. "I wouldn't murder another human for revenge.''

"How many times have you killed your own father in your heart?''

She winced. "That's different. You can't confuse the issues. I may have thought I wanted my father dead, but when I saw him . . . Damn your red soul, Wolf Shadow. I'm a healer. I save lives—I don't take them. I mean what I say. I won't condone murder and"—the image of a dripping scalp rose in her mind—"mutilation." She swallowed against the sour taste in her mouth. "I love you, but I won't stay with you if you murder Matiassu."

"And I will not be controlled by a woman. If you will not stay with me, you will not," he answered coldly. "I am the moon dancer. And I must do what I must do."

Wolf Shadow seemed a stranger to Fiona in the days that followed. Kitate departed on his quest to the Seneca Village, and Fiona and the shaman returned to Tuk-o-see-yah's camp. They traveled by night and slept by day, and not once did Wolf Shadow make love to her.

On the second day of their journey, Fiona's monthly bleeding began. She couldn't help feeling relieved. Despite her love for Wolf Shadow, she wasn't ready to carry his child.

Her old doubts and fears returned full force. She began to ask herself if she'd traded her self-respect for the pleasures of a virile man's bed. Why had she believed that she understood him . . . that they could find happiness together despite their vast differences? Why had she allowed herself to trust a man when no man had ever given her reason to trust before?

Wolf Shadow was a pagan—a barbarian—little better than Matiassu. She had sinned when she'd lived with him without benefit of the Church, but repentant sinners could receive forgiveness. If she left him . . . if she went . . .

Where? Where could she go? Her pride refused to

consider Stewart's offer. She'd die before she accepted help from him.

Timothy O'Brian. The rough frontiersman had said he would stand before a priest with her. Should she cast her lot with him? She didn't love him; she didn't know him. But many marriages of convenience occurred in Ireland. If a girl owned a patch of land and needed a man's strong back to work it . . . If a man had motherless children and needed a woman to care for them . . . A marriage, a real marriage blessed by the Church, would be something to hold on to. Her children would be legitimate, their souls safe from the dangers of purgatory. Her own soul would be safe.

Reason said that she should leave Wolf Shadow while she could. Leave him and take one of her own kind to husband. It was the logical thing to do.

But she didn't love O'Brian. She loved this great savage moving through the trees ahead of her like a ghost. She loved the sound of his laughter and the proud way he walked, as though he owned the earth.

She loved the things Wolf Shadow did to her body, the way he made her feel . . .

All of her life, medicine had come first. She had wanted to be a doctor, to heal the sick and comfort the dying. She'd wanted to bring new life into the world and ease pain. She could do that if she went with Timothy O'Brian . . . no less than she could among the Indians. Timothy's settlement had no doctor. Hadn't he said so?

A mosquito buzzed annoyingly around Fiona's head, and she slapped it just as another bit her bare forearm.

Wolf Shadow looked back at her. They were paddling a canoe upriver, which was not nearly as easy as flowing with the water's current, she'd discovered. His eyes rested on her for a few seconds, and her gaze locked with his.

Instantly Fiona was struck by the sorrow in his eyes. This was not a powerful shaman watching her, but a man . . . a man who loved her deeply and knew that their relationship hovered near the breaking point.

"The mosquitoes are bothering you," he said. "Why didn't you tell me?" He leaned forward on his knees and drove the paddle deep into the sparkling water. The birchbark canoe dipped slightly and turned toward the east bank. Wolf Shadow guided the little boat carefully against the shore, removed his moccasins, and leaped out in the shallow water. "Stick your paddle straight down into the sand and hold it," he ordered. When she obeyed, he climbed the bank and vanished into the thick growth of wild grape vine and foliage.

In a short time he was back with a handful of crushed, flowering pennyroyal. "Our people call this squaw mint," he explained as he got back into the canoe and rubbed the plants between his palms. "It will protect you from insect bites."

Fiona held the canoe against the bank as Wolf Shadow moved to the center of the boat and began to rub her arms with the oil from the plants. "Uhhhg," she complained. "It smells awful."

He smiled. "Would you rather stink or scratch?" He knelt before her and sensually anointed her throat and the back of her neck.

Her skin tingled where he touched her. She tried to ignore his callused fingers as they stroked and massaged the warm oil onto her body. His hands cupped her chin, and he brought his face close to hers. Fiona leaned away from him, and the birchbark canoe threatened to tip. "No," she protested weakly, "don't do that."

His firm lips covered hers, and she felt the old,

familiar thrill race through her body. "I promised to take care of you," he whispered huskily. "Do you think I want to see you covered with mosquito bites?"

The tips of his fingers dipped beneath the neckline of her deerskin vest, making her breathless. "I don't want to . . ." She trailed off, not certain what it was she didn't want to do. She gulped and drew in a deep breath. Her chest felt as though the weight of the river was pressing on it. And wherever his fingers touched her, her skin began to burn. "Ohhh," she sighed. "Don't . . ."

His hands moved down to the first rawhide tie that held her vest together. Fiona felt her nipples pucker against the inside of the deerskin. Suddenly the vest seemed too tight.

"I know you're angry with me," he murmured.

"Very angry." It was hard to remember that she wanted to leave him when his warm tongue was tracing her bottom lip and his fingertips were touching the inward curves of her sensitive breasts.

"I'm sorry," he said. He took hold of the second tie, and the paddle slipped through her fingers. He reached out and caught it with his left hand, then lowered his head to nuzzle the dampness between her breasts.

Fiona was trembling. She opened her mouth to protest, to tell him no, to tell him he couldn't do this, but nothing came from her throat. Ribbons of sweet, hot flame spilled through her veins.

The third tie parted, and he pushed open her vest. His mouth found her nipple, and he slowly circled the areola with his tongue, then took her swollen bud gently between his teeth and suckled it until she moaned with pleasure. He began to stroke her other breast, rubbing the warm oil into her skin, teasing the nipple to a hard knot of yearning.

"You must stop," she whispered. "I can't. This . . . this is my woman's time. I'm bleeding."

"Shhh," he soothed. "There are many ways to love, my Irish Fiona. Let me share them with you."

Then, somehow, she was lying in the bottom of the canoe, and he was on top of her. His long, silken hair brushed her cheek as she arched against him, entwining her legs with his. Her hands moved over his body, stroking, caressing as she moved her hips against his, thrilling to the hard, hot length of him.

The canoe drifted into the current and floated slowly downstream, but neither of them noticed. Neither cared. For an hour they were lost in shared rapture, and the sweet, wild notes of the tangled green forest were their love song.

Chapter 18

Despite the overwhelming joy of that afternoon of bliss on the river, Fiona continued to struggle with her doubts for the remainder of the five-day journey back to Tuk-o-see-yah's camp. Should she leave Wolf Shadow or not? Would she be better off among her own kind—with Timothy O'Brian or someone like him? And if she did decide to leave the Shawnee, would Wolf Shadow let her go?

When they reached the village late one rainy afternoon, Wolf Shadow's sister was waiting for them with a desperate message.

"Moonfeather needs you to come to Wanishish-eyun at once," Willow explained. "Ross Campbell's Englishwoman is near giving birth. Moonfeather and Cami went to assist in the delivery, but Moonfeather's runner says the mother is bleeding. The peace woman fears this birth is beyond her skill and that both mother and babe may die. She wants you both."

"Will you come with me?" Wolf Shadow asked Fiona after he'd translated Willow's plea. "Anne Campbell is a good woman—a woman you should know."

Fiona spread her hands impatiently. "If she's in danger, why are we wasting time?" Her personal problems receded to the back of her mind. She was a physician, and she was needed. Nothing else mattered. "You know I never deny a patient," she continued fervently. "If I can help, I must go."

"You would be safer here," Wolf Shadow reminded her. "Roquette's threat is not an empty one."

"I'm going."

He nodded. "As you say, if you can help, you must go. We will take warriors with us, but there are many places where death may find us between here and Wanishish-eyun—Fort Campbell, as the English call it. We travel south by canoe, and forest lines the river on both banks."

"How far is it?" Fiona asked.

"As the eagle flies? As the wolf lopes? As the river takes us?" He shrugged. "Two days maybe? Who can tell?"

"That far? Then we may be too late already."

"Messenger come when sun is high," Willow said in her softly accented English.

Fiona glanced at Wolf Shadow. "They sent a runner? Why would they," she asked, "if we can travel the river?"

"The river current will carry us south," he explained. "There are rapids and a waterfall to go around. We can move much faster than someone coming north."

"I come," Willow said firmly. "My husband, Niipan, he come. If Ross Campbell's woman dies, the peace woman will need me. I be of her family now."

"It might be better if you stayed in the village," Wolf Shadow said to his sister. Draping an arm around her shoulder, he took her aside and told her about Matiassu's visit and the bounty the Frenchman had placed on their heads. "You're newly married," he concluded. "You and Niipan should be taking joy in each other, not placing yourselves in jeopardy for my sake.''

Willow smiled up at him and touched his cheek with a fingertip. ''When have you ever done anything but lead me into trouble, little brother?'' she teased in their own tongue. ''The day I stay at home and hide under my rug for a dog like Matiassu is the day you'll see the sun come up in the west.'' She turned to Fiona and squeezed her hand. ''The sight of your . . .'' She struggled for the right English word. ''Your face make my heart smile. I have happy to see you, my sister.''

Fiona smiled back. ''And you, Willow. I'm glad to see you too.''

Niipan and Amookas—Fiona's adopted mother—joined them on the village dance ground. Amookas greeted Fiona with warm cries of welcome and hugged her soundly. Despite Fiona's embarrassment at such an emotional display, it gave her a good feeling, and she returned the embrace. Niipan merely nodded. By Shawnee custom, Fiona supposed she should consider the light-skinned brave some sort of brother. But Niipan wasn't looking at her in a brotherly fashion; his sloe eyes were as suspicious as Willow's had been when they'd first met.

''My mother comes also,'' Niipan said to Willow, ''and my father will not let her go without him.''

Fiona knew Amookas's husband was a white man, a one-legged Scot who lived with the Shawnee. She'd seen Alexander Mackenzie from a distance, but she'd never spoken to him.

Alex limped toward them now on his handmade crutch, a musket slung over his shoulder and two flintlock pistols stuck under his belt. He was a gnarled figure in a faded kilt and ragged Scots bonnet, and he looked to Fiona as stiff and tough as old leather.

''Aye, I'll go along wi' ye, shaman,'' Alex rasped.

"I'm nay much help on the trail, but put me in a canoe and I can fight like the devil himself."

Alex's Highland burr was so thick that *devil* sounded like *div-al* to Fiona, and she could hardly understand half of what he said. "Damned if a mon won't get auld sittin' aroond, gettin' fat as an auld squaw."

"We'll be glad to have you along," Wolf Shadow said.

"So." Alex peered into Fiona's face. "This be the lassie what's caused all the fuss. She's bonny enough, I'll gi' ye that, shaman."

Fiona mumbled what she hoped was an appropriate greeting and tried not to stare. She was frankly curious about the man who'd acted as a foster father to Moonfeather in her childhood. Wolf Shadow had told her that Alex Mackenzie was an educated man who'd taught her sister mathematics, French, and philosophy. Looking at Alexander Mackenzie, it was hard to imagine that he'd ever studied in Rome and traveled with British armies throughout Europe, as Wolf Shadow had related.

"Alex and your father were friends," Wolf Shadow had explained one evening a few weeks earlier. "They came to our land together many years ago. After Alex lost his leg in a battle, he decided to remain here in America with Amookas and his half-Indian sons. He knew he couldn't take his family back to Scotland, and he was happy here among the Shawnee. Cameron Stewart went back to Europe, but Alex stayed. Moonfeather learned much of the English world from what he taught her."

Had Alex ever regretted not returning to Europe? Fiona wondered. He didn't look like the sort of man who'd welcome personal questions—even from his wife's newly adopted daughter. But it was clear from the looks he and Amookas exchanged that the couple still deeply cared about each other.

He-Who-Runs, Yellow Elk, and Two Crows joined the group along with other Shawnee braves from Tuk-o-see-yah's village. Wolf Shadow decided that they would take six long canoes. The lead canoe and the last one would carry only heavily armed warriors. "We may still be attacked," he said, "but if we are, we'll be able to defend ourselves."

Wolf Shadow took Fiona in his canoe. Yellow Elk knelt directly in front of her with his musket cocked and ready to fire. Two fierce-looking Shawnee braves paddled, warriors so scarred and menacing that Fiona was afraid of them, even though she knew they were there to protect her.

The first leg of the journey was made without incident. The canoes sped along the river faster than Fiona would have thought possible. They continued on through the night and into the following day, stopping only once so that they could all tend to their personal needs. The only other people they passed were a young Delaware brave and his wife coming upstream on their honeymoon journey. Except for that, the river was serene and beautiful, a joy to see.

It was early morning when they reached the head of the falls and had to portage the canoes overland. Here, the Shawnee doubled their vigilance. Scouting parties searched the woods before the women left the boats. And, as they followed the descending path toward the winding river below the cascade, everyone maintained a tense silence.

At the end of the trail as the canoes were being lowered into the water, they were ambushed. Niipan was helping Yellow Elk slide a canoe over the edge of the sandy bank when a shot rang out from the far side of the river. One of the men who had paddled Fiona's canoe slumped forward and fell to his knees, a red stain spreading across his back.

The single shot was followed instantly by a barrage of musket fire. War cries echoed over the river as Wolf Shadow grabbed Fiona and shoved her face down behind a rock. He dropped to one knee, raised his musket, and took aim at a painted figure across the water. Fiona tried to lift her head, but he pushed her back down and pinned her there. His musket roared, nearly deafening her, but not so much that she didn't hear a man's agonized cry of pain immediately after the explosion.

Quickly Wolf Shadow began to load powder and shot to fire again. From her prone position, Fiona could see the Scotsman, Alex Mackenzie, half hidden behind a tree, firing one pistol after another as Amookas reloaded for him.

Suddenly Willow screamed a warning. Wolf Shadow whirled toward his sister, and Fiona scrambled up to see what had happened.

A whooping savage rose from behind the rocks at the base of the falls, drew back a bow, and aimed it at Wolf Shadow. In the split second between the time Fiona saw the man and the time he released the arrow, she recognized the face behind the Seneca warpaint. Matiassu! The arrow sprang from the bow as Wolf Shadow rammed his musket ball home and raised the gun to fire.

"No!" Willow shouted. As Fiona watched, Willow threw herself in front of her brother. Wolf Shadow's gun went off, his aim destroyed by the force of Willow's body. He caught his sister as a feathered shaft seemed to materialize in the center of her breast. Fiona heard her sigh as Wolf Shadow gathered her in his arms, and then her head fell back and she went limp.

He opened his mouth and uttered an inhuman howl of grief and anger, then lowered Willow's body to the ground, drew his knife, and plunged into the river.

Matiassu turned and ran, leaping from boulder to

boulder in his haste to reach the far side of the river. Mackenzie fired twice at Matiassu's retreating figure, but both shots missed.

Yellow Elk and Niipan charged after Wolf Shadow, seizing him and dragging him down into the shallows as the other men in their party kept up a steady hail of shot. Wolf Shadow struggled against his friends, throwing Yellow Elk off. The shaman had gotten to his feet again when Two Crows leaped into the fray and held him until Yellow Elk could wrest his knife away from him.

Fiona could understand only bits of what Wolf Shadow's comrades were saying, but it was plain to her that they thought chasing Matiassu across the river was nothing less than suicide.

As firing from the enemy became sporadic, Fiona ran to Willow's side and knelt beside her. Any notion she might have had of administering aid was dispelled when she saw the extent of Willow's wound, and realized she was dead. The arrow had pierced her heart and then continued all the way through her body. The ground around her was soaked with blood, and her face was pale and still. Weeping, Fiona closed her sister-in-law's eyelids and held her hand.

Yellow Elk and Two Crows forced Wolf Shadow back to the shore. Niipan was openly weeping as he picked up his bride and cradled her against him. Alexander Mackenzie fired a last volley and stepped out of his hiding place. "Little Hoof has a graze on his arm, and Afraid of Bears is dead. If I count right, we've nay more casualties but the puir lass."

Amookas began to wail a Shawnee death chant, a long, drawn-out keening that raised the hair on the back of Fiona's arms. Leaving Two Crows with Wolf Shadow, Yellow Elk assembled the warriors and sent three to retrieve a canoe that had drifted downstream.

Wolf Shadow's face might have been carved from granite. Fiona's stomach turned over as she gazed at him. The husband she loved—the man who'd howled with grief at the death of his sister—had vanished, leaving only a savage Indian shaman with eyes that were cold and heartless.

Fiona reached out to take his hand, then shivered and pulled back. "Wolf Shadow," she murmured.

At first he didn't seem to hear, then slowly he glanced down at her. "Fiona? You're all right?" His voice was so low she could barely understand him.

"I'm fine."

"I should have killed him before," he continued in Algonquian. "I let Matiassu live, and my sister has paid the price."

She clasped his fingers; they were cool and damp, as motionless as Willow's hand. She didn't speak— there was nothing more to say—but hot tears rolled down her face.

"There are three dead Seneca on the far bank, and a man I used to know from Seeg-o-nah's camp," Yellow Elk said gruffly. "Do you want me to take Two Crows and Niipan and go after them?"

"No." Wolf Shadow scanned the opposite shore with narrowed eyes. "We will give Niipan's wife back to the earth, then take the women on to Wanishish-eyun. When they are safe with Campbell, we will go together and find Matiassu. And this time, I will feed his bones to the wolves and cast his soul into a marsh so black that he will never see the sun again."

They reached Fort Campbell—the land the Shawnee called Wanishish-eyun, Thou Art Fair—that evening. Ross Campbell's father, Angus, had built a walled trading post here on the river nearly fifty years before. Angus Campbell, who had inherited the Scottish title Earl of Strathmar shortly before his death, had married a Delaware Indian woman and purchased fifty thousand acres from the tribes. His only legitimate son, Ross Campbell, was now the earl. Although Ross had come into a fortune when he'd married Lady Anne Scarbrough, an English heiress, he continued to make his home at Wanishish-eyun.

Ross Campbell was waiting for them when the canoes touched the sandy shore. He was a dark-haired giant of a man who clearly showed his Indian heritage. The strain of concern for his wife's condition and sleepless nights lay heavy across his handsome features. "I'm glad you're here," he said, extending a hand to Wolf Shadow. "Moonfeather's with her now, but it's not good." He glanced back at a boy holding two horses and lowered his tone. "She says the babe's crossways." His strong voice carried a Scots burr, softened by the flavor of Algonquian speech.

Wolf Shadow plucked Fiona from the canoe and set her down on the bank. "This is my wife," he said. "Moonfeather's sister."

One of Ross's dark brows rose quizzically. Wolf Shadow shot him a meaningful glance. "You're doubly welcome then. Stewart is here. He's back at the house with Anne."

It was Fiona's turn to look puzzled. "Cameron Stewart?" She wondered why he was here at Fort Campbell.

Wolf Shadow motioned toward his companions. "We were attacked on the river by Matiassu and his Seneca dogs." A muscle twitched along his jawline. "We buried my sister just south of the falls."

"You're sure it was Matiassu?" Ross asked. When Wolf Shadow nodded, the tall half-breed swore softly "Damn him to a fiery hell."

"He got away."

"Again. If any man has signed a pact with the

devil, it's Matiassu," Ross said. "He was a good man once. I used to hunt with him when we were boys."

"All boys do not grow into the same sort of men."

"I'm sorry for your loss," Ross said. "I met your sister. She was a good woman. If there is anything I can do . . ."

"Matiassu will pay for his deeds," Wolf Shadow promised.

"I'll send out extra sentries. We've had no attacks on Wanishish-eyun in years, but with Matiassu on the warpath, we'd best take no chances."

"First we will see to your wife," Wolf Shadow said.

"Aye." Ross sighed. "We'd best hurry back to the house." He motioned to the child to bring the horses. "This is our son, Royal."

Fiona smiled at the little boy. Royal Campbell was as comely as a girl, with great dark eyes and a mop of coal-black hair. He wore doeskin breeches and a fringed, open vest; his skin was tanned as brown as an Indian's.

Royal flashed her a shy grin.

When this boyo's grown, his father will have to beat off the colleens with a stick, Fiona thought. She tried to guess his age. Eight? He was still a child; his eyes were full of sweet innocence. She wanted to ask if he was Anne's son. If he was, that meant she'd already delivered one live child, which greatly improved their chances of delivering another. "How old are you?" she asked him.

Ross took the reins of the bay gelding. "He's six. Royal's big for his age. We've a wee bairn of three that favors Anne more than this one." Ross swung up into the gelding's saddle and pulled his son up behind him. Wolf Shadow and Fiona mounted the second horse. Fiona sat in front of Wolf Shadow and balanced her surgical kit on her lap.

The trading post, the stables, and the outbuildings lay some distance from Heatherfield, the stone manor house where Anne and Ross lived. Pausing only briefly to give instructions to his employees to be on their guard and to give Wolf Shadow's companions whatever they needed, Ross led the way down the valley toward the house. Amookas and Alex Mackenzie remained at Fort Campbell with the others.

When the four reached the front gate at Heatherfield, an English servant carrying a lantern ran out to take the horses. Even in the dark, Fiona could see that Ross Campbell's home was magnificent. Possessing five bays and gable-ends, the plastered and whitewashed stone house rose two and a half stories from the neatly manicured lawn. The massive front door was studded with iron nails, and the twelve-pane windows boasted real glass, and inner and outer shutters.

A middle-aged woman in a starched mobcap and apron opened the front door. "Thank God ye're here, m'lord. Lady Anne's callin' fer ye. Puir lass, she's sufferin' mair then most."

"Aye." Ross pushed the boy toward her. "Go wi' Greer now, there's a good laddie." His voice was near to cracking. "Put him to bed in your room, will ye?"

"Might as well; the little'un's there already." She tousled Royal's hair. "Would ye like a cake before ye go to sleep, now?"

"I want to see my mama."

"In the morning. You'll see her then." Still soothing the child, the housekeeper led him away toward the back of the house.

Fiona glanced around the marble-floored center hall. Heavy-framed oil paintings hung along the walls. Several doors lined the hall, all closed now. Beneath the largest portrait stood a mahogany hunt table flanked by two elegant chairs. Real Turkish carpets were scattered over the floor, and she could see a tall case clock on the stair landing.

Ross Campbell must be a wealthy man to afford such splendor, Fiona mused. She wondered why he had chosen to remain in the wilderness—far from any white settlement—and why he acted and sounded more like a frontier trapper than a great lord. And she also wondered why such a powerful man hadn't brought a real physician to see to his wife's delivery.

Almost as though he'd read her mind, Ross answered her last question. "We had a Virginia doctor here last week," he said, "but Moonfeather sent him packing. He tried to examine Anne with dirty hands, and he wanted to give her laudanum for her pains."

As they started up the wide staircase, Cameron Stewart appeared at the top. His eyes met Fiona's, and he halted. Fiona was shocked by his appearance; the nobleman seemed to have aged ten years in the weeks since she'd last seen him.

"Fiona," he said.

"I didn't think to meet you here," she managed. Ross and Wolf Shadow exchanged glances again, and Fiona looked back at Cameron. "Are you a friend of the lady?" she asked stiffly. She felt Wolf Shadow's eyes on her. Uneasily, she shifted her feet on the stairs.

"You might say that," Cameron answered. "Please, hurry." He stepped back. Fiona noticed that his eyes were red and puffy, as though he'd been crying.

Ross continued on, reaching out to touch Cameron's sleeve in sympathy as they passed him. Fiona and Wolf Shadow followed close behind. It was all she could do not to turn and stare at her father again.

The mystery of Cameron's odd behavior vanished from her mind as soon as Fiona entered the master bedchamber. Moonfeather looked up from her patient and gave an audible sigh of relief.

"You're here." She motioned for them to approach the tall poster bed.

Anne Campbell lay back against the pillows with a face as pale as tallow. She wore a lacy pink linen gown buttoned up to her neck with tiny pearl buttons. Her delicate face was contorted with pain, and it looked to Fiona as if someone had rubbed black smudges of charcoal beneath both eyes. Her lips bore traces of teeth marks and blood where she had bitten through the skin. Lady Anne managed a weak smile and tried to sit up. "Welcome, shaman," she rasped between cracked lips. "Welcome to Heatherfield, both of you. I wish your visit were a happier occasion. I'm afraid I . . ."

"Shhh," Moonfeather chided. "Save your strength."

Fiona's eye was drawn to the patient's swollen belly beneath the linen sheet. As she watched, a faint movement stirred the covering.

Anne gasped and clasped her stomach. She stroked the mound with loving fingers. "Still alive," she whispered. Tears welled up in her eyes. "Promise me you'll save the baby," she said. "Save my baby, no matter what happens to me."

"Nay." Ross went to his wife's side and knelt beside the bed. He took her translucent hand in his and kissed her tenderly on the lips. "Nay," he repeated. His deep voice cracked with emotion. "Save my bonny Anne. We have two children already, but there is only one Anne."

Moonfeather came to Fiona's side. "If you've Irish magic is that bag of yours, we'll need it, sister. I've done all I can for her, and it's not enough."

"We must wash and purify ourselves," Wolf Shadow said quietly. "I'll want to examine her myself. Will she allow—"

"Anne cares more for her child's life than for false modesty," Moonfeather answered. She broke off as Royal's voice came loudly from the hall.

"I don't care. I want to see her. I want to see my mama!"

"Not now," Cameron said. "Your mama's tired."

"Mama!"

"Bring him in," Anne whispered. "I want to see him."

Moonfeather went to the door and returned a moment later with Cameron, who was carrying the boy in his arms. Royal squirmed to get down, and Cameron released him. He ran to his mother, then grew shy. His lower lip quivered, and his brown eyes dilated until they seemed to fill his face, but he didn't cry.

Anne hugged him against her with more strength than Fiona would have thought the slender Englishwoman could possibly possess.

"I don't want you to die. Don't die, Mama. I'll be good, I promise. I won't bring my raccoon into the parlor anymore, and I'll be nice to my brother. I promise."

"Give your lady mother a kiss," Ross said, "and then it's off to bed with you."

Fiona saw Anne's belly tense, and she knew that another birth pain was seizing her. But Anne didn't cry out. She set her teeth together and forced a wan smile as Ross gathered the boy in his arms.

"No . . . wait." Lady Anne's breath was coming in short, hard pants. "I want you to have this, darling." She fumbled at the back of her neck and unfastened a golden chain. Dangling from it was a glittering amulet exactly like Fiona's. Her heart began to pound harder. "You must . . . you must give it . . . to your first girl-child, Royal. It's a magic neck—Ohhh." She clenched her eyes shut, and Ross pushed the necklace into the child's hand and nudged him swiftly toward the door.

"But I want to stay here with my mama," Royal insisted. "She won't die if I stay with her."

Cameron took the protesting boy from Ross and hurried from the room. Anne arched her body and moaned softly as sweat broke out on her forehead.

"I don't understand," Fiona said.

" 'Tis simple enough," Moonfeather replied.

"Cameron Stewart is Royal's grandfather. He's my father, and yours, and Anne's. Anne is our sister, Fiona, the English one whose name ye didna wish to know." She looked back to the bed where Anne writhed in agony. "She is our sister, and she needs us. Will you help her?"

Chapter 19

⌒◯◯⌒

An hour later, Fiona stepped away from Anne's
bed and looked up at Wolf Shadow. Acute disappointment filled her green eyes. "I can't do it,"
she said. "I can't turn the baby." Moonfeather
brought her a bowl of water, and she washed the
blood and birth fluid from her hands.

Wolf Shadow leaned over Anne and held his fingertips over her lips. Her eyes were closed, and she
appeared to be sleeping peacefully. He'd given her
a strong potion of powdered moccasin flower and
painted trillium. She was exhausted, her life spirit
clinging to earth by a spiderweb. He'd known when
he'd first looked at her what they would have to do,
but he'd allowed Fiona to try her skill first.

He regarded his wife with pride. Fiona was bright
and she learned quickly, but most of all she cared
about her patients. She would be great medicine
woman. Her white skin meant nothing; the Shawnee would sing of her and weave legends of her
magic for their children's children. He sighed. If
there were any children's children . . .

If he couldn't persuade his people to join together
against the flood of Europeans, there might not be
a future for the Shawnee. He wondered if he was
taking too much risk in keeping Fiona as his wife.

Hadn't he been the one who'd told the Shawnee and Delaware to reject all things belonging to the white race?

Inwardly, he smiled. Shaman . . . moon dancer. After his long years of training—after his exile in England—he was just a man like other men. A man who'd lost his heart to a slim, red-haired woman. His love for her was so great that it threatened to drive all else from his mind. To his shame, even when his sister lay dying in his arms, he'd been glad that it wasn't Fiona.

Willow. His beloved sister. He could speak her name silently, if he could not say it aloud. Her death had cost him part of his own soul, and he'd not rest until she was avenged. Later he would offer prayers for her spirit; he would sing the songs of transition and cut his body to honor her life. He would mourn her passing deeply and sincerely for the rest of his days. He would never, never forget her or the sacrifice she had made for him.

But as a shaman, he knew that the living must come first. His personal mourning could wait. Fiona's sister, Anne, would not live if they didn't take action at once. And even then, they might lose her and the babe.

So, first, before he hunted Matiassu to his death, he must use his power as a healer.

"Wolf Shadow," Fiona said, interrupting his reverie.

He blinked and focused on her face, yanked back into an awareness of where he was by the urgency in her voice.

"The bleeding is becoming worse. If we don't act quickly, the baby will die," she said.

"You know what we must do," he answered.

"I know," Fiona agreed, "but I'm afraid."

He gave her a half smile. "Courage is never the

lack of fear. Courage is doing what must be done in spite of it.''

He glanced at Moonfeather. ''Lay blankets on the floor and cover them with linen.'' Without waiting to see that she obeyed, he picked up Anne and carried her to the center of the room. ''We will need more lamps, as many as you can find.'' If it were daylight, he would have taken Anne outside, but it was night, and they couldn't wait until morning.

Fiona pulled a corner of the linen sheet taut. ''Wouldn't a table be better? I saw one downstairs in the hall. We could carry it up here.''

He frowned. ''A shaman does much of his healing on his knees so that the earth can give strength to the patient.''

Fiona's green eyes dilated with apprehension. ''Have you ever done this before?'' she asked him.

''Twice.'' Once, the mother had died and he'd saved the child. The second time, he'd not been able to save the baby either. ''Have you?'' he demanded.

''I've seen my grandfather perform cesarean sections. I helped him stitch a woman up, but I didn't do the actual surgery.''

Fiona was pale but calm. She'd scrubbed her hands until they were raw and washed her entire body, as Wolf Shadow had insisted. Both Fiona and Moonfeather were wearing Anne's clean linen shifts. Moonfeather had passed Fiona's surgical instruments through fire.

''I'll do the cutting,'' he said. ''I've not used your clamps, but you know how they should be placed.''

Fiona knelt beside her sleeping sister and laid a hand on her forehead. ''If we do it here on the floor, how will you tie her down?''

Moonfeather looked horrified. ''Nay, we willna bind her. Anne will sleep as she does now.''

It was Fiona's turn to recoil. ''My grandfather was

trained in surgery at the finest university. His patients were always awake."

"She has had enough pain," Wolf Shadow said.
"Would you give her more?"

"To save her life, yes," Fiona replied. She lifted
Anne's wrist and checked her pulse. "Her blood
flow is very slow. She may be dying already."

Wolf Shadow shook his head. "No, it is better this
way. She will lose less blood when I cut. The medicine makes her pulse slow." He laid his head
against her chest and was relieved to hear the strong,
steady beat of Anne's heart. He looked at Moonfeather. "Bring your father. Tell him to purify himself with water and prayer. He can hold the light for
us, and if your sister crosses over the river of no
return, he can hold the newborn child and keep its
soul from following."

"Cameron?" Fiona said. "I don't want him here.
We don't need him."

"Anne needs him, and perhaps his grandchild will
too," Wolf Shadow answered.

"No. Why not Ross Campbell, if you must have
someone else? Or Amookas?"

"This is no place for a husband. In his fear for her
life, he might do something that would cause great
harm. Amookas is at the trading post. Cameron is
her father. He understands what we are doing, and
he will not flinch from whatever comes. I say he
must be here."

Fiona bit back an angry reply. "I thought you
didn't trust Englishmen," she said.

"Cameron was always an exception."

"And me? Am I an exception?" she demanded.

"Since I've met you, I've changed many of my
ideas," he answered smoothly. "Moonfeather? If
you will call Cameron . . ." He closed his eyes and
uttered a prayer that his hand might be steady and
Anne's spirit strong. He was certain he could save

the child if he cut at once, but whether Anne would survive the ordeal was up to Inu-msi-ila-fe-wanu.

A few minutes later, with Moonfeather and Cameron watching, and Fiona close by his side, Wolf Shadow placed his palm on Anne's swollen belly and made a deft incision in her pale flesh.

He heard Fiona gasp as blood spilled over and stained the linen sheets. Again he cut, slicing the steel scalpel through muscle and tissue. Anne stirred, but her eyes remained closed, and she made no outcry. Carefully, Wolf Shadow widened the slit. "Now," he ordered Fiona. "Reach in and take the child."

She didn't hesitate. Her small hands plunged into the bloody opening nearly to her elbows. "I have an arm," she murmured. "Wait . . . there's . . ."

Sweat beaded his forehead, and time seemed to slow. Anne's lifeblood was seeping through his fingers.

"I have him," Fiona cried. "Cautiously, inch by inch, she drew forth the feet and legs of a perfectly formed male infant. "Ohhh, come on now, boyo," she murmured. She slipped one shoulder loose and then the head, and lifted him free from his mother. Cradling him in the crook of her arm, Fiona scooped his mouth free of matter, then tilted him upside down to clear his nose and throat.

The baby sneezed and let out a yell that would have done justice to a Seneca. His sturdy arms and legs flailing, he opened his eyes and began to howl. Quickly Moonfeather tied two knots in the infant's cord and cut it.

"Give him to Cameron," Wolf Shadow commanded Fiona. "I need you here, now."

She handed the baby to her father. For an instant their hands touched, and Wolf Shadow saw mutual caring leap across the chasm between them.

"Now," he said. "Clamp this."

Fiona pinched off a bleeding vessel and found a needle and thread. "Shall I stitch or you?" she asked. Her face glowed with the wonder of birth. One curling red strand had come loose from her braid and hung over her forehead. "I can do it. My sewing is neater than yours."

He nodded, and she began to close up the incision. It was slow, tedious, bloody work, but by the time she'd reached the second layer, he could feel Anne's breathing becoming stronger. If infection didn't set in, they would save both mother and child—he knew it.

Fiona pursed her lips and concentrated on each tiny stitch. Moisture glistened in the hollow of her throat above her amulet, and he had the strangest desire to lick it off.

He glanced over at Cameron. He'd swaddled the babe in clean, soft wrapping and was rocking him as gently as any woman. Cameron's cheeks were wet with tears, but his eyes sparkled. He was a good man, Wolf Shadow mused, no matter what he'd done in his life. He was a loving father and grandfather, and he'd be a good father to Fiona as well, if she'd give him half a chance.

"You're not bad at this," Wolf Shadow teased her. With the help of Inu-msi-ila-fe-wanu, they had snatched life from the Dark Warrior. He felt the shaman power surging up in him, and he wanted to dance and sing out his exaltation to the stars.

He wanted to lie down with this magnificent woman of his and make hot, passionate love to her.

Fiona raised her head and looked at the baby. Stewart grinned. "He's strong," he said. "I thought he'd be weak after all he's been through."

"It's his English blood," Fiona said. "The Sassenach are a stubborn lot; they don't give up easily."

"Neither do the Irish," Cameron said. "Thank you, Fiona, thank you both. They'd have died if you

hadn't . . ." His voice broke. He blinked back tears
and gently kissed the baby's head. "I guess it's time
that I took this young fellow out to meet his papa."

"Just another few minutes," Fiona said. "Let me
finish this, and we'll get Anne cleaned up, then he
can come in and see them both." She glanced at
Anne's serene face. "Still asleep. If I hadn't seen it,
I wouldn't have believed it."

"Then you and I will go and wash," Wolf Shadow
said. "There's a stream a few hundred yards behind
the house."

"In a stream?" She straightened up and eased the
tension on her back and neck. "I guess so, if you
think Anne will be all right."

"I'll stay wi' her," Moonfeather said. "She'll
sleep for hours, and when she wakes I'll give her
more of the medicine mixed with honey and tea.
She will be in pain for many days, and it's better for
her if she sleeps."

"Leave her here on the floor," Wolf Shadow ordered Cameron. "She's not to be moved for a day
and a night. I don't want her to lose a drop more of
blood than she needs to."

"Don't worry. Ross will do anything you say.
You've saved the woman he loves more than life
itself."

Wolf Shadow smiled. So, he thought, I'm not the
only one who feels this way. These three sisters have
a magic about them. They capture men's hearts and
make them believe that life without them would be
empty. He chuckled. And perhaps it would be. Perhaps it would . . .

The waxing moon was much lower in the night
sky when Wolf Shadow and Fiona finished washing
the last traces of blood and body fluids from their
hair and skin. Ross had directed them to a pool in
the bend of the wide stream that flowed several

hundred yards behind the manor house. The grateful Earl of Strathmar hadn't questioned why they wanted to wash in flowing water rather than in a scented bath attended by servants. He'd merely called a maid to bring them soap and thick towels, and then wished them enjoyment of his and Anne's private trysting spot.

Fiona was so weary that she waded into the pool still clad in Anne's linen shift. She dropped to her knees in the shallows and soaped and rinsed her hair until it gleamed like sleek otter fur in the moonlight. Wolf Shadow stripped himself naked and bathed from head to toe, but most of all, he watched her.

She was small and neat, as slender as a willow, with well-shaped breasts and buttocks, this wife of his. He never tired of looking at her fair skin. Tonight, in the moon's glow, that fair skin was as white as shell. Her glorious mane of hair, loosened from its thick braid, fell free nearly to her hips.

He held his breath and listened. There was no sound but the sighing of the trees and the laughing song of the stream as it hurried toward the mother river in the valley below. To the north, an owl hooted. Wolf Shadow, waiting for the answering call, mentally counted the space of time in his head. The sound came, and he smiled and relaxed. He'd brought his woman to this place of water and trees and star-strewn sky to be alone with her, but he was not so foolish as to risk her life by bringing her here without guards. Even now, two of his warriors prowled the forest, keeping watch for the enemy.

Fiona turned her head to look at him. Her large eyes were luminous in the moonlight. Desire pierced his chest and he moistened his lips. All his life he had watched almond-eyed women and thought them beautiful; now this fire-haired *equiwa* with eyes as round and liquid as a doe had driven all other women from his mind.

Warm eddies of water washed against his thighs, and he sank back into the pool, letting the buoyancy lift him as he stared up into the blue-black sky. The stars marched like endless campfires across the heavens, hanging so near to the earth that an arrow shot from a mighty hunter's bow must surely scatter the white-hot coals.

The water was warm and soothing, only slightly cooler than the muggy night air. His skin felt acutely sensitive, as though the space around him were charged with the same power that brought the fury of lightning bolts.

Fiona raised her arms above her head and shook the water from her hair. The motion drew her linen shift tight across her firm breasts. He could see the outline of her erect nipples beneath the thin cloth, and the sight sent a shudder of intense desire rippling through his body.

She smiled at him, a slow sensual smile that told him she felt the tension in the air as well.

"Come here, woman," he called to her. She laughed provocatively, and he felt his groin tighten. He swallowed hard. "I said, I want you here."

She thrust her breasts forward and cupped them with her hands. "I am a Shawnee woman," she teased, "a free woman. No man tells me when to come and go."

He stood up and waded toward her, but when he reached out to take her in his arms, Fiona spun and dove laughing into the deeper end of the pool. Instantly he plunged after her. He caught her ankle, but she twisted loose, turning and splashing water into his face. He dove on top of her, and they both went under in a tangle of intertwined arms and legs. She struggled against him, but it was no more than a pretense, and they both knew it. Still, the tussle thrilled him, heating his blood as he seized her and raised her high in the air over his head.

Still laughing, she slid down over his chest and wrapped her naked legs around his waist. Their lips met in a searing kiss of unleashed passion, and he crushed her against him so that her hot, wet opening pressed against his belly. The feel of her, the hot, sweet feel of her, made the blood pound like war drums in his ears.

"I don't think I'm tired anymore," she whispered. "I think I want more of those lessons you promised." Her fingers twined in his hair, and she opened her mouth to receive his seeking tongue. The musky woman smell of her was intoxicating. Sweat broke out on his skin as he thrust deep into her throat, tasting her . . . reveling in the exquisite sensation of her silken thighs writhing intimately against him. He held her against him, one hand cupped under a round buttock, the other roving down her thigh and up over her breasts.

Their kisses were like sparks on dry tinder. A fire leaped between them, caught the tinder, and flamed up. His stomach knotted with tension as he ran his fingers up the inside of her thigh to delve between her warm, wet folds.

"Make me hot tonight," she begged him. "I want to love you like I've never loved you."

His man-spear throbbed with engorged blood, and he longed to slide her lower and bury it beneath her russet triangle of damp curls . . . bury it deep and fill her with his hot, potent seed. "Fiona," he said, "Fiona."

She leaned her head back, exposing her creamy throat in the moonlight, and he shuddered with yearning. He nuzzled her breasts through the damp linen shift. She moaned with pleasure and tried to pull the neckline of her garment lower.

"Kiss my breasts," she urged. Her breathing was ragged. "Please. Suck them . . . suck them hard."

"N'wingandammen," he murmured hoarsely. "I like the taste of them. Like honey . . ." His nostrils flared as he took hold of the garment and ripped it down the center in one swift motion. She cried out with ecstasy as he buried his face between her warm breasts and sought her sweet, hard nipples with his lips.

His tongue flicked across her skin with tantalizing intimacy. His fingers stroked and caressed her secret places until the bittersweet anguish became a throbbing urgency. Never had she felt like this before. She squirmed against him, sinking her teeth into his heavily muscled arm and moaning deep in her throat.

She was consumed by the fire that raged between them. Her senses reeled. "Please . . ."

"I love you," he rasped. "I love you more than life."

"Now . . . now," she pleaded. "I can't . . . I can't . . ."

She inhaled sharply as she felt the swollen tip of his enormous, stiff shaft brush her quivering flesh.

"Is this what you want?" he whispered in her ear.

"Yes, yes," she cried. And then he guided her hips lower, and she felt him thrust deep inside her, filling her with his power, plunging deeper and deeper until she thought she could take no more.

"Ohhh." She gasped as he slipped back into the pool and she rode him into the warm, black water. He placed his strong hands on her hips and lifted her, then pulled her back until they were breast to breast and mouth to mouth. She laughed as she caught the rhythm, and she met him thrust for thrust.

Fiona felt her excitement building. She moved

faster and faster, and just as she neared her climax—
to her surprise—he pushed her away. "No," she
protested. "I haven't—"

He raised her up in the waist-deep water and
kissed away her doubts, then turned her so that she
faced away from him and taught her a new game.
He entered her with skillful ease while his hands
cupped her breasts and teased her nipples to aching
buds of desire.

Still, he held his rush of hot seed. He plunged
inside and withdrew while tremors of cold fire
rocked her body and soul. She cried out with joy as
she reached that elusive peak and was lost in the
warm, bright rapture.

Picking her up, he rained hot kisses over her face
and carried her to the bank. He laid her down on a
bed of moss and slowly began to make love to her
again.

I can't, she thought. I can't possibly . . . Not after . . . But the heat of his hard body permeated her
damp flesh, and his long, muscular fingers played
over her until she felt the tingling sensations of desire rising again. This time, when they joined . . .
when he filled her with his tumescent manhood,
they reached a mutual climax. And that moment of
supreme oneness was heightened for her by his
whispered words of love and the hot gush of his
seed within.

For a long time she lay in the circle of his arms,
sated by their lovemaking, utterly content. To her
surprise, Fiona felt no shame. Nothing as beautiful
as what they had just shared could be anything but
good, and right, and natural. In God's eyes, this
man was her husband. Never would she take another as mate. And if he died, she would be like the
wolf and live alone all the days of her life.

"You have taught me more than the joy between
a man and woman," she murmured, unconsciously

clasping her amulet between her fingers. "You've taught me—"

He placed his fingers over her lips. "No, my Irish Fiona, you have taught me. I was a moon dancer who knew the secrets of the spirits, but I did not know what happens in the hearts of men. You are the breath of my life, and without you, the sun would have no warmth and the moon no glory."

She giggled and nestled against his smooth, warm chest. "You look like a Shawnee, but you talk like an Irishman."

"I talk like a man who has lost his soul to a flame-haired witch." He rubbed a lock of her hair between his fingers. "What I say to you, I have never said to another woman."

"Or I to any man."

"*K'dahole, keega.* I love you." He kissed her with such slow tenderness that it brought tears to her eyes. "Now you," he instructed.

"*K'dahole, keeqa,*" she repeated solemnly. Her lips were swollen from the force of his kisses, and it was difficult to make them say the words right.

He laughed. "No. *Keeqa* is wife. You must say, *K'dahole, tshituune wai see yah.*"

She giggled. "Mighty husband?"

He nodded. "I am mighty, am I not? Who else could wield such a mighty spear?"

"Who else indeed?" she teased. "*K'dahole, tshituune wai see yah.*"

"We'll make a proper Shawnee squaw of you yet."

She sighed. "We'd best go back and see to Anne. I'm worried that she may bleed from the incision."

"Yes," he agreed, "we should." He kissed her again.

"What you did . . . the operation . . ."

"What *we* did," he corrected her.

"No surgeon could have done better. In Europe, you could make your fortune," she said.

"In Europe, I was a freak, a curiosity. The savage who walked on two feet and played cards like a gentleman." He inhaled deeply. "You must realize, my Fiona, that although I speak as you do, my heart, my mind, are Shawnee. It will ever be so. I was born with the ability to learn a foreign tongue, but I will never be civilized. I will never again live in a wooden house with square corners, ride in a gilded coach, or worship in an English church. I am Wolf Shadow, servant of my people. If you want to stay with me . . . if you want to be my wife forever—you must know these things. I will never change."

A single tear spilled down her pale cheek. He leaned close and caught it on the tip of his tongue. "I must change then," she whispered, "for if it means my immortal soul—if I am damned to hell for loving you—I must be damned. I will never leave you again—not for any man or church, or for all the gold my father possesses."

"Then from this night on, our marriage truly begins."

"Yes," she agreed sleepily, "from this night on."

He sat up and took both her hands in his. "There is a custom among the Shawnee—"

"No more honey."

He laughed. "None tonight, anyway. Although, I do believe you need practice in the ceremony. No, this is different—serious."

"What?" She was fully awake now.

"On a night such as this when a man and woman join and exchange vows, each may ask of the other one favor. By tradition, that desire must be granted if it is humanly possible."

She looked up at him in complete trust. "Anything. What do you want of me, Wolf Shadow? Whatever you ask, I will do." She had risked her immortal soul for him; anything else he asked would be less.

He gripped her fingers tighter. "You must forgive your father. Make peace with Cameron and lift the stone from your own heart."

"Him!" Angrily, she jerked away and scrambled to her feet. "Why does it have to be him? You'd think he was your father, not mine."

Wolf Shadow didn't move. He waited patiently, infuriatingly, knowing that she had given her word.

"You tricked me," she accused.

"You promised."

"I promised what was humanly possible. That isn't. He abandoned my mother." How harsh that sounded, even to her own ears. What if Cameron Stewart *had* tried to find them, as he claimed? What if he had told the truth and her grandfather had lied all those years ago? James Patrick O'Neal had despised with a pure, white hate the man who had ruined his only daughter. Grandfather could have lied to her . . . lied to cover his own shame. "I . . . I don't know if I can," she finished.

"I didn't ask that you love Cameron, only that you cease to hate him. And that you don't let that old hurt keep you and your sisters apart."

It was bitter medicine. Fiona grimaced as she wrapped a large towel around her waist and covered her bare breasts with what was left of Anne's shift. "Do I get to ask a favor?"

He grinned. "You do."

Fiona thought for a moment. "All right. You mean to kill Matiassu, don't you?"

"Don't ask me not to," he warned. "Matiassu is a dead man already. I cannot spare him, not even for you."

"No, I won't ask that. But I do ask that you not . . . not cut off his scalp." She shuddered. "No mutilation. If you must kill him, do it cleanly. You said you owed him a favor for warning us."

Wolf Shadow rose and walked into the darkness. For a long time he was silent, then he spoke. "It shall be as you say, Fiona. I will not take his scalp. For you, and for what is between us this night. I give it to you as a gift."

"Thank you. I know what it means to you."

"No," he answered. "You don't. You will never know what it cost me." He reached out his hand. "Come, it is time we—"

A man's agonized cry rent the still night. Wolf Shadow grabbed her up in his arms and began to run toward the house. Before they had gone two strides, a Seneca brave shrieked a war whoop close behind them.

Chapter 20

As Wolf Shadow whirled with Fiona in his arms to face their attacker, a pistol shot shattered the air. The painted Seneca staggered into the clearing and fell, facedown, on the ground.

"Fiona?" Cameron appeared at the edge of the trees with a Seneca arrow protruding from his upper thigh, a smoking pistol gripped tightly in his right hand.

"Here," she replied. "We're here."

"Back to the house," her father ordered. "A French and Indian war party landed near Fort Campbell, and they're headed this way. One of your Shawnee just brought word."

Wolf Shadow lowered Fiona to the ground and approached the prone warrior. He rolled him onto his back and felt for a pulse at the side of his throat. "Thanks to you, this Seneca will give us no more trouble," he said as he stripped the dead man of his weapons.

Cameron leaned against a tree for support. Blood was seeping through his breeches and running down his leg in a dark stream. Despite his obvious pain, he began to reload his pistol with powder and shot.

"You're wounded." Forgetting her disheveled state of undress, Fiona knelt to examine his injury.

Cameron shook his head. He was breathing heavily, and his face was white in the moonlight. "Leave it be," he said harshly.

"Can you make it back to the house?" Wolf Shadow asked.

"Yes, but there's not much time." He grimaced. "I killed another Seneca back by the wall. I think he was scouting for the main force. He's the one who gave me this." Cameron motioned to the shaft in his leg. "Fort Campbell's under attack. The French lugged a swivel gun downriver, but Alex Mackenzie blew it up with one ball from a light cannon mounted on the fort catwalk."

"Can Ross Campbell defend the house?"

"For a while. The fort's safer, but with the women to protect, we'd never break through the lines to get inside. It's the manor house or nothing. Ross's father built the fortified stone tower at the back to hold off a small army."

"We can't move Anne back to the fort," Fiona said. "It's too far. She'd bleed to death."

An owl hooted across the clearing. Wolf Shadow cupped his hands around his mouth and hooted back. Yellow Elk slipped from the woods as silently as a shadow.

"I've found the one you seek," he called in Algonquian. "Matiassu is here with his followers."

"Wait for me," Wolf Shadow ordered. "His last morning is about to dawn." He took Fiona's hand again. "Go with your father," he said calmly. "Tend to his wound, and see that Anne is kept still and quiet."

Fiona's heart was beating wildly. "You're not coming, are you? You're not coming with us." Her soft tone belied her wide-eyed terror.

"Take her," Wolf Shadow said to Cameron. "We'll cover your retreat until you're safely behind the walls."

"No," Fiona protested. "You can't stay out here. You have to—"

"Do as I say, woman."

Cameron handed Wolf Shadow his pistol and shot bag. "Here, you may need this more than I do."

The shaman slung the bag over his shoulder and stuck the pistol in his belt. For a moment, Fiona thought he might kiss her, but then he turned and followed Yellow Elk into the trees. Fiona hesitated for only a fraction of a second before she took Cameron's arm and supported part of his weight as they moved back toward the safety of the house. Her lips were moving in an unspoken prayer.

Minutes later, Wolf Shadow crouched beneath the sheltering boughs of a hemlock and watched as Matiassu moved cautiously through a small clearing. Dawn would break in another hour, and with the coming of the sun, Wolf Shadow was certain that Matiassu's combined Seneca and Shawnee forces would attack Ross Campbell's house.

Yellow Elk had reported that a battle was still waging at the fort while the renegade Shawnee, Matiassu, had brought his followers to surround the manor. Since the members of the Iroquois Nation rarely fought in darkness for fear of ghosts, Wolf Shadow wondered how the Frenchmen were controlling their Seneca allies.

Matiassu's warriors were not gathered together in rows like European soldiers; he had scattered them through the forest. Thus, although two score of hardened braves followed his eagle standard, Matiassu was alone here in the silent woods before sunrise.

This would not be the bright morning that the enemy hoped for; already heavy clouds shrouded the sky and a thick mist was settling over the forest floor. Wolf Shadow stared through the clinging fog at Matiassu's movement. He could no longer make out the man, but he could see his outline, dark against the trees, and he could hear the crunch of twigs under Matiassu's moccasins.

Taking a deep breath, the shaman cupped his hands around his mouth and uttered the hunting call of the gray wolf. The eerie cry echoed through the trees, and when the last note had died out, it was answered from the rise beyond Matiassu. But when that howl sounded, even Wolf Shadow himself could not say if the howl was a real wolf, a Shawnee, or a ghost.

Matiassu stiffened and quickened his pace.

Wolf Shadow smiled. His eyes narrowed, and he rose and took up the chase.

Cameron Stewart, Earl of Dunnkell, lay close to death. His skin was ashen, his breathing shallow. He was no longer conscious . . . no longer able to feel pain when Ross Campbell cut the Seneca arrow shaft in two and pushed the steel head through his thigh and out the back.

"We're losing him," Fiona said as she attempted to stanch the bleeding. "His heartbeat is becoming more erratic." She felt a raw pain deep inside her own body. This was more than the familiar physician's ache at losing a patient. Despite her attempt not to, she cared about Cameron Stewart, and she desperately wanted to save his life.

Wolf Shadow was right. Until she came to some sort of peace with her father, she'd never stop hurting, never be able to love and trust as a woman should. And if he died before they could come to an understanding, she would never be whole.

Cameron's strength had faded quicker than she could have imagined. He'd managed to walk the distance back to the house. He'd even made it partway up the inner stairs of the twenty-four-foot-square stone tower at the rear of Heatherfield before he'd collapsed and fallen into a coma.

Ross and a manservant had carried him to the second floor; the bottom floor of the battlemented tower had only a single iron door leading from the interior of the house and no windows. Triangular arrow slits in the thick stone walls let in a minimum of daylight on the second floor, and an iron grate could be secured across the narrow, winding stair. Furnishings were sparse, but this was the safest place for the women and children. The top floor was fitted out for defense, and it was there that the armed household men waited for the Indian attack to begin.

Moonfeather leaned over her father's head and kissed his cheek. Tears sparkled in her dark eyes, and her lovely features were contorted with sorrow. "He will die," she said. "Look at the arrowhead. No! Don't touch it, Fiona, it's poison."

"Poison? Are you certain?" Fiona asked. She tried to think clearly as her grandfather had taught her. Poison would account for Cameron's rapidly failing condition, but what kind of poison could act so quickly?

"Father's poisoned?" Anne lifted her head from her pillow and struggled to sit up. She and the infant were lying on a pallet on the far side of the single square room. A small sleeping boy of about three was curled up beside her, his thumb in his mouth. Fiona hadn't seen the older boy, Royal, since she'd returned. Moonfeather's daughter Cami, the housekeeper, and several female servants were also gathered in the room.

"You must lie still," Fiona warned Anne. "Your condition is still serious."

"My . . . father," Anne rasped.

"He's alive," Fiona said, putting pressure on Cameron's wound. "He's been hit by an arrow. We're

doing all we can for him. You must not excite yourself."

"He will die," Moonfeather repeated. "There is
no antidote for the Seneca poison. He will die before
the sun is fully up."

"No," Anne protested weakly. "Do . . . something. You must . . . must save him."

"Keep her still," Fiona ordered. "If she tears the
stitches, she'll bleed to death." Ross went to his
wife's side and took her in his arms.

"Father," she whispered. Her voice was strained;
she sounded like an old woman. "We're in the
tower. Where's Royal? Where's my son?"

Ross pushed her back on the pallet and leaned
over to whisper in her ear. The newborn woke and
began to wail. He picked up the babe and rocked it
against him with a tenderness Fiona had rarely seen
in so large a man.

"No," Anne whimpered. "No. You couldn't . . .
He's only a child."

"He's a Campbell," Ross answered. "Tusca's too
fast for anyone to catch him. The laddie will be safe,
never fear."

Anne began to weep softly.

Fiona looked at Moonfeather. "What is it? Where
is their son?"

Moonfeather's features grew taut. "When word
came that Fort Campbell had been attacked, Ross
put Royal up on his great black stallion Tusca and
sent him to the Delaware village for help. Ross's
mother was a Delaware. They will come."

"He sent that little boy out in the woods alone?"

"Our children are nay like your children, sister.
Royal knows the forest, and he knows the way to
his grandmother's village. If he got away before the
first scouts reached us, he'll be fine."

Fiona shook her head in disbelief. "But to send a
child—his own son . . . Why didn't Ross Campbell

go himself?'' Wolf Shadow was out there in the darkness too. Her fear for him made her light-headed. If only he'd come back to the house with her and Cameron instead of—

Moonfeather's answer cut through her musing with cold reality. ''If they attack, Ross will be needed here. Royal is too young to fight, but he can ride like a centaur.''

Fiona glanced at her sister in amazement. Where had a Shawnee woman learned about centaurs? she wondered. Then she felt a rush of blood to her face as Moonfeather's eyes revealed that she knew what Fiona was thinking.

''Alex Mackenzie educated me as though I were an earl's son,'' Moonfeather said. ''I learned Greek philosophy and the war games of Alexander before I was Cami's age. Ye ha' much to learn of me, sister.''

''It seems I do.''

Moonfeather laid a delicate, copper-hued hand on Fiona's arm. ''But we were not speaking of me—we were speaking of the war party that threatens us,'' she reminded in her soft Scottish accent. ''The Shawnee and the Delaware dinna make war on women, but the Seneca . . .'' She paused and pursed her lips as if she wondered how much to say. ''Seneca means 'eaters of men.' Before the white men came, even the Iroquois honored women. They never raped or tortured them. But now . . .'' She withdrew her hand and stared into Fiona's eyes. ''Now even my Cami would not be safe from their lust.''

Cameron moaned, and Fiona felt his forehead. His skin was clammy. The wound continued to leak dark blood despite her efforts to stanch the flow. ''There must be something we can do for your father,'' she said. ''Some Indian remedy . . .''

"For my father, Fiona? *Our* father," Moonfeather corrected.

Fiona threw open her surgeon's case and began to search through it. She could not remember what to do for poisoning. If only Wolf Shadow were here. He'd think of some antidote—she knew he would. She willed her hands not to tremble as she examined one container of medicine after another.

"Nay, not there," Moonfeather said.

Fiona looked up in confusion.

"Here." Moonfeather reached up and touched her amulet. "Your necklace, Fiona. The Eye of Mist."

Fiona clasped her necklace in her hand. Once again, the amulet was throbbing with that strange heat—so hot it almost scorched her fingers. She took a deep breath, wondering if she were dreaming or if this was really happening. "How? I don't . . ." She shook her head. "What are you talking about? Surely you don't believe that—"

Moonfeather grabbed Fiona's arms and shook her. "Aye. I do believe," she said fiercely. "The amulet has great power—the power to save him. Ye be the only one who can do it. My amulet has been used up—and so has Anne's. Only once can ye have a wish. If ye ha' never called upon the spirit of the Eye, ye can do it now."

A chill ran down Fiona's spine. "The legend," she whispered, and suddenly she heard her mother's voice. *One wish, my darlin' Fiona. Whatever ye desire . . . even unto the power of life and death . . .*

"Be ye a healer or be ye not?" Moonfeather demanded. "Forget your hate. He is your father. Can ye let him die without trying?"

Tears rolled down Fiona's cheeks, and she dashed them away with the back of her hand. "I don't know what to do," she admitted. "What do I do?"

"Ye maun say the words," Moonfeather urged.

"And . . . you . . . must believe," Anne gasped. "You must . . . believe . . ."

Fiona dropped to her knees beside Cameron and laid her gleaming gold amulet over his heart. "Please . . ." she whispered. "My wish is that this man will live."

At that instant, the first war whoop came from the woods surrounding the tower. There was a smattering of gunfire and the angry cries of men storming the house.

Matiassu was running. Branches lashed his face and clawed at his hair. His breath was coming in strangled gasps. He had never run away in his life, but he was running now. And close on his heels he could hear the slavering snarls of the ghost wolves . . . beasts larger and fiercer than any born of flesh and ,blood . . . ghost wolves with the eyes of haunted men.

The fog covered the ground at his feet; it sucked at his strength and blinded his eyes. His hearing was distorted, his mind confused. Was the howling behind him? In front of him? Should he turn left or right?

His foot sank into soft earth and he fell, sprawling. A jagged offshoot from a lightning-scarred stump dug a furrow in Matiassu's cheek, but he didn't feel the pain. He struggled up, fighting the tightness in his chest, and plunged through a green brier thicket. The thorns tore at his skin and tangled around his legs, but he didn't care. All that mattered was fleeing the fiends of darkness that pursued him.

He had lost all sense of direction. His weapons were gone, dropped somewhere in the fog. White-hot bands of steel crushed his chest; each breath was a torment. His ears rang with the echoes of the howling and the relentless pad of furred paws on the damp earth behind him.

The next time he fell, he could not muster the strength to rise. Weeping, he crawled on hands and knees into a small clearing. Here the fog was lifting, and he looked around, realizing with horror that he had come full circle. He was back at the spot where he'd heard the first wolf howl.

Exhausted, he fell flat, his face in the wet leaves. The forest around him was silent, so silent that not a single bird call broke the stillness. He pushed himself up on his hands and stared into the eyes of a massive wolf.

The fiery pain in Matiassu's chest became a molten ball of agony that radiated down his left arm.

Hackles rose along the gray wolf's back, and the beast's cold, black eyes seemed to grow larger and larger until the force of that inhuman gaze sucked the strangled breath from the war chief's throat.

Matiassu screamed once as the wolf bared ivory teeth, then the dying man pitched forward into a dark abyss, where the only sound was the wind rushing past his falling body.

Wolf Shadow knelt beside his enemy and rolled him onto his back. Matiassu's eyes were open wide, his mouth distorted in a silent shriek. "I did not touch you, brother," the shaman said. "Whatever weapon killed you came from your own quiver."

His fingers closed on the medicine bag that hung around the war chief's neck. With a twist of his wrist, he broke the rawhide tie and snatched it free. "You have no need of spirit magic where you're going," Wolf Shadow murmured, but then he remembered his own words to Fiona about hate. He placed the unopened medicine bag in Matiassu's left hand and squeezed it shut. "But on the chance that it will make you a wiser man in your next life, take it with you."

Then, leaving Matiassu's body where it lay, Wolf

Shadow turned away and began to run back toward Heatherfield and the sounds of gunfire.

Fiona wiped her father's forehead with a clean, wet cloth and tried not to flinch every time a musket fired over her head. She had no idea of how much time had passed since she had pleaded for Cameron's life. She only knew that bright sunshine filtered through the narrow window slits, and that he was still alive.

The terrible bleeding had stopped. It had slowed a little at a time, so that she couldn't be certain if her skill as a doctor or her wish had made the difference.

Cameron's eyes were closed. He was sleeping, but it was no longer the profound unconsciousness of a man slipping away from life; it was a deep, healing sleep. His breathing had become more regular. His heartbeat had slowed to normal.

If Fiona believed in miracles, she would have believed that one had occurred here in the midst of savagery.

Moonfeather had gone above to stand beside Ross and the other men, and shoot at the attackers. Cami rocked Anne's infant while the mother slept. Fiona was left alone to worry about the man she loved. Sweet Mary and Jesus, she prayed. One miracle isn't enough for me. I need another. I need Wolf Shadow to walk unharmed out of that hailstorm of fire and shot.

She closed her eyes and summoned his lean, dark face in her mind's eye. Where are you? she cried silently. Are you safe? I need you. I don't want to be safe behind these thick stone walls if you aren't.

"Fiona."

She opened her eyes and looked into Cameron's faded blue ones.

"Fiona," he whispered hoarsely.

"Shhh." She leaned over him. "I'm here."

"I have to . . ."

"Don't try to talk," she said.

"I must. You . . . you have to know. I've never claimed to be a saint . . . but I'm not the man you believe me to be. I didn't betray my marriage vows in your mother's arms. My wife knew . . . she knew, and she didn't care."

"Not now," Fiona said. "Later . . . when you're stronger. We'll talk of this matter then."

"Hellfire and damnation, girl. There may be no *later* for me. You . . . and your sisters have to know the truth." He swallowed and licked his dry lips. "I wed my . . . my English wife, Margaret, when she was thirty." His eyes pleaded for understanding. "I was sixteen, lass."

Fiona raised his head and gave him a sip of water. He seemed almost too weak to drink. "You need to rest," she said.

"I'll have rest enough in hell," he rasped.

"You're not going to hell or heaven yet. I'll not let you," she said stubbornly. "You're going to live, probably long enough to break some other woman's heart."

Sweat beaded his forehead, and Fiona wiped it away. "Margaret married me to gain her freedom," he said. "A marriage of convenience for us both. Margaret's parents were ambitious. The family had acquired great wealth in commerce, and they wanted a title for their only child. Margaret never wanted to marry, but she agreed to wed me because she thought a boy husband would be little threat to her."

"And you? Why did you marry her?" Fiona asked.

He forced a wry smile. "I had inherited the title of earl, but we were dirt poor, poorer than crofters. I had a widowed mother to support." He exhaled softly, and his burr thickened. "The Stewarts . . .

the Stewarts have always married heiresses. Fortune hunters, the lot of us.''

"There's no need to tell me," Fiona insisted.

"Damn me, but you're like your mother. There is a need. Our marriage was an arrangement, Fiona, a contract between two families. We each got what we wanted. I . . . I got the use of Margaret's unlimited funds, and she was a countess until the day she died."

His eyes drifted shut. For a moment he rested, then he looked at her again. "We were friends, Fiona. Never more. Margaret was bright and caring. I liked her, despite her . . . her peculiarities. I even bedded her."

"Don't do this," Fiona said.

"It was part of the bargain, you see," he went on. "Margaret loved children, and she wanted one of her own. She'd been such a disappointment to her family that she felt she owed them that, at least." His blue eyes clouded with pain. "I gave her bairns . . . but they never lived long enough to draw breath. Blue, shriveled, stillborn creatures. One after another . . . She never . . . never carried one to term, and she suffered more with each pregnancy. Then her physician told me that there could be no more. Another pregnancy would kill her."

Cameron reached for Fiona's hand and clasped it tightly. "I wept for our dead little boys," he whispered. "But I was only twenty when they said we could never sleep together again. Twenty, girl, twenty and full of life."

"It's all right," she soothed. "I didn't know."

"Margaret was a good woman. I always respected her. We laughed together, but we never loved like a man and wife should love. Margaret wanted a child, but she never cared for the getting of them. She was glad when that was over between us."

"Shhh, it's all right," she repeated. "Rest now."

"Margaret had her own pleasures, and I had mine. We made a pact never to interfere in each other's lives. She liked to travel to Paris and to Italy. She had her own companions . . . women companions." His gaze became hard. "Do you understand, lass? My wife was a woman who preferred the caress of another woman to that of a man."

"You mean, she—"

"I didn't hold it against her. Margaret was what she was. We got on well enough. *Never shame me publicly, so long as I live,* she said, and I never did. So long as we were husband and wife in name, she could hold her head up in society. She could entertain and be entertained in the highest circles. I kept her secret as long as she lived." He squeezed Fiona's hand. "Margaret and I lived our separate lives. I wasn't betraying her when I fell in love with your mother. Margaret wouldn't have cared if I brought you to England . . . not so long as I did it discreetly."

Fiona was too drained of emotion to speak.

"Your mother knew we couldn't marry in the Church, but we were handfasted. I loved Moonfeather's mother . . . but I loved yours most of all."

"She loved you more than anything."

"I searched for you, girl . . . I swear it. I offered a reward . . . for you and your mother. I never quit . . . searching . . ."

Fiona swallowed hard. "I believe you," she said.

"On my soul, I swear it. I would never have left her. I loved her. I still love her." He grasped Fiona's hand. "I know it's too late . . . too late to be a father to you."

"Maybe not," she whispered. "Maybe we can try."

Cameron offered her a wan smile, then closed his eyes. In a few minutes he'd drifted off to sleep again. Fiona bent over Anne to satisfy herself that she was sleeping peacefully, taking care not to touch Anne with her hands.

I am adopting Indian ways, Fiona thought wryly. Wolf Shadow had insisted that she not touch one patient after another without going through the entire purifying ritual again. He'd said it was taboo—an insult to the healing spirits. He wasn't even present to reprimand her now, and still she was following his odd instructions.

Fiona looked down at her hands and clothing. Cameron's blood spotted the simple skirt and bodice Greer had brought her when they had reached the house. She shrugged. All she'd ever wanted to be was a doctor. No woman doctor could be fashionable . . . or a lady, for that matter. She chuckled out loud. A lady? Fiona O'Neal? Living in the wilderness of America and wife to a savage medicine man . . . What would her grandfather say? Still smiling, she climbed the winding stairs to the third floor.

"Keep down," Ross cautioned when she appeared at the top of the steps. A broken arrow lay on the floor near one of the gaping windows. "They're still firing at us, but not as much as they were." He gazed out over the back of the house toward the trees. "Three warriors made it over the garden wall."

Fiona counted a half dozen men at the windows, some in servants' dress, others in rough buckskins. One of them turned and grinned at Fiona. "Them red devils lay where they fell, mistress."

"Timothy O'Brian. What are you doing here?"

"Workin' fer Cameron Stewart, as usual. It's good t' see ye alive, Miss Fiona." He snatched off his coonskin hat and nodded to her. "Are ye well?"

"I'm fine." Timothy was staring at her in an intense way that made her feel uncomfortable.

A volley of shots came from the woods, and Timothy ducked low. Bits of stone and lead showered

around them. "God rot their festerin' bowels," he
swore. "No offense, ma'am." He stood and
snapped off a quick shot. "Take that ye whoreson!"
He bit the cap off his powder horn and measured
powder into the pan with swift efficiency, then
glanced back at Fiona. "I trust ye've not forgotten
the offer I made ye?"

"No, but I'm content where I am." The thought
crossed her mind that it might be Wolf Shadow he
was shooting at, and gooseflesh rose on her arms.
"How can you tell friendly Indians from the attackers?"

Timothy grinned. "Musket balls ain't particular,
but I trust Ross's Delaware kin ain't shootin' at us."

Moonfeather was watching them.

Fiona looked at her sister. "All this shooting, and
none of you here have been hurt?"

"Nay so much as a scratch. If there are any French
out there with big guns, I've not seen them."

Fiona stooped low and moved across the room to
sit on the floor next to Moonfeather as another enemy musket ball ricocheted off the stone blocks. "I
don't understand," Fiona said. "Why didn't they
attack the front of the house?"

"They did," Ross answered. "But I've men at the
upstairs windows. Not many, but it doesn't take
many. My father built this house to be defended,
and I've arms and powder enough."

"Enough to stand off the whole French army if
need be," Moonfeather said. She took careful aim
and fired her musket. A cry of pain rose from the
trees. "One less Seneca," she boasted. "That's two
for me."

"I didn't see him fall," Ross protested. "They
don't count unless I see them go down."

Fiona looked from one to the other. "How can
you joke about this? Wolf Shadow's out there somewhere, and so is little Royal. This isn't a game."

Moonfeather smiled. "As I said, little sister, you have much to learn of us."

"Get down," Ross shouted, then swore a foul oath as a flaming arrow flew through the window and struck the wall behind the stairs. "Tend that fire, will ye, hinney," he ordered Fiona.

Moonfeather pointed to a wooden tub of water with a dipper hanging on the side. Fiona crawled across the stone floor, scooped up a dipperful, and doused the burning pitch on the end of the arrow.

"Aye, little sister, we take this serious enough," Moonfeather continued when Fiona returned to crouch beside her. She thrust a pistol into Fiona's hands. "Reload that, if ye ken how."

"I do. Wolf Shadow taught me."

"Then ye had a good teacher," Ross said.

Moonfeather's musket cracked, and Fiona coughed from the smoke. "Ross and I have been friends for years," Moonfeather said. "We played together as children." She traded the empty musket for the loaded pistol. "We hunted bear together," she said calmly.

The musket barrel was hot to the touch. Carefully, Fiona measured powder into the barrel, seated a ball on a patch, and rammed it down with a long wooden rod.

"Take care that ball's rammed tight," Ross cautioned before he fired and began to reload. "If it's not, the barrel will blow."

"Once, Ross and I hunted larger game than bear," Moonfeather said.

He grinned. "I nearly married her."

"I said no. If I'd said yes, he would have married me," Moonfeather answered. "Sweet sister Anne is right for him. He and I would have killed each other in two weeks."

"One," Ross corrected. "She—" He broke off as an owl hooted from the trees. "Hist! Listen there!"

There were two more shots, then silence. "Hold your fire," he ordered his men.

"Look!" Moonfeather beckoned to Fiona.

Fiona stood up and looked out the window. Her heart skipped a beat. Wolf Shadow was coming out of the forest with a small army of cheering Shawnee and Delaware braves at his back.

"He's safe!" Weeping and crying his name, Fiona ran down the steps and across the garden. And she flung herself into his arms and showered him with kisses.

Chapter 21

❦

Fiona sat on the grass in front of the small log cabin she shared with Wolf Shadow in the forest near Anne and Ross's home. It was a warm July day, and the air was heavy with the scent of the honeysuckle that grew thickly up the sides of the house. They had just finished sharing the noon meal, and Fiona was watching her husband craft an instrument for the dances and ceremonies that would be held that evening.

In the peaceful three weeks that had passed since Wolf Shadow's followers had helped the Delaware braves to defeat Matiassu's war party, Fiona had come to know her father and her sisters better. Every day they spent hours together, talking, laughing, and sharing their life stories. Anne—her newfound English sister—was a sweet and caring person, and much to Fiona's surprise, she was as drawn to this shy, quiet lady as she was to the incandescent Moonfeather. Discovering that she had a family after a lifetime of believing she was alone in the world filled Fiona with happiness.

She and Wolf Shadow had remained at Wanishisheyun to care for Anne and Cameron, and Moonfeather, as peace woman of the Shawnee, had called for the Grand Council to assemble here on Ross

Campbell's land. Already more than a hundred shelters had been raised in the valley, and more tribesmen and women were arriving every day.

Fiona and Wolf Shadow had been discussing Anne's uneventful recovery from surgery, and why the massive infection that Fiona expected Anne to suffer had never invaded her body.

"The amount of medicine you give is critical," Wolf Shadow said. "Too much and it can bring death . . . too little and . . ." He shrugged.

Fiona still couldn't believe that they had performed the operation under the most primitive conditions and saved both mother and child. Although Anne was still very weak, Wolf Shadow had insisted that she nurse the infant herself and that she be up on her feet and walking every day. The baby boy, still unnamed, was rosy and plump despite his unorthodox entry into the world.

"It still doesn't make sense," Fiona argued. "I'd think she would heal faster by lying in bed."

"Patients who lie in bed suffer lung fever," he replied.

"But what will happen to Anne later if she becomes pregnant with another child?" Fiona demanded. Now that she knew Anne and had accepted her as her sister, she had become fiercely protective of her health. "You can't expect her to live through an operation like that again. Shouldn't she sleep separately from Ross?"

Her brother-in-law had wasted little time in telling her that she had no need to address him as Lord Strathmar. "Titles in the wilderness be of less use than saddles on cows," he'd insisted. "Ross Campbell I was born, and Ross I shall be to my friends and kin. The only time I need to be called earl is when I'm dealin' with those rascals in the king's service back in Annapolis."

Wolf Shadow shook his head. "Anne should wait

two years before she has another child, if they ever choose to have another. Moonfeather can show her what plants to eat to keep her from conceiving. Shawnee women usually have only two babies, and your Anne now has three boys already.''

''You know of something that will prevent a woman from becoming pregnant?''

He smiled. ''Yes, but it is not a thing men should talk of. Ask Moonfeather. She will show you where and when to gather the roots, and how to prepare them. It is women's medicine, and a secret best kept by women. Some men resent the power it gives their wives.''

''And me? Would you resent it if I used it?''

''No,'' he replied seriously. ''It is a woman's right to decide, but I would hope that someday you will want to carry my child.''

''Someday,'' she promised. ''Someday.'' But that day had not yet come. Each month she waited nervously to see if she was pregnant. It wasn't that she didn't want children; she adored Anne and Ross's baby boy. It was that this life was still too new to her. She needed time, time to learn the Shawnee ways, and time to grow at ease with her husband.

''If it troubles you that I am not a Christian,'' he said, ''remember that I will never interfere with your religion or that of your child.''

''When the time comes, we will face the issue together,'' she assured him. The doubts that had troubled her before the attack on Heatherfield were still with her, but she hid them from Wolf Shadow. The thought of losing him during the battle had been so terrible that it still gave her nightmares. No matter how her conscience plagued her about the right of their union, her love for him was stronger.

She had never asked him about Matiassu. Instinctively, she'd realized the war chief was dead, and she hadn't wanted to know how Wolf Shadow had killed him. It was enough for her that her husband had not brought home Matiassu's scalp as a grisly trophy.

"Royal was a hero," Wolf Shadow had said, when she and Moonfeather had demanded news of the boy's safety. "Two Seneca chased him through the woods for miles. One circled around the road and nearly caught him. Royal charged them on that black devil of a stallion and rode right overtop of him."

Wolf Shadow's warriors had crept through the forest picking off the larger enemy force one at a time. When the Delaware braves had arrived on the scene, they had joined forces and sent what was left of the war party fleeing for their lives.

Fiona's husband had accepted her own news about Cameron's recovery from poisoning without blinking an eye. "I knew your spirit medicine was strong," he said. "I knew *you* were strong." He didn't add that he was proud of her—the look in his eyes said it all.

Early this morning, she had walked in the orchard with her father. The apple and peach trees had been covered with green fruit and the air filled with the buzzing of bees. The bees had brought back memories of the afternoon she and Wolf Shadow had spent together near the bee tree.

She smiled at Wolf Shadow. Since she'd left Cameron in the orchard, she'd wanted to tell her husband about the invitation her father had extended. Not certain of Wolf Shadow's reaction, she'd waited for just the right moment.

"Wolf Shadow."

"Yes." His eyes lit with affection as he looked at her, and she felt a warm glow within.

"Wolf Shadow, I have something to tell you. Cameron . . . my father . . . He wants me to go back to Annapolis with him," she said. "He says he wants my signature on some documents, and he wants to have the royal governor clear my indenture."

Wolf Shadow concentrated on pulling a piece of thin deerskin taut over a wooden ring and securing it with even stitches. He didn't look up at her, but his lips firmed into a thin line of disapproval.

"If I did go, it would only be for a few weeks, a month at most."

"So you say."

"He told me that he wants to change his will and leave all his fortune to me. He says that Moonfeather and Anne are both wealthy women, and they don't need the money. I suppose if he's an earl, he must be very rich."

"What did you tell him, Irish?" Wolf Shadow laid the flat hoop drum on the ground. The unfinished instrument was about twice the size of his hand and looked to Fiona much like a gypsy tambourine. Calmly, her husband glanced up at her.

"What do you think I said? I told him I didn't want his money." She folded her arms across her chest indignantly. "There was a time when even a little gold would have meant everything to us . . . to my mother and me. But not now. I told him to give it to my sisters or to his grandchildren." A thread of uncertainty crept into her voice. "We have no need of it, do we?"

He smiled. "No, little badger woman. We do not need English gold."

"Good. I don't hate him anymore," she said. "You were right, Cameron is a good man. But I'll not be beholden to him. I am thinking about going with him to Annapolis, though. Moonfeather and Cami are going. Her husband's plantation is there, you know."

"I am not Brandon. I will not have my woman live apart from me much of the time."

Fiona tried to keep her rising temper from show-

ing. "I didn't say anything about living apart from
you. I thought it might be a good thing to officially
dissolve my indenture so I don't have to constantly
watch over my shoulder for a sheriff with a warrant
for my arrest."

"So." He frowned. Cameron Stewart is an earl.
Cameron Stewart is rich. He is powerful." Wolf
Shadow turned a dark gaze on her. "He cannot dis-
solve the indenture without you?"

"I did agree to accept the gift of a medical book
and some new supplies. He says the apothecaries in
Annapolis are well-stocked. I can purchase almost
anything there that I could get in London. I need
ginseng root and laudanum, as well as some more
needles."

"Now you go for buying? Why do you go, Fiona?"

"Damn you, why are you being like this?" she
said, her anger flaring. "Didn't you say I was a free
woman? That I could come and go as I please?"

His jaw tensed. "I did not say you could not go.
But if you do, it may mean the end of our marriage."

She balled her hands into tight fists and rested
them defiantly on her hips. "By the holy blood of
good Saint Bridget! You were the one who insisted
I mend my fences with my father. I thought you
liked him."

"I like Cameron well enough. It is O'Brian I do
not like."

"O'Brian has nothing to do with my choosing to
go to Annapolis with my father."

"No?"

"Why would you think such a thing?"

"He offered to buy you from me."

"He what?"

"For three French muskets, a horse, and six steel
tomahawks."

"What did you say to him?"

"I threw him into the river." Wolf Shadow picked up the drum again and turned it between his big, hard hands. He scrutinized his stitches, then began to sew a strip of rawhide around the rim. Dozens of tiny white shells dangled from the leather so that when a dancer shook the drum the shells would clack together. "And," he added, "I threatened to make this drum of his hide instead of a buck's."

"You're jealous!"

"I'll kill him if he touches you."

She shook her head in amazement. "You've nothing to be jealous about. Timothy O'Brian is a good man. He offered to marry me, but I refused him. I told him that I'm happy with the husband I've got."

"I'm glad to hear that," he answered. "It seems to me that I can remember not long ago when all you wanted to do was get away from me."

"No gentleman would remind a lady of such a thing," she accused.

"No," he replied, "I suppose a gentleman wouldn't." He exhaled softly. "But I'm not an Irish gentleman, am I? I'm a savage—so you often remind me. Don't forget that, woman. I am like the wolf, and you cannot always know what I will and will not do."

"You jackass!" She dipped her hand in the bucket of cold water in which he'd been soaking ash strips, and splashed him. "Maybe that will cool your stupid jealousy," she declared, then turned and ran before she could tell if he was angry or not.

Torches flared in the night beneath a full moon, so low in the sky that Fiona could not keep from staring at it. Drums sounded, calling the people to gather. And they came by the dozens: Shawnee and Delaware, Seneca and Huron and Menominee— men, women, and children. Gray heads mingled with black, and adolescent boys too young to wear eagle feathers trailed enviously on the heels of young bucks, splendid in their ceremonial finery.

Young women at the height of their beauty moved in the shadows of the campfires, their huge eyes flashing, their soft garments rustling. Girl-children giggled and hid their round faces behind hands heavy with rings, and mothers swollen with pregnancy carried their burdens proudly.

Dogs barked and whined, babies cried, and horses snorted and stamped where they were tied. Bone whistles pieced the warm night air with snatches of melody, then fell silent. And the drums were joined by other drums, lending excitement and anticipation to the gathering crowd.

Pale-skinned men appeared on the fringes of the assembly: French, English, Irish, and Scot. All were unarmed, for the law of the Great Council was that no man should carry a lethal weapon. And the drums touched a chord deep in the hearts of the white men, calling upon emotions buried by centuries of civilization, and their pulses quickened, and their gazes followed the graceful Shawnee and Delaware women.

Roquette was there with a dozen followers, and Cameron Stewart and Ross Campbell watched them with wary eyes. The French party kept to themselves on the far side of the dance ground, and Fiona could tell that they were nervous.

"How can they show their faces after they attacked us?" she asked Anne indignantly. Servants had prepared a comfortable place of honor for the mistress of Wanishish-eyun to watch the dancing, and Fiona was sitting beside her.

Anne winkled her nose. "Indians." She shrugged daintily and spread her hands exactly as Fiona had seen Moonfeather do many times. "I've given up trying to understand Shawnee politics, and God knows the Delaware are probably worse." She clapped politely as a dignified old Indian woman finished the first speech of welcome. "In England, Roquette would have been drawn and quartered long ago. The thing is, we know that the Frenchmen who led the war party worked for him, but no one actually saw Roquette. Alex Mackenzie blew one white man up when they stormed Fort Campbell, but since he was dead, he couldn't implicate Roquette either. The Shawnee have this crazy idea that people are innocent until proven guilty."

She glanced up and waved at a handsome white man with blond hair who was embracing Moonfeather near the big campfire. "Brandon!" she called. "Welcome to Wanishish-eyun, darling." She leaned close to Fiona. "That's Moonfeather's husband, Lord Kentington to be exact. He used to be Viscount Brandon before his father passed away, and I've never gotten used to the change. He'll always be Brandon to me. Of course, our sister's Christian name is Leah, although few enough of us use it. Ross said Brandon was going to try and be here for the Grand Council. God knows how he manages without her. They made a bargain, you know, when they married. Very romantic it was, too. She was to spend half her time with the Shawnee and half with him. An odd way to run a marriage, I'd say, but it does suit them. Brandon says that our sister is a handful and"—she chuckled—"he says that their marriage never grows dull. When they are together, it's as though they're still on their honeymoon."

Another mature Delaware woman offered a welcome in Algonquian, then Moonfeather led a group of girls—including Cami—in the first dance. Both mother and daughter were decked in their finest doeskin dresses with long fringes and beautiful quillwork designs.

"Isn't she precious?" Anne confided, "I love

Cami like my own daughter. So far, she's the only girl." Anne touched her own amulet, strung on a golden chain around her slender throat. "Father says that if neither of us has a girl, we must leave our amulets to Cami—that's short for Cameron, you know. Moonfeather named her after Father. Father said he cut the Eye of Mist into four pieces. You and Moonfeather and I each have a piece. Father has the other—at least I think he does. I've never seen him wear it. But if there's a daughter, the necklace is supposed to be passed on to her. It's only right—don't you agree?"

Fiona nodded, too caught up in her own thoughts to pay much attention to Anne's chattering. She'd been going over and over in her mind the argument she'd had earlier with her husband.

Wolf Shadow had been wrong—absolutely, positively wrong. He'd been acting like a jealous fool, and she didn't like it. He'd deserved the wetting she'd given him.

Still, the argument troubled her. She'd dressed in Indian garb tonight to please him, refusing the lovely sky-blue silk gown Anne had offered in favor of this soft buff doeskin dress and moccasins. She'd left her hair loose, as he liked it, and she'd woven flowers into the tresses at the sides of her face, pulling them together at the back of her head. Anne had given her beautiful pearl earrings set in gold and a gold bracelet from India so heavy that Fiona was conscious of it whenever she moved her arm.

"Nonsense," Anne had said when Fiona had protested accepting the jewelry. "I'm disgustingly rich, and there's nowhere to spend it. You saved my life and my baby's. Please accept my gifts, not as payment but in return for the gift you gave us."

Fiona rolled the bracelet absently on her wrist. One of the reasons she'd never wished to marry was the possessiveness of men. She'd never wanted to be controlled by a husband, owned like a donkey or a cow. She hadn't been sure whether she wanted to go to Annapolis before, but now that Wolf Shadow had all but forbidden the trip, she'd go or die. She didn't want to risk what they had together, but if he couldn't trust her out of his sight, what kind of marriage would they have?

Indian men were carrying infants onto the dance ground. One by one, they filed forward, and three elderly women examined the children and then called out something in Algonquian.

"They're naming the children," Anne said. "It's considered good luck for a child to receive an official 'baby name' at a Grand Council fire. See!" She pointed out Ross, a head taller than the other warriors, with his own baby son in his arms. "We're naming him Geoffry Angus, but his Indian name will be N'mamentschi—Rejoice, in English." She laughed. "My mother would be horrified, but that's what the old women picked. I'm so happy to have him alive and well. They could have called him Little Skunk for all I care."

Ross turned and held the infant boy high for Anne to see, and she clapped loudly. There were general calls of approval from the onlookers, and Ross strode toward Anne, grinning broadly.

Fiona murmured her own congratulations and took the opportunity to leave. She wanted to look for Wolf Shadow, to try and have a moment alone with him to settle their disagreement.

"Wait," Yellow Elk called in his own tongue. He stepped into the firelit circle. "Another comes to receive a name this night." The crowd grew silent. "A child has died," Yellow Elk continued. Moans and cries of sympathy flowed around the assembly. "But . . ." The people listened eagerly. "But the child did not really die to his mother."

Fiona moved closer to the circle, not certain she

understood the words. Was the child dead or not? And whose child was it?

"He was the son of our peace woman, Nibeeshu Meekwon, who the English call Moonfeather," Yellow Elk proclaimed. Moonfeather joined him and fell on her knees, then began to wail in mourning.

Fiona stared at her sister in bewilderment. Yellow Elk had just said that Kitate was dead, but Moonfeather wasn't acting as though she'd lost a child. The mourning was plainly a charade.

"A mother has lost her only son," Yellow Elk went on. "And in his place stands a warrior of the Shawnee nation!"

The throng leaped to their feet and began cheering as Wolf Shadow led Kitate into the circle. Both the man and the boy were stripped to loincloths and moccasins; both wore their hair long and unadorned. Their skin had been rubbed with oil until it shone in the firelight, and they walked slowly with the pride of princes.

Wolf Shadow took Kitate's hand and lifted it high, bringing a roar of approval from the spectators. Then the boy turned and went to Moonfeather. He took her by the hands and raised her up. For an instant he knelt before her, to honor her above all people, then he stood and returned to the shaman's side.

Moonfeather joined Fiona at the edge of the circle. Her face glowed with joy, and she grabbed Fiona's hand and squeezed it.

"I'm so glad he's safe," Fiona whispered to her sister. "He's a fine boy." The words sounded trite to her ears as she spoke them, but Moonfeather smiled back with tear-filled eyes.

Yellow Elk made a great show of saluting Kitate, then he too left the circle and blended with the multitude.

"Kitate the boy is dead," Wolf Shadow said in his deep, resounding voice. "Here in his place stands the man." Kitate kept his eyes on the ground, his stance humble. "I, Wolf Shadow, shaman of the—"

"No!" A shrill voice broke through the moon dancer's oration. "I say you have no right to address the Shawnee. I say you are no true shaman. You have broken the laws of the people. I, Tuk-o-see-yah, say this." Men and women cleared a path for the old man as he limped feebly into the circle and pointed a painted stick at Wolf Shadow.

"Ahhh . . ." someone exclaimed.

"What is this?" called a Menominee brave.

"What can our shaman have done?" asked another man.

"It is the white woman," an old squaw croaked. "Wolf Shadow sinned when he took an enemy woman to wife."

Kitate's eyes dilated in astonishment, but he remained standing where he was and kept silent.

"You are not fit to stand in this circle," Tuk-o-see-yah said. "You cannot speak to us of forming a Shawnee Nation. You cannot speak to this council at all. You have no right to walk among the true men. You should be buried alive so that your evil cannot live after you."

Wolf Shadow looked at the old chief without anger. "Why do you speak so, Tuk-o-see-yah? Why do you accuse me in this sacred circle?"

Fiona's heart leaped in her breast. She wanted to run to Wolf Shadow. Never had he seemed so handsome, so magnificent as he was now with the firelight gleaming on his oiled skin, with his great black eyes full of compassion for an old man. Only Moonfeather's tight grip on her hand held her back. "Wolf Shadow," Fiona murmured, and suddenly she was afraid for him. Could his people turn on him for her sake? What would she do if they demanded he give her up?

"You have broken the law, Wolf Shadow," Tuk-o-see-yah said, shaking the feathered stick again. "You murdered my grandson Matiassu. You broke the law of the People when you killed a brother Shawnee, and you broke the greater law of the moon dancers when you used your spirit power to do evil."

"I did not lay a hand on Matiassu," Wolf Shadow replied. "His death was his own doing."

"You command the spirits!" Tuk-o-see-yah shrieked. "You ordered his death. It is the same as if you drove your knife into his heart."

"Matiassu stood outside tribal law," Wolf Shadow said. "He lost the right to be sheltered by that law when he caused the death of Beaver Tooth and my sister, Willow."

"You lie!" the old man roared. "Prove that Matiassu killed your sister." He turned to the crowd for support. "This moon dancer—this bad shaman—has accused my grandson of killing Beaver Tooth and Fat Boy. He!" He shook the stick at Wolf Shadow's chest. "He claims that my grandson was an evil man, but where is the proof that Matiassu killed anyone?"

"The proof is here," Kitate said.

Wolf Shadow cupped his hands over his mouth and gave the cry of the great horned owl, and the warrior Fat Boy stepped from the shadows. Cries of joy rose from the onlookers as the Shawnee brave joined Wolf Shadow and Kitate in the circle.

"It is Fat Boy!" shouted a woman.

"It can't be, he's dead," a brave argued.

"I know him," insisted another. "It's Fat Boy, all right."

"Where has he been?"

"That's my brother," yelled a young warrior. "Fat Boy, I'm here."

Fat Boy raised his hands for quiet. "I am the proof of Matiassu's sin," he shouted. "I saw Beaver Tooth fall with Matiassu's knife in his heart. I saw Matiassu take his scalp." He lifted a matted piece of hair high in the air. "This is the scalp of our friend and brother Beaver Tooth."

"I sent Kitate to the Seneca to steal a dance mask," Wolf Shadow said. "Instead, he stole away a Seneca captive."

The Shawnee were shouting so loudly that it was hard for Fiona to hear her husband's words.

"Kitate rescued Fat Boy from the Seneca," Wolf Shadow proclaimed. "Matiassu murdered Beaver Tooth and traded Fat Boy to our enemy as a slave. What say you to this, Tuk-o-see-yah?"

Dejected and broken, the old chief turned and walked weeping from the circle. Men, women, and children spilled onto the dance ground shouting Wolf Shadow's name and pounding both Kitate and Fat Boy on the back. Shouting and singing, two husky braves lifted Wolf Shadow onto their shoulders and carried him triumphantly around the fire.

Chapter 22

The moon had risen to its highest peak over the Wanishish-eyun by the time the council members had finished talking and the night had been given over to the younger people. Seasoned warriors had demonstrated their skills and boasted of their exploits in hunting and in war, and the newest braves had shown off their physiques and mastery of the most difficult dance steps. Old women with gray hair, their eyes bright with excitement, had shuffled around the fires while girl-children looked on enviously.

The Grand Council discussion would go on for days, but for now the Shawnee would forget political matters and dance and laugh together.

White men and women, Shawnee, Delaware, and Iroquois, all had eaten well. Kitate, whose warrior name was Sh'Kotai Olamaalsu, had been praised and showered with gifts by the tribesmen, and he in turn had given them all away to friends and relatives. The central fire had burned to a bed of glowing coals, and the children and elderly had found their beds.

The drums still sounded in the darkness, but their message was not the same as it had been earlier in the evening. At moonrise the drums had called all the people to the council circle. Now their muffled beat offered a more subtle invitation.

Fiona lingered by the edge of the clearing as Shawnee and Delaware squaws—blankets draped over their folded arms—formed a line and began a slow, stately dance. Onlookers, both male and female, began to chant softly. "Hih-yah, hih-yah, hih-yah."

"Come, little sister," Moonfeather whispered, pushing a red blanket into Fiona's hands. "Ye maun join in the Blanket Dance. It be for wives . . ." She chuckled. "And sometimes those who seek a husband."

"I don't know how—"

"Just do what this one does," Moonfeather insisted. "But be certain the man you choose is your husband."

"What?"

Moonfeather laughed again. "Come. Ye will like it, I promise."

Reluctantly, Fiona followed her sister to the end of the line. The slow, shuffling step was easy enough to follow, and after a few circles of the campfire Fiona could repeat it without thinking.

"Hih-yah, hih-yah, hih-yah," the dancers sang, and the cadence of the drums echoed through the moonlit forest.

Fiona became caught up in the repetitive rhythm. She lost her self-consciousness and began to enjoy the unity of the dance. The words were meaningless to her, but in some strange, inexplicable way, they filled her with an inner satisfaction.

Round and round the line of dancers snaked, weaving into the darkness and back into the light. A breeze brought the scent of honeysuckle, and that sweet smell mingled with the odor of burning cherry logs and the bite of tobacco.

A bone whistle joined the drums, followed by a

reed flute and the rattle of shells. The women kept
step as the cadence quickened and took on a frolic-
some air.

The woman at the head of the line shook out her
blanket and threw it around her shoulders. One after another, the other dancers followed her lead.
Fiona shivered despite the warmth of the summer
night and the nearness of the fire. Figures of men
moved in the shadows, and it seemed to Fiona as if
she could smell the clean, musky scent of them.

The teasing voice of a reed flute rose above the
drums. Across the dance ground, another flute took
up the melody. The braves edged into he clearing,
naked but for their minuscule breechcloths, their
bodies oiled and muscles glistening.

The line of dancers snaked close to the men, so
close that Fiona could see the outline of their craggy
features and hear the rasp of their breathing. Then
without warning, a man reached out and grabbed
her. She gasped in surprise and would have broken
step, but he tightened his arm around her and kept
her place in line.

"Wolf Shadow." She swallowed and breathed a
sigh of relief as shivers ran up and down her spine.
He hadn't spoken to her all evening. "I didn't—"

"Hih-yah, hih-yah, hih-yah," he sang. His deep,
rich voice made her feel weak inside.

Other couples were forming. As each of the
woman dancers pointed out her chosen partner, the
man joined her, and they unfolded the blanket and
spread it around both of them. Fiona saw Moonfeather point to her tall, yellow-haired English husband. Laughing, he came to her, and they pulled
her blanket over their heads.

Wolf Shadow took hold of Fiona's blanket and
tossed it away into the darkness. Her breathing came
faster as he led her out of the line of dancers and
into the center of the circle.

"I thought the woman was supposed to pick her partner," she whispered to him.

Mischief lit his dark eyes. He smiled a wolfish grin. "I was afraid you'd pick another." He held her lightly, fingertips to fingertips, but his gaze gripped her like an invisible ribbon of steel.

His moccasined feet moved to the beat of the drum, his hips and shoulders swayed sensually in the firelight, and all the while, he made white-hot love to her with his ebony eyes.

They circled the fire, inside the ring of chanting couples . . . within the dance yet apart from it.

His hair hung long and loose over his bare back, and his copper earrings jingled. His armband caught the glow of the coals and reflected their red-orange light. His bronze skin was a thin layer of satin over corded, iron thews.

She couldn't keep her eyes from the scrap of scarlet wool that barely covered his bulging loins. His flat stomach tapered to vanish beneath that bit of cloth, but the material did nothing to hide his smooth, hard thighs or his tight, well-shaped buttocks.

Fiona's body followed the steps of the dance, but her mind tantalized her with carnal desires. Her skin was acutely sensitive to the moisture in the warm night air. Her breasts felt tight and achy against the bodice of her doeskin dress; with every move she made, the soft leather scraped her swollen nipples. Shivers made gooseflesh rise on her neck, but she wasn't cold. She was so hot that trickles of sweat ran down between her breasts.

Wolf Shadow's fingertips seemed to be on fire. Her fingers burned where they touched his, and the flames shot down her arm to kindle a blaze in the pit of her stomach.

Wolf Shadow leaned close and brushed her neck

with his lips. "You were right to be angry with me," he murmured. "I was a jealous fool."

She opened her mouth to speak, but the words wouldn't come. She was trembling with anticipation, and all she wanted was to be alone with him. Anywhere . . . Anywhere that she could fill the rising hunger that burned within her.

"I had no right to tell you that you could not go with your father," he continued. "The choice is yours, Fiona. And if you go, I will wait for you, until you tell me that you want me no more."

Laughing couples were slipping away from the dance circle. She was vaguely aware of Moonfeather's departure, and the knowledge of what her sister and brother-in-law would soon be doing made her burn all the hotter.

"Will you forgive me?" he asked.

She nodded, light-headed with wantonness. She still could not speak. In answer, she undid the clasp at the back of her neck and stood on tiptoe to fasten her amulet around his throat.

His nostrils flared, and she saw his throat constrict. "I want you," he whispered hoarsely. "I want to make hot, sweet love to you." He placed his hands on her hips, and she felt the heat of him sear through her dress.

She drew in a strangled breath. "Yes," she managed. "I want you." And her knees went weak as he picked her up and strode from the dance ground with her cradled in his arms.

When they reached the shadows, he kissed her and she moaned with desire. She wrapped her arms around his neck and pressed herself against him. His bare chest was molten silk against her skin.

She lowered her head and closed her lips around his nipple, thrilling at the salt taste of him, reveling in the texture of his skin. He groaned as she tugged at his nipple with her teeth and nipped him until she felt him tremble.

Fiona arched against him, shaken by waves of fierce desire that brought a familiar wetness between her thighs. She wanted him as she had never wanted him before.

She told him so.

He kissed her again, filling her mouth with his hard, thrusting tongue, crushing her to him. Her heart thudded wildly as the inferno set her blood ablaze.

They made it only as far as the orchard.

He dropped to his knees in the clover and laid her back in the sweet-smelling grass. "Let me love you, Fiona," he begged.

"Yes . . . yes."

Not far away she could hear the moans of another couple locked in raw consummation, and the sounds of their passion inflamed her own. Whimpering with eagerness, she slid her dress up past her hips. He pulled it over her head and dropped it into the grass.

"Touch me," he dared.

Her fingers trembled as she unfastened his loincloth and let it fall.

His pulsating shaft thrust out boldly, huge in the moonlight.

"Touch me," he repeated.

Weeping and laughing all at once, she went down on her knees and took his smooth length between her hands. Her fingers stroked him lightly, and she marveled at his size and silken texture. He was tight and hard, swollen with proof of his desire for her. Shyly, she lowered her head and kissed him.

Wolf Shadow shuddered with pleasure.

Her confidence increased by leaps and bounds. She kissed him again, then cautiously tasted him with the tip of her tongue.

He groaned.

She chuckled and brazenly flicked her tongue against the taut skin of his swollen shaft.

"Yes," he managed. "Don't stop. That feels so good."

Instinctively, she drew as much of him into her mouth as she could take and sucked gently. He threaded his fingers through her hair and moaned.

"No more," he cautioned, breathlessly. He pulled her up and kissed her mouth, then nibbled a scalding path of kisses down her throat to her breast.

Her knees went weak as he circled her nipple with his tongue and tugged hard with his lips. Threads of golden joy spilled through her. "Now," she urged. "I want you now."

They sank together in the lush, soft grass, and he drove his turgid rod deep into her willing flesh. She met him thrust for thrust, entwining her legs with his and crying out with wild abandon.

They took and gave each other pleasure long into the warm summer night. And when at last they lay sated in each other's arms, Fiona was content. Her doubts were gone. For with the last barrier of their intimacy behind them, she knew that whatever adversity the future brought, she would rather face it with this man beside her than with anyone else in the world.

The first rays of the new sun had tinted the heavens a rosy purple in the east when Fiona and Wolf Shadow walked, hand in hand, back to their cabin to sleep. It seemed to Fiona that they had been unconscious for only a few minutes when a man's voice called Wolf Shadow from his bed.

She sat up sleepily and hastily pulled her deerskin dress over her head. Still barefooted, she walked out into the early morning light to see her husband talking with an Indian brave she didn't know.

"Seeg-o-nah wants to see me right away," Wolf

Shadow explained, unsheathing his knife and handing it to her.

Fiona recognized the name as one of the Shawnee chiefs with a large group of followers. "But why—" she began.

"Seeg-o-nah's wigwam is within the council area. "I may not carry any weapon capable of killing a man." He indicated the Shawnee brave. "This is Tek-ee. He says that Tuk-o-see-yah has changed his mind and will urge his people to vote for the establishment of a Shawnee Nation. Seeg-o-nah is one of those who hates the English. His family was massacred by British soldiers. Seeg-o-nah has not forgiven me for taking a white wife. Now he is willing to listen again to what I have to say."

Fiona rubbed her eyes and nodded a greeting to the grizzled old warrior, Tek-ee. "But what can you tell him at this time of the morning that you didn't say before?"

Wolf Shadow smiled at her. "I can say that I was wrong—that my own pride made me blind to the truth of my own mission." He took a step closer to Fiona, and his voice grew tender. "I can say that knowing you has made me realize that the Shawnee cannot reject all things European and go back to the way our grandfathers lived. We must take the best that your people have to offer." He exhaled slowly. "Liquor must be forbidden, for it is the curse of the Indian. But if we judge men by the color of their skin or the amount of Indian blood in their veins, we are no better than the English." He glanced at Tek-ee. "All men and women who are willing to live by Shawnee law must be welcome among us, if their skin is as fair as my Fiona's or as black as charcoal. We must judge men and women by their hearts, not the place of their birth. We must educate our children in the white man's reading and writing, as I have been educated, and we must welcome their religion—not to renounce our own, but to add to what we know of the Creator." Lightly with two fingers he touched Fiona's amulet, which now hung around his own neck. "This is the message I will give Seeg-o-nah, and I will tell him that even a moon dancer can learn wisdom from a small woman, if he is willing to listen."

Fiona's eyes moistened, and she swallowed a lump in her throat as she watched Wolf Shadow and Tek-ee walk away. She had traveled half a world away from Ireland and found a man she could respect and love. They would always argue, she knew that, but their quarrels would be like spice in a rabbit stew, necessary and unavoidable if she wanted a tasty meal.

She was still sleepy, but it was too late to go back to bed. She washed her face and brushed her hair, braiding it neatly in a single plait down her back. She was sweeping out the single room when Timothy O'Brian appeared in the open doorway. He wasn't carrying his musket, but he had a skinning knife strapped to his belt and a flintlock pistol tucked inside. He looked dressed to travel.

"Miss Fiona, can I speak to you?" He stepped into the room and closed the door behind him. "I know what he thinks of me, so I waited 'til I knew he'd be pow-wowin' with the chiefs."

Fiona leaned on her broom. "What is it? I hope you've not come to ask me to leave my husband again, because I'm not going to do it."

O'Brian's face fell. "But Mr. Stewart said . . ." His features turned a dark red. "Miss Fiona, ye got to listen t' reason. What if ye and him . . . Well, if ye get in the family way, it will be a mortal sin. Ye're too good a woman fer that. I offered t' make an honest woman of ye, and I'm still willin' t' do it. I thought if ye were comin' back with his lordship, then we could get t' know each other better. I—"

She met his stubborn gaze with one of her own. "I changed my mind, Timothy. I like you, but I love Wolf Shadow."

"He's a heathen red nig—"

"Don't say it. He's my husband and the finest man I've ever met."

"If that's the way ye feel, then maybe ye'd best come and tell yer father that."

"Maybe I will."

The door slammed open. "Why are you here?" Wolf Shadow demanded. "What do you want of my wife?"

Fiona flushed with embarrassment. "He thought I was going back to Annapolis with my father," she said, "but I told him I'd changed my mind. I'm staying here with my husband where I belong."

O'Brian's hand moved toward the pistol at his waist. "I want no trouble with ye, shaman. I'm just givin' the lady another chance to make up her mind."

Wolf Shadow took two strides and stood beside Fiona. "She is a free woman," he said softly. "If she tells you that she will not go, you have your answer."

O'Brian edged toward the door. "Ye're riskin' yer immortal soul, Miss Fiona. Jest ye remember that."

Warm relief flooded through Fiona. Wolf Shadow had had every reason to fly into a jealous rage, and he hadn't. He'd believed her without question. "My soul is my own concern," Fiona answered, taking her husband's hand and squeezing it tight. "I've no need of a heaven where he isn't welcome."

"Then there ain't nothin' more to say, is there?" O'Brian stalked out of the cabin with Fiona and Wolf Shadow following him. O'Brian stopped short as he confronted four men outside. "Roquette? What are ye—" He reached for his pistol, then uttered a cry

of agony as a Seneca warrior buried a steel tomahawk in his head.

Fiona screamed.

O'Brian fell back against the cabin wall, his mouth
opening and closing in surprise. He convulsed once
and then lay still with blood streaming down the
front of his contorted face.

"Get out here, both of you," Roquette ordered,
leveling the muzzle of a pistol at Fiona's head.

"Are you mad?" Wolf Shadow demanded.
"You'll never escape alive."

"We'll see about that. Just keep your hands where
I can see them, *sorcier*." Another Seneca brave and
a white man in a rawhide vest stood on either side
of Roquette. Both men held ready muskets. "You
have won the council," Roquette continued, "but
you won't keep the woman as well. She's still my
bond servant."

"Don't touch her," Wolf Shadow said. "She's
mine."

"Do as I say, or I promise you, I will leave you
with only a corpse to fondle."

"Stay where you are, Fiona," Wolf Shadow cautioned.

"No. It's all right," she said breathlessly. "I'll go
with him." Her heart thudded against her chest, and
she felt as though she was about to vomit. "I won't
risk your life."

"I paid for you, madame. I'll not have you warm-
ing this savage's bed." Roquette motioned with his
chin. "Get over here."

Fiona regarded him with utter contempt. How
could such a pitiful specimen of a man be the monster who was causing so much anguish to red men
and white on the frontier?

Roquette's long blond hair was streaked with gray,
and his pale eyes were rimmed with red. His once-
handsome face was criss-crossed with faint scars and

old pockmarks, and his thin nose showed evidence of having been broken and healed. He was freshly shaven, but he'd nicked himself twice in the process. His neck bore rings of grime above the clean linen shirt and blue military coat with wide red cuffs.

"You can't take me anywhere," she answered boldly. "I'm Cameron Stewart's natural daughter. Even you can see the futility of trying to kidnap an English earl's—"

"Bastard?" he finished. "All the better. Once I fill your belly with my son, your father will pay a great dowry to bribe me to marry you." He laughed. "I've always wanted to see if a lady's honey is any sweeter than a whore's."

Trembling, Fiona took several steps toward him. "My father will see you hang," she warned.

"Closer, madame."

Fiona took another step, and Roquette shoved her to the ground, took aim at Wolf Shadow, and pulled the trigger. The pistol spat lead and smoke, and Wolf Shadow fell back with a ball in the center of his chest.

Fiona hit the ground and rolled. The explosion momentarily deafened her, and her mind seemed to be working in slow motion. She turned her head and saw blood well up from her husband's terrible wound. He's dead, she thought, and the word echoed through the empty chambers of her anguished soul. *He's dead . . . dead . . . dead.*

Another shot cracked; this one seemed to come from a great distance. She heard a war cry and more shots. She was vaguely aware of a Seneca staggering across her legs and pitching facedown in the grass beside her. Numbly, she looked toward Roquette. The Frenchman was half turned away from her, raising a musket to his shoulder.

She groped in darkness for reality. Wolf Shadow was dead . . . and Roquette had murdered him.

Her grandfather's mocking words came loud in her head. *Quitter. Weak stock on your father's side. What more can I expect of an Englishman's bastard?*

"I'm not," she whispered. "I'm not a quitter." Her fingers touched Timothy's fallen pistol . . . and closed around the grip. The pistol had only one ball. She would have only one chance.

She rose to her knees and held the weapon at arm's length. She took careful aim at the back of Roquette's blue coat and slowly squeezed the trigger.

The Frenchman gave a gasp and fell as lifeless as a puppet with broken strings.

Fiona dropped the pistol. She was too blinded by tears to see her father, Brandon, and Ross Campbell come running toward her. She went to where her husband lay and stared down at his blood-covered chest. She cradled his head in her arms and felt his still lips for any sign of breath. There was none.

She closed her eyes and began to croon an old Irish lullaby. Her fingers tightened around her gore-stained amulet. All she could think was that Wolf Shadow was dead, and she had already used up her one wish.

Chapter 23

Cameron held Fiona in his arms as Ross knelt to examine Wolf Shadow's body. "He's dead," she sobbed into her father's chest. "He's dead. Roquette shot him through the heart."

She was cold . . . so cold. A numbness filled her body, her hands, her legs; she felt like a wooden doll. But a doll couldn't hurt as she did. A doll never felt as though its heart had been torn out . . .

"Why not me?" she cried out. "Why him and not me?"

Cameron's arms tightened around her. "Shhh, child," he said hoarsely. "You must have hope."

"I saw him. I put my fingers in the wound." She drew in a shuddering breath. "There is no hope. He's dead."

Hope was for fools. All her hopes and dreams had died when Roquette's bullet had smashed into Wolf Shadow's chest. She'd spent a lifetime watching other people's loved ones die and comforting them with meaningless words. She had always been a realist. Death was final, and she knew it.

Ross put Fiona's amulet in her hand and closed her icy fingers around it. The necklace was still warm and sticky with her husband's lifeblood.

"I'm sorry," Cameron said. "I'm so damned

sorry. If you hadn't wasted your—'' Suddenly he stiffened and pushed her away, gripping her shoulders. "Did ye try, lass? Did ye try the necklace?''

She shook her head. Tears streamed down her face. "No . . . it's no use. One wish, the legend said. One wish, even unto the power of life and death.''

People crowded around. There were shouts and curses. English voices . . . Algonquian. None of it meant anything to Fiona. Time stood still, and she was locked in a crystal teardrop of grief.

"You must try.'' Anne's soft voice came from behind her.

"Aye,'' Moonfeather agreed. She took Fiona's hand and held it to her own cheek. "Ye maun believe in the Eye of Mist . . . and ye maun try.''

Anne unfastened her own amulet and held it out. "Put mine with yours,'' she said. "They can't all be empty of power.''

"And mine.'' Moonfeather yanked her necklace loose, breaking the thin silver chain. "Father? Can ye add your section. If we put the Eye of Mist back together, then maybe . . .''

Cameron shook his head, and his voice took on the lilt of his Scottish childhood. "Nay, lass. I dinna ha' the last piece. Ye three must try with your own.''

Fiona dashed her tears away with the back of her hand. Was it possible? Could the necklace still retain enough power to save Wolf Shadow's life? Or was she deceiving herself? Hoping when there was no hope left . . .

"You must believe with all your heart,'' Anne said. "Let your love for him outshine death.''

Fiona gripped the golden charms fiercely. Following some inner fey command, she fitted the pieces of the necklace together; first Moonfeather's triangular section, then Anne's, and then her own.

"You must say the words,'' Anne reminded her.

"Aye, the words,'' Moonfeather whispered.

Cameron laid his hand on top of Fiona's. "To-gether," he told them. "The three of ye."

"Let him live," Fiona wished aloud. Her sisters' soft tones blended with her own. "By the power of this necklace and the love of God . . . let him live."

For long seconds, she waited, then let out her breath slowly. The invisible walls of her crystal prison seemed to evaporate, and she recognized other faces around her. Yellow Elk . . . Amookas . . . Royal. She was suddenly aware of the sickly-sweet smell of death and Roquette's sprawled body.

She looked into her father's eyes and read compassion and affection for her in his protective gaze. Her sister Anne, still pale and weak, leaned forward and kissed her cheek. Moonfeather held out her hands in a gesture that needed no translation.

I am loved, Fiona thought. No matter what, I have a family who cares deeply about me.

She sighed and looked down at the amulets in her hand. The familiar tingling sensation warmed the palm of her hand, and a shiver of anticipation ran through her body. And in gazing down, she noticed what she hadn't before, that Anne's piece and hers formed the eye at the center of the original amulet. Anne's charm was perfect, the strange inscriptions as bright as the day they had been carved thousands of years ago.

But her own . . . She glanced up at Moonfeather in confusion. Her own amulet contained a deep gouge. Frantically, Fiona wiped away the last of the blood. Surely, she would have noticed if—

"Fiona."

Wolf Shadow called to her from beyond the mist. His voice was cracked and husky, but she would have known it anywhere.

"Fiona?"

Her eyes dilated. The earth seemed to move under

her feet. Stepping back from her sisters, she spun and dashed toward the spot where her husband lay.

Brandon's and Ross Campbell's broad backs formed a wall that hid him from her sight. "Please," she cried. "Let me see him."

Ross turned toward her, and she caught a flash of triumph in his eye. "Hist, now, hinney. I'd nay ha' ye for a doctor if ye canna tell the dead from the living."

Fiona dropped to her knees beside Wolf Shadow. Her head was spinning, and spots of inky blackness threatened her consciousness. Her stomach turned over, and she gasped for breath.

Wolf Shadow was sitting up. His eyes were open— not glazed in death, but bright and full of pain. "Fiona," he rasped again. "Do you still draw breath?"

She kissed him. His lips were warm.

"You're alive?" she demanded. "But how . . ."

"The ball struck your amulet and glanced off," Ross said. "He's bleeding like a stuck pig, but there's no lasting damage done."

Fiona glanced at Ross in disbelief. "I'm dreaming," she cried in despair. "God rot your bowels, but this is some terrible dream." She kissed Wolf Shadow again. "You can't be alive," she protested.

Ross's laugh was a deep rumble. "Damn if she's not every bit as stubborn as my Anne."

"And Moonfeather," Brandon agreed. He pried open Fiona's left hand and dropped a flattened lead bullet into her palm. "It was lodged under his flesh. So shallow that I could extract it with my fingers."

She shook her head and laid her face against Wolf Shadow's chest, heedless of the blood. There was no mistaking the strong, regular beat of his heart. "It isn't possible," she murmured. "I know a dead man when I see one."

"And I know a live one," Ross said, getting to his

feet. "I'd say we don't even need to carry him to his bed. And good thing, from the size of him."

"I saw his wound," Fiona repeated.

"Typical hysterical female," Brandon remarked as he slid his arm under Wolf Shadow and helped him to his feet.

Wolf Shadow bit back a groan of pain and tried to grin at her. "Will you stop insisting I'm dead and do something to stop this bleeding?" he demanded of Fiona, "Or must I call old Amookas to sew me up?"

She followed him inside to the bed. "And if I am dreaming?"

"Then we must hope it's a long dream for both our sakes."

Two days later, Wolf Shadow walked unaided to the Grand Council and heard the members vote to create the Shawnee-Delaware Nation he wanted so passionately. And the following day, Alex Mackenzie was elected acting chief of Moonfeather's home village in place of the aging Tuk-o-see-yah.

"How can he be the chief?" Fiona whispered to her sister, Moonfeather. "He's a Scotsman."

"Nay," her sister replied, "he was a Scotsman. Uncle Alex has lived among my people for half of his life. He married here and fathered children. He has fought beside our warriors in battle and suffered in hard winters when there was little food. Alex Mackenzie may have been born Scot, but he will die a Shawnee."

"Does that mean that in time the Shawnee will accept me as one of their own?"

Moonfeather chuckled. "They already have, little sister. You have proven your worth by your tender doctoring."

Fiona grimaced. "Some doctor, if I cannot tell a live man from a dead one." Her gaze searched the warriors and chiefs gathered on the dance ground until she found the one she sought, and her chest swelled with joy. "It's not a dream, is it?" Her voice dropped to a whisper. "He is alive."

Moonfeather's eyes lit with understanding. "You and I and Anne share a special secret that none in all the world can know. We know the truth of the necklace. Dinna question, Fiona. Take your happiness and hold it tight. There is little enough in this world. Dinna trouble yourself by asking how or why. Accept each day as it comes."

"Yes," she agreed. "I will." Her lips thinned. "I've told Cameron. Father . . . that I won't be going back with him to Annapolis. I think he understands."

"Aye." Moonfeather smiled. "Name your first boy after him, and all will be forgiven. It worked for me, and Cami wasn't even a boy."

Fiona hesitated, and a question rose in her mind. "You said once that there were four sections to the Eye of the Mist." Moonfeather nodded, and Fiona went on. "You and I and Anne all have one. Where is Father's?"

The Indian woman shrugged. "I'm certain he'll spin a fine tale, if we ever insist upon an explanation."

"But he valued it so much. Why would—" Fiona broke off as Wolf Shadow came toward her, splendid in his wolfskin cape of office. She ran to him, and he caught her hands and squeezed them tightly.

"We've succeeded, Fiona," he said. "With Mackenzie as chief, his tribe will stand firm for the alliance."

"In spite of your white-skinned wife?"

"Perhaps because of her." He smiled. "I hear you've won your own victory."

"Yes. Father says he will set aside a trust for medicine and supplies. Anne wants me to use

Wanishish-eyun as a headquarters to provide care for the sick."

"All by yourself?"

She chuckled. "No, great shaman, not by myself. I still have a lot to learn from you. Perhaps in time we can train Kitate and other young people. Father has heard that a physician in Boston has had success in preventing smallpox. If I can find out what he's doing and how, we could save many Indian lives."

"So. You will be a gift to the Shawnee after all." His eyes twinkled. "The spirits do not lie."

Alex Mackenzie joined them. "Wolf Shadow tells me that ye follow the teachings of Holy Church," he said in his thick Scottish burr.

"I do," she replied, "but . . ."

"And ye wish t' be wed t' this breme heathen by the laws of that faith—knowin' all the while that once ye swear the oaths, there can be no divorce. None of this Shawnee divorcing whenever it takes your fancy. Ye are wed for so long as ye both live."

"I know that," Fiona answered, "but Wolf Shadow is not a Christian—not Catholic. No priest would—"

Alex Mackenzie's faded eyes narrowed. "This one would," he said. "If ye still wish it."

Fiona stared at him in confusion. "How—"

Moonfeather touched Fiona's arm. "Uncle Alex was once a priest," her sister explained quietly. "Long ago, before he came to America. He was a Jesuit, and he fought with the British army."

"Still am a Jesuit," Mackenzie corrected. "A bad priest I may be, a lost lamb in the Lord's flock, but I've never been stripped of my office. I am mortal flesh—a weak sinner, but the faith is true. And Wolf Shadow is a man that I'd judge fit for God's heaven, if any of us are."

A slow smile spread over Fiona's face. She looked up at Wolf Shadow. "Will you?" she asked. "For

me, and for our children to come? Will you pledge
your love to me in the eyes of the Church?''

She read the answer in his eyes.

They were married in the Grand Council circle
that afternoon before their assembled family and
friends and the members of the new Shawnee Nation. Fiona's father took her arm and led her to
stand beside Wolf Shadow.

"I promised your mother when you were born,"
he whispered in her ear. "I promised her that I'd
see you wed to a prince." She glanced at him and
saw tears fill his blue eyes. "I'm finally keeping that
promise."

She nodded, too full to speak . . . wishing her
mother could be here with her, but grateful for her
laughing sisters and her father and her many new
friends. She reached up and touched her amulet
where it hung around her neck once more.

Wolf Shadow had given it back to her before the
start of the ceremony. "It belongs to you, Irish,"
he'd said only half teasingly. "The magic is too
strong for a mere moon dancer. It's woman's magic,
not man's."

The amulet warmed her skin above the plunging
neckline of an exquisite, azure silk gown. The dress
was a gift from Anne—a bridal gown fit for a princess's wedding day. And on her head, over her long,
loose tresses, Moonfeather had placed a woven
crown of wildflowers.

"In the name of the Father, the Son, and the Holy
Ghost . . ." Father Alexander intoned. The words
flowed together like the days and nights of happiness that she'd known since Wolf Shadow had come
into her life.

"Do you, Fiona O'Neal, take this man . . ."

She did.

"Do you, Wolf Shadow, high shaman of the
Shawnee, take this woman . . ."

He did.

And then Wolf Shadow was reaching for her, and everyone was cheering. Their eyes met, and their lips touched. And Fiona put her arms around his neck and held him as though the magic of their embrace would last forever.

Epilogue

June 1733

Water cascaded thirty feet from the rocks above to feed the pool of blue-green water surrounded by primeval forest. The spray from the tumbling flow rose in a churning mist over the sparkling surface, lending an air of enchantment to the warm, lazy afternoon. No sound but the melody of birdsong and the rush of the falls broke the solitude. No sound but those and the shared laughter of two lovers.

Fiona and Wolf Shadow stood naked in the waist-deep water under the spray from the waterfall. Each held a handful of crushed leaves, and each was attempting to raise a lather on the other's bare body.

"Stand still," he shouted. "How can I purify you properly if you keep wiggling?" He cupped her left breast in his hand and proceeded to rub her nipple gently with the leaves.

She giggled and sank back in the water, wrapping her legs around his thighs and bringing her most intimate area close to his loins. Her head went under, then she bobbed up and released her handful of soap plant. "Come here, you," she teased. He was as aroused as she was; his swollen sex was proof of that, but she wasn't ready to satisfy his appetite yet.

He grabbed for her, and she let go of his thighs, twisted, and swam toward the deep center of the pool. He caught her, and they rolled over and over, sharing a kiss beneath the surface.

They came up laughing, and she dove under and took two strong strokes toward the shore. "You aren't taking this seriously," she chided, as her feet touched bottom and she waded into shallow water.

"Oh, but I am."

Her heart thrilled as he stood up. Water streamed down his bronzed chest and over his belly and thighs. Her gaze lingered on his huge erect shaft jutting arrogantly from a nest of dark curls. He caught her gaze and laughed, shaking the water from his long, midnight-black hair.

I'm a brazen jade, she thought. I'm ogling my naked husband like a lovesick cow stares at a bull, and I don't even have the modesty to blush.

God, but I still love him as much as I did on the day we married. And I know he loves me.

"If I am the high shaman," he said with mock severity, "and as far as I know you've not stolen my office yet, how is it that I've never heard of this ceremony?"

"Woman's magic," she told him. She climbed the bank and squeezed the water from her own waist-length hair. "Very powerful." She glanced toward the cradleboard hanging from a low tree branch to satisfy herself that their small son was still sleeping soundly and motioned Wolf Shadow toward her covered basket.

His voice grew husky. "Couldn't this ceremony wait?" he asked. "I want—"

"Shhh," she admonished. "You'll offend the spirits of the wild strawberries."

"What are you talking about, woman?"

Laughing, she took his hand and pulled him down onto the thick carpet of moss. She bent over him and kissed him, a long, tender kiss of anticipation. "Be patient, great moon dancer," she teased. "Lay back, close your eyes, and be still."

He obeyed, and she reached over and opened her basket. She laughed, and it seemed to her that the amulet around her neck radiated a warmth that caused her skin to tingle. She selected a ripe strawberry, put it between her lips, and kissed him again.

"Mmm," he groaned. "Sweeter kisses than I've had for a long time."

"Shhh, you're not allowed to talk." She kissed him again, this time touching his tongue with hers. He tasted of man and strawberry, and the warmth from her amulet unwound like a ribbon of delicious sensation that spilled to the soles of her bare feet. "Very serious," she repeated, selecting another strawberry. "The ceremony must be done exactly right, or we will offend—"

"Yes, yes, I know," he answered. "The strawberry spirits."

Slowly, sensuously, Fiona began to crush the berry against his golden-bronze skin. Concentrating, she drew a line around each male nipple and down the center of his chest. She chose another strawberry and rubbed it across his navel and then lower.

"I think I remember how this goes now," he said with a contented sigh.

"I thought you might."

"Every drop of berry juice must be sipped—"

"Every drop."

He opened one dark eye and winked at her as

she carefully picked another berry. She laughed, and they kissed passionately as a breeze gently rocked their son's cradle and played an endless love song through the green canopy of the sheltering trees.

Avon Romances—
the best in exceptional authors and unforgettable novels!

THE EAGLE AND THE DOVE Jane Feather
76168-8/$4.50 US/$5.50 Can

STORM DANCERS Allison Hayes
76215-3/$4.50 US/$5.50 Can

LORD OF DESIRE Nicole Jordan
76621-3/$4.50 US/$5.50 Can

PIRATE IN MY ARMS Danelle Harmon
76675-2/$4.50 US/$5.50 Can

DEFIANT IMPOSTOR Miriam Minger
76312-5/$4.50 US/$5.50 Can

MIDNIGHT RAIDER Shelly Thacker
76293-5/$4.50 US/$5.50 Can

MOON DANCER Judith E. French
76105-X/$4.50 US/$5.50 Can

PROMISE ME FOREVER Cara Miles
76451-2/$4.50 US/$5.50 Can

Coming Soon

THE HAWK AND THE HEATHER Robin Leigh
76319-2/$4.50 US/$5.50 Can

ANGEL OF FIRE Tanya Anne Crosby
76773-2/$4.50 US/$5.50 Can

The Passion and Romance
of Bestselling Author

Laura Kinsale

THE SHADOW AND THE STAR

76131-9/$4.99 US/$5.99 Can

Wealthy, powerful and majestically handsome Samuel
Gerard, master of the ancient martial arts, has sworn to
love chastely...but burns with the fires of unfulfilled
passion. Lovely and innocent Leda Etoile is drawn to
this "shadow warrior" by a fevered yearning she could
never deny.

Be Sure to Read

THE HIDDEN HEART 75008-2/$4.99 US/$5.99 Can
MIDSUMMER MOON 75398-7/$3.95 US/$4.95 Can
THE PRINCE OF MIDNIGHT

76130-0/$4.95 US/$5.95 Can

SEIZE THE FIRE 75399-5/$4.50 US/$5.50 Can
UNCERTAIN MAGIC 75140-2/$4.95 US/$5.95 Can